Hugh Brune

YOUR HOUSE IS MINE

SCEPTRE

Copyright © 1999 Hugh Brune

First published in 1998 by Hodder and Stoughton
First published in paperback in 1999 by Hodder and Stoughton
A division of Hodder Headline PLC
A Sceptre Book

10 9 8 7 6 5 4 3 2 1

A CIP catalogue record for this title is available from the British Library.

ISBN 0340 71867 6

Typeset by
Palimpsest Book Production Limited, Polmont, Stirlingshire
Printed and bound in Great Britain by
Caledonian International Book Manufacturing Ltd

Hodder and Stoughton
A division of Hodder Headline PLC
338 Euston Road
London NW1 3BH

Thanks to the Montini Experience and DJ Force.
Thanks also to Sarah, Arthur, Dinah, Neil, Fiona
and all at Sceptre

YOUR HOUSE IS MINE

Part One

∫

You don't notice it at first. You're sitting talking with your friends, drinking beer and someone, somewhere is playing some records. The music is indistinguishable from the general buzz of the conversation and laughter. Every now and then there'll be a tune that you recognise, usually an old one, a hip-hop track from the eighties or something, and you'll nod your head affectionately.

—Oh yeah, you'll say. —I think I've got a copy of this somewhere at home. Christ, haven't heard this in ages.

And you'll get to talking about places you used to go, people you used to know what seems like a very long time ago. And you'll talk about how things have changed and yet remained so much the same. And you'll realise that this is what you've been doing with your Saturday nights for pretty much ten years.

So you take another sip of beer and cradle the bottle with your hands. Nick says something about alcohol counteracting the effects of the drugs and you tell him he's missed the point. You're not drinking it for the alcohol content – there's fuck all alcohol in these poncey designer beers anyway. You're drinking it to have something to do with your hands while you wait for things to get going. You're drinking it because nursing an ice-cold beer bottle and occasionally raising it to your lips is one of the essential pleasures of life.

Clubs at around half eleven are like airport lounges. People sit and stand where they can, dressed in clothes they wouldn't dream of wearing at home and they wait. They wait with a sense of anticipation that becomes a crucial part of the whole experience. Airports could check people in more quickly, clubs could turn up their sound systems earlier; but they know how we love to wait.

Around twelve thirty Nick suggests dropping a pill. The place is full now. Some feet are starting to tap, some heads are starting to nod, the lights have gone down slightly. You try to imagine what the place is going to look like when it does start jumping. It's like looking at complete strangers and trying to picture them without their clothes on, only less sleazy somehow. Under the table you fish the wrap out of your watch pocket.

—Half for now?

He nods. You tear the tissue paper off the tablet, break it with your thumb nail and put half in your mouth. The other half you pass under the table to Nick.

Now the real waiting begins. Nick checks his watch. He seems to be conducting some kind of fucking experiment these days, measuring exactly how long it takes him to come up each time. You have the sad notion that he goes home and plots it all on a graph or something. Over the next half hour he will check his watch religiously every three or four minutes until it really starts to bug you.

—Fuckin hell, man, give it a rest, eh? Watched kettle, know what I mean?

—Yeah right, he goes, embarrassed that you even noticed.

You go for a wander, check out the different rooms. All the places that were empty when you came in are now packed to the roof and pretty much everyone seems to be moving around, not quite sure where they want to be, where the action's going to be. Because it's tangible now: there will be some action.

You come to rest at a vantage point over the main dancefloor. It's full of bodies and the music's certainly been turned up, but it's not exactly shaking yet. You watch the crowd swerve and move. There's a girl directly below you, eyes alternately open wide or closed tight, clutching her bottle of Evian for dear life, dancing away on her own in blissed-out oblivion. Short blue dress, long fair hair, star-shaped earrings, bright red lipstick, mauve silk scarf. She's got fluorescent bands on her wrists which she twists and turns in front of her eyes, making patterns in the dark, hypnotising herself as she dances. She is, it dawns on you suddenly, crushingly, the most beautiful girl you have ever set eyes on. Hey hey, here come the drugs!

The next thing that hits you is the beat. A persistent Bang. Bang. Bang. Bang. You raise your arm and jerk it vertically in time with the thumping. You point at the girl and the others with her. You can't imagine a life without these drums; you can't remember a time before they existed.

Over the top of the rhythm you begin to notice a synthesizer pattern. It repeats over and over and sounds like something you've known all your life. It changes occasionally – more evolves than changes – but the main pattern keeps coming back until it feels like an old friend.

Then the drums kick in even harder. BANG. BANG. BANG. BANG.

Then the synth pattern comes back. In your head you can hear all kinds of melodies and harmonies soaring over it. You look over at Nick and he's lost it completely, shaking his head and throwing violent shapes with his hands. You wonder if the silly fucker remembered to note down the time he came up. You smile so hard you can feel your face stretching.

Another tune is starting to creep in over these drum beats. It doesn't storm in, however. It waits politely until it's invited in, then it exchanges pleasantries with the first tune until that tune is ready to leave. Then it takes over big time. And it becomes clear straight away that the unthinkable has happened: this tune is even better than the first one. Meanwhile, before you've had time to get your head properly around this fact, there's a *third* tune, peering in through the window, just saying gently: look, man, no hurry, but whenever you're ready, like . . .

You look up at the DJ in his little glass box, spinning between three decks, fading up a little bit of this here, a little bit of that there, one ear in his headphones, one eye on the controls, blending together different parts of other people's music until he has a sound which is truly his own, a whole that is so much greater than the sum of its parts that it makes you want to cry. Every so often he looks out across the dancefloor at the effect his magic is having and beams proudly. Behind him his inner circle dance like crazy and shout compliments at him.

And so it goes. Each record blends seamlessly into the next. One doesn't end, the next doesn't begin: they merge. Like those computer-generated pictures in which one person's face is transformed stage by stage into another's. Or those games in which you turn one word into another by changing one letter at a time. You don't notice the steps of the journey but suddenly somehow you're somewhere completely different to where you were before.

Then without warning, BANG! The music cuts out and a voice comes booming over the speakers:

—If you ain't gonna dance, then what the FUCK did you come here for!

The beats come crashing back in and you look up at the ceiling and cry, WHOOEEE!!

And now it's *that* moment. That special, precious moment that comes in any great night out when you look around you and all of a sudden you realise THE WHOLE FUCKING PLACE IS JUMPING. They're dancing on the tables, on the stairs, behind the bar. Even the bouncers are moving a little. You close your eyes and shake your head and wag your finger as if to say: I fuckin told you, man.

The girl in the blue dress comes dancing your way, still waving her wristband around, still clutching her water. She still looks amazing, but of course now so does everyone. You smile at her and she smiles back, like, RIGHT AT YOU. You dance with her for a while, then the two of you slowly drift apart into other areas.

And you dance and you dance and you dance. And just when you think your legs will turn to jelly and won't be able to support you any more the drums cut out and you're bathed in great shafts of ethereal synthesizer sounds. You start moving like you're underwater and you can feel the tingling right to the end of your fingers. A green light starts flashing at one end of the dance-floor and you find yourself absolutely bewitched by it. Then it splits into rays and begins slowly to rotate. It is impossibly beautiful.

Then from somewhere far away the drums reappear, very quietly at first, nothing more than a distant rumble, then slowly getting louder and faster, louder and faster, louder and faster while one of the old familiar synth refrains is banging away again and the drums are louder and faster louder and faster building you up and up and up higher and higher and higher you raise your hands and shake them around open your eyes in wide-eyed fucking amazement at how high this can go upandupanduplouderfasterlouderfasterlouderfaster

BANG!

THEN the TUNE comes BACK much LOUDer THAN beFORE the BEAT is LIKE a PULSE that's PUMPing IN your SOUL you SHAKE your ARMS so HARD you FEEL they MIGHT fall OFF you COULDn't GIVE a FUCK it's WHAT you CAME here FOR you LOOK aROUND the PLACE and EVeryONE's the SAME they're GOing FUCKing MAD they ALL look FUCKing GREAT

Out of someplace or other there's some vocals:

> My house is your housey
>
> My house is your housey
>
> My house is your housey
>
> My house is your housey

You catch Nick's eye. You start mouthing the lyrics, pointing at yourself and then at him.

> —My house is your housey
>
> —My house is your housey
>
> Those fucking drums are building up again.
>
> —My house is your housey
>
> —My house is your housey
>
> This sounds fucking amazing man.
>
> —My house is your housey
>
> —My house is your housey
>
> —YOUR HOUSE IS MINE!

Fucking YEAH!

When the lights go up you feel like you've been dancing forever, yet somehow the evening flew by in five minutes. Among it all you found time to pop the other half of your pill, check out the Northern Soul tunes being spun in the chill-out room and, rather fortuitously, run into the girl in the blue dress at the bar.

—Havin a good one, she'd said after you'd been staring at her uncontrollably while she counted out her change.

—Yeah . . .

That's all you could think of to say, you smooth-talking bastard. You forgot all the other words in the English language.

—Yeah, you said again.

—Well great . . .

She took a long drink from her water, new from the fridge.

—Want some? They've turned the fuckin taps off in the ladies'. Bastards.

—Yeah, you'd said, somewhat predictably.

And she mumbled something about seeing you around and she was away. Back to her oblivion.

And now here you are, blinking in the light, trying to pick her out. Nick, absolutely drenched in his own sweat, says he'll see you outside. You peer at the slow-moving hordes of people shuffling past you but you can't see her; you check in the other rooms and she's still not there. You begin to wonder if you imagined her all along. They're playing the Stone Roses – they *always* play the Stone fucking Roses at kicking out time; it must be in the licensing laws or something. Eventually a bouncer collars you and shows you the door. You're practically the last person in the place anyhow.

Outside you find Nick sitting on a wall, humming to himself, drumming with his fingers. It's cool and it's quiet out here but your head is FULL of noise. All the records from this evening, in fact probably all the records you've ever heard in your life are playing over again ALL AT THE SAME TIME. You look over at Nick and it's clear he's going through the exact same thing.

—What kept you? he goes.

—Looking for someone, you begin to explain, but he's not listening, he's looking over your shoulder. He's seen something.

—Fuckin hell, I don't believe it, he says absently, jumping off the wall and walking right past you.

He wanders off into a crowd of people and taps one of them on the back, a tallish bloke with long, knotted black hair in a bushy ponytail. Motorhead hair. The guy looks over to see who's hassling him and it looks like there might be some trouble and . . . fucking hell, you know that face. It's W, one of your favourite actors of all time. This is great; you *love* seeing Famous People out and about in London. It's one of the real buzzes of living in the capital. In fact, this is even greater. Not only is this Famous Person actually someone you admire, as opposed to some half-arsed nobody from the telly, but Nick claims to know him. He interviewed him once for a magazine, way before he got famous, and they became buddies, going out once in a while for a drink or to shoot some pool (W's a shite pool player apparently). You've never been sure how much of this was bullshit but here Nick is, look, proving his point, slapping the Famous Person on the back and looking for all the world like his long-lost best friend ever. You hover and wait for an introduction.

W's in a bad way. Goes with the reputation, you suppose. Alternative counter-culture druggy actor. He wouldn't want to be seen out on a Saturday night if he wasn't off his tits; not good for business. But, you know, he's *really* in a bad way. Staring into space, slurring his words – in fact they're not even words, they're just slurs. You haven't got a clue what he's talking about. Still, there's a couple of girls with him who understand enough to laugh at every fucking thing he says. His mouth is all full of saliva and you reckon he might throw his guts up at any second. You think about the supercool films he's been in, the pimps and drug dealers and gangsters he's played. You look at him now. He looks like a fucking victim.

—This is John, says Nick finally, pointing vaguely in your direction. —John, this is W.

You shake hands. At least the guy seems sincere enough in his handshake.

—I'm a friend of Nick's, is all you can think of to say.

—Yeah, so am I, comes a sharp businesslike voice from behind you and you're almost shoved out of the way by a thick, tattooed hand coming forward for W to shake. W looks the guy up and down before he takes his hand. A big, beefy bloke, his skin's a mass of scars, tattoos, warts and straggley bits of hair. He could be a squaddie, he could be a psycho, he could just be pissed. He could be a pissed-up psychopathic squaddie. Whatever, even in the state he's in, W can see it wouldn't be a great idea to refuse the guy's hand.

—This is W, says Nick, who's still playing society host. —W, this is . . .

—Fat Cunt, says the bloke cheerily. —Everyone calls me Fat Cunt.

He's still holding on to W's hand. He tightens his grip slightly.

—With respect, mind, he adds.

A glimmer of recognition passes across W's glazed eyes. He smiles softly. —Fat Cunt, he repeats to himself.

Fat Cunt turns to Nick. —So Nick, how you doin?

—Yeah, good.

They shake hands.

Then he turns to you.

—And, uh . . .

—John, you say

—*John!* Course. How you doin, mate?

—Yeah. Okay.

—Nice one.

Fat Cunt's a vague acquaintance of Nick's. You're not quite sure what he does; you think Nick said once he was a photographer. Maybe that's how they got to meet, on a magazine somewhere. All you know is you see him around, he goes to clubs a lot and he and Nick usually nod to each other and sometimes exchange a few words. He looks like quite a handy bloke to be on nodding terms with.

Formalities over, Nick turns back to W, who's staring at his shoes, hopping from one foot to the other, still mumbling Fat Cunt's name to himself and dribbling.

—So what are you working on right now? Nick asks, like he's about to start conducting an interview in the middle of the street.

The question fails to register with The Finest Actor Of His Generation, but one of his girlfriends-cum-bodyguards answers:—Right now he's working on getting home without throwing up.

W burbles something in what might as well be Klingon but which Nick interprets as an invitation to all go back to his actor pad and take a bellyload of drugs.

—Come on man. Be a laugh, he says to you, looking for support.

You shake your head vigorously. You're scared. You're scared that you and Nick will just be pathetic hangers on, the only two people that nobody knows. You're scared that the whole thing will develop into a Drug Contest and you won't be able to keep up.

Fat Cunt doesn't take any persuading, though. —Fuckin A, man, let's go.

—Come on daddio. Don't be a . . ., says Nick and he makes the square shape like Uma Thurman in *Pulp Fiction*. Wanker.

—You go on. I'll catch you later.

—Your call, says Nick and he reels away into the night with his Famous Friend.

As they walk away Fat Cunt slaps his arm around W—Hey, man, is it true they won't let you into America cause you're an anarchist? you can hear him saying and you wonder what the fuck you're doing passing up an opportunity like this.

You half think about running after them. If only there was a way you could do it and still look cool.

—Hey, wasn't that W? comes a voice that makes you jump.

You spin round. It's HER!

—Yeah, you say. —Uh . . . yeah.

Shit, you're stuck in that groove again.

—Well, aren't you going with them?

—Nah. (A new word. Thank you God.) My mate's going back to his gaff but, you know . . . I fancy an early night meself.

You say this as brightly as possible. You are such a cunt.

—Well . . ., she cocks her head as she says this. —Do you fancy taking a short walk before your early night?

—Sure. Which way you headed?

She points and you have no idea whether this is the direction you want to go in or not. Like you're going to refuse her anyhow.

So you walk. You walk for a couple of minutes in silence, then she stops, puts out her hand and says:—Sally McKenzie.

You take her hand. You think of your own name. John. John's

such a dull, shite name isn't it. You're tempted to lie and say your name is Craig or Rory or Paolo or something with some fucking character at least. But she'll find out. If this goes any distance at all she'll find out. And then you really will look like a prize twat.

—John Santini, you say quietly, trying to prolong the handshake.

—Well that's got that out of the way at least.

—Yeah. I didn't want to say anything till we'd been properly introduced. You know, manners an that.

Wow. That was pretty much a whole sentence.

—So . . . you have a good time tonight? she goes.

—Yeah. Nice one.

Sally nods and takes this on board. She's making all the running here.

—You go to that club often? she tries.

—Yeah. Now and again. Good place. Good atmosphere.

Come on man. What the fuck are you doing? Do you want to walk with her or not? Show some fucking interest then. Ask her a question. Go on, ask her a question before she falls asleep on you.

Hey. If you ain't gonna dance, then what the fuck did you come here for?

—Sunrise looks pretty cool, you manage at long last.

—Yeah. Gorgeous innit. I love it when you stay up all night and see the morning in.

—Beats getting up for it. Did this summer job at the post office once. Had to get up at four thirty every morning. Fuckin nearly killed me. I had to sit in this tiny, piss-stinking room sorting out mail and I'd be completely fuckin zombied having been out the night before or whatever. Made so many mistakes they sacked me after eight weeks. Couldn't do it, man, couldn't do it.

—I just find it easier not to go to bed, she says.

You look up at her.

—Yeah? What do you do? You have to get up at four thirty every fuckin morning?

—Earlier than that sometimes, she says proudly, smiling. —I work at the flower market, you know, Columbia Road?

—Yeah, I know it.

—That's where I'm going now. Set the stall up around six, six thirty. Sometimes I have to go and get some stock before that, though.

—What, you're going to fuckin work? Now?

—Yeah! she says brightly.

—With no sleep or nothin?

—No sleep or nothing. I'll do my shift, pack up, have a big big lunch somewhere and then a long kip in the afternoon.

—Fuckin hell.

You're astounded.

—Fuckin hell, you say again to show just how astounded you are.

—It's not that bad once you've done it a couple of times.

—I dunno. I'm still on a buzz from the night. Don't think I could cope with having to think straight.

—The buzz helps. There's a real adrenalin rush to working the stall. You know, all the shouting and chatting up the customers and that. Kind of like coming up again really. It's the buzz that sees me through.

You walk on a bit in silence.

—Took some fuckin great Es tonight, you say finally.

Oh well done. That's going to impress her. Start bragging about how many pills you've done. And anyway you haven't taken *some* great Es; you took one. And you took that in two halves you screaming great ponce.

—Yeah, me too. I still feel tingly all over.

You look into her eyes. They're big and round and brown but you reckon she's down off the Es; she's just got killer eyes.

—So you wanna come and watch me at the market for a while? It can be a blast.

—Yeah sure . . . Might need some kip at some point.

—We have a van. You can stick your head down in that.

The van is probably the least comfortable place you've tried to sleep in your life. The floor is ridged metal and there's no blankets. It's also half full of boxes so there's no room to stretch out fully. Outside you can hear Sally and Petra, her partner, setting up their stall, laying out the punnets of greenery, labelling them, discussing prices. The quiet, sleepy street is beginning to fill up with tradespeople, all unspeakably cheery for this hour in the morning, greeting each other loudly and chatting inanely. You hope to Christ you can get some sleep before the punters arrive and it really starts going off. What time are they likely to get here anyhow? What time do people round here get up on a Sunday morning? How eager can people be to buy plants?

Eventually, despite the last remnants of the tingling in your fingers and toes, you drift off, asking yourself dumb question after dumb question. You don't notice it when it happens of course. Used to scare the shit out of you when you were younger. That you could just fall asleep like that without knowing about it. Was this how people died? Just click, like that, while you were thinking about something else entirely.

You dream fitfully. Weird, disjointed stuff that you won't remember in the morning. Stuff that it's probably just as well you won't remember in the morning. The last dream, the stark, vivid one just before you wake up is about gas ovens in the war. You come to and you're pouring sweat and feel sick in your stomach and it's fucking boiling in here. Someone's banging on the door. Just as you sit up they manage to pull it open. Blinding sun comes piling in. No wonder it's so hot; it's probably midday by now. Peering out you can see it's not Sally or Petra who's opened the door, it's a bloke. Fucking ugly bloke at that. Early twenties maybe, long greasy hair and a skin complaint that would confound specialists the world over. His face is all out of proportion too. Eyes too far apart, nose out of joint, mouth all lop-sided. Looks like his mum slept with her brother and they took the resulting offspring to Pablo Picasso for plastic surgery. You stare at him in dumbstruck awe. He's taken a couple of boxes out of the van before he notices you.

—Who the fuck are you? he goes.

It occurs to you that if you feel this shit, you must look pretty rough too. The sweat's still running down your back like a waterfall. You're trying to squeeze the images from your nightmare out of your head.

—I'm uh . . . I'm a friend of Sally's, you mumble.

—Yeah?

—Just sleeping off a bit of a long night, know what I mean?

—Another of Sally's friends, eh? he says under his breath. But he says it loudly enough under his breath that you know he wants you to hear.

—What do you mean—? you start to say.

He heaves the last box out and goes to close the door. —Good luck, he says, banging it shut.

Strange bloke.

You lie back and it hits you just how uncomfortable a night this has been. You can feel marks up and down your back where the ridges in the floor have dug into you. Neither this, nor the intense heat, nor even the now-bustling noise from outside, though, stops you from dozing off again.

When you next come to, you check your watch. Eleven fifteen. It's now really hot in here and fucking noisy outside. You kick open the door of the van and peer out. The street that was so desolate when you walked down it a few hours ago is now a riot of colour and sound. There are so many people they can hardly cram themselves down the thin strip between the stalls. The sun is out and people have dusted down their shorts and their sunglasses and their BRIGHT T-shirts. And everyone has bought something. Everyone has at least one houseplant the size of a small child or one cluster of brightly coloured flowers they're trying not to damage as they brush past everyone else. No one comes here to browse. Or maybe they do all come to browse but the wares are so tempting they end up buying something anyway. And on either side of these happy Sunday shoppers are the traders, these awesomely brilliant men and women who have persuaded this enormous crowd to part with their hard-earned cash for a product that serves no useful function whatsoever and will, in most cases, be dead and discarded within a week. These are people who could show some drug dealers you know a thing or two.

Sally's there in the thick of it, yelling blue murder.

—CAHM AWN! CAHM AWN LADIES AND GENTS! MUMS FIVE FER A PAHND NOW! FIVE FER A PAHND YER MUMS! ONLY A FEW LEFT!

Her voice is deep and hoarse, totally unlike it was last night. This accent is completely new as well.

You clamber out of the van and go over to her. She's changed her clothes from last night. All except the scarf which she has tied tightly around her neck and stuffed inside a long red woolly jumper.

—Hello sleepyhead, she says in her normal voice. —You okay?

—Yeah, you go, rubbing your shoulder where it hurts the most and rotating your arm.

—Stiff?

You nod.

—Yeah. Takes some getting used to, that van.

Then she turns back to the punters and her voice changes again. It's like she's been completely taken over.

—CAHM AWN! I'VE ONLY GOT FIVE OF THESE BUNCHES LEFT. FIVE LEFT NOW!

The voice reminds you of that little girl in *The Exorcist*. —YOUR MOTHER SUCKS COCKS IN HELL! you can hear her bellowing in your head. You can't stop yourself smiling.

—What you grinning at? she goes.

—Nothing really. Just the way your voice changes.

—Not very sexy is it. But it pulls in the punters.

—So . . . been a busy morning?

—Yeah, not bad at all. Sun always brings them out. Got shot of some rare old shite to a bunch of American tourists first thing. Can't shift these fuckin chrysanthemums, though. CAHM AWN NOW! FIVE FER A PAHND YER MUMS HERE! I dunno, maybe we've got nothing but the knowledgeable punters left and they can all see that these were picked a few days ago and've got forty-eight hours left in em at most.

An elderly-looking woman comes up to the stall and buys a tiny punnet of purplish flowers.

—That's a pahnd twenty-five darlin, says Sally in her Linda Blair voice. —Sure you don't want any chrysanthemums to go with that now? Only five fer a pahnd. Nah? Tell you what, as a special favour, how abaht I do you six fer a pahnd. Can't say fairer than that now can I?

The old woman shakes her head and blends back into the crowd.

—Oh well, I did my best. Hey, you wouldn't mind watching the stall for five minutes while I go for a piss, would you? I'm absolutely dying and Petra fucked off somewhere hours ago. Cheers, you're a pal.

—Hang on, I don't know shit about flowers. I don't even know what a fuckin tulip looks like.

—We haven't got any tulips an all the prices are marked, she's saying and already she's away. You put your hands in your pockets and stand there looking like a twat, hoping to God no one actually tries to buy anything while she's gone. If they do, you decide you'll just pretend to be another customer and shrug your shoulders. Either side of you the two traders, both young men around your age, are shouting their little raps.

—LAST FEW DAHLIAS. LAST FEW NOW!

—ALL THE BLUE BOXES ONLY A QUID!

—LAST FEW DAHLIAS. LAST FEW NOW!

—ALL THE BLUE BOXES ONLY A QUID!

You can feel the tingling coming back. Just a little bit but it's definitely there. You can hear some of the records from last night playing in your head.

—LAST FEW DAHLIAS. LAST FEW NOW!

—ALL THE BLUE BOXES ONLY A QUID!

There's a solid beat going now. You can feel it hammering underneath these two guys shouting.

—*LAST* FEW DAHLIAS. *LAST* FEW NOW!

—*ALL* THE BLUE BOXES *ON*LY A QUID!

(My house is your housey.)

—LAST FEW DAHLIAS. LAST FEW NOW!

—ALL THE BLUE BOXES ONLY A QUID!

My house is your housey.

—LAST FEW DAHLIAS!

—ALL THE BLUE BOXES!

My house is your housey.

—LAST FEW DAHLIAS!

—ALL THE BLUE BOXES!

You're tapping your foot and nodding your head. You're back in the club. Wouldn't it be great, you think, if you could shift some of these chrysanthemums for Sally. That would impress her.

My house is your housey.
My house is your housey.
—LAST FEW DAHLIAS!
—ALL THE BLUE BOXES!
—LAST FEW DAHLIAS!
—ALL THE BLUE BOXES!
YOUR HOUSE IS MINE!

Bang.

You take your hands out of your pockets and scream as loudly as you can.

—CHRYSANTHEMUMS ARE ONLY FIVE FOR A POUND!

Then you shut up immediately realising just how much of a cunt you sound. The two blokes on either side are looking over at you. You go bright red. You've started sweating again and your forehead is dripping and itchy.

The two men turn back to their own shouting.

—LAST FEW DAHLIAS. LAST FEW NOW!

—ALL THE BLUE BOXES ONLY A QUID!

—CHRYSANTHEMUMS! you try again tentatively. You're not even sure which ones are chrysanthemums.

A middle-aged woman with very fake blonde hair approaches the stall. Your heart sinks. You hope she doesn't ask you any awkward questions. You hope beyond hope she doesn't ask you any awkward questions.

—What are these little ones here? she asks. Awkwardly.

Fuck off and leave me alone you nosey bitch, you just manage to stop yourself saying.

—Uh . . . they're, uh, mauve, is what you actually say.

—Yes, but what are they *called*?

—Called? Uh, they're called . . .

You take a deep breath and say something long and Latin-sounding. Amazingly the daft cow buys it. Here's one who really is as stupid as she looks.

—And how much are they?

That's easy. All the prices are marked. You turn your head round to read it.

Of course. All the prices are marked except this one.

—Five pounds the bunch, you say firmly. Out of the corner of your eye you catch the bloke on your left shooting you an incredulous look.

—Mmm, five pounds, says the woman. —That seems an awful lot somehow.

—Tell you what darlin, you find yourself saying. —I'll do them for you at four fifty. How's that sound?

—Oh you dear young man! That's awfully sweet of you.

The woman peels off a fiver from a large wad of notes; she's obviously one who looks after the pennies and lets the pounds take care of themselves. You give her fifty pence out of your own pocket and hand over the flowers.

When she's gone you look over at the bloke on the left. He looks back and gives a nod of respect. Respect! You could get used to this job. Beats cutting people's hair off for a living.

There are no other sales while Sally's away. The music comes back and you have a little dance on the spot next to your collection of flowers. When you tell her what's happened she refuses to believe you.

—You're shittin me. You sold that tired bunch of crap for a *fiver*?

—Strue! Couldn't fahkin believe it, says the bloke on the left. Respect.

After the market you go for breakfast at a greasy spoon nearby.

—I'm paying, you say, flashing your fiver around like a wanker. Sally was so impressed with your salesmanship she'd let you keep the money.

When the plates arrive you can barely see the food for the steam. It dawns on you that you haven't eaten since around this time yesterday and the smell of the food is intoxicating. Forgetting for a second that you have company you take a chip and dip it gently into the yolk of your egg, delighting in the way the yellowey goo spills out over the plate. Mmm, how romantic. You look up at Sally to make sure you haven't grossed her out too much but she's already wolfing down great mouthfuls of sausage and bacon and fried tomato.

—Weird thing happened when I was in the van, you say when you can bear to stop eating for a second.

—Yeah? she says with her mouth full.

—Yeah. This bloke came to get some boxes out and he seemed to be telling me that I should watch out for you.

—Watch out for me?

—Yeah . . . he didn't say so in so many words, but the implication was that you seem to have quite a few guys sleeping in your van on a Sunday morning.

She laughs. —Huh. I wish. What did he look like, this bloke?

—Like . . . he looked like the ugly one in New Model Army, if you know what I mean.

—Great. That's like saying he looked like the short one of the Seven Dwarfs.

—Okay. He looks . . . longish fair hair, spots . . . how many ugly, an I mean *really* fuckin ugly people come and take stuff out of your van regularly?

—Must be Jimmy.

—Jimmy it is then.

—So he was warning you about me eh?

—Wished me good luck.

—An what did you say to him?

—Nothing. I can look after myself.

She grins. —I'm sure you can.

—So were you and he . . . you know . . . ?

She fakes a coughing fit and nearly spits out her food.

—You're fuckin joking aren't you! I mean he's kind of sweet I guess, but, you know, there are aliens out of *Doctor Who* I've fancied more. He obviously thinks you and I are . . . you know . . . though. Doesn't he?

You look at her and your balls freeze over. This is a Moment. It's exciting and flattering and terrifying all at the same time. You have absolutely no idea what to say or do.

The Moment seems to last for ever. Eventually she smiles and takes your hand.

—I'm whacked. I need to go home and get some kip.

You breathe a sigh of relief that the silence is over, even though you're disappointed at the outcome. You thought you might have been in there.

—I can call you though?

—You better, she says, scribbling a number on a napkin.

You walk home rather that take the bus. It takes the best part of a couple of hours but you love every second of it. The sun is out and you're whistling tunes to yourself. These sort of comedowns are in their way even better than the highs. Of course, you tell yourself to try and keep a sense of perspective, things can't be this great for ever.

Don't worry; of course they can't.

∫

No one in Misty's paid any attention to the tall, muscular drunk leaning on the bar methodically drinking his way through every spirit in the place.

No one paid him any attention but everyone knew who he was. There were seven old soaks propping up the bar but only one of them was famous. Only one of them had been decorated sixteen times by the Galactic Government. Only one of them had saved the planet, saved the lives of every man, woman and neuter-being in Misty's that cold and unwelcoming Saturday night; only one of them had a *really* good reason for drinking the way he was. They all knew why he was drinking and they all understood. Who wouldn't in his position?

Around midnight a fight broke out. Not a serious fight, just the run of the mill fisticuffs for a Saturday night. A couple of old fellows arguing about laserball, too much drink, things got out of hand. Punches were thrown; most of them missed.

Something inside the tall man stirred. He put down his drink and walked over to where the two old fellows were waving their arms around and cursing loudly. Conversation around the bar stopped, although the music continued to thump away. The fight, such as it was, also stopped.

The tall man didn't stop the fight. It just stopped when he

arrived. Both men, through their drunken haze, looked awe-struck.

'Come on guys,' said the tall man. 'What's this all *about*?'

'N-n-nothing!' they both said together.

'How about I get you both a *drink* and you can sort this out like *friends!* Okay?'

The old fellows shrugged.

The tall man turned and bellowed over to the barman: 'Hey Limey, a couple of *drinks* for these gentlemen!' Then he added, 'And fill mine up would ya. My glass looks pretty *empty* from here!'

'Sure thing Cap'n!' said Limey and he started pouring even though there were queues of people waiting right in front of him.

And that was that. Show over. The tall man walked back to his place at the bar and proceeded to get even drunker than he was already. The two old fellows slapped each other on the back and returned to arguing without fists. Conversations slowly resumed. There was murmuring about the tall man now he had drawn attention to himself. 'Isn't he . . . ?' 'Didn't he used to be . . . ?' 'Isn't it a tragedy . . . ?' 'And the boy was so young . . .'

And then four hours later, on his way home, he was picked up for being drunk and disorderly by a couple of rookie cops who couldn't believe their luck.

∫

Monday morning's a tough one. You sleep straight through the alarm, wake at quarter to eight and have to leave the house without ironing your shirt or having breakfast. You hate mornings like this: you know you're going to feel like shite all day. But if you roll in late Louie'll dock your wages. He's a cunt about punctuality.

You get there at eight thirty on the dot. Harry's just opening the door to the world as you leap off your bike and tie it to the railings outside. Louie's in the back brewing up some coffee. The coffee is the one true perk of working for Louie the Greek. His mother sends it over from Halkida and Louie brews it up in a strange contraption that looks like it was stolen from Dr Frankenstein's laboratory and serves it black and very, very strong in tiny white china cups. Normally you don't touch coffee, can't stand the taste of the stuff, but you can't say no to this. This is free drugs. You hold your breath and throw the drink back in two quick gulps. Immediately you can feel the caffeine shooting down every vein in your body like a heat-seeking missile. Zip! Bing! *Now* you feel ready for whatever the day has in store for you.

Except the day has nothing in store for you just yet because of course no fucker wants their hair cutting at eight thirty in the morning. You've tried pointing this out to Louie before, that every single morning he pays you and Harry for anywhere between half an hour and ninety minutes of sitting on your arses drinking coffee. Whereas you could really use an extra hour in bed. The old man's not having any of it, though. His line is that you stay open long hours so your customers know they can just drop in at any time. Convenience and reliability.

Convenience and reliability are two words that Louie the Greek uses a lot although his pronunciation of both is suspect.

So you drink his coffee and you talk.

—Good weekend then? you say to Harry as you do at this time every Monday morning.

—Yeah, bangin, he says maybe four Mondays out of five. Now and again Harry'll stay in on a Saturday night, usually when Charlton have lost that afternoon.

So Harry tells you where he went dancing and who he saw and you tell him where you went and who you saw. And Louie shakes his head in mock despair, murmurs something about young people today and disappears into his office to do the mysterious Paperwork that takes so much of his working week. (The business operates like this: you and Harry do the work, the actual cutting of the hair, while Louie sits in his office doing the Paperwork, which you have a hunch amounts to little more than finding new and more elaborate ways of counting his money. If the place is busy he'll show his face occasionally to sweep up the trimmings and empty the ashtrays; if not, he'll bark at you and Harry to do this instead of sitting around reading the magazines. You know Louie is a real barber because there's a yellowing certificate in Greek, dated 1962, from the Federation of Barbers in Athens that says he is. But in three and a half years of working here you've not once seen him lift a pair of scissors.) As soon as he's out of earshot you get down to the nitty-gritty of talking about drugs: when and where and how many. You both exaggerate wildly but you both know that you're both exaggerating wildly so it's okay. Even without making stuff up, though, your Saturday night beats his hands down this week.

—So what's W really like? goes Harry after you've finished your side of the story.

—Smashed out of his face when I saw him.

—Yeah man, but what was he *like*? You know, was he friendly an that or was he some stuck-up arrogant cunt?

—I dunno. He was smashed. Everyone's the same when they're smashed. He could barely stand up and he couldn't speak. He did shake my hand, though, rather than punch me in the face, so I suppose he must be a decent enough bloke underneath.

—You should have gone back to his gaff, though. That would've been some top do, that. Top-quality drugs available.

—Yeah, well Nick's coming in later. He'll tell us all about it.

—Can't believe you didn't go, man.

—I told you. There was this girl, right?

—Oh yeah, the *girl*, he sneers. —The one you managed to get so intimate with.

—She'd been up all fuckin night! She went straight from the club to work. There wasn't time. Anyway it wasn't like that; I think this is going to be a slower, gentler thing.

Harry snorts a laugh. —Yeah right. Just the way you like it, eh? You shrug your shoulders.

—Yeah, why not? I think this one could be special, you know? Harry shakes his head.

—You are *such* a wanker! If she could hear you actually spouting that crap. You say that every fuckin time! Every time you meet a bit and don't do nothing about it.

And he's right: you are a wanker. You want it slower and gentler like you want Harry to suddenly drop his trousers and piss on your shoes. You've thought of nothing but Sally since yesterday, how close you got, how far you stayed away. She was knackered you moron! You could have done anything you liked with her.

Ten past nine and not a whiff of a punter. Louie comes through and switches over the radio, much to your relief. There are only two radio stations allowed in this establishment. One is a Greek pirate station that comes out of North London and plays nothing but fucking awful bouzouki music that really begins to get under your skin after a while. This is, naturally, Louie's station of preference, but if the place is empty for too long he starts to worry, quite reasonably, that it's putting off the non-Greek punters. So then he switches over to the local news station which has inane phone-ins and debates and plays Top Forty tunes which are also fucking awful in the main but at least they're fucking awful in English.

Just before half past, Punter Number One marches bravely in and – oh fuck, it's Mr Noggin. Harry tosses a coin. You call tails. It's heads. Harry howls with laughter.

Mr Noggin is a charming, sweet man with a perfectly lucid brain and quick, dry sense of humour who just happens to have lost, in his old age, all control over his bladder. And like many men his age he has about a dozen hairs left on his entire head, yet he comes here every week. Every fucking week. Week in, week fucking out. And he stinks. And he insists on wearing light-coloured trousers that show up the piss-stains so you can see exactly where the damage has been done. —MR NOGGIN! you want to tell him (he's not deaf particularly but there's something about old people that makes you want to shout at them)—MR NOGGIN! YOU'VE GOT NO HAIR! YOU DON'T NEED TO COME HERE! NOW FUCK OFF HOME AND TAKE YOUR BASTARD BLADDER WITH YOU!

But you don't of course. You cut his hair as quickly as possible and breathe exclusively through your mouth.

The caffeine buzz soon wears off. Already you're starting to feel the effects of the weekend and the rushed morning again. The news comes on and it's *fucking* depressing, even for a Monday morning.

Some poor cunt in Leeds has died over the weekend, supposedly from taking a single E. He was out with his mates on Saturday night, down the pub. Didn't even want to go out clubbing after but his mates talked him in to it. They scored some pills off a dodgy geezer in the gents and all took one; the others had a brilliant time. This bloke had a good dance, but decided about one thirty that he needed some air so he went for a walk. They found him unconscious the following morning in a park some five miles from the club. Took him to hospital but were unable to revive him and he died overnight. He was seventeen.

Seventeen. Jesus.

And this is only a few months after some other poor cunt died in Bradford, supposedly from taking E, and that was splashed all over the news. What is it they're putting in their pills up there, for fuck's sake?

—Oh now that's terrible, says Mr Noggin.

—Just one tablet of ecstasy, the newsreader keeps saying over and over in his BBC tones. —Just one tablet of ecstasy was all it took.

You turn to Harry. He's stopped laughing now and he's staring at the floor.

They play a tape of the boy's mother speaking at a press conference over the weekend. She has the level, expressionless voice of someone who doesn't fully understand what she's reading, someone who is actively refusing to let the full weight of what she's saying sink in.

—David was such a lovely, sweet child As well as his loving family he was very popular and had lots of friends. He liked to go out and enjoy himself as most normal youngsters do . . .

Every so often her voice cracks with the strain.

—David was a normal boy. He'd never tried drugs before . . .

(Yeah right, you think immediately, but you don't say it. And neither does Harry.)

—We lost him to an evil, wicked substance peddled by evil, wicked men. We hope that our David's death will serve as a warning to other young people. Drugs are dangerous. DRUGS KILL!

David's father comes on next to appeal in a stern voice for witnesses to come forward to help catch the man who sold David the pill.

What's the fucking point? you think to yourself. The guy who sold it to him didn't know it was going to kill him. He's probably sold hundreds of Es in his life, never had punters die on him before. Now there's some small-time drug dealer up in Leeds shitting himself.

Louie comes out from the back. Somehow you knew he wouldn't be able to resist sticking his oar in on this one.

—See, is just like I told you . . .

As soon as he opens his mouth you know you've got about five seconds before you'll want to shove something very large down it.

—See, is like I told you. These little pills are very big danger. I'm sure his mother say to him every weekend, don't take the drugs, just like I tell you two boys here because I know you do. Don't take the drugs! But this boy, he didn't listen. And just like that other boy in Bradford, he didn't listen.

—So they both deserved to die then? you manage to spit out.

—That what you're sayin, Louie?

—Not *deserve* to die. A young boy don't *deserve* to die. But if they wasn't so stupid, they wouldn't be dead, that's all I say. You don't die of ecstasy if you don't want to.

Harry pipes up. —Yeah but he didn't actually die *of* ecstasy, did he? I mean, he actually died of heart failure or something, yeah?

Louie looks confused. Harry ploughs on.

—I mean, the doctor, when he does the death certificate, he's not gonna put for Cause of Death: Well, he was fuckin Ed out of his box wasn't he! He's gonna put Heart Failure or whatever . . .

—Yes yes, says Louie. —Heart failure from taking the ecstasy. Normally you don't die of heart failure when you are . . . how old is he?

—Seventeen, you tell him, feeling slightly ashamed. —They said it was going to be his eighteenth birthday in a couple of weeks.

—The poor mother, says Louie, shaking his head.

There's a short silence broken by Mr Noggin's high-pitched, croaky voice:—I spent my eighteenth birthday waiting to go over the top in the Somme.

Christ. *Did* you Mr Noggin? Well do tell us all about it; that'll cheer us up no end.

—I remember I drank whisky for the first time. One of the men had some he'd been sent from home and when he found out it was my birthday he insisted on sharing it. Just passed around the bottle, we didn't have cups or anything. It was a sort of party I suppose. We were all in quite high spirits. We had no idea what the next day held in store for us. I didn't have much of the whisky but I do remember the way it tasted and that warm glow it gave you all over. I'll tell you what though, I had a terrible headache the next morning.

He gives a hoarse little laugh. You start trying to do some mental arithmetic, an ambitious project for this time on a Monday morning. When the fuck was the Somme? 1915? 1916? Somewhere between 1914 and 1918 anyway. So if Mr Noggin was eighteen then, he must have been born just before the turn of the century, which means now . . . fucking hell, now he must be in his nineties. Jesus Christ! Suddenly you are prepared to forgive him the excesses of his bladder. Fuck his bladder. He can walk! He can speak! He can remember drinking whisky *seventy years ago*.

—Y'see, we'd been told that most of the enemy positions had already been taken out. That was the story going round the trenches. We were expecting an easy ride. We didn't know . . .

His voice trails off momentarily.

—Seven a.m. sharp we were up and at em. As I say, I had the most awful headache. We clambered over the trenches and we marched slowly forward and then . . . The chap who gave me the whisky, he was marching next to me, he was one of the first to go. Had his arm blown off. He staggered on for a bit, screaming and howling and then I think he got a bullet in the head. Put him out of his misery. I didn't feel so bad about drinking his whisky then.

You drift off while Mr Noggin reels off one horrific event after another. A thought occurs to you: suppose Mr N had been killed instead of his friend. Suppose it was him who got his arm blown off and a bullet in the brain. He wouldn't be here now, stinking out your place of work. But more than that, he'd have missed out on seventy whole years of his life. Seventy years! Think of the thousands of things he must have done in those years. Think of the thousands of little things he still does every day. Even being old and pissing your pants and having a life so empty you go to the barber every week although you've got no hair beats lying in an unmarked grave in a field in France with only one arm for seventy years.

Now. Think of all the people who *did* get theirs that day. Think of all the thousands of things each of those thousands of people could have done down all these years.

Think of that poor cunt in a park in Leeds. Seventeen.

Shit, you can feel yourself welling up. So no one sees you, you turn around and get a mirror to show Mr Noggin the back of his head. It looks uncannily like the front.

—That okay? you ask him.

Of course it's fucking okay; it hasn't changed since he walked in here. You just can't bear to hear any more of his story.

You help the old man clamber to his feet, take his bib from him, lead him over to the coat rack and help him on with his hat and coat. He gives you the exact change, as always. Then he shuffles towards the door, waving cheerily. —Toodle-oo then. See you all next week.

The second he's outside, Harry's running about squirting air-freshener everywhere.

—Fuckin hell man! I thought the old bastard was never gonna shut up. That was twice as long as he usually takes.

You sit down. You can't be bothered to argue with Harry about sensitivity. Louie sits down next to you and exhales noisily.

—Sad story, he says.

You nod.

—I could tell you some stories about my father and the Greek Civil War.

You look at him despairingly. —Fuck off, Louie.

On the radio they're now promising a live studio debate followed by a phone-in on the subject of young people and drug abuse. Hoo-bloody-ray.

—So if you're a concerned parent, or if you're a friend of someone who has a drug problem, or if you have a drug problem yourself, please call us now, and remember you can call us anonymously on oh eight hundred blah-di-blah-di-blah . . .

Anonymously. Sure. Phone up a radio station and speak to fifty thousand people anonymously. Your mum and all your friends aren't going to recognise your voice, are they?

—Yeah, I've got a fuckin drug problem, Harry starts shouting at the radio. —Every now an again I can't get hold of any cause my supplier's been sent down an I have to put up with sanctimonious cunts like you lecturing me on the subject!

You can't even manage a smile at this. Louie is still sitting, shaking his head. —Harry, Harry, Harry, he says quietly.

Okay, first you felt like shite. Now you feel like shite and you're fucking depressed. Have a nice day.

A doctor is speaking in that poncey, know-it-all voice that doctors have. Doctors on the radio at any rate.

—Of course, cases of ecstasy causing serious physical harm to users are actually quite rare.

—That's not to say ecstasy doesn't cause physical damage, though, is it.

—Well . . .

—Because we know that it does.

—We don't actually *know* that for certain . . .

—We've got proof right here! There are people dead. Only a matter of weeks ago Peter Bartlett, aged nineteen, found dead in his bedroom in Bradford; now David Samuels, aged seventeen – *seventeen* – found dead in a park in Leeds.

—Now, we don't know for sure what killed them.

—Drugs killed them. They were alive. They took ecstasy. They're dead. End of story.

—Mmm, not quite . . .

—To be frank with you, doctor, I think it's rather disturbing to hear a medical man such as yourself trying to suggest that this killer drug is somehow safe.

—Ah now, I never said ecstasy was *safe*. It's far from being safe. What I'm trying to say if you'll just let me, finish, Bill, is that we tend sometimes to concentrate too much on the physical effects of ecstasy, and cases of physical damage like this are, whatever you say and I know you don't want to agree with me, actually quite rare. However, it is the long-term *psychological* effects that are of great concern to me. An estimated quarter of a million people take this drug on a regular basis . . .

—What sort of psychological effects are we talking about?

—Oh, the usual: depression, paranoia. Paranoia especially.

—I should think they are pretty paranoid. Chances are they're going to die very shortly!

Cue studio laughter. Bill, the presenter, the Voice of Impartiality, has cracked a joke.

—As I say, an estimated quarter of a million people take this drug on a regular—the doc tries again.

But Bill cuts him off. —Mmm. That's very interesting. But I'd like to focus for now, if we can, on the physical nature of this deadly drug. I believe we have Lesley on Line Five. Can you hear me, Lesley?

A woman's voice sounds like it's coming from Mars. —Hello? Hello?

—Hello Lesley.

—Hello Bill!

—Hello Lesley. What's your point?

What is her fucking point indeed.

—I just wanted to say, Bill . . . love the show by the way, really good—

—Thanks Les.

—I just wanted to say that a friend of my sister's, her son goes to a school where someone died of drugs a couple of years ago. So this problem really does affect us all. And what I'd like to see is the bringing back of the death penalty for these people.

—Which people exactly, Lesley?

—You know, drug dealers, drug pushers, drug takers.

—So just for drug offences then?

—Yes.

—I see. Interes—

—And maybe for Asian drivers.

—I beg your pardon, Lesley?

—They should bring the death penalty back for these Asians who can't drive an all. I don't know what it's like round your way but round here it's terrible, they cut you up at roundabouts, they don't indicate—

Click.

—Thank you Lesley! An interesting point. The death penalty for drug dealers. It works for Thailand, it works for Singapore. Professor Stuart Brockwell, could it work for Britain?

—Jesus fucking Christ, you say under your breath, but louder than you think.

—Ouch! yells the poor bastard whose hair you're cutting.

—Shit! Sorry, man. I was just listening to that bollocks on the radio, you know.

—Feeling guilty are you? he goes.

—What me? No mate, I don't deal drugs. I cut hair for a living.

—Yes, but I get the feeling that you and your friend . . . well, perhaps I'm jumping to conclusions.

He's a well-spoken gent with not much on top of his head, but one of the ugliest, bushiest moustaches you've ever seen.

—And what conclusions would you be jumping to? you ask him innocently.

—Well, I would imagine that you and your friend . . . uh, *dabble* occasionally.

You bite your lip to stop yourself laughing.

—Dabble? you roar. —Hey Harry, this bloke thinks we might be dabbling. What d'you reckon? Do you dabble?

—Dabble! Harry roars back. —I don't dabble. I fuckin *indulge*, mate. I *overdo*.

He gives a quick flurry with his scissors. The young lad he's doing looks completely bewildered.

Your gent chuckles good-naturedly. This is good. At this point he either laughs along or he stands up and punches you out. And, crap as this bloke looks, you're not really up for a scrap right now: it's Monday morning and you feel like shite. Anyway, you're only having a laugh, aren't you?

—I'm sorry if I've offended you, says the gent.

—No mate, you're all right, you go. —I'm just curious as to how you arrived at these conclusions.

—Well, you know . . . your clothes, your hair, your friend's nose stud, the music.

He has a point about the music. Louie's gone out on his Errands and Harry, still muttering about *indulging* and *overdoing*, has taken the opportunity to bung in a bootleg DJ mix tape he picked up at Camden Market yesterday afternoon and he's whacked the volume up. This is brutal, unforgiving techno and it sounds fucking magic to your ears on a Monday morning, especially after those pompous arsewipes on the radio. But you have to admit it's as likely to alienate as many punters as Louie's bouzouki shite.

Harry starts grooving to it, snapping his scissors to the beat. —*Da*bble, *da*bble, *da*bble, he begins to chant to himself.

His customer is looking positively scared now.

—Okay. Fair point about the music, you concede. —But, anyway, whether I dabble or whether I indulge or whatever the fuck I do, why should I feel guilty? I didn't sell him the E. Kid knew what he was doing anyway.

—Mmm, that's debatable, says the gent. —But no, you're right, you shouldn't feel guilty. It had nothing to do with you.

—Exactly, you say hesitantly.

—It's just that you sounded a little touchy about the subject just now.

—I'm not fuckin touchy! you say touchily. —I'm just bored of the subject, that's all. We've been talking bout it all fuckin morning and it's been on the radio and I'm sick of being lectured about it.

—I see.

You stop cutting. Part of you wants to do a Mr Blond on this guy for getting you so wound up, but you know it's not really his fault.

The phone rings and Harry gets there first. You hope it's for you. You desperately want to talk to someone, anyone about something else. Football, last night's telly, Marvel super-heroes; politics or Russian history or your horoscope for the week; anything except drug-related deaths.

—It's your dealer, says Harry, holding out the receiver.

You wish he hadn't said that. It's Ian, of course, and Ian *is* in many ways your dealer. But not in the way the gent in front of you thinks. You see the sparkle in his eye and now you definitely want to Mr Blond him.

—Hey Ian, what you got? you say, taking the phone.

—Hey Harry, turn that shit down, you yell when you realise you can't make out a fucking word at the other end.

Ian repeats himself. —I got a little something that might be of interest to you.

—Yeah?

—Issue Three of a certain American super-hero comic.

—Is it—?

Ian cuts in. —A certain very-difficult-to-get-hold-of American super-hero comic. Featuring a certain American super-hero who inspires a certain devotion among his followers.

Ian irritates the fuck out of you when he's in this kind of mood, which is basically all the time, but he has the goodies you need so what can you do?

—Look man, is it what I think it is or what?

—Now that would depend on what you were thinking.

—Don't fuck about, man. Is it Captain Midnight?

Ian pauses while he tries to find a suitably wanky way of saying yes. —You wouldn't be far wrong in that assumption, is what he eventually manages.

—Yes! you grunt to yourself and you punch the air with your

fist. All you've managed to do is score an obscure comic book from an annoying git in North London but you celebrate it like a winning goal at Wembley.

The gent with the moustache gives you a wink in the mirror, but you're smiling now and not even this cunt can bring you down.

Harry, meanwhile, is showing his punter his own back and sides.

—Yeah yeah, the kid says impatiently. Poor fucker can't wait to get out of here. If Harry had given him a Phil Oakey, he'd still be itching to split.

—Can you wait for me till six thirty? you ask Ian down the phone.

—As always, comes the reply.

You hang up as the young lad scurries out the door.

—Don't forget your change now, Harry calls after him, slamming the till draw shut. —Oh yes, I do like a tip.

Your guy is not so easily intimidated, though. You finish his cut once and he asks for a bit more off the top. You take a bit more off the top and he wants it tapered at the back. Any more of this shit and you're actually going to start humming 'Stuck In The Middle With You'.

Still, at least he shuts the fuck up. The rest of the cut passes almost in silence. Harry turns the music back up and you both groove to it a little. The punter tries to nod his head, but you point out to him that if he carries on doing this you'll more than likely cut a hole in his scalp. He gives one of his good-natured laughs. But he stops doing it.

When he comes to pay, though, he leans over to you and whispers:—Look mate, do you think you could sort me out a little something for the weekend?

You don't fucking believe this. You look over at Harry and his jaw's hit the ground.

—I told you man, that's not my job. My job's cutting hair.

—Yeah, but obviously you know some people—?

—Y'see, there you go jumping to your conclusions again.

He looks at you imploringly. You raise your hands in a final gesture. He shrugs his shoulders and turns to leave.

—Keep the change, he says sadly.

He wanders out into the street, absently dabbing the tissue you gave him at the beautifully-tapered nape of his neck.

—Jesus, what a tosser, says Harry.

Six o'clock takes forever to come round. The day started off badly and it doesn't get worse so much as slow down. So it's a bad day for much, much longer.

Louie comes back shortly after lunch, looking a little red in the face (his Errands, which he runs most days, consist of meeting up with a bunch of his mates at a Greek café, playing backgammon and putting away a few bottles of retsina). He shouts at you both about the music.

—What is this? You bastards trying to put me out of business?

You refuse to have the phone-in show back on because you *know* they'll still be droning on about drug scares. So you compromise on Louie's bouzouki bollocks. You try and blank it out of your mind and concentrate on the job in front of you, but that doesn't work so you try and imagine what this music would sound like with a great thumping backbeat underneath it. Ah! That's better!

Nick never shows up and you're both disappointed and relieved. Disappointed because you're quite curious to hear what he got up to on Saturday night, relieved because no doubt he'd have gone on and on about it for ages. *And* he'd have wanted to discuss the drug panic story at inordinate length.

You leave on the dot of six and cycle through the rush-hour traffic up to Ian's grotty little shop in Camden. It's a hot day and tempers are beginning to fray among some of the drivers. The car windows are all down and you catch snippets of the news as you skim by the stationary vehicles. Is there no escaping this fucking news story?

The shop is closed when you get there so you bang on the window to get Ian's attention. He emerges after a while, scratching his scraggy beard and clutching a doubtless very rare, rolled-up Spiderman comic.

—*Willkommen, bienvenu,* welcome, he says, opening the door to let you in.

The smell of the place hits you full force. You always think you're prepared for it, but it gets you every time. The whole place stinks of musty old paper; of cigarettes and coffee; of *Marvel* comics T-shirts worn by young men on hot summer days with a total absence of under-arm deodorant (hey, why waste money on vanity products when there are entire series of *Uncanny X-Men* back issues to be bought?). The whole place stinks, essentially, of Ian.

—Fancy a brew? he says, manoeuvring between the boxes and piles of old comics on the floor.

As it happens you're dying for a cup of tea, but you've had cups of tea made by Ian before and death is infinitely preferable.

—No, you're all right. Come on then, let's see what you got.

He starts flicking through a bunch of envelopes behind the till, looking for the one with your name on it. Naturally they're all misfiled and it takes him an age. Or is he just being a cunt?

—Come on, man

—Christ, I can feel you trembling from here, he goes.

—Yeah right.

Finally he remembers he's already looked out your envelope and stashed it under the counter. He fishes it out, tutting to himself at his own stupidity – you want to punch him in the mouth – and hands it over.

And you tear open that fucking envelope. You tear it open like a kid on Christmas morning. You tear it open, but you're *very* careful not to damage the goods inside. You slide the magazine out carefully and turn it over to look at the cover and . . . and it is! IT FUCKING IS!

It's Issue Three of *Captain Midnight Saves The Earth*.

Jesus Christ, *look* at you. You're twenty-fucking-eight years old, going weak at the knees over a fucking comic book. Even wank mags wouldn't be as sad as this.

Of course, now you've got your goodies you've absolutely no desire to talk to Ian at all. Now he's just a smelly cunt in a crap T-shirt. You want to get yourself home and shoot up.

—So how are things with you anyway? he asks hopefully. But he knows the score; pimps and pushers all do.

—Yeah, all right.

You can't afford to be blatantly rude to him: you're going to need him again after all. But you do want to get the hell out of his shop.

—Haircutting business going okay?

—Yeah. Fine. We keep cutting it, fucking stuff keeps growing back. Always busy . . . always busy . . .

You're sure you've had exactly this conversation with Ian before. Word for word. You roll up your precious comic and begin drumming listlessly with it on your left palm as you gently reverse towards the door.

—Yeah, comics are doing all right too, he says, presumably in response to a question he imagines that you asked.

—Hey, you gonna see the film? he continues.

—What, the *Captain Midnight* film?

What other film is he likely to be talking about? Your all-time hero is about to be turned into Hollywood product and he wants to know if you're *going*?

—Yeah, I might check it out, you say. By which you mean, of course, that you'll be first in the queue the night it opens.

—Yeah. It'll be shit, though, says Ian.

—Course it will.

—But we'll still have to see it.

—Absolutely.

Conversation dries up. You have to think of something to say before Ian asks if he can come to the cinema with you.

—So, when you expecting Issue Four? you ask, seizing on the one thing you actually give a flying fuck about.

Ian draws in breath loudly through his teeth like a motor mechanic looking at a woman driver's dodgy carburettor.

—Couldn't say, he frowns. —Three to four weeks I should think. Six weeks tops. I'll give you a call. But . . . you know . . . we should meet up before then. Go for a beer.

Hand on the door. Almost safe. You want to 'go for a beer' with Ian like you want to fuck your mum's cat. Not now, not ever. You grab the door handle behind your back, you turn it slowly. It's bastard well locked.

Ian produces the keys from his pocket and dangles them tantalisingly in front of your face. Fuck. You're his prisoner. He's going to hold you to ransom. Not let you go until you've signed a sworn promise in your own blood to meet him at a stated time at a stated place to 'go for a beer'.

But he's merciful. He unlocks the door and you escape out into the sweet, warm evening air.

—See you later then, he goes.

—Yeah, see you round.

And you're so grateful to be away that you actually give him a couple of pats on the shoulder in something approaching a gesture of friendliness and male bonding. Steady on.

You clamber on to your bike and pedal away furiously past all the same cars that were queuing here in the heat on your way up. Christ, who'd be a motorist in London in the summertime.

When you get back, you're pleased to discover your flatmates aren't in. The chief function in your life of your flatmates is to be so resolutely square they make you feel cool. They're nice guys as far as it goes but right now you really don't want to hear about their day, or listen to their records, or watch their TV programmes, or meet any of their friends who may happen to have dropped by. You just want some peace and quiet.

Before you've even got your bag on the table, though, your little urban idyll is shattered by the familiar squeak squeak *grunt* from the Incredible Shagging Neighbours who live behind the paper-thin walls next door. Squeak squeak *grunt*. Squeak squeak *grunt*. It's eight o'fucking clock! What do they think they're doing? Any normal, healthy married couple ought to be watching *Brookside* in glum silence or arguing about whose turn it is to do the washing-up around now. Not fucking on the sofa! The very idea brings a nasty taste to your mouth.

You switch on the radio and turn it up loud. But that only encourages them. The bastard starts taking his stroke from the click track on the record they're playing. You get *grunt* click *grunt* click *grunt* click until it makes you want to scream. You put a couple of slices of toast on and get a beer out of the fridge. When the toast's up, you take it through to the front room and settle down with your headphones, Harry's mix tape which you took while he wasn't looking this afternoon, and Captain Midnight.

The tape bursts in halfway through a track the way mix tapes always do, as if to suggest that there is no beginning or end to this music, just an endless loop and you're hearing only a tiny fragment of it. The track grabs you immediately. An insistent synth riff that gradually opens out and then closes again, like a mouth blowing smoke rings. Now let them grunt and squeak all they like, the bastards. The track gets increasingly manic as it goes on, the riff getting higher and higher in pitch until it sounds like it's going to explode.

An hour passes in a flash. When you get to the end of your comic – and a banging good issue it is too – you flick back through it slowly, reliving the story in flashback. This is how you're supposed to dream, isn't it? Backwards at double speed. Then, just at the point you wake up, your brain flips the dream over and slows it down so you can make some sort of sense of it. That's how come you always wake up at the most interesting bit. Once you're back at the beginning you start reading again from the top. And just as you're starting to read, you get one of those blinding moments of self-revelation that if you could distil it into pill form, you'd have the drug of the century and be very rich and completely fulfilled for ever. Just as you're starting to read your poxy kiddies' comic for the second time, it occurs to you that you're purely, blissfully, unequivocally happy. This, really, is all you need from life.

Christ. Little things please little minds or what? Look at you! Bottle of beer. Slice of toast and butter. Tape of some mindless, faceless techno bollocks. And a comic you should have grown out of when you were eleven. And you're a pig in shite. No other people, you'll notice, in this little paradise of yours. No friends. No mates. No social skills required. You'd be better off as a fucking hermit on top of a pillar. Or in some squalid bedsit somewhere with your old *Marvel* collection and your 'exclusive' remix tapes. Rent'd be cheaper. You could give up your job: why exactly *are* you working all hours to buy creature comforts you don't really need? And you could live on your own: no more having to hope the wankers you share with won't be in when you come home at night. In fact, if it wasn't for your job which you hate and your flatmates whom you tolerate, you'd never have to go out or speak to anyone at all, would you? What kind of sad, lonely, antisocial, fucked-up individual are you? You know, it's people like you who suddenly snap one day and go and shoot up little children in shopping malls.

And what about that new girlfriend of yours? Eh? What's she going to think when she finds out what a complete headcase you are? And she will find out. Of course she will. You can't keep shit like this buried for long.

And there you have it. No sooner has it struck you how great you're feeling than you're feeling like shit again.

Have a nice evening.

∫

Commander Tiff Rimini sat at the battered communication desk and prepared to make the most painful broadcast of his life. All around him was carnage. Throughout the city, the only settlement on this tiny, far-flung moon, buildings were gutted and burned. There were few people left and those not already dead were close to death, including Rimini himself. He could feel the life ebbing away from him with every movement he made.

EEEAAARRRGGHH!

In the adjacent room another one of his men perished. Lieutenant Howell, a young father of two, had set fire to the computer records room and sat in the flames.

Rimini switched on the transmitter and was relieved to find it still working. He searched for the signal of the Galactic Government Headquarters but was unable to get a fix on it; he then scanned for any suitable frequency, anyone at all who would be able to pick him up and hear what he had to say, but the airwaves were completely jammed. So he just sent his message out into the ether. He didn't have time to wait for a strong signal. Someone would receive the message eventually: space was infinite, that was the one thing you could be sure of.

He caught himself smoothing his hair back as the screen in front of him flickered into life, even though he knew he would be long gone before these images reached anyone. Vanity was the last to die. He cleared his throat and began.

'My name is *Commander Tiff Rimini*, Governor of the city of *Kahtoom*, the only outpost on the third moon of the planet *Jowa* in the Serpicus Six system! For the last twenty-four hours we have been under *attack* from a race of beings known to us only as the *Ancients*! These aliens have completely *destroyed* our city and caused *unimaginable devastation* to its citizens! This is not a Mayday call; by the time I am received it will be too *late* for that! This is intended as *information* for any interested party who receives it and also as a final log entry for the *Galactic Government*, with whom I serve, should it ever reach them. This race of beings are the *deadliest* I have encountered in my long career of deep space exploration! Their threat is not a *physical* one. They have damaged physically only our *buildings* and *vehicles*. Not one of our citizens has perished directly at the hands of the Ancients, *and yet . . .*'

Rimini paused. What was the point of trying to explain it all? He should have sent this message many hours ago if it were to achieve anything. Many hours ago, however, his sense of duty seemed to have deserted him completely. He was comforted to find the last dying ember of professionalism that had led him to at least attempt the broadcast before it was all over. Now his duty was done though. No more.

'Rimini *out*!' he said and snapped off the transmitter. He reached inside his uniform jacket and took out his laser pistol. He checked the energy levels, set the controls to full and placed the nozzle in his mouth. Thinking of his mother, he squeezed the trigger with his left thumb.

∫

So when's a cool time to call Sally? How long should you leave it before calling to show that, yes, you're interested – keen even – but you're also pretty cool about it and not in any way completely fucking desperate. Christ, it's so long since you've done this kind of shit. What's the protocol? Monday's too early, obviously. Tuesday you decide Wednesday would be better. Wednesday night you decide Thursday would be better still.

Anyway you can't phone her Wednesday night – at least this is what you tell yourself as the evening progresses – because Nick shows up at long last and you spend the whole evening with him. He rolls into the shop around half five wearing, you're sure, the same clothes you saw him in on Saturday night, his hair looking like it's glued together by grease, and three days' growth scratching away at his chin.

—Fuckin hell, it's Captain Oates back from his little walk, you go.

—Doctor Livingston, I presume, is his response.

—All right matey! yells Harry from across the room, looking up from his crossword. —How you doin?

They rap for a couple of minutes about Charlton Athletic and their dismal prospects for next season. The commotion brings Louie out of his little den.

—Hey, hey, what's all the fuss, he goes to Nick. —You want a haircut or you just come here to chat to my staff?

—Yeah, cause we're far too busy to chat, says Harry without even bothering to look up from the crossword this time.

—No, it's cool, man, says Nick. —You can give me a cut. Just a Number One all over. No frills.

Louie gives you the nod.

—Fuck off. I'm not cutting that, you say flatly.

—He's a customer, he wants his hair cut, says Louie like he's explaining it to a small child.

—Louie, look at this shit. It's got fuckin animals living in it.

Nick makes a show of looking hurt. —John, man, I thought we were mates.

—Course we are. Mates got nothin to do with it. Your hair's a fuckin disgrace, that's all, an I'm not touching it.

Louie's wagging his finger furiously.

—He's a customer. Customers are customers, he points out, as though this will settle the matter once and for all.

—How bout giving him a wash and cut? says Harry.

Nick protests. —What's the fuckin point in washing it when I'm just going to get it shaved off?

—Okay, okay, okay, says Louie, raising his hands. —How about this, John gives you wash and cut but you only pay for cut?

And with that he beams as though he's just negotiated a peace settlement in Cyprus.

—Why, that's a very kind offer indeed, Mr Kouliadis, says Nick, looking directly at you.

Oh, bollocks.

You lead Nick over to the basin, sit him down in the chair and gently tilt his head backwards. You wrap a towel round his shoulders and tuck it in snugly. You fetch a tunic and attach that to his front, making sure it doesn't grip his neck too tightly. Then you turn the shower-head on and let the water play on your left hand to test the temperature.

And then, when you're sure it's really fucking scalding, you aim the jet at his head.

—OUCH! he screams.

—I'm sorry, sir, you say smoothly. —Would you like the temperature a little higher or a little lower?

—Lower, you cunt!

So you turn off the hot altogether, whack up the cold, and give him another blast.

He practically leaps into orbit. —JESUS FUCKING CHRIST!

Louie comes scurrying back out of his den.

—You're a fucking CUNT, Santini, says Nick when he can get his breath back.

—John, I'm warning you, says Louie, although as usual he doesn't say exactly *what* he's warning you.

Harry's pissing himself laughing and you can't help joining him.

—Okay, I'm sorry, man, you say between giggles. —I won't do it again, I promise. Come on, sit down.

Nick looks at you suspiciously and mutters.

—I'm warning you, says Louie again before disappearing to count some more money.

Number Ones are a piece of piss. Maybe that's why they're called Number Ones: they're the first, basic, most primitive haircut. Easiest thing to learn. You get your electric razor, fix the attachment, whizz whizz whizz, job's done. Fucking monkey could do it. And *everyone* wants Number Ones these days. Time was when it was just the Nazis wanted a shaved head; now everyone's in on the act. Gay blokes; techno heads; weird New Age characters; crusties; blokes in their thirties just starting to lose it; anyone, in fact, who can't be arsed with their hair any more. Naturally you love doing Number Ones. Five minutes work and they cost the same as any other cut. But you really want to spin Nick's cut out so you can go for a drink with him at six. You don't think Louie's going to be in the mood to let you go early after your little jape. So you run the razor over Nick's head very slowly, savouring every last beautifully clean hair that's plucked. Then you delicately sculpt some shape into his sideys and neck-line.

But it's still all done by quarter to.

—How bout a shave? you say

—Fuck off, says Nick, quite reasonably under the circumstances. —You think I'm going to let you anywhere near my neck with a razor?

—Come on, man, I was only messing about. I don't actually want to kill you. Anyway, you need a shave; your beard's longer than the rest of your hair now.

He peers at himself in the mirror. It's true: his lovingly crafted sideys do look kind of ridiculous set against the tangled bush directly below.

—Okay, he says reluctantly. —But you better be *fucking* careful.

—Sure thing, you say gleefully.

This is great. You love doing shaves. Makes you feel like a barber in an old Hollywood movie.

Conversation is still stilted, though. Louie's right next door and you two know you couldn't talk for five minutes without mentioning drug stuff. And you suspect Nick is still a bit sore at you about that shit with the water.

Harry's chatting away to his customer, though; an amiable-looking bloke in his fifties. They're talking about house prices. Harry knows as much about house prices as you do about netball, but that doesn't usually stop him. Here he is, in fact, prattling on about the inherent risks of endowment mortgages against the grim life-enslavement of repayment mortgages, exchanging negative equity horror stories with the customer (are there any more boring stories in the whole known universe?) and even attempting to predict the ebb and flow of interest rates over the next five years. Of course, if he actually knew anything about any of this shit he'd be retired by now, having made a killing on the property market, instead of cutting people's hair at six fifty an hour.

At five to six you pluck the last hair from Nick's chin and wash the lather off with water: water so beautifully, satisfyingly warm it could have come directly from a natural spa rather than out of your rusty, grungey tap. You towel him off and give him a squirt of the three-year-old cheap shite aftershave that Louie once bought at the duty free shop at Gatwick.

—Fancy a pint then? you ask Nick, extremely quietly.

—IT'S ONLY FIVE TO! Louie barks from his den before you've even finished the question.

Nick grins as he hands over a fiver. —How bout I just see you in there?

You spend exactly four and a half minutes pretending to sweep up Nick's shavings while listening to Harry's inane chatter; now the punter's trying to persuade Harry that estate agents are not, in fact, the complete wankers they're often made out to be, but a bunch of essentially good guys doing a difficult job as well as they can. OF COURSE THEY'RE FUCKING WANKERS! you want to interject, but you don't. It's an unwritten rule that you do not interrupt a man in conversation with his barber. It's a sacred relationship.

By the time you hit the pub, Nick has already downed half his first pint.

—You get me one in then? you ask him hopefully, although it's perfectly obvious he hasn't.

—No, but if you're going I'll have another.

You've never managed to work out if Nick earns more money than you, or less. Unless there are stacks of articles in obscure publications that he chooses to keep quiet about, he's not exactly the most prolific journalist in the world. And how much does this kind of shit pay anyway? Presumably the odd pieces he's had in the national press have paid reasonably handsomely, but you can only recall a couple of those in the last year or so – and you *know* when one of the dailies has run a piece by Nick because he buys all the copies in his local newsagent and presents one to everyone he knows.

Whatever his income, though, he is *fantastically* tight-arsed with his money. This stunt with the drinks is so typical of him he could copyright it.

You have plenty of time to ponder Nick's financial status while waiting at the bar. It's not that there's a queue or anything, it's just that you have the bar presence of a gnat and the barmaid has some really important glasses she has to finish washing before she serves you.

When it finally dawns on you that you are more likely to grow old and die in here than you are to ever get a drink, you call over softly to her:—Two pints of Kronenbourg, please.

—Just coming, love, she says and carries right on washing those glasses. How'd they ever get dirty anyway? You and Nick are the only punters in here and you haven't managed to dirty a fucking glass yet.

Behind the frantic scrubbing of glasses, you catch a glimpse of Barry the Landlord flitting into the kitchen.

—HEY BARRY! you yell at him desperately. —ALL RIGHT, MATE!

Barry turns round with a startled expression. The barmaid looks a little concerned.

—Oh hi . . . er, Jim, isn't it? says Barry, coming through to the bar.

—John.

It's perfectly okay for him not to know your name. You've only been coming here every week for three years.

—John, yeah right!

—From the . . . you know, place next door. Ever need a cut . . .

You grin at him moronically. But it's had the desired effect; your pints are now being pulled; the bimbo barmaid has finally twigged that you are a Regular and this is your Local and you deserve some Respect.

Nick's finished his first pint by the time you get back to him. He pushes the empty, froth-stained glass away and pulls in the fresh one, lifting it to his lips immediately – without saying thank you, you note, the ungrateful bastard. You sit down.

And you stare at each other for a short while, neither of you sure who should start.

—So . . ., you both say, simultaneously, eventually.

Then you both laugh.

—So how was your drugfest with W Saturday night? is what you start to say.

—So what about you and that girl, eh? is what Nick manages to get out fractionally ahead of you.

You shrug, trying to look as noncommittal as possible. —Yeah, nice one, you say airily.

—Have you . . . you know . . . ? asks Nick and he makes a jerking movement with his elbow which you know he means to signify sex, but which resembles no sexual manoeuvre you have ever come across.

—No, man, it's early days.

—Aw come *on*. God had created land and sea by now.

He makes a big show of looking away in disappointment like he's just had a crucial goal disallowed. All you can do is shrug again.

—Anyway she had to go to work.

—When? Monday morning?

—No, man, Sunday. She works the flower market up Columbia Road. She had to start at six so we went straight there from the club. I had a kip in the back of her van while she set up the stall, then I helped her out a bit, then we went and had lunch.

—An that's it?

—That's it. I told you before, I'm a smooth operator; I like to take things nice and slow.

—Bollocks, says Nick. —So you gonna see her again or what?

—Yeah. Reckon I might phone her tonight when I get in.

—It's Wednesday, he tells you.

—Yeah. I figure, Saturday night: promise to call, Wednesday night: call. Keeps em guessing. It's long enough to show that you're not gagging for em, not so long that they . . . you know . . .

—Get fucked off with you and go off with someone else.

—Yeah . . . Anyway, she hasn't called me.

—Does she have your number?

—I'm in the book.

—Does she know your surname?

—Yeah . . . I told her.

—Do you think she was listening?

Fair point.

—So what about you? you ask him to change the subject. —Where the fuck you been? I thought you were coming round Monday.

—Been to Leeds, he says secretively, obviously as glad as you are that the conversation has switched over to him.

—Leeds? you say thickly, waiting for him to expand.

—Yeah, it's a long story, he says, taking a long gulp of his drink. Then he just looks at you.

It's half past six, you're thinking to yourself, how fucking long a story can it be?

—Ask me about my Saturday night first, he goes. He's obviously been planning exactly how he's going to tell this story for some time.

—Okay, you say, and you adopt the voice of a four-year-old:—How was your Saturday night, Nick?

—Fuckin *storming!* he says, leaning into you. —I have never consumed so many unidentifiable substances in my life.

This is exactly what you were afraid of at the time. You're glad you didn't go. He reels off a long list of minor celebs who were there: it sounds like a sort of alternative *Hello!* diary piece. The only people you're sorry to have missed are two top-name DJs who apparently played all night and most of the following day. Not having their own collections to hand, they had to make do with what was available, alternating between fairly recent club classics and some really old retro shit: Abba, Dexy's, Chic, Blondie, Tears For Fucking Fears.

If it were to get out to the music press that a certain DJ had been playing Tears For Fears tunes at a house party, it would kill the guy's career. Either that or it would kick-start Tears For Fears' career back into action.

The more Nick tells you about it, the sadder the whole thing sounds. Later on in the evening, W and a few members of his Inner Circle settled down to a game of Pass the Parcel. Attached to each layer of the parcel was a little bag with a powder or pill of some description. W and his mates threw the package violently at one another and whoever had it when the music stopped had to unwrap a layer and consume the drug. The game continued until all the layers had been removed and there was a winner, or until an ambulance had to be called.

—I mean, fuckin cool or what! says Nick, who gets impressed by stuff like this.

You shake your head.

Various wasted-looking, scantily-clad girls passed among the guests with trays of pills, some brightly coloured, some deathly-white, some large, some small. Nick contented himself with dropping one of these every so often and dancing to the peculiar cocktail of music. W didn't talk to him all night. There again, after the game of Pass the Parcel W didn't talk to anyone much. So when Nick was bored of dancing he went up and nodded to Fat Cunt.

Fat Cunt nodded back.

And they both stood in complete silence for an age, nodding to the music.

—Fuckin hell, this is Tears For Fears, innit? said Fat Cunt eventually.

They both laughed. Long, deep, drug-induced belly laughs. Then suddenly Fat Cunt looked at his watch.

—Shit, what time is it?

—I dunno, said Nick—Bout four thirty, I think.

—*Fuck!* My watch is broken.

He ripped the strap off and flung the watch across the room.

—Stupid fuckin thing!

A few people looked over at him. Then they looked away again pretty sharpish.

—Listen, is there a TV in here?

—A TV? said Nick.

—Yeah! A fuckin TV!

Nick was scared by the tone of voice. —I, uh . . . I dunno. Yeah, there must be. Guy's an actor ain't he. Let's have a look upstairs.

They went upstairs and found a portable telly in one of the bedrooms. There were two girls doing lines of coke on the bed and just starting to undress each other. They looked up with bewildered expressions as Nick and Fat Cunt stumbled into the room.

—Fuck off now! Fat Cunt barked at them. —I wanna watch TV.

One of the girls looked like she was thinking briefly of complaining. Then she caught the glint in Fat Cunt's eyes and started putting her clothes back on.

—What the fuck you wanna watch at four thirty in the morning? Nick asked as the girls scurried past him.

—Programme bout Roswell. Documentary. New footage an everything. I forgot to set the fuckin video before I came out an now my fuckin watch is broken. I've missed five minutes of this already.

Nick started to ask him something else but Fat Cunt held up a hand to silence him.

—Look, I wanna watch this, all right? Now, why don't you stand by the door an make sure no one comes in an disturbs me, yeah?

Nick wasn't going to argue. He went over and stood by the door. He could still see the telly, but he wasn't really interested. All it was, as far as he could see, was blurred black and white video footage of a bunch of men in white coats poking and prodding what looked very much like one of the puppets off *Sesame Street*. He smoked half a joint someone had given him earlier and had passed out before the programme ended.

He was woken roughly by Fat Cunt shaking him.

—Nick. Come on, wake up man.

Fat Cunt looked white as death. He looked like the Roswell alien had got up off the autopsy table and come round to pick a fight.

—What's goin on? Nick asked blearily.

—It's the news, Fat Cunt hissed at him. —Come and watch the news.

By the time Nick was sufficiently awake to take anything in, the bulletin was finished, so Fat Cunt filled him in on the story, which was just breaking, of the dead kid in Leeds. The seventeen-year-old.

—I tell you, there's more to this than they're letting on, he said urgently. —Listen, you still writing?

Nick nodded.

—I think you should get up there, do some digging around. There's a story to this, I fuckin know there is.

—Okay, said Nick. —I might ring a few people tomorrow.

—No, man, this is serious. You gotta go now. Right now.

Now? It was nearly dawn. Nick was just thinking about making his excuses and leaving. He was fucked. The last thing in the world he was about to do was get on a train and go to Yorkshire.

—Now, said Fat Cunt firmly.

On the other hand . . .

Fat Cunt babbled on about the story and Nick's poor, mashed brain tried to make some sense out of what he was saying. It sounded like a perfectly straightforward event; tragic, but hardly mysterious. Something was firing Fat Cunt up, though. Maybe he'd just been watching too many TV programmes about aliens.

Then Nick remembered him saying once he had family in that part of the world. Maybe there was some kind of personal connection.

—So, you know this dead kid or something?

Fat Cunt shook his head. —Never met him.

—So . . . ?

—Look, it's just a hunch I got. You're the journalist. You go up there, see what you can figure out.

Nick started to protest, but he was silenced by a frazzled, menacing stare. —You gotta do it, man.

It didn't seem wise to discuss the matter any further.

—And *that*, says Nick loudly, emptying his glass and thumping it down on the table dramatically,—*that* is how the rest of my weekend started!

You look nonplussed. This sounds more like a *Boy's Own* fantasy than anything else. Maybe Nick took too many of those funny-coloured pills on Saturday night and set off on an almighty trip he's not quite returned from.

He's staring at you with wide eyes.

—This is it, John! he goes. —This is the story I've been waiting for. This is the one that's going to make my name.

Then he does something quite eerie. He takes out his wallet.

You've never seen Nick's wallet before. You feel numb and slightly awed. He's opening it slowly, delicately, respectfully. He's fingering the handful of yellowing notes inside. You can feel him forming the words in his mouth, strange, unnatural sounds:—W-o-o-o-u-l-d y-o-o-o-u l-i-i-k-e . . . ?

You can hear the news headlines already.

Bong! Aliens land in Luton.

Bong! Peace declared in the Middle East.

Bong! Nick Jones buys round in London pub.

Then abruptly he snaps it shut and announces:—I'm marvin, aren't you? Let's go for a curry.

Over a lamb vindaloo that tastes of raw fire you get the rest of Nick's weekend. Fat Cunt impressed upon him the importance of getting up there right away. There was more to this story than met the eye. Shit was going to hit the fan from all around and there'd be some glory to be had for the guy who threw the most. Before Nick had made his mind up, Fat Cunt had called him a cab to the station.

He had a fry-up at the station and a couple of hours' sleep on the train. Despite the excesses of the night before, he felt completely together by the time he arrived in Leeds mid-morning. He got a bus into town and went to the hospital where they'd taken the boy and pronounced him dead. He obviously wasn't the first visitor that morning as there were a couple of security guards on the steps refusing entry to anyone who wasn't actually dying of something. There would be a post-mortem conducted to determine the precise cause of death and then the body would be released to the parents and that was that, they said. No entry to anyone. Under any circumstances.

Nick made a few notes and then, unsure what to do, got a cab to the park where the body was discovered. On the way he heard a radio report outlining the facts of the case as far as they were known, which seemed to correspond more or less exactly with Fat Cunt's version of events. The scene itself was easy to find: there was a small crowd of cops, other journos and a few ghoulish hangers-on, and loads of red and white police tape. Disappointingly, there was no white body outline to show where the boy had fallen. Perhaps that was because he was still alive when they moved him from there.

There was a modest buzz of activity. The cops were hunting through the undergrowth inch by inch for clues and barking at each other down walkie-talkies. The journos were shouting the occasional question and getting terse, one-word answers. Nick jotted down a few more notes and wondered where the hell this great story was supposed to be. It all looked pretty straightforward to him. Obviously he wasn't digging deep enough, but where should he start to dig?

One of the other reporters, a red-faced man in his fifties, wearing a Columbo mac, approached him

—You're not local, are you? said the man, and Nick felt like a cowboy in a B-movie Western who'd just wandered into the wrong saloon.

—No, he said.

—So where you from then?

Nick gave the name of a prestigious national newspaper which had once, several months ago, published one of his articles, and then argued with him for weeks afterwards about how much they were going to pay him.

The man raised his eyebrows. —Oh, so the big boys are getting involved now, are they. Must be more to this than I thought.

—Just a hunch, said Nick.

The man held out his hand. —Gavin Armstrong, he said.

Nick smiled and took his hand and for some reason gave the man a false name.

Armstrong worked for a local rag. It was a fairly clear case as far as he could see. Kid got unlucky. Still, he had to admit it was a good thing for the paper to get another juicy drug story so close to home. They could run forever with this. Once the actual facts of the case were out of the way, there'd be front-page coverage of the funeral; profiles of the shady world of nightclub owners and, by way of contrast, the school and community devastated by their loss; hard-hitting editorials; and *features*. Boy, the features you could run around a story like this! Twenty Things You Never Knew About Ecstasy. (Number One: IT KILLS CHILDREN!) How To Tell If Your Child Is On Drugs. (Point Two: if your child is unusually lethargic, he's probably smoking dope. Point Seven: if your child is lively and active, chances are he's on speed. Underlying context: whatever your child's like, whatever they do THEY MUST BE ON DRUGS! LOCK THEM UP NOW!)

Armstrong rubbed his hands with glee. His numbers had come up.

—And drug stories *do* help to sell papers, he added, taking a swig from a hip flask. —You may remember there was a similar thing in Bradford a few months ago, kid about this age. I tell you, the papers over there had a bloody field day with that.

Nick refused a drink – he was still feeling kind of fragile – but agreed to go for lunch with the local man. There was to be a press conference at three and there didn't seem to be much else to do until then.

—So what's this hunch of yours, then? asked Armstrong,

raising a glass to his lips. His lunch consisted of a pint of astonishingly cheap Yorkshire bitter and two shots of whisky.

—Oh, I dunno, said Nick. —I mean, that's all it is. A hunch. It's not based on facts or nothin.

He could hardly say that he'd been at a party in London the night before and this fat bloke he vaguely knew had told him there was some serious shit going down in Leeds and to get his arse up there straight away.

—It all just seems so convenient, Nick went on unconvincingly. —You know, not just for your paper an that, but for anyone who wants to attack this culture. Sweet kid takes an E for the first time, winds up dead an it's not just the drugs, it's the music, it's the clubs, it's all the people who are a part of it, they all get implicated. So I dunno. I'll nose around a bit, see if I can dig anything up. An if not . . .

—And if not?

—I'll bugger off home, I guess.

—NO! roared Armstrong. —That's not the answer at all. If not . . . you'll MAKE SOMETHING UP! Christ, how did you ever end up on a national?

The press conference was a predictably sombre affair. Nick bummed his way in by sticking very close to Gavin Armstrong and flashing an out-of-date NUJ card. The mother was in floods of tears throughout; the father was putting a stern, brave face on it, but his voice cracked when he was called to speak; the senior policeman had that grave, saddened, determined look that cops always have on these occasions. The mother read a brief statement and Nick could feel himself choking up. Poor bastards; none of them deserved this.

—David was such a lovely, sweet child. As well as his loving family, he was very popular and had lots of friends . . .

The conference yielded very little in the way of new information, other than that young David was not actually a mortal at all but an angel put on Earth by God to show Mankind the error of its ways. Afterwards Nick tried to make his way over to the family. He felt brutally intrusive, but he'd come a long way to try and get some kind of story. No chance, though. They were surrounded by cops and clearly had said all they were going to say. Reluctantly, he set off to try and interview David's friends, the ones who were with him, who bought the pills, who were having such a great time till it all went wrong. They'd all seen lawyers, though. No dice.

By the end of the evening he'd got exactly nowhere and was on the verge of jacking it in and coming back to London. What would he tell Fat Cunt, though? He felt like a loser for turning up nothing whatsoever. Of course he could always do what Gavin Armstrong suggested and MAKE SOMETHING UP! But he believed Fat Cunt knew more than he was letting on and would see through this immediately. So he decided to stay the night, have one more go the following day and if that didn't produce something, he was fucking off and Fat Cunt could say what he liked. He got himself a cheap and nasty B and B near the station and caught up on some of the sleep he'd missed from the night before.

He got up bright and early the following morning and headed for the boy's school. They'd be holding some kind of memorial assembly and he might be able to glean something from talking to the other kids. He wasn't the only person to have had this idea, though. Gavin Armstrong was among a group of six or seven hacks already there when he arrived. The headmaster had seen the opportunity to garner some free, wholly sympathetic publicity for his school and welcomed the ladies and gentlemen of the press to join the school for morning assembly, provided they agreed not to approach the children or upset them in any way.

For Nick, the assembly brought back unpleasant memories of his own school days. They even sang All Things Bright And Fucking Beautiful. He made a few more scribblings and, flicking through his notebook, realised he might yet salvage a half-decent human-interest story out of this. If the papers weren't interested, there were plenty of glossy magazines who lapped up shit like this.

Naturally, he and all the other journos ignored entirely the headmaster's request not to talk to the children. They all spent morning break roaming around the playground asking probing questions about this kid, David, and what he was like. But they didn't really turn up anything new. Unsurprisingly, it turned out David wasn't quite the angel painted by his mother. In fact, by all accounts he was a bit of a tosser (he was a big Simple Minds fan apart from anything else). But the stuff about drugs was all true: as far as anyone knew, he'd never touched them before.

And then Nick had his brainwave. The one angle he'd not explored yet, the one piece of the puzzle he'd not looked at, perhaps the most crucial piece of all: the guy who sold David the pill. No one seemed to have asked much about him. The police had issued a description and an identikit picture based on the testimony of the other boys, but that was it. And this was when Nick realised that he had one significant advantage over the cynical old soaks around him – he was twenty years younger than most of them and he was on the scene. He could hang out in clubs and not look like a journo sniffing out a story.

So that's what he did with his Monday night. He got fifty quid out of a cashpoint, the most his bank was prepared to let him have, he picked up a listings magazine and he did a tour of the groovier nightclubs in Leeds. In each place he scored an E and quizzed the seller gently about the scene in general and what was going down since Saturday night. When he ran out of money, he sold on the ones he'd already acquired and then bought some more. That way he got to talk to buyers and sellers. And once he'd talked to all these people . . .

Once he'd talked to all these people, fuck all. Buying and selling Es in clubs in Leeds turned out to be exactly the same as it is in London. Fifteen quid a throw for a little white capsule that could contain anything and a blind eye was turned by the management so long as you were reasonably discreet about it. No one knew anything. No one was saying anything.

Three o'clock in the morning, in his last port of call, Nick decided to call it a day. He'd try and flog his remaining pills – he didn't want to take them himself; he didn't know where they'd been, did he? – and then he was out of there.

A youngish guy with a scrawny goatee approached him in the chill-out.

—Hey man, got a spare pill?

Nick nodded towards the gents. Once in the cubicle, he reached into his pocket for the drugs, but the guy put up a hand to stop him.

—Hear you've been asking questions bout Saturday night.

Nick froze.

—Bout the guy who sold the kid the E.

Nick shat himself. This must be the guy! This was the guy who sold the lethal pill. He'd heard Nick asking around and now he was going to kill him to cover his tracks. Nick was sure he could see a knife in his jacket pocket.

But, instead of cutting out Nick's liver and eating it, the guy leaned towards him and said, very, very quietly:—Can we talk?

—Sure, Nick said when he was able to speak.

—Not here.

Nick looked around. It looked pretty private to him. —Okay . . . ?

—Follow me.

The dealer was still speaking in frightened, clipped sentences. Nick reassured himself with the thought that this guy seemed even more scared than he was.

They left the club. The guy had a brisk, agitated walk and Nick found it hard work keeping up with him as they ducked and dived through the empty streets. He started to get cold feet again. Maybe he was just being led to an ambush where this bloke and a bunch of his friends were going to beat the shit out of him. Maybe he should just cut his losses and disappear now.

Eventually they stopped, though, on a wide, brightly lit main road. The dealer held out his hand.

—Danny, he said.

Nick took it.

—Nick, he returned, still wheezing slightly from the walk. He thought about giving a false name again, but he couldn't be bothered in the end. Life was complicated enough.

—So, said Danny. —What you wanna know?

—Here? Nick asked.

There was no one about on the street, but every so often a taxi would rumble hopefully by. Actually it was a perfect place to stop: no one could hear what they were saying, but if they started murdering each other someone would probably notice before long.

—Here.

—Okay . . ., Nick took a deep breath. —I'm a journalist, right?

—Oh fuck right off, man.

Danny started walking away in disgust. Nick shouted after him. He couldn't believe he was going to lose him now, having nearly killed himself chasing the bastard halfway across Leeds.

—Hey, wait up . . .

Danny gave him the finger without turning round.

—I'm on your side! Nick tried.

This provoked a response at least.

—Yeah? I thought you were supposed to be on the side of truth or something.

Nick prepared himself for a speech. —Whose fucking truth, though? You can't see the truth unless you're gonna look at both sides of the story. Far as I can see no one else is bothering to do that here. Come on, you could do with someone on your side, couldn't you?

Danny stopped walking. He still looked unsure, though.

—Look, man, I go clubbing, Nick continued. —I deal a little myself. I'm cool.

Nick was getting desperate now. Telling someone you're cool is completely self-defeating. If you have to say it, it's not true. Danny seemed to buy it, though.

—What's your angle, then?

—Nothing. I don't have an angle. I'm just trying to work out what's going on, that's all. I reckon there's more to this than meets the eye, know what I mean?

Danny shook his head. —Nah. Kid got unlucky.

—I've heard that phrase too many times the last couple of days.

—Yeah? What you reckon happened then? This all part of some government plot?

—I dunno.

Nick shrugged his shoulders.

—I dunno, he said again. —How bout you tell me what happened. Can you tell me who your supplier is?

Danny sat down in a shop doorway.

—It wasn't my regular guy, he said. —That's what's got me worried.

Nick sat down next to him. Thank Christ, it looked like he was finally going to open up.

—Who was it then?

—This guy I bumped into Saturday afternoon outside Elland Road; there was a friendly on. Like I say, I didn't know him but this guy seemed to know me. He certainly knew I dealt a bit. Came right up to me, said he had ten Es he wanted to sell for a fiver. Job lot, quick sale, no questions. Well, I just thought he was Old Bill so I told him to fuck off, but he kept pestering me, followed me practically the whole way home. So I eventually I bought the pills, you know, just to get rid of him. I never had any hopes for them, they had to be duds at that price, but I tried one anyway, while I was watching *Blind Date*, and actually it weren't too bad. You know, not pure by any means, but quite a nice little buzz. Now I can't believe my luck. I've just bought these for fifty pence each from some dodgy guy outside the football ground, I'm gonna be able to go out tonight, sell em fifteen quid a throw no bother. I'm fuckin laughing. So I go out, I do my rounds like I usually do on a Saturday night and I rake it in. Next morning, I wake up, see the news on the telly, I remember the face and all of a sudden I'm a fuckin murderer.

Nick nodded slowly, taking this in. Danny now looked exhausted with fright.

—Have you seen some of the shit they've been writing about me? Calling me the scum of the earth, saying I've got connections with Manchester gangs and stuff. It's bollocks, man. I don't know which way to turn, though. I knew someone was gonna catch up with me, I knew there was no way I was gonna get away with it . . .

—Don't worry, Nick said quietly. —I ain't gonna shop you, you needn't worry bout that. You're a protected source. I just . . . I just wanna work out what's happening here.

They sat in silence for a while. It was an interesting story, but Nick couldn't see where to go with it. He got a description of the mystery man from Danny, but it wasn't going to be much help. A middle-aged man with black hair and a moustache; shit, how many of them were there around?

Eventually, Nick scribbled down his telephone number, patted Danny on the shoulder and told him to call if anything further happened or if he remembered anything else important.

And then, feeling more knackered than he can remember feeling ever, he got a cab back to his hotel . . .

—What? An that's it? you say, unimpressed. —That's your great story, Mystery Man Sells Killer Pill?

—Wait, there's more, says Nick, stuffing a great forkful of curry into his mouth. You finished yours ages ago, but he's hardly touched his with all his talking.

—That's all I got while I was in Leeds an, yeah, I was pretty disappointed. But I went round to see Fat Cunt last night an he was fuckin made up bout all I'd been doing. Couldn't believe I'd had that much initiative. You know, I've never seen him quite that . . . animated. What was the guy like again? he kept going. Middle-aged? Dark moustache? And he wanted to know all about Danny too, what he looked like, whether I was going to be able to contact him again. And then he'd nod and grin with this faraway look in his eyes. Really kind of, you know, enigmatic.

Off his fucking rocker more like. But Nick's not done yet.

—An then this afternoon, bout four o'clock I got a call from Danny . . .

—Yeah?

—An guess what. The guy's phoned him!

—What guy's phoned him?

—The dealer! The mystery man! He's phoned Danny up an started threatening him. Tellin him not to get cold feet, not to even think about calling the police cause he's got connections an it could all get very unpleasant.

—So what's he gonna do?

Nick beams at you triumphantly. —He's gonna sit tight till I get up there again tomorrow, and then we're gonna put my Masterplan into operation.

—Masterplan?

—Yeah, that's what it is.

And waving a curry-stained fork in front of your face, Nick explains his Masterplan to you in great detail. And it turns out to be so monumentally stupid you have to get him to repeat it to make sure you heard him properly.

—You're kidding me.

He shakes his head.

You throw a lump of cold nan at him. —That's fuckin ridiculous, man. That's the most fuckin ridiculous thing. I've ever heard.

Nick looks at you like you just suggested the Earth was still flat.

—What else do you expect me to do? he says. —Apart from my journalistic ethics, I think Fat Cunt is going to beat the shit out of me if don't turn something up.

You let it ride. You know better than to try and argue with Nick when he's as wired as this. You're going to come back to it later in the evening, though, when you've thought up a few more convincing arguments. You're certainly not going to let him just waltz off and do something as insane as this.

Masterplan indeed.

After the meal, Nick suggests going on to a club. He's blagged some freebies for an opening night. A new place on the Charing Cross Road. (Of course it's on the Charing Cross Road. How original. You wonder if there's a single building within half a mile of Centrepoint that hasn't at some time or another been a nightclub.) He's not making any promises but it might be, you know, okay-ish in a kind of dull way.

So you go along and it's, you know, okay-ish in a kind of dull way. Nick has to argue a little to get you in on the guest list, but not too much. It's a small, cramped place – the listings will describe it as 'intimate', no doubt – stuffed full of journos and other minor celebs. The professional liggers of London. Presumably someone somewhere has paid to get in but you're buggered if you can spot them. Maybe the forlorn-looking Japanese couple at the bar. The music's not bad. It's generally records you've heard a thousand times before and they're being overlapped rather than mixed, but it's not bad. You get a drink and it's free and you have a little dance and you end up having quite a good time despite yourself. Nick's on nodding terms with a few of the people here and you have a chat with them. Mostly people are enjoying themselves, but then so they should be with free beer. No one's *really* going for it, though. The place isn't jumping like it should be; to be honest, it's barely limbering up. Normal mid-week club night really. Everyone's got half an eye on the alarm clock tomorrow morning. Even the journos will be expected to put in an appearance some time before lunch.

You tackle Nick about his Masterplan a couple more times, you go through it step by step with him, unable to believe he can't see what a stupid bastard he's being, but he's refusing to be swayed.

He's booked his ticket back up to Leeds in the morning and that's that. So you figure, what the hell? You've been a mate and done your best; it's his funeral. You make a point of asking him, though, whether if the worst comes to the worst, you can have his record collection.

The main thing about the evening, of course, is that you don't get home till half past two. Which is far too late to call Sally.

So that's it; it'll have to be Thursday.

You wake up Thursday morning what seems like five minutes after you went to bed and already you're thinking about her. You think about her for so long in the shower that you don't have time for breakfast. You think about her while cycling into work and almost cause a pile-up on the Highbury and Islington roundabout. You think and think and think: when's the best time to call her – during the day? in the evening? before supper? after supper? And what are you going to say when you do call her?

Yeah. What the fuck are you going to say to her?

You get through the day in a dream. Harry asks if you're doing anything tonight and you have to stop yourself from saying, yeah, actually I'm phoning my girlfriend tonight. So instead you say, nah, not really. So he asks you if you want to go for a drink after work and you say, nah, not really. And he looks at you kind of weird. Come the end of the day, you find yourself sweeping up after the shop's closed. Louie asks if you're feeling okay.

You cycle home slowly. The decision's been made: before supper. That way, if it's a success you can have a pizza and a bottle of wine to celebrate. And if it's not a success you can have a pizza and a bottle of wine to console yourself.

Your plan of attack is mapped out with military precision. You get home. You have a wank. This seemed like a good idea when you thought of it: relieve sexual tension, reduce the chances of coming across like you're desperate for it, and besides, you haven't jerked off for months and you're scared you'll forget how. But it backfires on you. Instead of warmth, satisfaction and fulfilment, you end up with that kind of empty self-loathing you only get from wanking, and it sticks around all evening.

Next, you roll a spliff. This is for after the wine and pizza, when the whole show's wrapped up. Suddenly you're Will Smith in *Independence Day* and this simple phone call is your mission to fire cruise missiles into the alien mothership. The spliff's your cigar for mission accomplished; when the fat lady sings.

Now you're sorted. You go to the drawer by your bed where you carefully filed the scrap of paper with her number on it somewhere between a three-month-old bank statement and a letter from your mum. You know exactly where it is, in that special place that you reserve for items of supreme importance. Without even looking, you reach a hand into the drawer and pick it up.

And it isn't fucking there.

Your balls freeze over. You rifle through all the scraps of paper in the drawer again; Christ, why do you hang on to so much *crap*? Then you tear the drawer out and empty the contents on the floor. Then you tear out all your other drawers and empty their contents on the floor. Then you look on the mantelpiece and under the bed and through all the pockets of all your clothes and behind the stereo . . . Then you go back to the first drawer. It must be in here, you must just have missed it. You only ever put your important shit in this drawer. It's your Important Shit drawer. You try and retrace your steps when you got home on Sunday afternoon. This isn't easy since you were completely out of it, but even so, you remember – you can *distinctly* remember – putting the piece of paper in that drawer. So why the fuck isn't it there now?

—Why aren't you there now? you wail at the tauntingly useless bits of paper that are there.

That helped a lot.

You march over to Richie's room and barge in without knocking.

—YOU'VE BEEN IN MY ROOM, YOU CUNT!

Richie is lying upside down on his bed wearing nothing but a bright red pair of Y-fronts, cutting his toenails.

—No I haven't, he answers simply without changing position.

—YES YOU FUCKING HAVE! THERE'S A PIECE OF PAPER MISSING!

—John, I haven't been into your room. What the fuck would I wanna go into your room for? An I don't know anything about a piece of paper.

He sounds angry now.

—Well, *some*thing's happened to it, you argue logically.

—It wasn't me neither, says Tony, wandering in from the front room where he's been watching *Emmerdale*. —You doin yoga or something? he says to Richie.

—What's happened to it then?

—I don't fuckin know. You must have misplaced it.

—What was on this precious piece of paper? asks Richie.

—A phone number. A very important phone number.

Tony and Richie look at each other. Fuck me, they're both thinking, don't say he's gone and got himself a girlfriend.

And you look at both of them and all of a sudden you feel like the wanker you are. Of *course* neither of these two stole your piece of paper. Why would they? These people already have girlfriends; they have normal, regular, healthy sex lives. They don't need to steal women off you. Anyway, the piece of paper didn't say whose number it was, it was just a bunch of figures.

So Tony's right then. You must have misplaced it. You dopey cunt. The one time you manage to meet a girl and she likes you and she gives you her phone number and what do you do? You lose the fucking thing. And now you'll probably never see her again and there's nothing you can do about it. There's nothing whatsoever you can do about it.

Actually there is something you can do about it. There's something very straightforward you can do. You can go back to that same club on Saturday night, back to the scene of the crime. Even if no one will come with you. Even if Nick is too busy researching his scoop and Harry is going to a wedding and your flatmates and their respective girlfriends and even your sister, who has the social life of a skunk, have better things to do, you can still go. You can go on your own.

You'll need to get there really early, of course; just in case she's just going there for a bit before going on somewhere else. But that's okay: you can always spend the first three hours spinning out a single bottle of Becks, propping up the bar, trying to engage strangers in conversation, being given a wide berth by everyone. By one o'clock it'll be perfectly obvious whether or not she's coming (she isn't; of course she isn't; she's not the kind of girl who'd be going to the same place two weeks running; she'll be at some ultra-trendy new place you haven't even heard of; right now, right this instant while you're sipping the last sad dregs of that warm German lager, she'll be doing cocaine in a toilet cubicle with a children's television presenter), but you won't leave. You won't leave just in case she comes on here *from* someplace else, someplace that wasn't as cool as she hoped it was going to be, just to catch the last set. You'll allow yourself the occasional dance, but mainly you'll spend your time cruising the joint looking for that elusive, one-in-a-million face. Anyway, you can use this opportunity to actually *listen* to some of this music you're always banging on about, actually listen to it without the benefit of being mashed – for you won't dare to do drugs tonight: it might just push you over the edge. But you may not want to do this for long. You may find that, listened to soberly and objectively, when you're feeling depressed and not at all 'up for it', not 'largin it', not 'havin it big time', when you're plain and simply pissed off, this music is nothing more than an irritatingly repetitive, tuneless dirge. And the people are nothing more than robots. Look at them all. Drop a pill: dance. It's so fucking easy.

No, you may not want to listen too long. You might end up vowing never to go out again.

So what now? You could just give up and go home. But that would be the quitter's thing to do and you've come too far, you can't let go now. After all, up to now the whole thing's been a bit of a gamble. You had no idea what she'd be doing with her Saturday night, it was all a wild, clutching-at-straws guess. But you do know where she's going to be in a couple of hours' time.

So, you see, you have to do it; you really have no choice in the matter. Knackered and fucked off as you may feel, what you have to do is trudge wearily off to the flower market. Even if you get lost and wander round in circles and get completely freaked out by this part of London at this time of night and don't get there until well after the stall's opened, you've got to stick with it. There's simply no alternative.

You never know; it might be worth it. You might just be rewarded with the following conversation:

—Hi, stranger. How you doin?

—Yeah . . . uh, great. How bout you?

—Not bad. So . . . Thought you were gonna call me. How come I never heard anything?

—Yeah . . . I, uh . . .

—What was the point of taking my number if you weren't gonna use it?

—I, uh . . . I lost it.

—You *lost* it?

—Yeah. That's why I came . . . To see you.

She smiles. There. Wasn't it worth it now?

—You look completely fucked, she says brightly.

—Yeah . . . long night. How bout you? You go out tonight?

As expected, she gives the name of some place you've never heard of. You attempt a nod of recognition but it doesn't really come off.

—It was okay, she says. —Nothin special. You look like you had a good night, though.

You raise your eyebrows wearily and pluck from thin air the name of a place you heard Nick mention recently. Obviously you don't want to let on you've been back to the same place you were in last week.

—Any good?

—Yeah, bangin. Got a bit fucked on the old doves, you know . . . But we had a good crowd together.

You wanker. You've been standing on your own drinking beer all night.

She laughs. —An you came all the way over here after to see me!

—Yeah . . . Only way I knew how to find you.

—That must mean you wanna ask me out, yeah?

—Well, I . . . uh . . .

—I mean, that's quite a trek to make in the middle of the night just to make small talk.

—Yeah, I guess.

—Looks more like the actions of a man who's about to ask for a date.

You're utterly lost now. You were never any good at playing these games. Does this mean she likes you or not?

—Well, yeah . . . you know . . .

—Go on then!

What does she want? Bended knee? If she says no after this, you're going to fucking deck her.

—D'you wanna go out sometime then? you mumble.

—How bout Tuesday night? she says immediately.

—Yeah . . . great.

—Pictures?

—Uh . . . Okay, why not?

She senses some hesitation on your part. You thought you'd just go dancing together again. You forget sometimes that there are other forms of entertainment. And there *is* a film out this week you're quite keen to see.

—I don't really like going clubbing mid-week, she explains.
—And anyhow, it'd be good for us to do something different together. See how compatible we are when we're not off our faces.

—Yeah, whatever.

—Right. You give me your number this time. I'm not trusting you again.

She hands you a pen and you find your hand shaking as you scribble down your number.

She takes the piece of paper and examines it before – are you watching this? – folding it up and putting it carefully in her purse.

—Okay, I'll give you a call Monday and we'll sort something out for definite.

You stand there grinning dumbly, silently. Of course, you know this is all a dream. You'll wake up in a moment and it'll all be over. But, all in all, it has to be said, this is a pretty good dream.

—You look wasted, man, she says. —Go home. Get some kip.

—Okay, you say happily.

On the way up to the tube, just as an experiment, you pinch yourself.

Ouch!

Fuck, this is real. You're awake. You found her. You asked her out. She said yes. She's giving you a call Monday to sort something out for definite.

And she's not the sort of twat who'd lose a phone number that was given her.

Fucking hell!

You jammy bastard. You *jammy bastard*! You know that you don't for a moment deserve any of this, don't you?

ſ

A special convocation of the Galactic Government was a rare event. Even the oldest delegate, Mr Ziammi from Petulus who had been representing his people for some hundred and thirty galactic years, could only remember seven such occasions previously. It meant there was an emergency; not a trivial localised affair, but a very grave danger that might threaten the whole galaxy.

The media of fifteen solar systems was gathered outside the Great Hall. For most of these reporters, whatever was being said behind those imposing, ornate doors would be the greatest story of their careers. They waited quietly, with none of their usual banter, for the debate to finish and for the Media Delegate to report.

Inside the Great Hall there was silence. The delegates had just finished watching what remained of Commander Rimini's final broadcast by the time it reached this side of the galaxy. All were moved. Some were moved to tears. All eyes turned towards President Quanchard for some kind of explanation or guidance. Quanchard looked lost and bewildered.

'There are a couple of *records* in our computer banks,' he began falteringly. 'Records that show that the Ancients have visited us before, *several thousand years ago!* All the *evidence* suggests that they come from . . .,' his eyes flickered around the room nervously, '. . . *beyond the Barren Gulf!*'

There were gasps and cries of No! The Barren Gulf lay out beyond the Serpicus Six System. For as far as instruments could measure, many thousands of light years, there was no habitable planet in the Gulf. And therefore no way of crossing it. No known life form could survive for a fraction of the time it would take to cross the Gulf without needing to stop for fuel and fresh water. Several foolhardy explorers had set out, trusting in themselves and God. None had returned.

The Appalatian delegate rose to his feet. 'Do you mean to *suggest* to us, Mr President, that these creatures are *immortal*?'

Quanchard shook his head. He looked very uncomfortable indeed. 'No, they seem to have found another *solution* to the problem!'

'Yes?' urged the Appalatian

'It appears,' said Quanchard, and then he stopped to clear his throat. Words were sticking. 'It appears that the Ancients are able to *reproduce* very quickly! They produce many *hundreds* of offspring, many more than they need to *replace* their numbers, and the *surplus* are used for . . .' His voice lowered as he desperately sought a more palatable way of saying this. 'They *feed* on their young!' he said eventually.

There were widespread murmurs of disgust.

The Appalatian tried to clarify this. 'You mean the poor wretches of Kahtoom were *eaten*?'

'No, no,' said Quanchard hurriedly. 'As far as we can tell, the Ancients are *cannibals* but not *carnivores*! No, in fact it looks as though they didn't actually *kill* the people of Kahtoom . . . !'

Before he had the chance to explain further, the youthful, zealous delegate from Hamus shouted out, 'Look, this is all very *tragic*, and obviously our feelings go out to the families of these innocent *victims*, but let's get this in some kind of *perspective* here! These events occurred right the other side of the *galaxy*! There is no evidence that the aliens plan to *encroach* further on our space! In fact, for all we know they could already be on their way *home*!'

'Yes, but for all we know as well, they might be plotting a course directly for *here*!' said Quanchard sternly. 'They have sophisticated *cloaking* systems and our instruments are having diffi-culty *tracking* them! Fellow Galacticans, I cannot *conceal* from you, we could be in very *serious danger* indeed! I have put all armed forces on *full alert!*'

There was a pause while this sank in. The young Hamusian was quiet.

Then the Appalatian, who was still on his feet, said, 'What about Captain Midnight? Does anyone know his *whereabouts?* Is there any possibility that Midnight Patrol might be reconvened to help with this *situation?*'

It was unlikely. The last Midnight Patrol mission had ended in success but had cost the Captain the life of his son. Since then Captain Midnight, it was common knowledge, had become a drunk and a recluse. And, disillusioned, the rest of Midnight Patrol had gone their separate ways.

'I've already been *considering* this option.' said Quanchard.

'The man's a *wreck!*' cried a delegate from the back. 'We can't rely on him!'

The President held up a hand to silence him. 'Actually, the Captain's current *psychological* state makes him *ideal* for this job!'

The delegate snorted. 'Last I heard he was being held in *custody*. Seems he had a little too much to *drink* on Saturday night . . . !'

'Now look here, Captain,' explained Cadet Nigson, who still couldn't believe what was happening to him. Captain Midnight is in the back of his patrol car! 'I have every respect for who you *are*, and for what you've *been* through just recently, I'm a big *fan* of yours, I used to *hero worship* you when I was at school, but I'm afraid that doesn't make it okay! We're still going to have to *turn you in!* Even *super-heroes* don't have the right to break into *old ladies*' houses and *piss* all over their furniture!'

The tall man leaned towards the young police cadet and threw up all over his bright, clean uniform.

∫

And where do you end up meeting her? Burger King on Leicester Square. Possibly the least romantic place on Earth. It was the only place in the West End you could both agree on, though, and it is handy for all the cinemas. So Tuesday night you find yourself picking through the hordes of tramps and tourists, looking again for that one-in-a-million face.

You've got there early but you're pleased to see that she's beaten you to it. That's a good sign. Shows she's keen. She's managed to get one of the window seats on the top floor and she's sat there smoking a cigarette slowly. She looks stunning. She's got a small black beret and scarlet lipstick and a long tartan scarf draped around her shoulders, even though it's summer and still quite warm. The way she smokes is immediately seductive; stealthily, hungrily, like she's smoking underwater. You've seen her smoke before, she must have got through a packet and a half just working the stall that Sunday morning, but that was all frantic and fussy. You haven't seen her *smoking* before. Not like this. You stand by the stairs and watch her devour half a cigarette across a crowded room. If the room wasn't a fast food joint and the crowds weren't exclusively Italian teenagers, this could almost be a film. Or one of those poncey black and white posters students put on their walls.

You, needless to say, have made absolutely no effort whatsoever.

You've come straight from work in the clothes you've been wearing all day. Trainers. Faded jeans. A crumpled red and black shirt that looked really cool when you bought it about four years ago. You look, even by your peculiarly low standards, like shit.

You're suddenly overawed by this vision of beauty in front of you. You can't possibly go over to her when she looks like *that* and you look like *this*. You'll have to go home. Think up some excuse. Phone her tomorrow and say your cat died or something. Just as you decide this, though, she catches your eye and gives you a little wave.

Too late.

—SALLY! you yell and most of the people in the room turn round and look at you.

You feel yourself reddening. You hope to Christ she hasn't seen you standing over here like a moron for the last ten minutes gazing at her.

You go over to her. To your delight she stands up and kisses you hello. You go even redder.

—How you doin? she goes.

—Yeah great. Sorry I'm late.

—You're early.

—Yeah I, uh . . . sorry?

—You're early. It's just that I'm even earlier. I didn't have much to do this afternoon so I thought I'd come down and wait for you.

She looks around.

—Can't think of any place I'd rather be, she says. And she smiles.

Just in time, you realise this is a joke and you laugh just a little too loudly.

—So you want anything to eat? you ask her.

—I don't touch the shit they make in here.

—No, me neither, you say hurriedly. —Fuckin pig swill, but I thought I might get a Coke or something.

—Okay. Coke would be good.

She pauses to think for a moment.

—Actually, I am kinda hungry. Could you see if you can get me some chips that haven't already been buried in salt. I'm not allowed salt. Doctor's orders.

—Okay. Comin up.

You fight your way downstairs. There are no queues at the individual counters, just a mass of people pushing hopefully. You push along with them and thanks to some subtle manoeuvring just about manage to get to the front before you're old enough to qualify for a bus pass.

—How may I help you please? says the girl behind the counter without moving her lips.

—Yeah, can I have a portion of chips with no salt please.

—How may I help you please? she says again a little more firmly.

—Chips. Without salt.

—Cheeps? she says.

—Yes. Without salt.

—Large cheeps?

—No, regular'll do. But the important thing is no salt, yeah? She looks confused.

She decides to start again. —How may I help you please?

Of course. She's a fast food employee. The only words of English she knows are those on the menu. You look up at the boards to see if you can construct a meaningful sentence from the words available.

People behind you are getting impatient. If they were cars they'd be sounding their horns.

—Look, what I want is chips . . .

You point to the chip fryer.

—Yes, cheeps! she nods enthusiastically.

—Except without any salt.

You look around desperately for some salt to point to.

—Yes, large cheeps. What else you want?

Something large and heavy to beat you about the head with please.

Eventually you manage to get chips, a Quarter Pounder and two Cokes. The chips have got salt all over them but if Sally doesn't want them you'll have them. The Quarter Pounder you stuff down your throat before you go back up to her so she won't know. You eat it so fast you feel like puking, then you fight your way upstairs again.

Sally takes one look at the chips and says:—They're fuckin smothered in salt, I can see it from here.

—Yeah, sorry. The assistant turned out to be from Venus and we had no common language.

—Ugh, she grimaces, pushing the things away. —You have them.

—Okay.

You munch away slowly at the chips, still feeling slightly queazy from the burger and not quite sure what to say next. Obviously you're looking pissed off because the next thing Sally says is:—Don't worry, I forgive you.

—Eh?

—The chips. I forgive you for getting me chips with salt on.

—Oh yeah, right . . . Sorry.

—I said I forgive you . . . Hey, John, you okay?

She takes your hand and looks concerned. You like this.

—Yeah, yeah, I'm fine . . . well, no actually.

—What's the matter? Shit at work?

—No, it's nothin like that. It's my mate, Nick, you remember? The guy I was with at the club that night I met you.

—Oh yeah, the guy who was going off with W to that party, what happened to him?

—Well he came away from the party in one piece . . .

—Yeah? What was happening?

—Oh, you know, minor celebrities taking drugs.

You shrug nonchalantly as though this is the most tedious thing you've ever come across. You *wanker*.

—So what's the matter with him? Sally asks.

—Well, you know he's a journo?

—No . . . really? What's he write about?

—Oh you know, whatever . . . Whatever he can get paid for. That's how come he knows W, he interviewed him once. Anyway, he picked up this lead on a story at that party at W's house and he's been chasing it ever since an, you know, I'm worried. He's really into it, but I'm scared it's going to land him in some real shit.

She fumbles for another cigarette without taking her eyes off you. —Wow. How exciting. So tell me, what's this story?

She's staring at you intently, those killer eyes boring into you, dying to find out what you've got to say. So you tell her the story, the whole story from Fat Cunt out of his head at the party to Danny ringing Nick in blind panic and Nick's great Masterplan. She hangs on your every word and you feel like you've died and gone to Heaven.

Actually, the whole thing's a cynical and desperate ploy. Understandably you're not too sure of your chances of bedding this beautiful and intelligent woman on your own merits, but you figure that if you go on about your fearless, talented journalist friend some of the glamour will rub off on to you and she'll be peeling off your boxer shorts before you can say Kate Adie. It's tortured logic, but lust plays funny tricks on the brain.

—Masterplan? she says.

—Yeah, this is what I'm worried about. Nick's got this crazy idea bout going up to Leeds an helping Danny.

—Help him do what?

—Track down this fuckin psycho who keeps phoning him up an threatening him. One who sold him the dodgy pills.

—Hmm . . . That doesn't sound like a particularly clever idea to me.

You're relieved Sally's with you on this one. Nick just looked at you like you were a jerk when you suggested this might not be the greatest idea ever. Fucking psychos are not for *tracking down*, you wanted to tell him, they're for avoiding if you can and obeying if you have to and that's all.

—But how, she asks. —How is he going to track him down? I guess this guy doesn't leave a calling card.

—No, but he has a phone number. This is the Masterplan. Nick told Danny that the next time the guy phoned he should trace the call; you know, you can get the information off the exchange now bout which number called you last. Then, when Nick gets there, they're gonna call the guy's number, pretending to be selling him something or whatever an get his name, then they're gonna look up that name in the phone book, find an address that matches the number . . .

—And then . . . ?

—And then . . . I dunno, investigate I guess. Do whatever journalists do when they're checking out a story. Maybe they'll just give the guy's name and address to the police, but I doubt it. Danny is kind of implicated in this.

—Shit . . .

Sally breathes out. The whole plan is so scary because it might actually work.

—You ought to try and stop him, John.

You shake your head. —Too late. I tried. I fucking argued with him about it for hours before he went, but he's stubborn as shite when he gets into something like this . . .

—What do you mean? He's already gone?

—Yeah, he went last Thursday . . .

—Last Thursday!

—Yeah . . .

—So he'd already gone when you came to see me on Sunday morning . . . an you didn't say anything about it.

—Well, shit, I was kinda knackered, you know . . . we didn't really talk much Sunday, if you remember . . .

Now she's shaking her head. —I don't believe it. I don't believe you actually went clubbing while your best mate was off chasing gangsters an you didn't try an stop him.

—I did try an stop him! I just said I did!

She looks at you the way your teachers used to when you were explaining what had happened to your homework. You're not too pleased with the way this conversation is going. She's supposed to be impressed with your tales of adventure and mystery, not sitting in fucking judgement on you.

—Look, maybe nothing's happened. The plan might not have worked . . .

—Have you heard from him?

—No . . . I left a couple of messages for him on his mobile, but he hasn't called back. I'm telling you, I'm sure he's fine.

She rolls the killer eyes. —This is fucking dangerous, John! she says. —I've been reading bout some of this stuff in the papers, they're saying there's Moss Side gangs involved an all sorts . . .

—They were saying that about Danny as well. It's bollocks. No one knows who's involved.

—Well it's not the Salvation Army, is it. Whoever this guy is who's making these phone calls, he's a villain of some sort. An he's not exactly gonna be thrilled bout a hack phoning him up out of the blue . . .

You hold up your hands. —Okay, okay, how bout this? I'll try him again tonight when I get in and if he doesn't answer, I'll leave a message and *insist* that he calls me back tomorrow. An then I'll phone you straight away to let you know he's all right, cause obviously this is gonna cost you sleep otherwise. How's that?

That shuts her up for a bit. What fucking business is it of hers anyway? He's *your* mate; she hasn't even met him properly. If you want to let him go charging around chasing gangsters, surely that's between him and you.

You both fall silent. You don't want to talk about this stuff any more.

—How bout we pick a film? you say eventually

You notice with alarm that while she was waiting Sally has been browsing a listings magazine and circling possible films in ominous red biro. One of those circled looks like it might be in French.

It hadn't occurred to you that there'd be any debate over which film you were going to see. You'd just assumed it would be the *Captain Midnight* film. Didn't everyone want to see that?

—So what do you fancy? she says.

You don't want to commit yourself at this stage.

—There's quite a few here I thought looked kinda interesting, she goes on.

—Mmm.

You crane your neck to try and read her magazine upside down. They all look shite to you.

—What about this one? she asks, pointing, inevitably, to the French one.

Tricky situation. It's not that you don't like French films as such – there have been some really cool ones. And you'd love to pretend that you want to go and see this particular film with her; it would make you seem cultured, sensitive, intelligent, all those qualities you're laughingly trying to convey to her. But the thing is, there's only one film you want to see tonight and that's that.

—I heard it had some dodgy reviews, you try.

—Yeah? That's surprising. His other films were great.

She reels off a couple of names.

—Okayyy . . .

She runs her finger down the page of films.

—How bout this one? you ask tentatively, pointing at your favourite which remains resolutely uncircled.

—*Captain Midnight?*

—Yeah.

—You're kiddin me. *Captain Midnight?*

—Yeah. Why not?

—It's big-budget Hollywood bollocks!

—Special effects are supposed to be amazing.

She slams her palm on the table in exasperation.

—I *hate* that. When people try and justify really shit films just cause they've got cool special effects. It's like buying a book cause you like the feel of the paper. If it's a sci-fi film it fuckin ought to have amazing special effects. What's important is the story and the characters.

It's your turn to reel off a list of films. —Have you *seen* the effects in any of those?

She's forced to admit she hasn't.

—Well there you go then! See, it's the same guy does all the special effects in those films and he's a fuckin genius, man. The effects are like a whole other dimension to the film. Like a completely different character in their own right . . . so you see it *is* about character after all.

Hey. Not bad. She's starting to waver.

—So they're really something else are they?

—Yeah. And you've really gotta see them on a big screen like they have in the cinemas round here. Really big screen, big sound system, the whole bit.

—Mmm.

What you really want to do is tell her that you have to see this film, you must see this film because you have been collecting *Captain Midnight* comics since you were fourteen, you have every issue ever published for over a decade, some of them worth good money now, you have followed the Captain loyally through many fantastic adventures and now, unbelievably, there is someone in Hollywood who shares your passion and has enough clout to get a fifty-million-dollar movie off the ground, hire an energetic, trendy young director to make it and persuade a genuine, bona fide A-list star to play the title role, and now this film is here and you must see it. And that really is that.

But you don't tell her this. You haven't reached that stage in your relationship yet. You don't tell her this because you don't want to tell her about your comic collection. Because there is one simple rule, one ancient law passed down from generation to generation that you can never forget: it's comics *or* girlfriends. Not both.

She's wavering, though, she's definitely wavering. One more solid argument should clinch it.

—Please? you say.

—Eh?

—Please can we go and see this film?

She throws up her hands in resignation. —Better be fuckin worth it.

The cinema is an adventure right from the word go. You persuade Sally that the best place to see a film like this from is the very front row and you're both delighted to find that not only are the seats fantastically comfortable but they also tilt backwards like a dentist's chair so you don't get a sore neck. The lights are lowered slowly and then, before the curtains even open to reveal the screen, there's a short laser show, accompanied by various spooky noises to show off the impressive sound system. This ends with a giant thud that sounds like an explosion going off five miles away.

You look over at Sally. She's grinning madly. At last something seems to be going right.

—Wish we had some drugs, you say.

When the film starts, it starts loudly and doesn't let up. The screen is the size of a house and completely engulfs your field of vision. At times you actually feel like you're inside the film. And you *love* this film. The special effects are as mindblowing as you said they'd be, there's an exciting story, some funny lines and great action sequences. Moreover, everyone around you is loving it too. There are whoops as baddies get whipped, gasps as our hero is plunged into yet further danger, complete silence at the achingly moving part where Captain Midnight's son is killed, and loud, long laughs at the comic relief. About an hour into it you figure that this is probably your favourite film of all time. And it's LOUD. When you emerge blinking on to Leicester Square your head is still FULL of all those sounds. It's like coming out of a club.

—So what d'you reckon? you ask Sally.

—We paid seven pounds fuckin fifty for that, she says stonily.

—You didn't like it then?

—No! I *knew* it was going to be shit . . . I suppose you loved every minute of it.

You're not sure how to respond.

—Nah. Bit disappointing really.

—Special effects *were* good, though, she concedes.

—Yeah, they were okay.

—But you know what I think about special effects.

—Yeah. Too right.

That seems to be the end of your little film debate.

—So . . . which way you going? she asks with a sigh.

Actually you had been hoping to go back to her place to shag her senseless, but somehow you feel you might be pushing your luck now.

—Home, I guess.

—Yeah. Which tube?

You nod towards Leicester Square station.

—I'm going up to Tottenham Court Road, she says quickly. —I'll see you later.

She gives you a peck on the cheek and adds:—I'll call you later in the week, yeah?

And with that she's off.

Will she fuck, you're left thinking to yourself, but you give her a weak smile and a wave. The crowds of Chinatown swallow her up in seconds and you stand there for a few moments feeling like a burst balloon.

Well you fucked that up, didn't you. You fucking fucked that up, you fuck. Not only does she think you're a shit best friend to have, she hates your taste in films as well. And she probably has her suspicions about your comic collection. Face it, she's no more likely to call you than the Queen Mother. And you can't go crawling back to her flower stall *again* on Sunday.

But . . . but for some unfathomable reason she seems to like you. So the following night – the following night! less than twenty-four hours after that last goodbye! – this is what happens.

The phone rings. It's just after eight and you and your flatmates are watching some unspeakably shite sitcom. You haven't shaken off the depression from last night and you can't be bothered to do anything but watch shit on TV. You hate your friends. You hate your flat. You hate your life. You feel you deserve this sitcom.

The phone rings. No one wants to answer it.

—It's your turn, Tony tells Richie.

—Fuck off, says Richie.

—Come on, man. I'm watching this!

—Hey John, why don't you go, says Richie. —You just said you thought this was a pile of wank.

—Yeah, but it's not gonna be for me, is it, you say morosely. —It's gonna be for one of you two Casanovas.

And you sit there stubbornly.

The phone keeps on ringing. Tony's the first to crack.

—Okay. But it's someone else's turn next fuckin time.

He's back seconds later.

—Hey, Fuckin Casanova. It's for you, he says angrily.

—It'll just be my mum, you mutter as you drag yourself out of your chair.

—Didn't sound like your mum.

There's a particularly loud burst of canned laughter.

—Shit, I missed that, says Tony.

—It wasn't funny, you tell him.

—Course it was funny. There was laughing, wasn't there?

You groan loudly at him. —Why do you think they have canned laughter on sitcoms, Tone?

—I, uh . . . eh?

—I mean, they don't have canned crying on sad programmes or canned gasping on exciting programmes. Do they?

Tony looks bewildered.

You carry on. —I'll tell you why they have canned laughter. It's because even the people who made this shit know it's not fucking funny. If they didn't put the laughter in for you, you wouldn't have a clue where the jokes were.

—Uh, John, I think your call's waiting, says Richie.

—Yeah, well . . .

It was a point worth making. You leave Tony to think about this and amble off down the hall to the phone.

—Hello? you say unenthusiastically.

—Hi.

—. . . Sally?

—Yeah. Just calling to see how you were doing.

—Fine, yeah, great . . . thanks for last night.

—Yeah . . . heard from Nick yet?

—Nah . . .

Just in time you remember your promise. —I did leave him a message but he hasn't got back to me yet. Course, it could be his phone's not working.

—I guess . . .

—Seems the most likely explanation. I still can't see him being kidnapped by baddies.

There's a silence at the other end. She doesn't seem convinced. Then she changes the subject completely.

—Listen, you doing anything at the weekend?

Of course you're doing something at the weekend. You're trying to escape from the mind-numbing shallowness of everyday life by taking a shitload of drugs and listening to primitive music being played at dangerously high volumes. What a stupid question.

—Don't think so, you say.

—I'm not working the stall Sunday an I could really do with getting out of London for a bit. Would you like to come away with me?

—Does the Pope shit in the woods?

—I, uh . . . does that mean yes? she says hesitantly.

—Yes it means yes!

—I thought we might go to Brighton. It's kinda cool there.

—Heh, heh, dirty weekend? you say before you can stop yourself.

She sounds indignant. —Doesn't have to be a dirty weekend. We could have a clean weekend instead.

Her voice drops to a whisper. —Take lots of showers maybe.

You nearly explode. This is the single most erotic thing anyone has ever said to you.

She reads out a bunch of train times and tells you where to meet her and you write it all down, gushing and cooing down the phone as you do so.

—I'll see you then, she says finally.

—Okay. See you later.

—An see if you can't get some news before then, eh?

—Oh yeah . . . right.

Oh boy. Oh fucking BOY! You can't believe this is happening. She's the girl of your dreams, you met her a week and a half ago and now you're going to fucking BRIGHTON with her!

Right, this is how happy you are: when the Incredible Shagging Neighbours strike up later in the evening, *you don't care*. You think it's *sweet*. And for the next few days your flatmates hate you even more than you hate them.

∫

It was a strange and uncomfortable meeting of Midnight Patrol. They had been rounded up at short notice and only seven of them were present in this small shuttleship, which had been donated to them especially for this mission by the Galactic Government. Some had put so much distance between themselves and the tragedy of the recent past that they were not able to make it; some refused point blank to come. The seven were: Chaymar, next to the Captain himself, the most senior member of the Patrol; Roltan, the bizarre mutant with the power to make himself invisible; Karlax, the strong man; Pleysium, the computer genius; Matrix, his creation, the android; and Zanzi, the beautiful Appalatian with laser-eyes. None of them would have believed they would be gathered together again. None would have believed they would be called upon to deal with a crisis like *this*.

The Captain, who had been bailed out of prison especially for this, called for attention and began to explain the gravity of the situation. He went over the points arising from Commander Rimini's broadcast and President Quanchard's speech.

Chaymar voiced the fear that was troubling them all. 'Captain, I'm not sure we're *ready* for a mission like this! We're all still a bit of a *mess* . . . !'

Captain Midnight's voice was urgent. 'Listen, as well as *feeding* on their own *children*, the Ancients receive their nourishment by sucking the *lifeblood* out of other beings! This is a race with no sense of *joy*, no sense of *happiness*, so they *steal* those things from other people! That's how the people of Kahtoom died! The Ancients didn't strictly speaking *kill* them, they took away their *will to live*. Which of course had the same *result!* Now, am I right in thinking we all still feel our *pain*, our *loss*, our suffering?'

There were nods from around the room.

'Well, don't you *see?* That makes us *perfect* for this mission! We'll be less *susceptible* to the parasitic attacks of the Ancients! One of the most important aspects of our *preparation* for this mission will be to *cultivate* our *grief!* We must learn to *encourage* our pain, to feel *more* of it! That way my son will truly not have died in *vain!*'

The Captain looked around at his loyal team. He hadn't wanted this. He had resigned himself quite happily to a life of nostalgic drunkenness, seeing no more action than breaking up the occasional bar brawl. But now he was here he couldn't help it; he was pleased to have them – most of them anyway – back together again. Pleased to have one more mission, one more chance to save the galaxy.

But he had to suppress these feelings of pleasure; they could prove fatal to them all.

There were no questions from the team. Captain Midnight gave the signal and Chaymar fired up the ship's engines.

∫

You're in a flap all the way down to Brighton. You haven't been on a train (a big, proper train with a pointy front, not the tube) for ages and even though it's stuffy and dirty and full of suicidal-looking commuters and moving about as fast as a push bike, you're unbearably excited. YOU'RE GOING TO BRIGHTON! WITH A GIRL!

Okay. Get a grip.

You chat away incessantly to Sally and she makes a fair show of looking interested; or at least looking like she's still listening. Of course the only thing she really seems to give a damn about is Nick and his little adventure. This is starting to bug you a little; sometimes she seems more interested in him than she is in you. He's only a bloody journalist following up a rather dodgy-sounding story, for Christ's sake, not James Bond. At least you have managed to get the bastard on the phone now so she can't still accuse you of being callous and uncaring. Yes, his Masterplan did come off, you tell her, although it took some time, but no, he hasn't been captured by the baddies and isn't being tortured by Mr Big. She seems almost disappointed by this.

In fact it took three days for the bloke to contact Danny again with more of the same threats. Three days during which Nick just hung out at Danny's flat and they went clubbing a couple of times and got to be quite matey. Nick was just about to give it all up and come back down to London when on the Monday evening the call came. This time the bloke sounded even more scared and deranged than before. He started accusing Danny of already having gone to the police and said he had Danny's number, he knew where he lived, he was going to come round and teach him a lesson. Had he seen the scene in *Scarface* with the chainsaw and the bath? Danny was quite shaken when he put the phone down, but once Nick had spoken to him, it just made him even more determined to find out what was going on and get this psycho off his back.

So Nick dialled 1471 and got the number and, taking a deep breath, phoned the guy back. He gave him some bullshit about doing some kind of market research and asked if he could just check the spelling of the gentleman's name? The guy sounded puzzled and said he didn't think there were too many ways you could spell Roger Macmillan. Nick thanked him and apologised for being so stupid; of *course* he knew how to spell that. He was sorely tempted to push his luck and ask straight out for the guy's address but in the end he bottled it. He asked a few more dumb questions so the guy wouldn't get suspicious and then he hung up. When they looked the name up in the phone book, though, sure enough there was a Macmillan R. with this number and there in black and white was his address. A posh-sounding road out in the suburbs. They looked at each other, they couldn't believe it – they'd found the guy! They'd only gone and fucking found this nutter!

—And then what? Sally asks, absolutely transfixed by this.

Well, then it all gets a bit dull. Nick insists they go and spy on this bloke Macmillan, stake out his house. Danny's a bit worried about this, worried that Macmillan or maybe one of his associates will recognise him. So they agree that Nick will go with a mate of Danny's called Carl, who has his own car and is unemployed and could use a little action to brighten up his life. And starting Tuesday morning they park up the street from Macmillan's house and watch his comings and goings. Carl's got his dad's binoculars, Nick's got this really fancy camera with a zoom lens that Fat Cunt lent him, they feel like paparazzi at the Oscars. Mr Macmillan looks just as Danny described him: middle-aged, black hair, moustache. Only he acts less like a drug dealer than anyone Nick has ever come across.

He leaves the house at ten o'clock every morning and walks down to the little off licence he owns, which he opens up at ten thirty (and which, as Nick is keen to point out, is nothing more than state-sanctioned drug dealing anyway). He stays there until six or six thirty, when he leaves it in the hands of the two lads who work for him. He never, *never* seems to go out in the evening. His wife, Pat, works in a café about a mile from their house and also doesn't have much of a social life. According to the neighbours, he's from London, she's a local girl, they moved up here about five years ago and they've got two grown-up children. And they're lovely, lovely people.

And that's pretty much it. As far as you're aware Nick and Carl are still at it. While you're here on a train to Brighton – with a girl! – they're sat in a car outside a boring old bastard's house playing I-Spy, waiting for the boring old bastard to suddenly nip out and finalise some huge cocaine deals. Bloody stupid, in your opinion, and you wonder how long Nick's going to stick it out for. Surely it's a classic no-win situation. Either this guy *is* a major villain, in which case Nick and Carl are in huge danger; or, as looks more and more likely, he's nothing of the sort, in which case they're getting numb arses for fuck all.

—An this doesn't bother you at all? Sally says. —That your mate's sat outside some psychopath's house while you're breezing off down to the seaside?

Of course not. You're way too happy to be bothered by anything like this. But you were prepared for this eventuality. You fucking knew she was going to ask you about Nick.

—I got the number of this place we're staying at an gave it to Nick, you tell her proudly. —If anything goes off, we'll be the first to know.

—Well, good. I'd never have asked you down here if I'd known all this was going on, she says. And then she folds her arms, stares out of the window and looks cross. That seems to be all she has to say on the subject of Nick, which is fine by you.

You do want to keep on chatting, though. You're still all fired up by this whole weekend-away thing. Sally's looking absolutely fucking amazing and you're pretty sure she likes you now, and not just because you've got a brave journo friend who knows some famous people. So you yap away to her about all kinds of boring stuff. You tell her about Shirley, Richie's girlfriend, who works too hard and never has time to see him and when she does she's too shagged to spend quality time with him, and Laura, Tony's newish girlfriend, who's a total fucking nympho and completely mad about Tony, but he can't quite shake off the memory of Bryony who left him for a university student about three months ago. And Sally nods and smiles but doesn't really contribute much to the conversation until she suddenly cuts in to the anecdote about how Tony and Laura met with a question:

—So do you think relationships can ever work out?

—Eh? What do you mean?

—Well these two mates of yours have these two women who appear to be far more trouble than they're worth and everything you've been saying seems to suggest that you don't think relationships can ever work out in the long term . . .

—Maybe they can't.

—. . . which I have to say I find a bit worrying.

—Worrying? How?

You great fucking shit-for-brains. You don't see where this is leading at all, do you?

Sally suddenly becomes animated. —*Because*, she says, gesticulating with her right hand in a very French manner and scaring the passenger sitting next to her. —Because here we are going down to the seaside and we're . . . together, and it may work out and may not but, you know, I'd like to think there was a possibility that something might come out of it. And it'd be quite nice if you thought so too.

Now you see where the conversation's going. Once it's already got there.

—No, no . . ., you protest quickly. —I mean I do . . . I do think that . . . I mean . . .

And that's it. That's pretty much the only thing Sally says all trip, the only light relief in an otherwise uninterrupted flow of vacuous bullshit from you. You spin a few more yarns about your friends and family, some true, some embellished, and when you've run out of these, a couple made up entirely as you go along. What the hell.

Eventually, even you become thoroughly fed up with the sound of your own voice. You're still excited, though. You lean over to Sally and whisper conspiratorially:

—How bout we go to the bogs and drop a pill? Get us in the mood for this evening.

—Fuck off, man. You're talking enough shite as it is. You haven't let up for a second since we left Victoria. You do an E an you'll probably shoot yourself into orbit.

She has a point.

—Spliff then. Calm me down.

Sally is tooled up with drugs. She told you so before you left. And what a wonderful thing that was for a new girlfriend to tell you.

—Give it a rest. There's probably smoke alarms in the toilets. If you want drugs go get yourself a beer from the buffet.

You think about it for a moment, then stand up.

—An get us a cup of coffee while you're at it, she adds.

Maybe you're just being paranoid but you're sure you catch an audible sigh of relief from the entire carriage as you leave them to a brief spell of peace and quiet.

For the price of a modest meal for two, you manage to buy two cans of Red Stripe and an extraordinarily large plastic mug of coffee. The lager is warmer than the coffee.

As you shuffle back to your seat, trying desperately to prevent your drinks ending up in someone's lap as the train lurches around corners at full tilt, you think back on that conversation with Sally, that small intermission in your monologue. Did you fuck up again there? You really should have seen that Relationship shit coming. There is one positive thing you remember, though, and suddenly you feel all warm inside.

What was it she'd said . . . ? We're going down to the seaside . . . *together*. Together! That means she intends to sleep with you . . . doesn't it? . . . yeah, together . . . what else could together mean? . . . you're coming down to Brighton together, as a couple, you're staying in a guest house and you're going to sleep together.

This has been worrying you for quite a while. Obviously the signs were there that a wriggle was on the cards. Brighton. Weekend. Just the two of you. But that hasn't stopped you from believing that things could still go horribly wrong. That you'd get there and check into separate rooms. Or she'd be meeting a bunch of her friends and you'd spend the whole weekend in a gang of ten. But no . . . she'd said *together*. What else could together mean? She might as well have said, come fuck me now.

The train spins round a corner particularly violently and you topple over on to a snoring old lady. You manage to keep the drinks intact, though.

The old girl looks startled.

Getting laid tonight, you want to tell her. But she wouldn't appreciate it.

Sally has this whole thing worked out. She's booked the guest house, she knows which club she wants to go to tonight, which spot on the beach she's heading for tomorrow, which restaurant she wants to eat at. Clearly she's been here before. For all you know she comes down on a fortnightly basis with a different bloke each time. Like you give a fuck anyway. Even if she had another bloke with her this weekend you'd still be here. This is too great for words.

The sun's more or less gone down by the time you arrive, but it's still hot and sticky and you break a sweat lugging your bag from the station to the guest house. You had absolutely no idea what to pack so you packed everything. This is what your mum used to do on family holidays and it used to piss you off no end: now look at you.

You're expecting some seedy dive of a guest house, but you're pleasantly surprised. The place is bright and clean and the woman behind the desk is friendly. She calls Sally by her first name. And the room. The room is just unbelievable. A huge circular room with an enormous double bed (double bed! *yes!*), a couple of armchairs and a coffee table and its own little bathroom.

—This is almost bigger than my whole flat at home and there's three of us live there.

Sally smiles. —That's why I always come here. Always get this room if I can.

You do a couple of circuits of the room while she starts to unpack.

—Right, she says. —Quick shower and change an we're outa here by ten thirty. Okay?

She takes her top off so casually that it takes a moment for it to register.

Instantly you're embarrassed. Without thinking you begin removing your own clothes. Somehow it seems impolite not to. But Sally holds up a hand to stop you.

—I know what I said on the phone about showers. But these are just *quick* ones before we go out. So I think we better go separately, yeah?

—Oh . . . yeah. Course.

She disappears into the bathroom wearing nothing but her knickers. You wander round the room in nothing but your underpants and socks, listening to her shower and hoping your erection dies down before she gets out.

It doesn't. She emerges with a towel wrapped round her and you quickly grab your towel and hold it in front of you so she won't see the bulge. Not that you've got a great deal to worry about in this department: your erection merely looks like another man's natural pouch. But maybe it's better not to raise too many false hopes for Sally.

You have the quickest shower ever in the hope of getting out before Sally has time to put on fresh underwear. She's way too quick for you, though. She's already got on a bright yellow dress and she's standing at the mirror applying that fabulous bright red lipstick of hers. Shit. Now you've got to find a way of getting changed without her seeing you. You walk slowly over to your bag and then hop around awkwardly while you try and pull on a clean pair of boxer shorts underneath your towel. Fortunately she's too busy with the eyeliner to notice. You hadn't planned on getting changed for this evening, but she has so you figure you ought to. You pick out a crumpled red T-shirt that's lying on top of your groaning bag and attempt to uncrumple it by stretching it in various directions and when that doesn't work, by swearing at it loudly.

When she's finished with her make-up, Sally catches your eye in the mirror. —Zip me up? she says.

You zip up her dress in what you imagine to be a slow and

seductive manner. No bra, you're pleased to notice. You don't dare hope that there's nothing down below either.

She puts on her fluorescent armbands and turns to face you.

—Okay. Let's go!

Sally takes you to a club down on the seafront. It looks pretty drab from the outside and you begin to wonder if this was such a great idea after all. Clubs in the provinces are never as good as the ones in the capital are they? There'll be some third rate local DJ, a crappy sound system and loads of beery blokes trying to cop off. Perhaps you should have just stayed in that amazing room and had sex all night.

There's a small queue of people waiting outside. Mostly blokes in jeans and trendy-ish T-shirts. Much like yourself. Some women, who've made a bit more effort. You're reassured to find you're not going to be the least trendy person there, but it doesn't do much to dispel your fears about the place as a whole. The best-dressed people are the bouncers who are wearing bright red Guardian Angel outfits and whispering secretively into walkie-talkies. They could be extras off *Star Trek*. There's one guy, one girl and they search everyone thoroughly on the way in which means that, although it's a small queue, it still takes ages for you to get in. That airport-lounge syndrome again. A group of blokes just ahead of you get turned away, presumably for looking too young. They certainly don't look threatening in any way, nor are they noticeably any less cool than other people in the queue. You, for example.

When it comes to your turn to be searched, you suddenly worry about Sally and her stash of drugs. But they're not looking for those, they're looking for weapons. After the search you're handed a leaflet headed ECSTASY AND WATER warning you of the dangers of drug use in the light of recent events. It's their way of saying, we know what you've got on you, we weren't looking for that, we don't give a shit.

Inside the place is nothing special either. A small room with a balcony upstairs and an even smaller chill-out off that. People mill about and check their coats in and drink alcopops and a DJ lays down some cool, gentle rhythms while snatches of the *Prisoner* play on a large screen. It's a mellow groove but you can get into it.

The joint fills up quickly, though, and once full starts to move. Before midnight even, there's a bunch of people on the dancefloor and they're all shaking something. You realise you're in danger of getting left behind here so you give Sally a nudge and ask her for a pill. She fishes one out of a compartment in her bag. There's a couple more Guardian Angel types patrolling inside so you decide to take no chances and head for the gents to unwrap it.

Too late. The tiny room is already crammed full of wide-eyed lads coming up and getting the shits. There's one cubicle. *One* fucking cubicle. Don't they know the effect these drugs have on some people's insides? There's a half-hearted flush and a young bloke emerges looking relieved and happy and gives a knowing nod to the cross-kneed people in the queue. You haven't got time for this. You peel off the paper, knock back the pill and head back out to the dancefloor.

It seems to take an age to kick in, but there's a good enough general vibe and some top tunes being spun so you have a lengthy dance anyway. After an hour or so your feet start getting tired. This shouldn't be happening. You're thinking maybe you got a dud. And then you're thinking maybe it doesn't matter; this is a cool place, I'm with a beautiful woman, they're playing good music, maybe I'll just have a dance and actually appreciate something for a change. It occurs to you to ask Sally for another E, but you don't want her to know that the first one was shit. She seems to be having a good enough time on hers. Your feet are beginning to ache, though. You catch Sally's attention and tell her you're going to sit down for a bit. She looks puzzled but nods okay.

You're seized on the way up the stairs to the balcony. It shoots down your arms and your legs and tingles exquisitely in your extremes. It hits you with such force that you nearly fall over and have to grab on to a stranger for support. He gives you a huge grin and a slap on the back. You go and sit down anyway but you know it won't be for long. You take a seat on the balcony and watch the people go by and are pleased to notice that everyone's dancing already, everyone from the dancefloor all the way up the stairs to the tables on the balcony and even those people sitting down like yourself are dancing in their own way, stamping their feet or waving their arms or nodding their head or just rolling their eyes, and it's not just the drugs either because there's plenty of people here not on drugs at all, for example the girl right in front of you with the short auburn hair, tight midriff T-shirt and cycling shorts, she doesn't look like she's on anything, not anything artificial anyway, she's just high on the drugs her own body is able to manufacture and pump around itself and all she has to do to keep this going is dance and dance and dance all night and there's a guy over the other side of the room who's in exactly the same state, stripped down to football shorts and trainers and working his body like he's training for a marathon and you realise that for these people that's what tonight is, it's a workout, it's a more interesting way of keeping in shape than staying at home with a Jane Fonda video, or rather about six Jane Fonda videos on the trot, and you're intrigued by this and you make a point of watching these two and they don't stop dancing all night, not for one single record, and you marvel at the power of this scene, this culture, whatever you want to call it, this vibe, to bring such disparate people together, because these two presumably hang out in the gym a lot – that guy didn't get his muscles for free – and you'd no more voluntarily go to a gym than you'd go to a morris dancing convention, yet here you all are getting off on the same tunes, and just a little further down from you there's three heavy metal kids, greasy old hippies with beards and faded Metallica T-shirts and they're getting off on this too, off their faces and headbanging, and this of course is great headbanging music, and you *hate* heavy metal and you hate people who like heavy metal, but what the fuck, more power to them, and there's indie kids here and soul boys and fashion-victim young mods and old-school punks, black and white, boys and girls, and you suddenly understand what that disco band were on about all those years ago when they sang about one nation under a groove and isn't it fucking *great*, but you decide to stop thinking about all this, you decide to stop thinking about it there and then and listen to the music, just for a few minutes you're going to concentrate on the music because it's the music that really counts in all this, it's the music that's bringing all these people together, more than the drugs, more than the design and the style, more than the clothes, more than the attitude even, it's the music that's got this thing nailed firmly to the mast, this swirling, hypnotic music that was born with the technology of the late eighties, was born of many other musics – Hi NRG, northern soul, Krautrock, Chicago House – but mutated into something original, and is mutating still, taking on board jazz and African rhythms, creating something new and fresh right in the face of those tired old cynics who were moaning that art was dead and history was doomed to repeat itself and they'd heard it all before and they'd seen it all before, so while art and film and literature and most of the rest of contemporary culture spiralled in ever-decreasing circles, this music shot out on left field raising its hands and partying, constantly changing, constantly re-inventing, and so surely it deserves to be listened to *very closely indeed*, and that's just what you're going to do, you're going to listen very closely indeed, try to learn, try to understand, listen to how the beats of one record fuse into the next, how patterns come and go, how sounds open and close, how shapes appear and disappear, and without thinking about it you're up and dancing on the spot, your brain didn't command this action, your body just did it, natural reflex, and Jesus, how you dance: you dance as though you were afflicted and your very life depended on how hard you could dance and all thoughts are driven from your mind, you're not concentrating on anything now, not thinking about anything, you couldn't if you tried, your brain is empty but your head is full and for this short spell your body and soul are united in pure motion, until eventually you dare to open your eyes and allow one or two thoughts to creep back in and the first thought, of course, is of Sally so you inch forward to the balcony railings so you can peer over and pick her out on the dancefloor and there she is, in the middle, in the thick of it all, she's got her wristbands on and she's waving her arms around, hypnotising herself like she was doing the first night you met her and, break your heart, she looks even more beautiful now than she did then and you're just grinning to yourself about this when you get another HUGE rush and you grab on to the railings and swing backwards and forwards, letting yourself go and pulling yourself back again and you know you must look like a complete twat doing this but you really couldn't give a toss and you try and catch Sally's eye so you can give her a smile and a wink to let her know every-thing's okay, the E was a good one, the club's good, the music's good, you're having a good time, you're having a fucking good time, but you can't get her attention because her eyes are shut and she's blissed out so you decide to go down and join her, after all you are supposed to be on a date with her, so you make your way through the crowds of dancing people and you run into the guy you nearly knocked over on the way up and you give him a little hug and you clamber down the stairs and dance your way across the floor to Sally and when she sees you she throws her arms in the air and then throws them around you and gives you a big, wet, rubbery kiss and just as she's doing this the music seems to go up a notch so you let each other go and both punch the air and you get to thinking, once you've had your fill of punching the air, you get to thinking that *this* is what you want to do with the rest of your life, you want to pop pills and dance to loud music with Sally, and that's it, and why the fuck do you let so much shit clutter up your life, why do you spend so much time cutting smelly bastards' hair when you could be here doing this all the time, you could go out dancing every night, no reason why not, so you start devising cunning plans that will allow you to adapt your lifestyle so you can do this every single night and obviously the first and most important thing is to give up your job, tell that cunt where he can stick his barber's pole, although in his way Louie's not so bad, you'd probably miss him if you did leave, but leave you must if you are to pursue your dream, so you'll need to find alternative sources of income as this lifestyle is not particularly cheap and you think maybe you'll become a DJ, that way you could combine work with pleasure, but it would involve quite a considerable outlay on decks and records, not to mention tracking down a hitherto undiscovered talent, so you fall back on the old standby of dealing drugs, which you reckon you probably wouldn't be very good at, or – most likely of all – winning the Lottery, and when you've won the Lottery, which you feel you surely will do just as soon as you start buying tickets again, then Sally can give up her job too and you can get married and go clubbing every night, in London, down here, in Leeds, wherever, and once you're married you can have kids and that needn't interfere with your clubbing because you can just get babysitters every night and they'll understand at the school that you can't make parents' evenings because you're supercool and you're fucking *out* every night and your kids will be proud of you and other kids will be in awe of you and want to be friends with your kids because their parents are so cool and you have this beautiful vision of you and Sally as old timers, rocking chairs on the porch, smoking spliffs and dropping Es as the sun goes down and you want to reach out to Sally and share this with her but you can't tell her because the music's so loud and she won't hear you and the music's so loud and fast and loud and fast and loud and fast and loud and fast. And loud. And fast.

So all in all it's a good little night. You do come down – eventually – but as with all great comedowns, you're only coming down to a plateau way above where you started off from, so you can deal with it okay. You and Sally sit in the chill-out, grinning stupidly and stroking each other's hands, sucking on ice-pops. You haven't had one of these since you were about seven: how did Sally know this was exactly what you needed?

—So what do you think to this place? Sally asks.

—Yeah, not bad. Almost as good as some places in London.

You don't want to sound too enthusiastic. Heaven forbid she would think you *uncool*.

—Almost? she says. —It's better than any place I know in London.

You cast an eye around. It's starting to empty a little.

—We-ell. Wouldn't say *better*.

—You will in a moment. She takes your hand. —Come on, I wanna show you something.

—Where we going?

—We're leaving.

You haven't finished your ice-pop yet.

—What. Now?

—Yeah, come on.

She stands up and tugs on your arm.

—I thought you were gonna show me something. Something to convince me how great this place is.

—Yeah, I am. It's outside.

You work the last chunk of ice-pop up the plastic tube with your fingers and then you stick the tube in your mouth and suck out the rest of the liquid. When you're done you smack your lips and say:—Okay, let's do it.

Sally giggles. —Your tongue's bright purple!

You take this as an invitation to give her a full kiss on the mouth. She doesn't resist. She can't talk anyway: hers is bright orange.

You go through to the main room and pick up your coats. There's fewer people here, but it's still alive. You wouldn't mind another quick dance as it happens, you've still got a small buzz going, but Sally seems dead set on leaving. And you're kind of curious to see what she's got to show you.

What she's got to show you . . . well, you see it the second you step outside. Of course. The beach. This is where this place scores over any place you've ever been in the capital; you're not stepping out into some dingy East London back street, or Camden High Street, or Charing Cross Road, you're not going to have to wait hours for a night bus or pay a fortune to a dodgy mini-cab driver, you've stepped out on to the beach, there's the sea right in front of you and your pretty little guest house is ten minutes' walk away.

The beach, bathed in the soft light of the moon and the not quite so soft lights of the pier to your left and the plush seafront hotels behind you. Up and down its length are small groups of people, some huddled around fires or torches, others visible only by the glowing orange dots of the joints being passed between them. You find your own spot and start doing the exact same thing. As soon as you sit down, Sally starts skinning up, and pretty soon, in addition to being extremely happy, you're stoned as well.

—So . . . get the picture? Sally says.

You smile. —Yeah, I think so. You win.

—It's not about winning, it's all about taking part, she replies, putting the finishing touches to her roach. You love the way her tongue sticks out when she's concentrating. It's one of a list.

How long do you do this for? An hour or two? It can't be more than a couple of hours because it's still dark when you leave, but while you're there you have no concept of time at all. A guy drifts over, asks for a light and ends up sitting and talking to you. Later on a couple of his friends join him. You end up talking about the daftest things you've danced to on E. It's a conversation you've had before.

—A fridge, says Sally and shoots into the lead.

The others laugh. —A fridge? one of them says.

—Yeah. When I was living in a bedsit I used to have this fridge that made this kind of blip noise every time you opened the door and the light came on and I came in late one night off my tits and I opened the fridge to get a drink and it went blip! And I shut the door while I was swigging out of the milk carton and it went blip! again. And I thought, wow, that's a cool noise. So I stood there *op*ening the door and *clo*sing the door again, dancing around getting off on these blip sounds. And the girl who lived next door, who I was friendly with, heard these strange noises and shuffling around and came through to see if everything was okay and there I was doing a tango with my fridge.

They all laugh again and you laugh with them.

—I used to come home and dance to the air filter in the bathroom, says one of the guys.

—Yeah, I've done alarm clocks before now. You know, that tick tick ticking . . . man, that can sound good sometimes.

You all nod. Everyone's done alarm clocks.

They all look over at you.

—Uh, I've danced to the sound of my next-door neighbours making love.

They look at you even harder. You're going to have to explain yourself. So you start telling them about your flat and the paper-thin walls and the Incredible Shagging Neighbours . . .

—Hey, they're in love, give em a break, interjects one of the guys who's probably in love himself.

. . . and how it really pisses you off when you put a record on and they start up next door and he takes his stroke from your music. So you came home one night and they'd been at it when you left at eight and they were still at it when you got in at four and for all you knew they'd been at it solidly for the eight intervening hours, and you were happily off your face, so instead of getting mad and banging on the walls like you usually do, which never has any effect, you started to get into it and you were imagining a beatbox starting up behind the noise and you were replaying all the tunes of the evening with this grunt . . . squeak . . . grunt . . . squeak . . . grunt . . . squeak in the background . . .

They're looking at you very strangely indeed now.

—I hope that doesn't make me sound too weird, you say hurriedly.

—Nah, man, whatever gets you through the night, says the first guy, inching away from you.

Sally throws you over her gear. —Innit amazing what you can learn about someone on a second date. Go on, John, roll us another.

You've been dreading this secretly. Rolling joints is not among your social skills. Face it, you're not exactly laden down with social skills and rolling joints is not among the few you do have. You like to blame your school: how come they never teach you the useful stuff at school, the stuff you might conceivably use in later life, like how to type, how to drive a car, how to mix a Bloody Mary, how to prepare and consume soft drugs? Why do they insist instead on filling your head with useless shit like periodic tables and cosines and irregular verbs? Why, you might have gone in a bit more often if you'd thought you were learning something. Hurry up with the breakfast there, Mum, I can't be late today, I've double spliff building first thing . . .

So when you first started dabbling in illicit substances you really hadn't a clue what you were doing. You watched other people, you tried to copy them and by and large you made a complete arse of it. It didn't matter too much, though: for the year you were a proper dope friend you thought joints were a bit poncey anyway. You'd discovered hot knives, altogether less fiddly once you'd mastered the art of knocking the bottom out of a milk bottle. And then when you quit smoking you gave up dope completely for a while. So you never really progressed from making a complete arse of it.

Tonight must be your lucky night, though. The papers stick together, your fingers find a natural rolling movement, the contents pack tightly together, the roach you construct fits snugly in the end. It's a spliff of distinction. A Rolls-Royce among reefers. You hold it up in front of your eyes and admire its silhouette against the moon. You bang the tip against your hand expertly until everyone has had a chance to see just what a wonderful creation this is.

—You gonna light that fuckin thing or what? says Sally.

—Oh . . . uh, yeah.

You spark it up. What a fantastic feeling sparking up is. You vow to start smoking again first thing in the morning. Well, if Sally smokes already it'll be easier in the long run.

You take a couple of hits and pass it on. You want everyone to have ample opportunity to admire your handiwork. And anyway . . . what were you thinking about? . . . oh yeah, anyway you really don't need more than a couple of hits because . . . why exactly? there was a reason why you don't need more than a couple of hits . . . Christ it's hard work keeping this train of thought going . . . oh yeah, the reason you don't need more than a couple of hits is because . . . YOU'RE ALREADY STONED! Hey! What have you got to say about that?

You lie back on the pebbles. From here on you drift in and out of the conversation. But mainly out. You stare at the sky and marvel at the number of stars. There are about three stars in London; the rest are gobbled up by the streetlights and the smog. But here they're laid out in all their sparkling glory, arranged in the patterns you remember reading about as a kid.

You look at all the other little lights flickering up and down the beach and feel an immediate, affectionate bond with these people. All these people. The mods, the rockers, the soulboys, the students. Even the crusties with dogs. This is your generation. And this is what your generation likes to do: get stoned, lie on a beach at night, look at the stars, listen to the waves.

You're just a bunch of fucking hippies when it comes down to it.

You're so happy, so content, it's scary. You wish all your friends could be here. You wish Nick could be here and not be so uptight. You wish your mum and dad could be here and understand. You wish poor old Mr Noggin could be here – having cleaned himself up a bit first, maybe.

Poor old Mr Noggin. How come he got born into his generation and you got born into yours? Twist of fate or karmic justice: discuss. You think of him on his eighteenth birthday, cowering in a muddy, shit-stinking trench, clutching on to a flask of whisky. His first sip of whisky. You think of that kid in Leeds, alone in a park, choking with fear as his heart gives out. You think of all those millions of Mr Noggins who never made it into old age and incontinence. In those days the older generation really knew a thing or two about shitting on their young. None of this tutting and wringing of hands and praying it's all just a phase: pack them off to a few fields in Belgium and mustard gas the little fuckers. Show them who's in charge.

Eventually it starts getting cold and you feel like you might doze off any second. Your new friends have drifted away and anyhow this idyll, this oasis of perfection for the last couple of hours has been shattered by some cunt with a guitar playing Levellers' songs. The terrifying thought strikes you that this could actually *be* one of the Levellers. Time to make tracks.

Away from the beach reality hits you full in the face. It's easy to forget that not everyone likes to spend their Friday nights the way you do. That ten years down the line there are *still* people who don't get it. Plenty of them. And here they all are in the centre of town, rolling out of nightclubs that prefer to call themselves discotheques and require gentlemen to wear jackets, rolling out of lock-ins, curry houses, all-night amusement arcades in their smart casuals, the blokes drunk and belligerent, the girls drunk and teary. It's a depressing sight. It's a really fucking depressing sight.

Behind you a woman with smeared make-up takes off her high heels and chases in stockinged feet after her boyfriend who's further up the street chasing after another bloke who's committed some kind of indiscretion. Called his pint a poof or his bird a pint or something. The woman is poured into a dark top and bright red mini-skirt that are both about two sizes too small for her. How the fuck she managed to get into them you can't guess. You're reminded of trying to stuff your sleeping bag back into its container after you've used it.

—GARY! she's screaming hoarsely. She's clearly had a long night of singing along to La Macarena and Young Guns Go For It! at full throttle and she hasn't much voice left for trying to dissuade her boyfriend from murdering someone. —LEAVE IM GARY! E DIDN'T MEAN IT . . . GARREEE!

Gary catches up with the other bloke and starts pummelling him about the head.

—GARY! FUCKIN HELL GARY, STOP!

You feel sick. What the fuck are you supposed to do about this? Intervene? Go call the police? All that's likely to achieve is diverting Gary's attention away from his current victim and on to yourself. But you're approaching them now. You can't just walk past a guy having seven shades of shit beaten out of him and not do anything about it. Can you? Apart from the moral implications, Sally will think you're a coward and won't want to sleep with you.

Just as you decide that you really must do something, though, the other bloke manages to get a punch to Gary's mouth. Gary goes down and the other bloke makes his escape. The woman screams.

—GARY! GARY! ARE YOU OK? WHAT'S E FUCKIN DONE TO YOU?

—Fuckin ave that cunt, Gary mumbles through the blood. —I will. I'll fuckin ave im.

His girlfriend cradles him in her arms. You keep your head down as you walk past. Sally grabs your hand. You put your arm around her protectively – although obviously if anything goes off you're just going to run like buggery and hope she can keep up. She'll understand.

But nothing happens. As you walk by him Gary's still mumbling excuses to his bird. —Gave im a good fuckin pasting though. Before e clobbered me. I was avin im good an proper . . . just got a lucky punch, that's all.

And she starts crying. Drunk and belligerent; drunk and teary.

You and Sally pick your way through the fights and vomit and blood back to your pretty guest house. You can't handle shit like this when you've been on E. Why can't everyone just be cool and love each other?

—Wonder if Nick will have phoned, says Sally as you reach the guest house. But there are no messages.

Back in your room you head straight for the toilet. For an awful moment you think you might throw up but it passes and you settle down to a routine bowel movement. Sitting with your trousers round your ankles, you wonder whether sex is still on the cards for tonight. On balance you hope not. Keen as you are to get your end away with Sally before she realises what a complete tosser you are and refuses all further contact with you, you still haven't quite come down yet and shagging on E is not all it's cracked up to be. While it sounds great to be able to keep going for ages without fear of premature ejaculation – which is quite some feat as far as you're concerned – in practice it poses all sorts of logistical problems. For example, if you have no chance of coming ever, how do you know when to stop? You've resorted before now to timing yourself to records, calculating that by the end of track five, say, you'll have been at it for twenty minutes so you'll pull out then before you both start to bleed. But there's no CD player here. And anyway you're knackered. It's as much as you can do to tease your arse muscles into action; you're not sure you can stay awake another twenty minutes. Falling asleep immediately after sex is one thing, but *during?*

Also there's the conceptual problem with shagging on E: namely, if you have no chance of coming ever . . . what's the fucking point?

So you're quite happy to find as you emerge from the bathroom Sally is already in bed and fast asleep. A little disappointed maybe that she's kept her T-shirt on but that's okay. There's tomorrow morning for making love, there's the rest of the weekend, the rest of your lives.

You slip into bed next to her and nuzzle up against her shoulder. She murmurs something softly. You are amazed to discover that she's *even more beautiful* when she's asleep. Oh boy. You drift away to sleep thinking about what a great evening you've had and what a great weekend you're going to have and . . .

BRRINNGG!

. . . you're dreaming of bright flashing lights and endless beaches and being hugged by strangers and . . .

BRRINNGG!

. . . somewhere in your dream there's a phone ringing. Someone get the phone. Someone get the phone . . .

BRRINNGG!

. . . and you're in a house . . . you answer the phone . . . you answer the phone and it keeps on ringing . . . Oh Christ . . .

BRRIINNGG!

. . . it's the phone from the start of *Once Upon A Time In America* and you're Robert De Niro out of his box in an opium den and . . . someone get the phone . . .

BRRINNGG!

. . .

BRRINNGG!

Someone get the fucking phone!

BRRINNG!

You're finally shaken awake. You look around for this damn phone . . . but it's not a phone at all, it's an *alarm clock* . . .

BRRINNGG!

Sally has brought a fucking alarm clock with her!

She too finally stirs and hits the clock to switch it off.

BRRIN/click.

Thank fuck for that. The silence is heavenly. Enormous.

You peer at the clock and chuckle to yourself. For a second there you thought it said half past eight. It can't be half past eight, though; you only got in just before seven. You start to drift pleasantly back to sleep . . .

Sally sits up suddenly.

—What you doing?

—Breakfast! she says brightly.

—You're fuckin kidding me.

—No, come on. The breakfasts here are out of this world and they stop serving at nine.

—I don't want any fuckin breakfast. I've only been asleep five minutes.

—You'll want this breakfast. Come on. You can catch up on your sleep on the beach later on.

And without warning she's naked again, prancing across the floor to the bathroom. Your erection goes from nought to sixty in a couple of seconds. That's that then. You won't be getting back to sleep now and if you did you'd only end up having a wet dream probably, which would be . . . well it doesn't bear thinking about. So you haul yourself out of bed and find the loosest pair of trousers in your bag. Something to give the old fellow a bit of camouflage. Erections like this are like local anaesthetics, they can last anything up to four hours, so it's best to just carry on and work round them. You'd rather it wasn't *too* obvious for Sally, though. Don't want to play all your cards at once.

The smell of breakfast comes wafting up the stairs as soon as you open the door. Sally leads you down to a small room where half a dozen other people are eating in complete silence. The only sound is the soft clink of cutlery on plate. But the lack of sound is more than amply made up for by the smell . . . man, that *smell*.

First strike is a glass of orange juice which you sink in one and it sends shivers of wholesomeness up and down your body. So how come MDMA is a Class A drug and Vitamin C isn't?

Next you're taken to a sideboard and invited to choose a cereal from one of those little Kellogg's Variety packs. Oh wow! You haven't had one of these since you were about six. Some cunt's had the Frosties already, though, so you have to make do with a bowl of Rice Crispies. As ever, they fail to go either snap, crackle or pop.

While you're still slurping away at these, a matronly waitress comes over and asks if you'd like the full breakfast. You look over to Sally for guidance and she nods so you nod too. Vigorously.

When the breakfasts arrive, you discover that this place has a rather different understanding of the word 'full' than yours: a more generous understanding, a more expansive, *fuller* definition. On the plate in front of you – and it's an extremely large plate – there appears to be one item of every foodstuff you've ever heard of. There are sausages and tomatoes, bacon and roast potatoes, poached *and* scrambled eggs, mushrooms and black pudding . . .

And in five minutes flat it's all gone.

—Hungry were you? says Sally, mopping up her juices with a bit of fried bread.

—Yeah. Must've been.

—Told you it'd be worth it.

The waitress reappears. She wants to know if you'd like any more toast.

She's having a laugh, isn't she?

—Oh yeah, man, you gotta have some toast! Sally insists. —They have the best homemade marmalade ever here.

You stare at her incredulously. She's not an inch over five foot and light as a feather. Where is she putting this shit?

So the toast arrives and you force some down and, while you've never managed to get particularly excited about marmalade before, there is no denying this is good marmalade. You manage a couple of little triangles and then raise your hands in defeat.

You're just sitting back in your chair, willing your poor startled stomach to digest this stuff more quickly, thinking how lovely it would be if you never had to get up from this table for the rest of your life, when the waitress comes back over and says there's a phone call for you. You and Sally look at each other; it can only be one person . . .

By the time you get through to reception, Nick has hung up but left a message for you to call him back. The woman at the desk changes a pound coin into ten pence pieces and points you to the pay phone in the corner.

The phone is in a small cabin off the reception area. The cabin is no bigger than a regular phone box, so you both have to squeeze in, which is enjoyably intimate. Sally feeds a coin into the slot while you dial Nick's mobile number.

—Hello? comes a crackly voice at the other end.

You balance the receiver between you so you can both hear, but neither of you can actually hear properly.

—Nick, it's John . . .

—And Sally.

—Yeah, hi, how's it goin?

Nick sounds half asleep.

—Yeah, good, you reply. —Just had the biggest fuck-off break-fast of my life. So . . . what's been happening?

There's a loud fizz and crackle which eventually develops into something like:

—Fuckin hell, mad stuff John, mad stuff . . .

—This guy actually done something then? asks Sally, who looks just a little pissed off that Nick only used your name just then.

—Shit, I'll say he has.

—You actually caught him shifting a few more pills?

—It's worse than that, man, it's much worse than that.

Sally unloads the rest of the coins into the phone. This sounds like it might take a while.

Nick goes on. —This is it, man. This is fuckin *it*. This is the story that's gonna make my name. I'm telling you, it's *huge*.

—So go on, says Sally. —Tell us what's happened.

—Okay. Last night, bout seven o'clock, Macmillan and his wife go off for a little drive. Carl didn't even want to bother following them; you know, I think he was fed up just following these unbelievably dull people to and from their jobs every day. We'd been hangin round that offie like a couple of fuckin winos, eating lunch at the wife's caff, seeing them home again for four whole fuckin days. But I said, if we were gonna bother sitting outside their house for four whole fuckin days, supposedly staking them out, then we might as well follow them when they actually go somewhere . . .

The line goes fizzy again. You have a wonderful mental picture of Nick and this other bloke cramped up in a car for days on end, getting so pissed off with each other that they wind up arguing about whether or not they can be bothered to follow the bloke they're supposed to be trailing.

Shit, they must have been going out of their minds in that car. Four days and nights. How many games of I-Spy is that?

—So anyway, we follow Mr an Mrs M to a house on the outskirts of Bradford, another big house just like theirs. We wait outside an there's several more people arrive. Looks like they're having some kind of dinner party or something. I see my opportunity to get some concrete evidence so I leap out of the car, hide meself behind a bush an start snapping away with Fat Cunt's camera. Carl's doin his nut in the car cause he's convinced I'm gonna get both of us caught, but I figure what the hell, we've come this far . . .

You glance at Sally; she looks awestruck. Bastard.

—Mostly they're all well-to-do types like the Macmillans, but . . . *but* . . . guess who was among them . . . ?

There's silence at the other end. Obviously he wants you to name names so he can look clever.

—Jimmy Hill, you say to get it over with.

—Mr and Mrs Bartlett! he says triumphantly.

—Who are . . . ?

Sally's nodding in recognition. —The parents of that kid, what was his name?

—Peter Bartlett, says Nick. —The one who died from taking an E a few months back. In Bradford. You know, an then they launched this huge crusade in the media against drugs and raves and dance music.

—I remember . . . So what, though?

—Don't you see? Nick sounds incredulous. —Don't you see what this means?

—No, you say flatly. —I don't.

—Well, okay, I didn't either to begin with. It was Danny who worked it out after we told him what we'd seen. But it makes perfect—

He's cut off by the pips. You can't believe this has used up a quid already. Fucking mobile phones. You look over at Sally, but she's shaking her head. You fish around in your pocket; all you have is a couple more pound coins . . .

—I just put another quid in here, Nick, this had better be a good fuckin story.

—I told you, man, it's the story that's gonna make my name, it's gonna be known as the Nick Jones story.

—Okay, fire away.

—Right, this is the deal. You remember how these Bartletts were really fired up with all the anti-drug stuff after their kid died?

—Understandably, says Sally.

—Well, yeah, whatever. But they did, though, didn't they? They went mad with it. Poster campaigns, adverts, appeals, the lot . . . yeah?

—Yeah, I remember.

—Well, suppose that wasn't enough for them. Suppose once they'd been on the telly, had the press conferences, they still felt they hadn't achieved enough? What could they do then to stop kids taking this drug they hated so much?

He's waiting for an answer again.

—I dunno, you say. You haven't a fucking clue what he's getting at.

—Look at it from your point of view, he goes. —What would be the one thing most likely to stop you from taking this stuff again?

Once again, you're totally lost.

—How about, he says, slowly and deliberately, and you sense that finally the point of all this may not be too far away. —How about if the number of people dying from ecstasy suddenly increased enormously? If it really did start to look as though it was as dangerous as some people wish it was?

—I guess . . .

Suddenly you see where he's going with this.

—Surely you're not saying . . . ?

—YES! Nick shouts. —These people are manufacturing deadly pills to scare kids off taking E. The Bartletts, Macmillan, who seems to be the dealer, their friends, they're all in on it. How bout that for a fuckin story? Crazed Parents In Drug Revenge Death Frenzy!

You're alarmed, but not for the reasons Nick thinks you should be.

—Please tell me you don't believe this, you say to him.

—Of course I do! What other explanation is there?

—I dunno. There must be bout a hundred more believable ones than that.

—What's not believable about it?

Jesus. What's not believable about Father Christmas?

—Well, okay, for a start, this mate of yours, Danny, he bought ten pills off the guy outside the football ground, yeah?

—Yeah . . .

—But only one of them was a killer. He sold all ten that night an far as we know the other nine were all okay. If this group wanna increase the number of people dying significantly, how come they didn't sell him ten dodgy ones?

—Cause it's got to seem random, hasn't it? If ten people dropped down dead in one place in one night, it'd look like a plot.

You don't believe it; he's serious.

—For fuck's sake . . .

Now he sounds hurt. —Come on, man, you're supposed to be my mate. Supposed to stick by me. This is my big chance. What does your, uh, friend think?

—My name's Sally, says Sally firmly. —I dunno. I guess it sounds plausible. You're gonna need some proof, though.

—Yeah, course I am. I'm gonna stick around up here now, see what I can dig up.

—Well, take care, Sally says anxiously.

Shit, this is getting worse by the minute. She's *worried* about the bastard.

—I suppose there's no point in me trying to point out that this is completely fuckin ridiculous an persuade you to come home?

—Fuck off, man, says Nick.

Sally's glaring at you. Looks like you might have to concede defeat on this one.

—Okay then, take care from me too, you add quickly, staring back at Sally. See, you do care. —Look mate, this is costin me a bomb. I'll be back home tomorrow night, give us a bell then an let me know how you're doing . . . And don't do anything stupid . . .

With that you hang up.

—Shit, John, that's so exciting, says Sally after a moment to get her breath. —God, I wish I had the guts to do something like that. I feel I'm just pissing my life away selling flowers to people sometimes . . .

—Yeah, you say in a suppose-so kind of way, to try and convey the impression that you and Nick discuss things as exciting as this on a pretty regular basis actually.

The two of you waddle back up to your room, flop down on the bed and watch a bit of *Rugrats* on the telly. Okay, you're thinking to yourself, half an hour to digest this lot, forget about Nick and his lunatic adventures and then we can start thinking about steering the conversation around to sex. For your erection, which had abated slightly while you were eating and talking, has returned with a vengeance, and it's brought reinforcements. You have firmly decided that there's been enough fannying about. This is Brighton, you're with your gorgeous new girlfriend and you want to shake some action.

No luck, though. Five minutes later Sally's up and about, packing stuff into a little day bag, demanding to go to the beach. Wearily you haul yourself out of bed a second time and switch off the telly. It's not going entirely to plan so far.

On the way down to the beach, Sally stops outside a small restaurant.

—This is my favourite restaurant in the whole of Brighton. I thought we might book a table for tonight.

Oh great. More food. Just what you want to think about right now. You've just decided that you've had enough of this and you're going to make some cutting, sarcastic remark, when you see her line of reasoning. Of course. Saturday night. Candlelit dinner for two. Slow walk back along the beach . . . sex! She's a girl; she wants to do the thing properly; create the right atmosphere and all that. Very nice.

—Yeah, why not? you say.

You have a look at the menu stuck on the window. Your extensive experience of eating out ranges all the way from McDonald's to Burger King, with the odd pizza and curry on special occasions, so this seems on the pricey side to you. But it's a guaranteed wriggle at the end of it, so what the fuck?

The rest of the day you spend doing seasidey stuff. You have a little kip on the beach. It's a nice enough day, but not so sunny you'll burn. Then Sally persuades you, against your far better judgement, to go in for a dip. And the water's FREEZING. You can feel yourself turning blue all over. Still, puts paid to that fucking erection. You have a good old splash about and throw water at each other and generally frolic about like ten-year-olds. Afterwards you go for a walk along the pier and go on a couple of the rides and play some amusements. And somewhere along the way you have your first kiss. Not like the brief, loved-up snogs you had in the club last night. This is your first proper tongue down throat, hands on arse kiss. And it's magic.

Lying on your bed while Sally puts her make-up on – she's got her top off again but you're getting blasé about this now – you think back over the events of the day. Seems weird. You spent all day acting like kids and now here you are, getting ready to go on a very grown-up evening out. You've never been to a restaurant with a girl before and you're kind of nervous. Are you going to be able to sustain a conversation for a whole evening? It's okay in a club: you've just got to nod every so often and shout, yeah, nice one! But you can't really get away with that in a restaurant. And will you be able to understand the menu? None of it seemed very familiar when you were looking at it earlier on. No burgers, you noticed. Suppose you order something and it tastes like shit; you'll have to eat it all and then pay through the nose for it. Suppose you do something wrong and end up making a right tit of yourself . . .

Suppose, in fact, you spend most of the meal sitting in faintly embarrassed silence. The two of you keep trying to ignite a conversation, but nothing will catch. Pretty soon your mind is a gaping void. None of your usual topics of conversation seem appropriate here: music, comics, bitchy comments about your friends. On top of this, you're now seriously concerned about Nick and his gentle slide into insanity. You can't get him and his stupid idea off your mind. No point in trying to talk about it to Sally, though: she still seems to think he's in with a shout for the Pulitzer Prize, and you don't want to end up arguing with her. Not here. Anyhow, you have a distinct feeling she's going to bring the subject up herself at some point.

So you ask her a few questions about herself and she gives you a few one word answers. And she asks you a few questions about yourself and you give her more or less exactly the same one word answers. It's not small talk, it's fucking microscopic.

—Mmm, this is good, says Sally, wiping her mouth. She has some kind of chicken casserole thing, which she has been eating slowly and stealthily, savouring every piece.

—Yeah . . . yeah. so was mine.

You're aware suddenly that you've been eating twice as quickly as her. While she chomps away delicately, raving about how great this is, you casually flick a couple of remaining peas about your plate and check out these surroundings.

You're really not comfortable here, no two ways about it. Sure, the ingredients are all there: the low lighting, the candles, the music you can barely hear. But it all seems so safe, so *conformist*. Pretty much all the other people here are couples, mostly older than you. There's no one here drunk or having an argument or a food fight, or, as far as you can tell, a really good time.

It's okay, though, you have to keep reminding yourself, this is what adults do, you'll grow into it. You can't stay up all night dancing to loud music the whole of your life; there are other ways of having fun. Anyway, it's a means to an end, isn't it?

And Sally does look kind of gorgeous in here.

—So what about Nick's little adventure, then? she says finally.

Here we go.

—Isn't it the biggest pile of festering wank you've ever heard in your whole life? Jesus, Nick's spewed out some prize bullshit in the time I've known him, but this takes the fuckin biscuit. Vigilante parent groups cooking up lethal pills and killing off clubbers one by one! Fuck's sake . . .

This is what you *want* to reply. This would be your honest, personal reply. However, at long suffering last you are slowly but surely learning the value of tact and consideration and politeness. Especially when you want to get laid.

So what you actually say is more along the lines of:—I'm not sure I'm totally convinced by this idea.

—What idea?

—Of this Macmillan an his gentle, middle-class cronies making up killer tablets.

Sally shrugs. —I dunno. It fits the facts as far as we know them. An it's no weirder than a lot of the shit you read in the tabloids.

Yeah. And you're not wholly convinced by any of that stuff either. But once again, something between your legs stops you from telling her this.

—But he's right, you know, she goes on. —If this story turns out to be true, it really will make his name. He'll be able to sell it all over the world. God . . . it must be so exciting.

You try and look enthusiastic. Of course the downside of all this is that if it all turns out to be a crock of shit, he'll look like a prize twat all over the world.

—Oh come on John! He's your mate. You ought to be giving him all the support he needs.

—Yeah . . . yeah, you're right. I'm pleased for him, I really am, you stutter, and you desperately try to think of another topic of conversation.

—So how long have you two been mates? she asks, not letting up for a second.

—Oh, uh, I dunno . . . six or seven years.

—Yeah? Where'd you meet?

—Stone Roses, Spike Island. We both got split up from the people we were with. Ended up hitching back to Camden together. We'd both just moved to London. I was doing this foundation course, or rather I wasn't doing very much of it. I was bunkin off most of the time. That's how I ended up cutting hair; never did me studies properly. Nick, though, he was the clever one. He was at university, just started that year. So neither of us knew anyone much in London, we were living pretty close to each other, so we just kinda stayed in touch.

—An how come he knows so many famous people?

Jesus, what a shallow question. If she just wants to fuck celebrities, she's hitting on the wrong two guys.

—He doesn't know that many really. He's a journalist. You know, he interviews loads of people an some of them he gets to know.

—Like W?

—I never knew he was mates with him to be honest with you. I mean, he used to brag on bout it an that, but he brags on bout so much stuff that you don't really take much notice. I thought he was just bullshitting me.

There's a sudden sharp pain in your stomach; it feels like you just swallowed a bread knife. You stop talking, convinced you're going to start choking any second, but it passes as quickly as it came. Sally seems not to have noticed.

—I think W's great, though, don't you? she gushes. —What was that really cool film he was in again?

She starts reeling off names of films. You have no idea which one she means; you thought they were all pretty cool.

—So did Nick have a good time back at his gaff then?

—Yeah, think so. They just took bucketloads of pills basically. W an some of his mates ended up playing Pass the Drug Parcel.

You start explaining the rules but she's way ahead of you.

—Oh wow, man, you shoulda gone! she says.

—Yeah, then I'd've got talking to Fat Cunt and ended up chasing psychopathic parent groups around Yorkshire as well. No thanks. Anyway . . .

You take a deep breath. You're going to try and say this without sounding too smarmy.

—. . . I wanted to be with you.

You failed. Miserably.

—Thank you, she whispers back. Amazingly, it seems to have worked. You've got another Moment on your hands.

She takes your hand across the table and gazes into your eyes.

She mouths another thank you. You want to tell her that you love her, that you have loved her from the very first moment you saw her and that you always will. Time has stopped. The other people in the restaurant have ceased to exist. It's a beautiful Moment, one that could last for ever and ever . . .

But it doesn't last because you are suddenly gripped by an urgent need to go to the bathroom.

—I'm sorry, you'll have to excuse me, you say, standing up and pulling away from her.

The toilets are at the other end of the room. You practically run towards the door. You have that sinking feeling of your trousers filling up. All the curries you've ever eaten pass before your eyes.

Inside the cubicle you wrestle with your belt, your fingers and thumbs conspiring against you, and yank down your jeans. The stuff starts tumbling out of you before your bum has even reached the seat.

Aaaahhhh!

This feels eerily like sex.

You know there's more to come, though. In fact, this turns out to be one of the longest dumps in the history of the world. When you're finally done, you half expect Norris McWhirter to be standing outside with a stopwatch and a gold medal.

The stuff just keeps on coming. Some of it's liquid, some of it's solid; some of them are real fucking porcupines that burn up your cheeks and have you clinging on to the radiator, wide-mouthed in agony. Every now and then you think you're done and you wipe yourself, only for your hateful body to dredge up another load and send that on its way. You're getting through a rainforest of bog roll here. You have a bloodcurdling fear that it might run out before you finish.

As you weren't able to bring a comic with you, you have plenty of time to sit and think. Think and worry. You worry first and foremost that you have completely spoiled the evening. This is not only deeply embarrassing, it's also somewhat unromantic. You're also concerned about all her questions about Nick. It's easy to become paranoid when you've been sat on the dumper for twenty minutes, so you get to thinking: what if she's just using me to get at him? She saw him at the club that night and she finds him kind of glamorous. She's only with me now because I know someone who knows someone who's vaguely famous.

Another load comes sploshing out. Ugghh. You feel sick. You feel sick and absolutely fucking miserable.

When finally the torture is over – for the time being at any rate – you have to prise yourself off the seat. It's left a sharp red ring around your arse. You pull up your jeans and flush the chain. And . . . nothing. You feel the panic rising. You pull the chain vigorously, several times. Come on you fucker! There's a half-hearted flushing sound and a cupful of water splashes into the bowl. It's full of paper and mess all the way up to the rim. It's going to take a fucking tidal wave to flush this lot away. You give it one more go and get a proper flush this time. Most of the shit is sucked noisily into the U-bend. There's still quite a bit of stuff left float-ing but fuck it, you've done your best. You wash your hands and leave this putrid hell-hole.

You're almost too embarrassed to go back to Sally now. You can sense the perfumed aroma of your deposit wafting across the room. Everyone's turned to look at you.

—Are you okay? Sally asks as you sit down. She looks concerned at least.

—Yeah . . . fine . . . don't know what happened there . . .

You both sit in silence. What do you say when you've just spent twenty minutes on the khazi? What do you say *to* someone who's just spent twenty minutes on the khazi? The romantic mood's well and truly buggered.

You don't particularly want to start talking about Nick again, but wasn't that roughly where the conversation left off? You've got to talk about *something*.

—Nick's never had a girlfriend, you know.

Not *strictly* true.

—In fact, a lot of people reckon he might be gay.

Complete lie.

—Yeah? says Sally sweetly. —How come?

—Well, you know . . . cause he's never had a girlfriend.

—Has he ever had a boyfriend?

—Uh . . . no. Not that I know of, but, you know . . . that doesn't mean—

—Well there you go then, he's as likely to be straight as he is to be gay, isn't he?

You shift gingerly on your burning butt.

—Actually, there is quite a good reason . . .

No there isn't, there's no good reason at all why anyone might suspect Nick was gay. But you're spared from having to make one up because your bowels have another announcement to make.

—Sorry, you gasp.

It's a slightly shorter visit this time. A mere quarter of an hour maybe. But it's a more painful one, a *much* more painful one. When you emerge this time, you feel ill. And you obviously look ill because the first thing Sally says when she sees you is:

—Christ, John, you look green. Come on, I'm taking you home.

The head waiter is terribly worried about the way you look. He ushers you both through the door without letting you pay. Green patrons are not good for business. It wasn't their fault, though; if anything, it was that fucking breakfast.

—Hey, that's a great way to beat the bill, says Sally outside.
—Have to try that one again.

But you're too miserable to see the funny side of it. You can't even raise a smile.

So your new girlfriend takes you home and puts you to bed. So much for the guaranteed wriggle. You lie there feeling like shit, she watches a film on TV. In the morning, she goes for another one of those breakfasts, you lie there feeling like shit. You stay in bed until you have to vacate the room. Then you struggle up to the station with your bag full of clothes you never wore.

You and Sally hardly speak on the train. In the afternoon it starts to rain and you watch the drizzle run down the window of the carriage. It feels like the end of more than a weekend. You came away to Brighton with the girl of your dreams and you didn't sleep with her. You can't believe it. You can't believe how shit your life can be.

You know what your mistake was? You let yourself get carried away by hope. Whatever made you think things were going to work out between you and her anyway? How could you possibly imagine that someone like you could end up with someone like her? Go on.

Get back to your haircuts and your comics and your sad, lonely little life. You fucking loser.

You look over at Sally. She's reading a newspaper. You know now that you will never sleep with this woman. You will *never* sleep with this woman.

Part Two

∫

You spark up a joint. Sally's already asleep, which is slightly discon-
certing. Isn't it the blokes who are supposed to fall asleep straight
away? And the girls who are supposed to lie awake, as you are now,
feeling empty and lonely? Still, you haven't grown tired yet of her
beauty as she sleeps.

You wonder if maybe your sex life is already growing stale.
Maybe that's why she's fallen asleep so quickly. It hasn't been going
long but already it's settled down into a pattern. One evening
through the week you go out someplace quiet and then back to
either yours or hers, then Friday night you'll go out clubbing and
you'll be too tired or drugged up for sex when you get in, so it has
to wait until the morning. And you work Saturday mornings so
you have to be quick about it. Saturday night you go out again, but
then she goes straight off to the market from wherever you are.
And that's about it. Your relationship needs to move on, get to the
next stage. You want sex on a Tuesday afternoon. Outdoor sex.
Kinky sex.

Maybe it's the fact that you've got stuck on telling her that you
love her. Maybe that's what's holding the relationship back. You *do*
love her. You've known that for some time. And you want to tell
her, but it's just a question of finding the moment. You can't really
do it when you're Ed up – you love everyone when you're Ed up –

and you seem to be spending a lot more time Ed up these days. Nor can you tell her immediately before, after or during sex; that would be crass. You need a romantic, neutral setting where you can say what you have to say without fear of it being misconstrued.

What you should have done, of course, is tell her in that restaurant in Brighton. You could have got it all sewn up back then. That was easily the most romantic moment you've shared so far. And you were going to tell her, your lips were just forming the words, she looked so beautiful that night you couldn't not tell her. But your body rebelled and that was that.

—Gis a toke on that, Sally mumbles without opening her eyes.

—No, you can't have any.

—Why not?

—Cause you're asleep.

—No I'm not.

—Yes you are. You're just pretending to be awake.

She opens her eyes. —There. I'm awake. Now gis a fuckin toke, you bastard.

—Mmm . . .

—Gis a toke now or I'll never give you another blowjob as long as you live.

—You only had to ask.

You finish off the joint between you and both drift back to sleep. That's better. Stop worrying, you've got a beautiful girlfriend there, better than you deserve. Enjoy it. Relax . . . relax . . .

You wake with a start. You're panicking already but you don't know why. You look over at the clock. Eleven thirty. Saturday.

SATURDAY! ELEVEN THIRTY! SATURDAY! ELEVEN THIRTY!

Hang on, though, it's your Saturday off. That's how come you had such a late night. You're not going in today.

You lie back on the pillow, the happiest man alive. It's your Saturday off. *Yes!*

It's your first Saturday off since you started going out with Sally and she's gone and arranged a bloody meeting for today. You were well pissed off when you first found out, but now you're kind of looking forward to a day on your own. You give her a prod in the back.

—Hey, what time you seeing that bloke?

—Uh . . . twelve thirty, I think.

—It's eleven thirty already.

She makes a lunge across your chest to pick up the alarm clock and look at it.

—*Shit!*

She clambers out of bed, pulls on a T-shirt and heads for the bathroom. While she showers, you have another little doze. When she gets back, though, she's woken up properly and starts chatting away.

—Good place last night, eh?

—Yeah.

—Those doves were the business.

—Yeah.

—An that DJ . . . what was his name?

You tell her.

—He was pretty good, she says.

He was fucking out of this world.

—So what you gonna do with yourself today?

You give a big yawn. —Oh, I dunno. Potter about, I guess. No plans.

Now that isn't entirely true. You know exactly what you're going to do today. You're going to go round to Ian's shop and pick up the new *Captain Midnight* comic. He phoned you Thursday to say it was in and you haven't had the chance to get round there yet and now, not to put too fine a point on it, you're gagging for it.

But you don't want to tell her that, do you?

—Well . . . have a good time.

—Yeah, you say sleepily. —You too.

—Yeah, right. What you fancy doing tonight?

—Dunno.

—I thought we might just stay in. I wouldn't mind a quiet night. I might even get some Lottery tickets. I haven't done the Lottery in ages.

—Whatever.

She gives you a kiss on the forehead.

—I'll see you later. Give me a call, yeah?

—Course.

Well. You're awake now. Might as well get up.

You don't bother with breakfast; that's how keen you are to get your hands on your fix. Although you're heartbroken at having to wait two whole days for your comic, you actually much prefer to go to Ian's on a Saturday when the shop is open, rather than in the evening during the week. There are other people there to deflect his interest. People who enjoy talking to him. This should just be a quick in and out job, then you can retire to the caff round the corner, get yourself a huge fry-up and read your new story. This is what days off are meant for.

The only downside to this is the smell. A dozen smelly people smell a whole lot worse than one smelly person on his own. About twelve times as bad. And it's a hot day today, a really hot day. You're sure you can smell the stench from halfway down Camden High Street. But when you get there, it's even worse than you feared. It's the Body Odour Olympics in here. You hold your breath and make your way to the counter where Ian is engaged in a heated *Spawn* debate with a fat bloke in a Ramones T-shirt.

—Hey, Ian.

—Hey, John. Just a second. I'll be right with you.

—Yeah, I'm in kind of a hurry.

—Just coming. I'm trying to persuade this idiot that the first issue of *Spawn* wasn't in fact the biggest selling comic of all time . . .

—Yeah, an important point, but like I say, I'm in a bit of a hurry . . .

—Okay, man, keep your hair on . . . hey, you all right? You sound kinda funny.

You're still not breathing through your nose, which makes your voice sound like you're doing Dalek impressions.

—Yeah, got a bit of a cold. Nothin serious. But I don't want anyone else to catch it.

—On a day like today?

—Yeah . . . summer cold.

You wave a fiver hopefully in front of his face. Ian looks at it, then looks over at the fat bloke and points at him.

—Don't go away; I haven't finished yet.

He retrieves your comic from the mess of envelopes and hands it over. You pay him.

—Cheers. Have to go for a beer sometime, he goes.

—Yeah. Some time soon. I'll give you a call, you lie.

You manage to make it to the door without breaking into a run. Outside you exhale loudly through your nose and then breathe in great lungfuls of pure, sweet-smelling North London smog. Then you head for the caff. Now, *that's* a proper, wholesome smell. The smell of grease and frying oil. The smell of clogged arteries and heart failure. You get a large plate of the works and are very careful not to get any ketchup on *Captain Midnight*.

When you get back to your place, not only are the Incredible Shagging Neighbours up to their usual tricks, but Tony is entertaining his girlfriend in his room. It's grunting and grinding in stereo. On a Saturday afternoon as well. You don't care, though. You've had a good seeing too already today. You've done your share of disturbing the peace.

You got yourself a couple of records from the market while you were up in Camden, so you slap on one of these and turn up the volume. They're names you only vaguely recognise, ones you've read in a magazine somewhere, but you've got to take a punt sometimes. It's so hard to keep on top of this music as obviously none of the records in clubs are introduced, and even radio DJs are now starting to consider themselves too cool to let their listeners know what they're listening to. If you're honest with yourself, you don't even particularly like playing techno music at home – you'd just as soon stick with your Primal Scream records – but you'd feel a complete fraud if you didn't make some token effort to keep up. And Harry's madly enthusiastic about it all, and a lot of this rubs off on you. You wonder if Sally has a lot of records. It's so weird to have a girlfriend who likes the same kind of stuff as you. Your most recent girlfriend was the last person in the world to realise how shit Big Country were and, criminally, you'd overlooked this character flaw in order to get laid.

As soon as it starts, the record's familiar. You've heard this quite a few times out and about. A big, square beat with some kind of Eastern chanting going on over the top of it, and sitars and stuff. It's a good one. You think they played this down in Brighton when you were there . . . fond memories. Fuck, you were out of it that night.

You pick up your comic and start flicking through the best bits again. Good comic, good sounds.

Five minutes later Tony comes through wearing nothing but his boxers. His face looks flushed.

—Hi John.

—Tony. Nice pecs, man.

—Yeah . . . thanks.

It was a joke, you fucking moron.

—Uh, Nick called, he goes on. —He wants you to call back. I think it's kinda urgent.

—Okay. Cheers.

—Oh . . . and another thing . . .

—Yeah?

—You couldn't change the music, could you? I mean this is cool an everything, but it's wearing me out, man. You got any reggae or something?

—Fuck off, Tony.

—Yeah . . . uh, right. See you later.

Bollocks. You were just getting comfortable, now you've got to go and phone the intrepid journalist. You don't believe for a second that he has anything urgent to say to you, not since his elaborate conspiracy theory about the mad Yorkshire parents fizzled out, but you're kind of curious so you amble over to the phone. Anyway, Sally would never forgive you if you left your best friend waiting, if you didn't *support* him. So you dig his mobile number out of the mass of little scraps of paper that serve as your address book and dial the number.

When he finally answers it, it sounds like he's in a submarine. PSHHTTCCCHHH. —Yeah? Hello? PSHTTT. —Hello? —Nick?

PSSSHHTTCCCHHHARRRCCCK—. . . is it?

—Nick? Can you hear me?

Suddenly the line clears.

—HELLO? HELLO? IS THERE ANYONE FUCKING THERE?

—Nick, it's John. How you doin, man? I heard you called.

—John, yeah! Sorry bout that. Shit line.

—Where are you?

—On the train comin down from Leeds. I've got some more news bout that story. It's all opening up again, man.

—Yeah?

The line fizzes out once more. When you can hear him again, he goes:—So what you doing tonight?

—Nothing much. Thinking of staying in actually.

—Fuck that, man. It's Saturday night!

—Yeah, I know . . .

—Warehouse party. Tonight. Illegal squat warehouse party. Eighties-style. You gotta go, man. Gonna be storming.

—I dunno . . .

—Come *on*, man! This one's gonna be historic. You'll hate yourself if you don't go. You'll be telling people you were there in ten years' time . . .

—Okay, okay . . . whereabouts?

He gives you the name of a pub in Hackney. Closing time. —I'll tell you what I've found out when I see you, he says. —It's some fuckin heavy shit, I tell you.

And then the line dissolves again. You hang up.

You walk over to the stereo to pick out an appropriate tune for Tony. You select the fastest, jitteriest drum and bass track in your collection. Luckily it's on an LP. You put it on at 45.

What a happy, happy man you are.

Sally takes a bit of persuading, but she comes round once you tell her Nick is going to be there and he has some news for you. The pub is one she knows and she likes the beer garden so you get there early. The garden and surrounding park are already full of trendy-looking young things sitting around in small groups, drinking cider and passing around surreptitious spliffs. It's a party waiting to happen.

Nick hasn't arrived yet and there's no one else you really know, but there are one or two familiar faces. Including Fat Cunt, who's leaning up against a tree, smoking a giant spliff on his own. You want to show Sally that you know *someone* here, so you wander up to him.

—All right? you go.

—All right, he says.

Silence for a bit.

—Here for the rave?

—No, there's a bring and buy sale up the road I'm going to. You manage a little laugh. —Yeah, right.

Funny guy.

—Nick's not here yet, you say.

—Doesn't look like it.

—He's coming though.

—Yeah. Think so.

—I spoke to him today. On his way back from Leeds. Reckons he's uncovered some amazing shit up there.

Fat Cunt holds a finger to his lips. —Let's leave it for Nick to decide when to tell everyone, eh? He might not want it to come out yet.

His voice suddenly becomes more menacing. —I'm sure what he told you was in complete confidence.

You look at the size of his arms, his tattoos, the body piercing, the T-shirt that says DON'T FUCK WITH THE TRUTH. You decide to agree with him.

—Hey, Jim – he says.

—John, you tell him. However big a meathead he is, he can get your fucking name right.

—Whatever . . . you ever seen a UFO?

—Uh, no . . . don't think so.

—Never had any recurring dreams about strange operations being performed on you?

—No.

He nods, apparently satisfied with your answers.

—Why? you ask him.

—Oh nothin . . . just curious, you know.

He hands you the rest of his spliff.

—I gotta talk to some people over there. See you round, yeah? You take a couple of tokes and pass it on to Sally.

—That was . . .

—Fat Cunt? she hazards a guess.

A band strikes up inside the pub and they relay the music out to the garden through speakers. They're not a particularly good band, but it's something to listen to while you drink your beer and watch a fantastic smoggy sunset over the skyline.

Is this the moment? you think to yourself. Is this the moment to tell her? Is that sunset Hollywood enough? But you bottle it.

Closing time comes around and you don't want to be the first people at the party and there's nowhere else to go on to, so you spin out your last drinks. Eventually, a spotty youth in a badly ironed shirt demands your glasses (—Empty or not, I gotta have em NOW!) and he waits, snapping his fingers impatiently, while you drain them. It's eleven thirty; he probably stopped getting paid half an hour ago so you can't really blame him. Still. Doesn't stop you from questioning his parentage. He gives you a hard stare and you decide to call him a cunt. So he says, what did you say? And you say, you heard you cunt. And Sally has to put a hand to your arm to restrain you or this is going to end up in fisticuffs. Oho, look at you! One of those rare occasions when you meet someone who's a bigger tosser than you are and you're Charles Fucking Bronson all of a sudden.

About half the people have left the beer garden. You follow a straggley line of party-goers down a few quiet side streets. Sally starts having a go.

—What you think you were playing at back there?

—What? you say thickly.

—All that stuff with the barman.

—Yeah, well. He was getting on my nerves.

—He was only doing his job. Christ . . . reminded me of that wanker we saw in Brighton.

—Who?

—The one beating up that bloke in the street.

—Oh yeah . . . him.

—I don't really go for stuff like that, I have to tell you, says Sally. Sounds like she's serious.

—Yeah, I'm not really like that, though. You know me . . . I don't really know what came over me there.

It's a sobering thought. The only real difference between you and the guy in Brighton is that he could handle himself in a fight once he'd started it.

—I'm sorry, you say feebly.

Fortunately you get to the place before this conversation can get too much further. It's not much on the outside. A giant run-down warehouse in the middle of what looks like a building site with SQUAT NOW! painted on it in large black letters. The A is in a circle to make the Anarchy sign. There's a faint thud of music coming from inside, but you can only hear it when you're right up close and apart from that there's nothing to suggest there's anything going on. One of the group of lads in front of you knocks secretively on the door. It opens and you're all ushered in quickly by a tall, lanky bloke with blue hair so a conspicuous queue doesn't develop outside. Next to him is a much shorter black girl who asks you apologetically for two pounds.

—It's just for hire of the systems, she says. —The DJs are doing it for free.

You hand the money over readily. You're not sure if it's a good sign or not that the DJs aren't being paid.

You walk through into a large room with rudimentary decorations. There's a few balloons and streamers hanging from the ceiling and strange patterns have been painted on the walls in Day-Glo colours. At the far end is a guy who looks about fourteen spinning the records. There's a few people milling about, but no dancing as yet. That's okay; it's early days.

You decide to go for an explore. The stairs are highlighted by the word STAIRS painted in luminous green above a door. They turn out to be nothing more than the fire escape on the outside of the building: black metal steps leading up to the two other floors. A couple of steps are missing. Someone'll do themselves an injury on those before the evening's out, you catch yourself thinking.

From the second floor you can see out over the garden that belongs to the building, a sizeable, overgrown piece of land with a large wire fence around it that's turned into a dumping ground for other people's shit. There's a bizarre selection of stuff here: an old sofa, a wheelbarrow with no wheels, lots and lots of boxes full of cut up newspaper, an old broom, a filing cabinet; and strewn among all this are shadowy men pissing.

The room on the second floor is the drum and bass room. It's almost completely bare. At one end there's a DJ, his decks and a relentless strobe; in the whole of the rest of the large room there is a complete absence of furniture and precisely one person, a shaven-headed bloke with no shirt on and a *lot* of tattoos, dancing maniacally. You peer in briefly from the door and move on up.

Top floor is chill-out. This is where the action's happening at the moment. Groups stand around drinking cans of beer and talking while a long-haired, bearded hippie bloke, who could easily be in his fifties, spins the kind of weird ambient shit you only hear in chill-out rooms. Or elevators. The great thing, you notice, about being a chill-out DJ is that all of your tunes last about twenty-five minutes and there's no real mixing required – the whole point of this music after all is to be unobtrusive – so you can just bung on a record and then bugger off for a drink or a spliff or even a dance on one of the other floors and it'll be ages before you have to do anything else. Just as well the cunt isn't being paid.

This room is also where the squatters live by the look of it. There are old copies of the *Guardian* and battered paperbacks on the floor and some beanbags and a couple of chairs that look like they've been ripped out of a bus, on which people are sprawling and skinning up rather more openly than they were in the pub. A guy with puffy red eyes, wearing a leather jacket moves among them, proudly offering trips!-Es!-whizz! It's a weird place all right: part factory, part nightclub, part someone's front room.

You scan for familiar faces. Nick still isn't here and there are few other people, as far as you can see, who weren't in the pub. Fat Cunt's standing on his own again and smoking another big fat one, but you don't feel like trying to start another conversation with him. You and Sally get a couple of bottles of water, pop a pill each and settle down to wait for things to happen.

—Where's Nick then? Sally asks.

—Dunno . . . delayed, I guess. He'll be on his way. He sounded like he was really up for this on the phone.

—Yeah? Looks pretty quiet so far.

Sally looks round, unimpressed.

—Just wait. It'll all kick in later. So . . . what do you think of this place?

Sally still looks unimpressed. —I dunno. It's like a club in a parallel universe.

—Yeah?

—I mean, on the surface it *looks* like a club but there's all these little differences. It only cost two quid to get in, instead of, I don't know, fifteen or something. And this bottle of water cost no more than it would in my corner shop. They're not trying to rip people off, which is cool. They're just doing it for the music and the sake of doing it, which is doubly cool. Also, cause it's illegal anyway, people can take drugs without having to be all secretive about it . . .

—So it's better than a regular club?

—On the downside, cause it's illegal, there's no safety requirements or anything. Couple of those steps on the fire exit are missing.

—Yeah, I noticed that. Someone'll do themselves an injury . . .

Damn. There, now you've said it.

—Careful, Sally says, smiling. —You'll turn into your mother.

You shake your head.

She continues. —And I've only seen one toilet so far and it didn't have a lock on the door. It's okay for you, you can just go out in the grass, but if I need to go, you'll have to stand guard for me, okay?

—Yeah. Just say the word.

—Of course, if people don't have to go to the toilet to score or skin up, there'll be less of a queue.

—There's that.

She lights up a cigarette and starts flicking absent-mindedly through a copy of *Marie Claire* that's lying next to her.

—So what do you think Nick's found out today? she asks.

—Who knows? Who knows if he'll want to tell us?

—I'm looking forward to actually meeting him.

—Yeah, well, he's even less likely to open up in front of someone he doesn't know.

She looks hurt. —Not even if it's someone he knows you trust.

—I dunno. He's quite protective about shit like this. An I've never seen him quite so passionate about a story before.

—Mmm. That bloke, though, Fat Cunt . . . I really don't want to call him that, hasn't he got another name?

—Don't think so.

—Come on. His mother can't have called him that.

—I dunno. Mr and Mrs Cunt have a podgy little baby boy . . . they've not got much imagination . . . could happen.

Sally stares at you.

—Seriously, though, rumour has it he changed his name by deedpoll, you go on. —He's a very peculiar man.

—Anyway, *he* obviously thinks there's something to it.

—Mmm . . .

Conversation fizzles out. The drugs haven't kicked in yet. The DJ returns, puts on another record and fucks off again. This tune sounds exactly the same as the first one.

—Shall I skin up then? asks Sally.

—Yeah. Nice one.

So you share a joint and Sally reads you some stuff from her magazine and then, once you're feeling nice and relaxed, if not exactly stoned, you go over to the fire exit and look at the view. As you expected, it looks rather nicer now. There's a constant stream of people pushing past you, coming up and down the stairs, but you and Sally just stand there, holding hands, gazing out over the skyline: the rows of silhouetted brick terrace, the moon and the stars, the tower at Canary Wharf winking in the distance.

Sally, I think I love you, you're thinking to yourself over and over again. Sally, I think I love you. Sally, I think I love you. Sally, I think I love you.

But you don't say it.

A dishevelled-looking Irish guy joins you at the top of the stairs. He's clutching a can of Special Brew and he's drunk or stoned or something.

—Ah yesh, he slurs. —I love to look at the shtars. You know what I always say? It's reassurin. That's what it is. Reassurin. Whatever happened, wherever you are, you can count on the shtars. The shtars'll always be there . . . I like that . . .

He stares out in wonder.

—Actually a lot of them aren't there at all, you tell him. —Lots of the stars you can see burned up thousands of years ago, but they're so far away that their light is only now reaching the Earth.

—Eh? he goes.

You explain it to him again, more slowly this time.

—Oh yeah, shatter me illusions why don't you? Bashtard!

And he stomps off down the stairs.

—That was such a horrible thing to do, says Sally.

—Are you kidding? I love talking bout this stuff when I'm stoned. I thought he'd groove to it. I mean, doesn't it freak you out to think that when you look up at the night sky, you're actually looking into the past, I mean *straight* into the past. What you're seeing is not the sky as it is now, but how it was years and years ago, before you were even born. In fact it's not even that, it's like a *mixture* of histories. Each star operates on a different time scale depending on how far away it is. That does my head in . . . fuckin cosmic, man . . .

Now you're stoned.

Sally looks at you blankly. —Shall we go for a dance? she says.

You go back down to the main room on the ground floor. The volume's been turned up a bit in here, the heat's been turned up a bit too and the place is starting to move. As soon as you start to dance, the E begins to flow. You give Sally a big grin; she's got the same thing going. And for the next hour or so you put your head down and dance. The music's pretty good. There's a rapid turnover of DJs – all the young guns of the area getting a turn – but they all have an impressive selection of records, most of which you haven't heard before. Some of the mixing, it has to be said, is shambolic. One guy in particular just plays two records simultaneously and flicks back and forth from deck to deck: thirty seconds of one tune, then thirty seconds of the other. After a few records of this you want to throttle him. But this is the cutting edge, you have to keep reminding yourself. A lot of these tunes will have been recorded very recently by the DJs themselves, or by friends of theirs, and in many cases you'll be listening to the only copy in existence. If they're lucky, a bigger-name DJ will pick up on their tune and incorporate it into his set, then more and more club DJs will get hold of it, it'll get played on specialist dance radio and make the dance charts, at which point the original champion will drop it like a hot stone and move on. Then it might get included on a compilation album, Forty Bangin' Hits In The Mix! or some such, and start making a bit of money. And then, if it's really popular, in about twelve months' time a major record company will rerelease it with massive promotion and it'll go straight into the Top Ten. And you'll be able to say, truthfully, that you were there when it first got aired. Except you won't of course, because you won't remember any of the tunes you hear tonight tomorrow morning, let alone sometime next year. You're off your face. You wish they'd put the names of the DJs up; one of them might just make it through the net and achieve something and you'd be able to boast that you were here. It'd be like having seen the Sex Pistols at the 100 Club. Only cooler.

The party's really pumping now. People are still coming in; the word's gone out on the grapevine to pubs and clubs and house parties, via pirate radio and mobile phone. And as you watch the blue-haired guy peering nervously out every time he opens the door just in case this time it's not more ravers but the Old Bill, you think to yourself: what the fuck is this doing being illegal? What in God's name is wrong with a bunch of people playing music and dancing to it if that's what they want to do? It's fucking insane; while there's murder, robbery, rape and God know what else going on all over London, if the police drive by here and hear the happy sound of people enjoying themselves they're going to have to come in and break it up. And then there'll be trouble.

And still they come. All kinds of people, some in groups, some on their own. Most of them are already up for it by the time they get here and move straight on to the dancefloor. A studenty type in round glasses wanders up and down, shouting to himself and anyone else who'll listen:—It's just like the eighties, man, just like the eighties. Yeah!

A foreign-looking guy with dark skin and an enormous rucksack comes in. Looks like he was just passing on his way to the airport or station or something, heard some noise and decided to check it out. He scores a pill off the trips!-Es!-whizz! guy, has a wander round while he waits to come up, then goes back to the main floor for a brief, but vigorous, dance before strapping his rucksack back on and leaving. He's going home a happy man. It's a beautiful sight, you think to yourself. He's going to go home and tell his mates, Fuckin England, man, it's the greatest place on Earth.

At long last Nick shows his ugly mug. You go up to him and give him a big hug. He hugs you right back; he's off his face too.

—Where you been? you shout at him above the music.

—Got delayed.

—Yeah? What's been happening?

—A lot . . . I'll tell you bout it later. I gotta have a dance.

You lead him over to where Sally is. She's still well out of it, water in one hand, cigarette in the other, eyes closed.

You give her a prod. —Sally! This is Nick!

—Oh hi! she exclaims in delight. —Pleased to meet you!

—Yeah, likewise, says Nick.

And then you, all three of you, dance.

And you dance and you dance and you dance. And you dance until all of a sudden the lights go out.

Black.

Silent.

Shrieks.

A couple of people light matches.

Sally grabs your hand.

—John, are you still there?

—Yeah . . . you wanna get your lighter?

—Yeah, I wasn't thinking.

She fumbles for it.

Once you've got over the shock, it starts being quite funny. The lack of music is a drag, though. Most people keep on dancing; they can still hear the records in their heads.

The black girl who was at the door appears with a torch. —It's okay, she tells everyone. —There's a fusebox round here somewhere.

It takes her and her friends five minutes or so to sort stuff out. When the music comes back on, it sounds louder, better; the streamers look prettier.

You dance some more.

Eventually your legs turn to jelly and you want something to drink that isn't warm tap water. You catch Nick's eye and ask him if he wants to have a look around. Sally's still flying. Wild horses wouldn't drag her off this dancefloor, so you leave her to it and go upstairs.

—Mind yourself, there's a couple of steps missing, you tell Nick as you climb up the fire exit.

On the second floor, the drum and bass room is doing better business. The mad tattooed skinhead is still there occupying centre stage; you get the feeling he hasn't moved from this spot or stopped dancing all night, nor will he for another eight hours at least. But he's now joined by a roomful of other folk, none quite as scary as him but a few not far off it. And the strobe is still strobing. Once again you peer in briefly and then make tracks.

In the chill-out you and Nick get a couple of cartons of Ribena – at cost price – and crash out on some beanbags. Nick says he fancies a joint, but he hasn't got any gear and neither have you. Sally's got it all downstairs. You decide you don't need a joint that much after all. Nick spies Fat Cunt standing in the corner – he doesn't look like he's moved all night either – and goes to blag a hit off him. You stay where you are. They chat for a bit, and you're sure at one point Fat Cunt looks over at you and says something serious, and then Nick comes back over with Fat Cunt's spliff.

—So what's been going on? you ask him as he sits down. —I thought this whole Mad Parents Ecstasy Club thing had blown over. I mean, people haven't exactly been dropping like flies just recently . . .

Nick shakes his head. —Maybe, but I reckon it's gonna start again pretty soon.

You try to catch his eye to see if he's serious.

—What? You're kiddin me. How come?

—I don't know . . ., he sighs. —I don't know how much I should tell you.

—Why not?

—I mean for your own protection, like. Less you know, the better.

—Oh fuck off.

You give a little laugh. You can't help it. Nick looks pissed off.

—I'm sorry, man.

—John, I'm tellin you. This is serious.

—Okay. So tell me.

Another long sigh. He looks pained, like he's trying to weigh up all sorts of delicate pros and cons.

—Okay, okay, he says finally, and he lowers his voice and leans in towards you. —I think there's gonna be another death this weekend. Another E death.

—Yeah? How can you be sure?

—I can't be *sure*, he says in little more than a whisper now. —But I got a pretty good idea.

You look at him and wait for him to expand. Maybe this is it; maybe this mate of yours has finally, irrefutably lost it. You can't say it wasn't on the cards the way he was going.

It becomes clear, though, that you're not going to get any more out of him without further prompting.

—So where does this pretty good idea come from?

—Last weekend. Macmillan went on a trip.

—Yeah . . . ?

—Yeah. To Scotland. I was sitting outside the offie watching him as usual. Bout two thirty on the Friday afternoon he leaves, looking all suspicious, he goes up to the station, buys a ticket to Edinburgh . . .

—And you followed him?

—Yeah. Then I gave Carl a bell on the mobile an he came up on the train after me. Now, we knew he was going up to Scotland cause we'd been talking to one of the guys who works in his shop. But, get this, he said he was going up to some whisky convention. *But . . .*

He stops to labour this *but*, wagging an index finger around, and you realise he's completely out of his box. Either he's had some on the way down or Fat Cunt rolls mental spliffs.

—Let me guess, you say. —There was no whisky convention in Edinburgh that weekend.

—None that we could find. *He* certainly didn't go to any fucking convention . . . Least not while we were following him.

—You mean you lost him?

—Yeah . . ., Nick says, reddening slightly. —Briefly, on the Saturday night. It's a pain in the arse cause it meant we missed him actually dealing the stuff; but I know exactly what he was there for. Obviously they've decided another death in Yorkshire's gonna look a little suspicious, so they're widening their net. An I bet you any money someone dies this weekend. Whichever poor fucker Macmillan sold the pills to will have sold them on during the week, or they'll be selling them at a club tonight, and some other even poorer fucker's gonna be headline news tomorrow. Who knows, maybe he sold a whole bunch of bad ones this time. Maybe they've stopped fucking about.

—Shit! Why don't you do something then? Tell someone?

Nick looks at you despairingly. Even through the haze of dope and God knows what else, you can see he's completely drained.

—Cause I'm only ninety-five per cent sure. And anyway I've no idea who or whereabouts. What can I do? Call the police and get them to close down every club and every illegal rave in Scotland? It's not exactly practical, and these places would never get reopened again. And anyway maybe it's an acceptable sacrifice . . .

You look at him in horror. —What the fuck are you talking about?

He casts his hand around the room. —One person dies so all these people can enjoy themselves. An all the other people all across the country. It's the sort of sacrificial statistic that works for cars. So many thousands die each year in order that so many millions can get to and from work easily every day. And alcohol; same deal.

—Fuck off, man. You don't really believe that.

He doesn't respond.

—But this one person doesn't have to die! you shout.

—Yeah, he says quietly. —Exactly.

You can't believe Nick's attitude to this. Even allowing for the fact that he's scared and he's paranoid and he's obviously smoking too much spliff right now and he's keen to get his story, this is pretty fucking callous. You can almost see him sitting in front of the news tomorrow willing people to die so his story will be vindicated.

But now he's told you, what should *you* do? Should *you* tip off the cops and get them to close down every club in Scotland? If you don't and someone dies, are you responsible? But how would you explain it? How would you get the story across without sounding like a complete headcase?

Maybe that's why Nick doesn't want to do anything about it. Because he knows no one would believe him.

Or . . . maybe, deep down, he doesn't believe any of this shit himself. Maybe it's more complicated than that, even. Maybe part of him believes it's all true, the part of him that desperately wants to break this story and establish a name for himself; but part of him knows that if he tried to approach the authorities with his wild hunches, they'd think he was taking the piss.

You try and broach the subject gently. —So you didn't actually *see* this guy offloading any pills in Edinburgh?

—No, but I know he must've done. That's what he was there for.

—Yeah . . . yeah, course. So . . . what did you see him do?

Nick looks puzzled by the question, but he tries to remember. —I dunno. He checked into this hotel, quite a nice-looking place, on the Friday afternoon. That evening, he met up with a woman—

—A woman?

—Yeah. Scottish woman. I reckon she must be one of their gang . . .

—So he's told a lie bout what he's doing at the weekend, an then he's gone to meet a *woman* . . . ?

—Yeah, Nick nods. He can see where you're going with this.

—Shit, there's any number of reasons why you might lie an then sneak away with a *woman* . . .

—Oh bollocks, man! Nick shouts. He sounds like a spoiled child now: a spoiled child on drugs. —He went there to offload more of his dodgy pills, I'm tellin you!

—Did they have separate rooms?

—Eh?

—Macmillan an this Scottish woman, did they have separate rooms?

—Uh . . . no, don't think so.

—There you go then, you try to say as kindly as possible. You're relieved you've managed to work this through to a logical conclusion; you were getting kind of scared for a moment there. Now, if you could only make this fucking idiot sitting next to you see sense.

No chance. —Okay, maybe he was shaggin her . . . That don't mean he wasn't up selling pills as well, does it?

—Nick, you tell him gently. You want to hold his hand or something, but you think he might object. —There'll be other stories, man. You're a good journo. You'll make it without this, believe me . . .

He stands up suddenly. —Fuck it, this isn't just about me. It's nothin to do with me. I just got a hunch about it, that's all. A hack's hunch. I *know* I'm right, I fuckin know it.

There's a pause. What's the point of arguing with him any further?

—Anyway, he says quietly. —We'll know by the end of the weekend.

You knew it! He's going to spend all day tomorrow shouting at the news bulletins, Come on, die you fuckers, die! Because if no one dies tomorrow he looks like a jerk.

—Course, I hope I'm wrong, he adds quickly.

You can feel the tingling coming back to your fingers and toes. —Come on, you say. —Let's go for a dance.

You stand up quickly and give Nick a hand up. He's still lost in thought.

—Snap out of it, man. Like you say, there's nothing you can do about it. Forget it. Enjoy yourself.

The drugs are coming back. You don't want to think about this shit any more. All you want right now is mindless hedonism. With music.

You go out to the fire exit and pause to show Nick the view and tell him about the Irish guy you were talking to. You look out at the moon and stars and Canary Wharf and the nearby rooftops and down to the garden where hordes and hordes of youths are breaking in over the fence, breaking it down completely, running across the grass and stopping to beat up those having a piss. Suddenly bricks are being thrown and there's shouting. More and more people come piling over a fence like ants out of a nest.

You're rooted to the spot. What the fuck is going on?

The frontrunners get to the bottom of the fire exit and start running up the stairs.

—Fuckin hell, man. I think we better get inside, says Nick. —Looks like it might turn nasty.

You manage to get inside and away from the door just in time. The first guy bursts through and smacks the nearest bloke to him in the mouth. He goes down in shock, lip bleeding. Reinforcements arrive very quickly and line up behind the leader. The music stops. The place falls silent. Knives are drawn.

Shit, you're thinking to yourself, where are the bouncers? Where are the meatheads in dinner suits? Where are the pigs?

The main man, an enormous bloke with a shaved head and Mr T jewellery, spots his quarry. The trips!-Es!-whizz! guy who's shitting himself behind the DJ's decks.

—You owe me money, the main man shouts across the room.

—Yeah, man. I don't have it, says the dealer, his voice high-pitched with fear. —I don't have it right now, but I can get it for you. Real soon. I'm working on it.

You've never heard a man sound so petrified in your life.

—YOU OWE ME MONEY!

Mr T starts to walk slowly across the room. No one else moves. He picks up an empty bottle of Becks, smashes it on the floor and starts waving the broken end around in front of the dealer's face.

—YOU . . . OWE . . . ME . . . SOME . . . FUCKING . . . MONEY!

—Y-y-yeah, man. Like I say, I-I-I don't have it r-right now . . .

—BOLLOCKS!

He kicks the dealer in the balls. It's a perfect shot. All the men in the room wince.

—YOU BEEN DEALIN TO THESE CUNTS ALL NIGHT! COURSE YOU GOT SOME FUCKIN MONEY!

He beckons over a couple of the others. They start going through the dealer's pockets while he's still on the ground clutching his groin. They tear strips off his clothes while searching him.

—Okay, what you got? Mr T asks them when they've finished.

—Couple a hundred quid. And some gear, Es, speed, bit of dope, some dodgy-looking acid.

—That gear's worth two fifty on its own, the dealer manages to say in gasps.

Mr T kicks him again, in the stomach this time.

—The gear ain't worth fuck all. The gear's what I get for having to come here in the middle of the night and sort you out. You still owe me fifteen hundred.

The dealer starts wailing. —I told you, man. I ain't got it. Gonna take me some time.

Mr T drops to a squat so he can bring his mouth close to the other man's ear.

—Look, what you want me to do? You want me to take this out on that little girl of yours . . . what's her name?

He snaps his fingers impatiently.

—Emily, boss, says one of his hoods. —Seven years old last March.

—Yeah, that's right. Emily. You want me to take this out on her? Is that what you want? Cause it's not what I want. It's not what I want at all. I didn't get into this to go around cutting up little girls. I'm a businessman for fuck's sake. But if I do, if I do have to go round there and cut up her pretty little face, then you'll find the money won't you? Then you'll find the money so fucking quick you'll look like Paul Daniels. So why don't you do the decent thing and find it before I have to do that? It'll be much less painful for you, and me. And Emily . . .

He stands up and gives the poor bloke one last kick before turning to his cronies.

—Okay fellas, have some fun.

They all pile in. But Mr T can't resist, he has to turn around and stick a couple more boots in himself. He doesn't use the broken bottle, though, you notice. And the others don't appear to be using their knives, although the weapons are still very visible. That's okay. They're just teaching this guy a lesson; they're not actually going to kill him.

A cold fear grips you suddenly. What about Sally? If this is going on up here, what the fuck is going on downstairs? There were loads more than this in the gang surely. Are the rest of them sorting out another grudge down there? And who's to say that once they've seen to business they won't start beating up anyone else they don't like the look of? These guys look like they enjoy their work.

You start to inch towards the door.

—Where the fuck you going? hisses Nick.

—Gonna check on Sally.

—You fuckin crazy? You want em to do you next?

But the door's unguarded now, they're all laying into the guy they came for and no one notices as you sneak slowly out. You've got to find Sally. You've also got to get away from this sickening noise. There's not a sound in the room apart from boots and fists and yelps of pain. Nick's too chickenshit to stay on his own so he follows you against his better judgement. You go down the first flight of steps gingerly, then run down the rest.

The music's still playing on the other two floors. On the ground floor there are still people dancing. The other gang members are nowhere to be seen. Maybe that was all of them upstairs; maybe it just looked like there were more of them when they were coming over the fence. Maybe they're hiding somewhere. You make your way across to Sally who's still dancing with her eyes closed, oblivious to all this.

—WE GOTTA GO! you yell at her.

—WHY?

—CAUSE THERE'S FUCKIN MAYHEM GOING ON UPSTAIRS.

She looks at you nonplussed.

—SALLY, THERE'S GUYS WITH KNIVES BEATING SHIT OUT OF PEOPLE. WE'RE OUT OF HERE!

You yank her off the dancefloor and over to the door.

—Oh come on, John, we can't go yet, she wails. —Let's just wait here with the others.

Word's got around. Most people are now milling by the door where they can make a quick escape if they need to.

You're not sure. You want to leave.

—If you go, leave the area completely, says the guy with the blue hair, who looks concerned. —Don't go hangin around outside drawing attention to the place.

—This is okay, reckons Nick. —We can stay here awhile till things settle down. Looks like they only came for that one guy;

they'll be off in a minute.

He's barely finished making this wildly optimistic statement when the dealer staggers through the door, his clothes ripped, his torso slashed to ribbons and a massive gash across his left eye. A couple of people scream. You feel like throwing up.

So much for the cunts not using their knives.

He's followed by the black girl who's organising the show.

—HAS ANYONE GOT A MOBILE PHONE? she yells. —HAS ANYONE GOT A FUCKING MOBILE PHONE?

—Give her your phone, man, you tell Nick.

—I thought we were leaving, he says. —Like right now.

—Come on. The poor cunt's gonna die if they don't get him an ambulance.

He tosses his phone over reluctantly. The girl signals for the music to stop.

—Okay guys, she announces. —Smoke em if you got em. The gang upstairs are taxing people on anything they're holding an I'm just about to call the cops.

You turn out your pockets; two pills left. It's pop them or drop them. You don't want to hand them over to knife-wielding maniacs and you certainly don't want the pigs to find them. Sally and Nick both shake their heads, they don't want any more, not under these circumstances. So . . . you do them both yourself.

You silly fucker.

The black girl makes a couple of quick calls, then hands Nick his phone back.

—Okay, he says. —Let's get the fuck out of here.

You just make it out the front door when you hear the gang coming from upstairs. You can hear Mr T shouting:—Okay, who's got some lovely sweeties for daddy? Come along now, children, don't be shy.

The three of you leg it across the road and then Nick ducks down behind a parked car to hide. Sally joins him.

—What the fuck are you two doing? Let's just get outa here.

—No, man, let's wait, says Nick. —Wait an see what happens when the Old Bill get here.

—Wait and see what happens? They'll break up the party and arrest everyone, that's what'll happen. Come on, let's go home.

—Nick's right, says Sally. —I think we should wait and see.

You don't fucking believe this. They're both still dancing. They're crouched down behind this car, bobbing up and down, *dancing*. Sally must have slipped herself an extra couple of pills when you weren't looking and Christ knows how much Nick's had. They're at that stage where they'd truly rather die than give up the dance. There again, you've just popped two more pills; you're going to be as fucked as they are before long. You crouch down with them.

You wonder why the gang didn't come down immediately after their poor victim, the trips!-Es!-whizz!-guy. What kept them? Then you remember the skinhead with the tattoos in the drum and bass room. He didn't look like the type to just stop dancing and hand over his drugs without a fight. Fuck. You wonder what those bastards have done to him.

It takes a few minutes for the first police car to arrive. Two coppers jump out, bang on the door and rush in. You're not sure this is entirely wise. Has no one told them how many blokes there are inside? And how many knives they have between them? But within seconds there's two more cars and a van and the whole place is crawling with Old Bill. Then the ambulance arrives and the dealer is carried out on a stretcher. His head isn't completely covered by the blanket, you notice; he must still be alive. He has one small consolation, of course: the cops aren't going to catch him holding.

It doesn't take long. There's muffled sounds of shouting and punches being thrown; you can't really hear much with the door closed. Then the various gang members; together with some ravers who presumably got a little over-zealous in their self-defence, including the drum and bass skinhead, who, you're pleased to see, doesn't appear to have a scratch on his face, they're all marched out, hands behind their heads, and put into the van.

Then a very strange thing happens.

They all leave.

The ambulance, the van, the squad cars and all the coppers, the whole bloody lot, they all leave. There's no evacuating the premises, no body searches, no taking down of everyone's name and address. They just go.

You feel like you've been dropped into the parallel universe Sally was talking about, a bizarre place where the police exercise common sense and restraint. They've come along promptly when called, put themselves at risk protecting the public, arrested the guilty parties and then buggered off again without throwing their weight around.

Well fucking hell.

You all run back across the street and bang on the door. You can hear the music's started up again already. The guy with the blue hair is not impressed.

—I thought I told you to leave the area.

—We did, says Sally. —But we got lost. We wandered round in a big circle and now we're back again.

—Come on, Jez, says the black girl from behind him. —This is the guy lent me his phone, let em in.

Jez opens the door as reluctantly as he can manage. You run in and hit the dancefloor immediately. It's a strange record the DJ's chosen to start things up again with, but in a way it's a stroke of genius. It's a crossover tune, one that was hip maybe six months ago and is now riding high in the charts. It's gentle, poppy, accessible; handbag stuff, the sort of cheesy thing you'd never expect to hear in a million years at a do like this. But it's also familiar, safe and reassuring. And judging by the reaction from the crowd, it's exactly what they wanted to hear to express their collective relief. People shout and wave their hands in the air and blow whistles. The drugs start flowing again, those two extra pills kick in big time, the fear is driven out and the joy let in once more.

And you *dance*.

At dawn the three of you go and sit in the garden, smoke a spliff and watch the sunrise. Sally asks Nick how his investigation is going, but he's reluctant to tell her the whole story. Maybe he is slowly beginning to doubt his own convictions, or maybe he's just too fucked up by the events of tonight. He just mumbles something about still following up one or two leads and leaves it at that.

—Shit, it's a shame you weren't able to get some proof. I'm sure there was something to this story an it makes me sick to think of those bastards getting away with it.

Nick's eyes light up; your heart sinks. This was all he needed: someone to believe in him, someone to trust him. Now he'll be off again on his flights of fancy and Sally'll just encourage him and there'll be no bringing them back to Earth.

But it doesn't happen. Nick really doesn't want to talk about it. Instead Sally stands up and announces that she has to go to work.

Nick looks distraught. —You're kiddin me!

—Hey, I'm a working girl, she shrugs.

She gives you a peck on the cheek and then she gives Nick one too, and yours is no bigger than Nick's, you notice, and she thanks you for a memorable evening and leaves.

Nick shakes his head in disbelief. —Fuck, I don't know how she does that.

You go for a piss up against the broken wheelbarrow and Nick joins you.

—YOU GOTTA FIGHT! you shout for no apparent reason.

—DURR! DURR! goes Nick.

—FOR YOUR RIGHT! you continue.

—DURR! DURR! goes Nick again.

And then you both yell in unison:—TO PAARTY!

And you fall about laughing.

You go back inside and dance on till mid-morning. You don't start coming down till about ten thirty, then all of a sudden your legs feel crumbly and it's time to go home.

—Well, that was an interesting evening, says Nick as you settle down in the top front seat of the bus.

—Yeah. Right. You'll have to let me know if they plan any more raves there.

—Serious?

—Yeah!

You're at that stage of fatigue where everything you say sounds like you're taking the piss.

—Sally's nice, says Nick.

—Yeah, you say. —I know.

And then you sit in silence until just before you reach Nick's stop when you grab his arm and say:—Nick . . . ?

—Yeah?

—About that thing . . .
—What thing?
—That thing you said would happen over the weekend.
—Yeah?
—I hope you're wrong.
—Yeah, he says. —Me too.

∫

Kahtoom was a picture of desolation. As far as the eye could see, buildings burned and nothing else moved. The few people that were visible were clearly dead, swinging from lamp-posts or lying in gutters.

In their shuttle, hovering over the carnage, the Midnight Patrol fell into awed silence.

'Chaymar, any readings of *life* at all?' asked Captain Midnight.

'*Sporadic*, Captain! A few isolated signs dotted about the city!'

'Okay, take us to the nearest and set us down! It looks like we're too *late* to be of any real *use* here, but we may be able to find out where our *friends* have moved on to!'

They landed in a park. No one came to watch and stare at them. The shuttle nearly took the roof off a nearby house but it scarcely seemed to matter.

The readings took them to a small building a couple of streets away. Chaymar knocked on the door, but there was no answer so he blew it off its hinges with a laser bolt.

Inside they heard groaning. Faint, frightened moans from another part of the house. They followed the sound through to the bath unit at the back, where a young, scruffy-looking man lay on the floor in a pool of greenish vomit. Beside him was an empty bottle of pills.

Captain Midnight knelt down beside the man, who was roughly the same age as his own son. Would have been.

'*Why?*' he said softly.

It took a moment for it to register with the man that there were other people in the room with him, and for the question to penetrate his consciousness.

'Why *not?*' he mumbled finally.

The Captain shook his head. An entire *city* succumbing to despair like this?

'We need to find out where the aliens have moved *on* to! To stop this happening again! Can you *help* us?'

There was no reply. The man's eyelids began to flicker.

'Can you tell us where the Galactic Government buildings are, so we can access their *radar* records?'

'What's the *point?*' The man's voice was getting fainter. He was slipping away.

Karlax moved forward and grabbed the man's arm. 'The *point,*' he growled, 'is that if you don't tell us what we want to know, I will *break* your *arm!* And I'm sure you don't want to spend the last few *minutes* of your sorry life in screaming *agony!* Do you?'

The young man made a noise which went something like: 'NNNNNGGH!'

The simple directions were the last words the young man said. When they got there, the Midnight Patrol found the government building was in a similar state to the others in the city. Captain Midnight had hoped that the Galactic officials would have been made of sterner stuff than ordinary citizens, that they would have been able to hold out for longer against this crushing sense of futility. But he was wrong. This building, like all the others, was strewn with the corpses of people who had been driven to various and ingenious methods of suicide by the visit from the Ancients. They passed through the foyer where the security staff had formed a circle and shot each other simultaneously; they passed the computer records room where Lieutenant Howell's charred body still sat, staring eerily, mouth agape; and they passed the communication desk where pieces of Commander Rimini's brain still clung to the controls. Eventually they found the radar room. Here too there were bodies to be walked around. Captain Midnight was relieved to notice, though, that the machinery in this room had not been burned out. It all still looked operational.

'Okay,' he barked, 'let's get the information we *need* and get *out* of this place!' None of them wanted to stay in this godforsaken city a moment longer than was absolutely necessary. They wanted to get out there and catch the creatures who had done this.

It was a simple business to run the recent radar reports and track the path of the Ancients' fleet as it left the Serpicus Six system. It produced a puzzling answer, however.

'I don't *understand* this, Captain,' said Zanzi, staring in bewilderment at the screen in front of her. 'According to this, they carried straight on past the sun of this system, following an *absolutely straight* path until the radar lost them!'

'That takes them back into the *Barren Gulf*, doesn't it?' said Karlax. 'Maybe they're heading back to wherever they *came* from!'

'No, it doesn't quite take them *into* the Gulf,' said Pleysium. 'It takes them on the *fringes* of it. But there are no inhabited *planets* on their current course!'

Chaymar shook his head. 'There is *one* inhabited planet out in that direction! It's not a member of the Galactic Government! In fact, we have not even made *contact* with its people! They are not considered *developed* enough to receive alien visitors!'

'They may be receiving them *soon enough!*' said Karlax.

'I've *heard* of this planet too,' said Captain Midnight. 'I *read* about it somewhere! I believe it's known to its inhabitants as . . . *Earth!*'

∫

—Hey John, man. You okay?

You're sat on the floor, white and shaking, surrounded by tufts of hair. You don't remember feeling like this before. It's not fear exactly, although there's an element of fear about it; it's more a sense of overwhelming dread. You're not in any personal danger, but you're still completely terrified.

—You okay? Harry says again. —You look like you've seen a ghost.

—Yeah . . . I think I did.

You're over the worst of the shock, but your legs are still trembling. You try to stand up. It isn't happening. You collapse back on the floor and Harry can't help a snort of laughter. You look fucking ridiculous.

Louie comes out of his office to see what's going on.

—What the hell you doing? he shouts.

—Well, it's like this, Harry starts explaining, and shaken as you are, you're keen to hear what he's going to come up with. —It's been a pretty quiet morning, no customers at all in fact, so we thought we'd liven things up by having an Acting Pissed competition.

—John's winning, he adds.

Louie, predictably, explodes. —Ah, so you think you can just play around! I told you before, no customers: sweep, clean, tidy. Always things to do . . . John, your face is white. Have you seen a ghost?

—Harry just asked me that.

—And . . . ?

—I've just had a bit of a shock, that's all.

—What sort of shock?

—Just a shock . . . a shocking kind of shock.

—But you're white! What has happened?

—Fuck it, Louie, I don't wanna talk about it.

This is what you just heard on the radio. This is your shock.

The Edinburgh girl who collapsed in the early hours of Sunday morning after taking a single tablet of the drug known as ecstasy has died overnight in hospital. She has been named as Alison McCormack, aged sixteen, from Marchmont. Her parents are expected to make a statement tomorrow morning, but in the meantime police are asking for witnesses who may have seen or been with Alison on Saturday night to come forward.

You feel cold despite the heat outside. So Nick was right. Why didn't he do something to stop this? If he knew, really *knew* this was going to happen, why the fuck didn't he do something to stop it?

Why didn't *you* do something?

—Look, Louie, I'm sorry. I need some fresh air. And I need to talk to Harry for a minute, alone. Is it okay if we nip out to the caff over the road? We'll keep a careful eye in the shop and if anyone comes in, we'll be straight back, okay?

—No. You can't just leave your work like that.

—Oh come *on* Louie, give us a break. I just need to rest up for a coupla moments an I'll be fine. Otherwise I'm gonna end up taking the rest of the day off.

This sways him. —Okay . . . but very quickly.

—Hey, good call, says Harry as you leave the shop. —We'll have to try this one again.

—Yeah, right . . .

—So what's the deal? he asks. —This has got something to do with that Scottish girl, hasn't it?

You nod.

—So . . . what? You know her or something?

—Knew her, you correct him. —No, never met her.

—So . . . ?

You push open the door of the caff. —Come on, let's get a drink an I'll tell you all about it.

You get yourselves two steaming mugs of tea. You don't get any food; the smell of the place is filling enough. Through the window you can watch Louie strutting and fretting.

—It's Nick, you tell him, piling twice your normal amount of sugar into the mug. —Saturday night, he told me there was gonna be another death this weekend. In Scotland.

Harry looks puzzled. He probably still thinks this is some elaborate wind-up on your part, some scheme you dreamed up to take the piss out of Louie and get off a morning's work. —Shit. How'd he know? he says.

And you tell him. Staring into your tea, stirring the whole time, watching the freckles of on-the-turn milk swirl into infinity, you tell him the whole story. You tell it all from your point of view, of course. The whole idea sounded ridiculous: Nick getting carried away by one of his own daft theories, egged on by Fat Cunt, who knows a thing or two about insane conspiracy theories, and a petrified small-time drug dealer in Leeds who'd believe anything to clear himself from blame. How could there possibly be anything to it?

What you want is for Harry to tell you it's okay, that no one could have expected you to believe Nick's story, that anyone would have done the same in your position, not to blame yourself. Instead, what he says, after a short pause while he takes all this in, is:—Fuckin hell, man, why didn't you do something?

—What could I have done? you yell at him, moving your arms violently so you nearly knock his tea into his lap. —Who could I have told? How could I have made them believe me?

You give him Nick's argument about cars and alcohol and acceptable levels of risk. You still think this is a crock of shit, but Harry seems to buy it. —Yeah, suppose you're right, he says with a shrug after considering it.

And that seems to end his interest in the matter. He starts gazing out of the window and then he comments on the weather.

You yank him back. —Fuckin hell, Harry, don't you see what this means?

—What?

—This girl dying in Scotland?

—Uh . . . ?

—They exist! There go your arms again. —They're real! There's a group of mad, middle-aged psychopaths somewhere up north making deadly pills that look exactly like Es an they're gonna flood the market with these things an kill people. An they're not doing this for profit, they're not criminals in the normal sense, they're on a fuckin crusade. You can't blackmail them, you can't buy them off, they're just gonna keep on and on killing people until they've achieved their aims, until there's no more Es, no more dance music, no more raves, until the whole fuckin culture is dead on its arse.

Harry's response surprises you. —Well . . . had to end sometime, I suppose.

—What do you mean?

—All this. Raves, techno . . . I mean, couldn't go on for ever, could it?

Is he taking the piss?—Why not?

—Well, can you imagine still doing this when we're forty-five? How sad would that be?

—Well . . . yeah! Why the fuck shouldn't we?

Harry doesn't reply, but just looks at you as if to say, if you can't see how crap that would be, there's no point in trying to explain it.

—Anyway, you bluster on. —We're not the last generation, you know. When we're forty-five there'll be other people in their mid-twenties. Why shouldn't they have a good time? Telly's not about to end, football's not about to end, why should this?

—That's exactly it! Harry slams his hand down on the table, animated suddenly. —This was supposed to be a brief, spontaneous flourishing, the kind of thing that you could look back on an say yeah, I was there, I was part of that for five or ten years or whatever at the end of the century, a kind of pre-Millennium thing. The worst thing that could happen is it just turns into a nice, respectable, comfortable lifestyle entertainment choice. I mean, it's happening already, isn't it, with these 'superclubs' branding their own T-shirts an stuff an these top-name DJs poncing about, acting like film stars. Fuck it, man, far better the whole thing dies now than turns into a fuckin pantomime.

You have no answer to this so you don't attempt one. You're just thinking about what on earth you're going to do with your Saturday nights if he's right.

—Of course, he carries on, more quietly now. —It might all be a coincidence

—What might be?

—This girl dying. People do die, you know; it's not exactly a hundred-per-cent-safe pastime, popping pills, is it?

Jesus, hasn't he been listening?

—Look, Nick's been following these people. His mate Fat Cunt had got wind of something and sends him up to Leeds on a tip-off. Turns out the bloke who dealt the pill that killed the kid there is going to meetings with the parents of that other kid that died in Bradford a few months ago. That's scary enough. Then Nick follows the same bloke up to Edinburgh an lo and behold, one week later another poor kid dies there. Three deaths linked to one gang. That's pretty cut an fuckin dry to me.

—Yeah, maybe, says Harry, still sounding unconvinced. —But why do they only make one pill in each batch a bad one? An why leave it so long between strikes? It's not really a logical strategy, is it?

—I dunno. Nick reckons it's cause they don't want to attract too much attention; each death has got to look like an isolated incident, otherwise the whole thing'll be blown.

He still looks unconvinced.

—Look, I'm telling you, it's happening, all right!

—Hang on, he says, ignoring you. —Looks like something's going on.

Over the road Louie is waving frantically at you. There's a customer! Fucking hell. Quarter past eleven on a Monday morning and the first customer of the week is here.

—Come on. We better go. An listen, don't worry about it.

Whatever's going on, it's not your fault; there's nothing you could've done.

Thank you.

You amble back over to the shop. Harry's kind enough to take the customer. You sit around and read some more old magazines. You switch the radio on to the bouzouki station so you don't have to listen to another bloody phone-in about drug use. Louie's delighted and calls out from his office:—Ah, so you do like my music! I knew it!

—Yeah, that's right Louie, you shout back wearily.

Then, shortly before lunch, with not a sign of another customer, you get a phone call.

—It's your dealer, Harry says, holding out the phone.

—What? Ian?

—No, your *dealer* dealer, he says in a much softer voice.

Shit.

You're not sure what to do. You're out of pills; you popped your last two in a fit of panic on Saturday night. But in the light of recent events maybe that's no bad thing. Maybe it's time to be out of pills for good.

Checking that Louie is nicely occupied, humming along happily to his music, you take the phone.

—Yes? you hiss.

—Mr Santini, this is Mr Wilson from the Happy Days Insurance Company . . .

Ah. He's pretending to be an insurance salesman. That'll fool the cops or MI6 or whoever the fuck it is he thinks is tapping his phone.

—We have a special offer on life insurance this month, Mr Santini, which I thought you might be interested in.

Wide-Boy Wilson, being a professional drug dealer, is completely fluent in the language of Drug Euphemism. He speaks it like a native. You, on the other hand, being an occasional user and not that quick on the uptake, never got beyond the Linguaphone Learn-In-A-Week stage. You know not to use certain words on the phone – ecstasy, marijuana and so on – but that's about it. Consequently, most of the time you haven't got a fucking clue what Wide-Boy is going on about. It's really quite simple, however. In fact, there's only one rule to remember. Wide-Boy doesn't phone up for chats; he's not that kind of guy. So whatever it is he tells you, whatever you *think* he's talking about, what he actually means is: look, do you want to buy some drugs?

—Uh, perhaps you could give me a quote on this policy, Mr Wilson, you ask him, entering into the spirit of the thing.

—Seventy-five pounds.

—I see. That's a higher premium than I would normally pay. What sort of cover could I expect for that?

Hey, you're getting the hang of this.

—Well, let me see . . . you have ten children, don't you Mr Santini?

—No, I haven't got any fuckin children. I'm not married.

—Oh, excuse me, my records must be incorrect. I was under the impression you had ten children. Ten . . . *little fellers?*

The penny drops.

—Oh . . . uh, yes. Yes, of course! you splutter.

Brilliant. You *forgot* you had ten children for a moment.

—And this seventy-five quid, this would cover all ten children, would it?

—Yes, that's right Mr Santini.

—Well, that sounds quite reasonable.

—Fine. Shall I drop by this evening and discuss the finer points with you?

—Yes, that would be convenient.

Are you out of your fucking mind? What have you and Harry just been talking about? There's a gang of psychopaths out there selling death tablets to small-time dealers exactly like Wide-Boy Wilson and here you are going, duh, yes please, seventy-five pounds for ten rounds of Russian Roulette in pill form, sounds like a good deal to me. You fucking moron.

Louie comes out of his office, nosing around. —Who was that? he asks.

—Oh just some insurance salesman.

—And you invited him to your house? What are you doing? He won't leave until he's made a sale, you know.

—Yeah, well maybe I could do with some life insurance. I don't feel too good today.

The afternoon's just as slow as the morning. One old guy comes in just after lunch, Harry does him a quick short back and sides and that's it. Not even Mr Noggin puts in an appearance. Business goes on like this and you'll be out of a job pretty soon; but frankly, today you couldn't give a toss. You try Nick several times during the day, at home and on his mobile, but no joy. You hope he's okay; you're anxious to speak to him about what's been going on.

The rest of the day you idle around on your skinny arse, looking like shit, feeling like shit. At four, Louie takes the unprecedented step of allowing you to go home early.

—What? On full pay? you ask him, just to be sure.

—Yes! You are very ill. You go home, have some rest and come back tomorrow when we will be very busy. And work!

You cycle home slowly, stopping off at a cashpoint. When you get back, Wide-Boy's already there, feet up, watching *Grange Hill*.

—All right Wide-Boy, you greet him. —How'd you know I'd be home so early?

—I didn't. You don't mind me making myself at home, do you?

—Hey, *me casa*, *su casa*, buddy.

—Just thought I'd come an hang out here for a bit an wait for you, he goes on. —Don't worry, I've been very well-looked-after.

The only other person in is Laura, so presumably she's been doing the looking after. Flirting with him outrageously all afternoon probably. You're not sure if she's cool about drug stuff, though, so you go into your bedroom to do the deal.

—Good scam, the insurance salesman bit, innit? says Wide-Boy, laying the pills out on your bedside table.

—Yeah. Nice one.

You give him the money and hope he'll leave, but he's not showing any inclination.

—So what about the news, eh? you ask him.

—What news?

—You know, from Scotland.

He shakes his head slowly. —Nope. Don't know bout any news from Scotland, he goes. Clearly Wide-Boy doesn't allow his life to become cluttered up by news media of any kind. You tell him, briefly, about what's been going on. He thinks about it.

—Shit happens, is his measured response.

Then, bless them, the Incredible Shagging Neighbours start up. It's not even tea-time yet.

Wide-Boy looks disgusted. —How long do they keep this malarkey up for, then?

—Oh, till breakfast if we're lucky.

—Fuckin hell.

He stays for a few minutes longer, but then he can't stand it any more. You reckon it's some time since Wide-Boy got laid.

—Well, must be off, he says. —People to see, things to do an all that.

—Okay, see you round then. Thanks for the . . . uh, insurance.

—No problem. See you later.

As soon as he's out the door, you give Nick another try. Still no answer. Where is the cunt and why's he got his phone switched off? Then you try Sally. She's engaged.

Fuck.

You decide to go round and see her anyway. You've got to talk to somebody about this. And she's obviously home.

Laura catches you on the way out of the door. —Your friend's nice.

—What? Wide-Boy? Yeah . . . nice bloke.

—Wide-Boy? Is that what you call him? What's his real name?

—Uh, dunno . . . Nigel, I think.

—Oh, she says. —I see . . . Tells me he's in insurance.

—Yeah, that's right.

She tries leaning coquettishly against the wall. She almost ends up falling over.

—Must have some money then? she enquires sweetly.

—Yeah, I think he does okay. He works odd hours. You know.

—He left very suddenly. You wouldn't have . . . uh . . . you wouldn't have a phone number for him by any chance?

—Somewhere. Not on me. But I can get it . . . what you gettin at, though? What bout you an Tony?

You really don't want to get into this.

She sighs heavily. —Between you and me, it's gone off the boil a bit with Tony. It's all got a bit predictable. I thought that maybe if I got a bit of excitement elsewhere, that might actually liven things up with Tony. Might actually be good for the relationship in the longer term.

Why, of course.

—Look, I gotta go, you say. —There's someone I gotta see. Why don't you try an patch things up with Tony and if in a few days there's still nothing happening, give us a shout an I'll see if I can dig out Wide-Boy's number. How's that?

—Okay! she says brightly and turns to walk back into the front room.

Sally looks surprised to see you.

—John! You . . . uh . . . you didn't call.

—But you're still pleased to see me, right?

—Course. Come in.

You go in. It's much messier than usual, drawers open, clothes all over the floor.

—I tried to call you, you tell her. —But it was engaged.

—Yeah, I suppose it was. I was talking to Nick for a while.

—Yeah? I've been trying to get hold of him all day. How'd he get your number?

More to the fucking point, what's he doing phoning Sally and not you? Whose mate is he?

—Uh, I think I gave it him Saturday night . . . You know he's really beating himself up over this girl dying in Scotland.

—Yeah, I was a bit too. But I had a long talk about it with Harry today an, you know, Nick was right with what he said on Saturday night. What could we have done? Who'd've believed us if we'd even tried?

—Oh it's not that so much. He's just really angry with himself for losing Macmillan on the Saturday night last week. If he could've seen the guy who bought the pills, he could've said something, stopped this all from happening. *And* he could've turned the pills over to the cops to analyse them and got his story an been the hero of the hour. I tell you John, he feels so responsible about all this.

—Where is he?

—Staying with a friend somewhere. He's going up to Edinburgh this evening.

Now there's a surprise.

She looks guiltily at the clothes strewn about the place and a stuffed blue holdall in the doorway of her bedroom. It's pretty obvious what's going on.

—I'm going up to join him.

—You're doing *what?*

—I got a few days off work, some of the stalls have been cancelled, so I thought I'd go up an join him. I've always wanted to go to Edinburgh an this stuff really intrigues me.

—Intrigues you? you say in disbelief – It doesn't scare you at all? That you'll be off chasing a lunatic group of killers. You just find that *intriguing?*

—Look, I was brought up in a tiny little village in the middle of nowhere, I've done fuck all with my life, the most exciting thing that's happened to me was coppin off with a bloke whose mate knew W, the actor . . . I wanna *do* something, something I can tell people about, something other than sell fucking flowers.

You raise your voice. It must be the first time you've raised your voice at her. —Fuckin hell, Sally, this isn't a game! These people are killers and they're not gonna be over the moon at finding you an Nick on their trail . . .

—But—she starts to say.

—And they will find you, course they will. Cause they're professionals and you two are just a couple of amateurs. Whatever you think of Nick's investigative skills. You'll be like the pesky kids off *Scooby-Doo.*

It's meant as a gross insult, but Sally just smiles. —Far as I remember the pesky kids always caught the baddy, didn't they?

You're way too wound up to see the funny side, though. —It was a fucking *cartoon!*

She loses the smile and lets out a deep sigh. —This is exactly the reason I wanna go. I'm worried about Nick. Worried that he's so bent on cracking this story an easing his conscience he might do something stupid. So I figure if I go too, I can stop him taking unnecessary risks. I think he has this romantic notion of himself as some kind of self-sacrificing, interepid news hound, willing to risk anything to bring home the story. I reckon he needs someone there who actually cares that he brings himself home in one piece too.

There's something about the way she says *cares*. You're getting deeply paranoid now. Didn't she just say the only reason she fancied you was because your friend knew a film star? Didn't she say that? Just now?

She senses your thoughts. —You know this has nothing to do with us, don't you?

Ah yes. Us.

—I fuckin hope not, you say.

—Course not, silly.

How come she mentioned it then? There's an awkward silence while you decide whether or not to voice this thought and make an issue of it.

—Look, I got a couple of hours before I need to catch my train, she says eventually and she pulls the last few Rizlas from a ripped-up packet on the table. —How bout I skin up?

Yeah, that'll solve everything.

You watch her, both of you lost in thought, as she licks a cigarette along its length, then peels off a strip of paper to release the tobacco. She looks intensely beautiful, eyes focussed in concentration, brow furrowed with worry. You are absolutely, completely head over heels in love with her.

So why don't you tell her? Go on, just tell her. Break this deadly silence and tell her that you love her. It's more important than arguing about whether she goes to Edinburgh, isn't it? Stop waiting for the moment and fucking tell her.

—Sal—, you begin nervously, but she starts speaking at exactly the same time and you let her talk over you. Not that you were really going to tell her anyway, were you, you pathetic sack of shit. You'd've bottled it before the end of the sentence.

—Anyway, we've got a plan, she says.

A plan. How reassuring.

—Danny an Carl are comin up too, so there'll be four of us. Even safer. And we're gonna do pretty much what Nick did in Leeds. Except with four of us working in two pairs it ought to be quicker. We'll hit all the clubs in Edinburgh till we get a lead on who dealt the girl the fatal pill, then when we track him down, we'll see if he can identify Macmillan from the photographs Nick took in Bradford . . . and then we'll have a case!

—Yeah, but what sort of case? This guy's gonna be a drug

dealer. Him an Danny, they're never gonna testify, they just wanna get this whole thing behind them.

—It's first degree murder against a bit of small-time drug dealing, course they'll testify . . . Fuck!

The joint comes apart in her hands. The papers are old and keep coming unstuck. She throws it on the table in exasperation.

—Here, let me have a go, you say.

She looks at you hesitantly. She knows how crap you are at skinning up at the best of times.

She tells you some more about the Plan while you're wrestling with the joint. Initially you make an even bigger arse of it than she did, but eventually, triumphantly, you get something smokable together. It doesn't look too pretty, loose and flabby, but it's holding together more or less. For the moment. You spark it up and a giant flame takes hold at the end. Sally bursts out laughing.

—Things we do to get high, you mutter.

It hits the spot, though. A few minutes later and you're both feeling giggly and not wanting to talk about frightening or confrontational things. Sally curls up on the sofa next to you and you talk about all kinds of other stuff until she has to go.

But not the stuff you really want to talk about.

She even asks you straight out at one point:

—So what were you going to say when I interrupted you a few minutes ago?

—Oh, I dunno . . . I don't remember, you lie.

And the moment passes, yet again.

You see, you really are a sad, pathetic sack of shit. Aren't you?

∫

It looked like a quiet, unassuming planet. Quite an ugly planet, in fact. Most of the surface was covered in water and the rest had little in the way of geographical interest.

Kommandant Salena Machtbar snorted as she peered out of her porthole at this puny little world. Little did it know what to expect!

She was looking forward to this assignment; all the signs were that it would be the easiest yet. The only remotely intelligent life on this rock was still hopelessly primitive and emotionally immature. They would yield their positive thoughts with even less resistance than the poor fools in the Serpicus Six system. It would be a feast!

It was Machtbar's job to lead the first reconnaissance team. It was a dangerous and responsible task and one she was proud to perform. She was the youngest officer ever to attain this position in the Ancients Space Corps and somewhere on the other side of the universe, her parents were busy telling all their neighbours and friends how well she was doing.

She summoned her reconnaissance team. Four other officers hand-picked by herself. Four other officers she knew she could trust to work with her, to be brave and loyal and not lose their heads. Their mission was simple: to blend in with the people of this planet, to discover where the centres of power lay in order to make the final takeover that much smoother. This was not some one-city outpost like the last place, this was a full, teeming, independent world. A world with literally billions of emotions to access. She needed well-disciplined soldiers who would not go crazy and run amok.

After a short debriefing in which they were warned about common substances on the planet that could be highly dangerous to Ancients, such as salt and coal, the five of them marched down to the Replicator. This machine would transform their appearance into that of the creatures below and inject their brains with the alien language and culture. This was the part Machtbar was looking forward to the least. She had studied pictures of these creatures in the computer library and she was appalled by their appearance. At least she counted herself lucky she was a female. The male of this species had, of all things, external genitals, which looked, frankly, ridiculous. It was like new-fangled modern buildings back home where they put the pipes and wiring and escalators on the outside of the house.

There was much joking and laughing when they emerged from the Replicator. They explored their new bodies by prodding and tweaking each other to see which parts gave pleasure and which gave pain. They were issued with alien costumes which made them feel even more stupid and were uncomfortable and irritating against their fresh skin.

The laughter and good humour died down as they approached the shuttle pod. The mission was close at hand and it was time to be serious. The captain shook them all by their bizarrely-shaped hands and wished them well.

They climbed into the pod and set off for the planet known as Earth.

On the planet below, radars were briefly alerted to the appearance of an unidentified flying object, but it passed so quickly that in most cases it was dismissed as equipment error. There were enough *X-Files* creeps making stuff up as it was without giving them any encouragement.

∫

You don't hear from her for three days. Three whole *days*. By Tuesday lunchtime you're already beside yourself with worry. By Wednesday morning you're a wreck. Where is she? Why doesn't she call? Don't they have fucking phones in Scotland?

Nothing you can do, though. Nothing you can do except sit tight and go out of your mind.

So you cut hair and you keep mum. Harry asks you how things are on a regular basis and it's nice to know he's concerned; he's a mate. You tell him things are okay and he doesn't believe you, but he can see you don't want to talk about it so he lets it go.

And in the evenings you immerse yourself in music and comics. Immerse yourself almost to the point of drowning. You start thinking, what would Captain Midnight do in this situation? How would he dispatch justice to this insane band? It's an innocent little thought on its own, the kind of notion that can creep into your mind and leave you chuckling at your own foolishness. Captain Midnight indeed. Why, he's a fictional comic superhero! But careful you don't let it go any further; this is a very dangerous road to go down. You could start seeing things. You could find yourself picturing Captain Midnight flying around Leeds and Edinburgh beating up unlikely-looking baddies in suits and shoul-derpads. You could start seeing yourself as a member of Midnight

Patrol. You could even give yourself your very own name and identity.

You *could* find yourself, on Wednesday evening, standing in front of your full-length mirror, wearing nothing but your boxer shorts, announcing in a booming voice:—I AM SANTINI THE SUPREME! MY SPECIAL POWERS ARE MY EXCEPTIONAL INTELLIGENCE AND MY ABILITY TO TRANSFORM MYSELF INTO A PUMA AND RUN AT GREAT SPEEDS! I STRIKE FEAR INTO THE HEARTS OF VILLAINS EVERYWHERE!

And if Tony suddenly marched into your room and caught you doing this, you'd feel a right cunt, wouldn't you?

—Oh . . . uh, hi, you say.

—Hi . . . ? he says nervously.

Shit. This is even more embarrassing than being caught wanking. There's only one thing for it, only one way you can get out of this with any shred of dignity.

Act stoned. Act really stoned.

You move away from the mirror and the door and Tony, and collapse on your bed. You start giggling as furiously as you can manage.

—Sorry, mate, I'm completely fucked, you tell him between snorts.

—Oh . . . right.

—Been out with Harry. He had this wicked skunk, man.

There's a pause while you giggle some more.

—Anyway . . . nice boxers, says Tony, who's starting to panic a little now. —Where'd you get them?

—The Planet Jowa in the Serpicus Six system! you shriek and burst into more cackles.

Careful. You might be overdoing it a little here.

Tony gets all serious suddenly. —I was just gonna to see if you wanted to go for a drink. Me an Laura have just had a bit of a bust-up an I could do with a drink.

You're clearly in no state to go out and confront the general public, but he suggests bringing through a bottle of wine and this sounds like a terrific idea to you. You've forgotten momentarily that the only kind of wine Tony drinks, or the only kind he buys at any rate, is the very cheap, very nasty red kind. While he's out of the room, you slip on some clothes and give thanks that at least you weren't stark bollock naked when he came in.

Why didn't the bastard knock anyway?

It takes him about two hours to tell you all his woes. He does all the talking. You just listen, try manfully not to wince every time you take a sip of wine and laugh manically every so often when you remember that you're supposed to be stoned. He does ask you at one point about Sally, but you just shrug noncommittally and he takes that as a sign to talk about himself some more. Stoned or not, you manage to nod off before he's left the room. You come to in the middle of the night to find an empty bottle and two glasses on your bedside table and Tony gone.

Finally on Thursday afternoon she calls. You nearly piss yourself with the relief. —Are you okay? Are you okay? Are you okay? you ask her over and over again, not quite believing she keeps saying yes.

—Tell me what's happened.

—There's been too much to tell, she says. —I don't know where to start. And I don't really wanna talk about it over the phone.

—Okay . . . you're okay, though?

—Yes!

—Okay . . . so when can we meet?

—When can you get away?

You shout over to Louie in his office.

—Louie, I'm sorry. I need the rest of the afternoon off.

That brings him out in a hurry.

—I'm sorry. I'll make the hours up Saturday, I promise. But I really need to go.

You're in no position to make that promise until you've spoken to Sally and found out what's going on, but you need to make a fast getaway. You need to see her. She says she's okay, she sounds okay on the phone, but you won't be sure until you've actually seen her face and touched her.

—What is the problem? Louie asks.

—I can't talk about it. I just need to go. Now.

Louie shakes his head. —I am not sure I can employ somebody like this . . .

—Louie, this won't happen again. But just this once, cut me some slack. Please.

He's still not sure. —Maybe when you've finished this customer . . .

—I'll finish him off, pipes up Harry.

You could French kiss him.

—That okay with you, mate? you ask the customer, a young, studenty type in a black jacket and collarless shirt. —I'm shit at doin flat tops anyway. You're better off with Harry here.

What can the bloke say? He nods.

Louie throws up his hands. —Okay, okay. But next week we must have a little talk. You and me.

He wags a finger sternly. It's one of the things he's good at.

—Can't wait, you mutter. Then you pick up the phone and say:—Just coming. Your place?

—No, says Sally. —I don't really want to hang around here.

She gives you the name of a café near her flat. You slam down the phone and leave before Louie can change his mind.

It's quite a lengthy cycle across town, so you have time for some top-quality worrying on the way. What did you think you were doing letting her waltz off into trouble like that? Anything could have happened. If half what Nick suspects is true, these people are dangerous. Why didn't you stop her going? Or go with her yourself? Why didn't she call? How come Nick didn't answer his mobile phone for three days?

You've worked yourself up into quite a state by the time you get to the café. It's one of those mock-French café/bar affairs that would look quite charming and original if there wasn't a chain of identical places all across London. Sally's sitting at a table outside with a coffee and a newspaper. You go up to her and grab her hands. She jumps.

—Are you okay? you ask her urgently before you've even said hello.

—Yes, I told you, I'm fine, she says, sounding slightly annoyed.

—But really . . . ?

179

—But really.

You breathe out. You can relax a little now. You chain up your bike and go inside to get yourself a coffee. A blonde woman in a white blouse with a daft bow tie tells you firmly that it's waitress service only and ushers you back outside.

—So tell me all about it, you say, sitting down.

—You haven't even given me a kiss yet. Aren't you pleased to see me?

—Oh yeah. Sorry. I . . . uh, I've been worried. You know.

She smiles. Secretly she's pleased you're so concerned; you can tell.

She puckers up. You oblige.

—There's nothing bout it in here, she says, folding up her paper. —Guess that stuff's not newsworthy any more.

—Up to you to give me all the info, then.

—Okay then. Ready for a story?

—Sitting comfortably. Begin.

She drains her cup and starts talking.

They didn't talk much on the train going up. Sally wanted to ask Nick further about this poor girl in Edinburgh, she hadn't had time to read all the newspaper reports. But Nick didn't want to discuss the case at all. He was convinced the whole carriage was full of hacks waiting to steal his scoop. Sally tried to point out to him that even if there were other journalists going up to cover the story, they would only be doing it from the conventional angle. No one else suspected what they suspected. But he just put a finger to his lips to shut her up, which made her feel foolish. When she did manage to persuade him to go over some details of the Plan they hadn't finalised, he insisted they go into one of the toilets so no one would hear. It was ridiculous. They snuck in one after the other and stood cramped between the toilet and the sink discussing how they would go about scoring Es in Edinburgh nightclubs. The toilet was blocked with paper and stank to hell and the sink was half full of still, yellowish water, Sally felt humiliated and somewhat nauseous. She also felt slightly scared. Nick was being so intense about this; if he decided he was going to do something reckless, would she be able to stop him?

When they returned to their seats it was clear that Nick wasn't going to talk any more, so Sally decided to try and get some sleep. She had barely shut her eyes, however, when there was a roar from halfway down the carriage.

—HALES!

Christ, what now, thought Sally.

An enormous man with a large, bushy beard and a hideous beige raincoat was coming towards them. He looked like one of the Wurzels training to be a Sumo wrestler.

—HALES, IT'S ME! GAVIN ARMSTRONG!

As he approached them, he lowered his voice. Slightly.

—Been for a quick bit of how's your father in the bogs, have you? Can't say I blame you, mate.

—Yeah, actually . . ., Nick began.

—Brought your young lady with you, eh? Mixing a bit of work with pleasure?

—I'm not his young lady, Sally said firmly.

Nick interrupted her. —No, this is a colleague of mine . . . uh, Linda Watson . . . we were just chatting privately.

—Course you were, course you were, said Armstrong and then he turned to Sally. —So you're a fellow hack. Pleased to meet you, my dear.

He held out a hand, but hardly seemed to notice that Sally refused to take it; he just kept on talking.

—That's quite a crowd your rag's sent up for this one, then. I ran into Ken Nightingale at King's Cross and he's covering this one too . . . you are still with the same paper, I take it?

Nick had to think for a moment. —Oh yeah . . . yeah, course. We're, uh . . . just covering different angles, Ken an me. Know what I mean?

—Beginning to look like there might be something to that little hunch of yours after all, Armstrong said, fishing for leads. —Got anything further to go on?

Nick shook his head. —Nothing at all . . . Whole thing's a bit freaky, though . . .

—You're telling me. Still, bit of a result for me, getting to follow up my original story. Very rare I get out of Yorkshire these days, very rare.

He beamed at both of them and dug his hip flask out.

—What about the little lady? She got any theories? he said, offering the flask.

Sally'd had enough of this. She tugged Nick's arm. —Come on, weren't we gonna go up to the buffet?

Armstrong held his arms up. —No offence meant!

—Yeah, anyway, we gotta go, said Nick. —See you around.

—At the press conference?

—Yeah, right . . . when is that again?

—Tomorrow at ten. Princes Hotel.

—Course . . . yeah. See you tomorrow then.

Armstrong gave Nick a hearty slap on the back as he turned to leave. —See you tomorrow, Derek, my man.

—Derek? said Sally when they got to the buffet.

—Yeah, first name I could think of. Don't know why I gave him a false name. Seemed like the right thing to do at the time.

—And Linda Watson? Who the fuck's she when she's at home?

—Okay, I'm sorry! I'd given myself a false name so it seemed rude not to give you one too.

Sally hadn't intended to get any food; she'd simply used it as an excuse to get away from the fat fool in the raincoat, but now they were here she was feeling kind of hungry. They both got sandwiches and the mood between them lightened a bit.

However, when they retook their seats they sat in silence for most of the rest of the journey. Sally never got to ask any more questions. Eventually she drifted off and managed to doze a little.

They got to Edinburgh around four in the morning. The rest of the hacks were whisked off to their plush expense-account hotels; even Gavin Armstrong, the local paper man from Leeds, was last seen climbing bleary-eyed into a taxi. Nick and Sally hung around the station for a couple of hours, trying to stay awake and not get beaten up by the strange people who make it their business to hang around railway stations at night looking menacing. They did a little speed that Sally had brought with her to keep them going and sat on the pavement waiting for the sun to come up.

Danny and Carl were due in on a train from Leeds at six thirty. They were delayed and all four of them were starving by the time they finally met up. They went into the first café they came across, ordered enormous breakfasts and discussed the Plan.

Which was this: Nick and Sally would try and get into the press conference; Danny and Carl would go to the girl's school and see if they could glean any information from her friends. These were both long shots. In the afternoon they'd find themselves a cheap place to stay, get some kip. Then they'd get hold of a listings magazine and hit the clubs.

The press conference was, as they had suspected, a bit of a washout. All they managed to learn was that Alison McCormack had been an intelligent, lively, popular girl, she didn't do drugs, didn't hang out with the wrong kids, her teachers expected her to go to university . . . pretty much the usual stuff. And they had to suck up to Gavin Armstrong and sneak in with him, which disgusted Sally.

Danny and Carl fared even less well. Hanging around outside a girls' school asking questions nearly got them arrested. Their claims to be private detectives working for an anonymous benefactor were not wholly believed by the school authorities and they had to split before they had found out anything useful.

So when the four of them met up again at lunchtime, they were pretty despondent. Not to mention absolutely knackered.

Nick tried to cheer them up a bit. —Come on, we knew we probably wouldn't have much luck with things this morning; we'll go an find somewhere to crash out an then we'll get a result this evening, you'll see.

The others didn't look convinced. They were all too busy looking tired and pissed off.

It seemed to take them an age to find a suitable, cheap place to stay that wasn't already fully booked. Eventually they came across a shabby-looking guest house run by a grumpy old woman. It was dirty, unwelcoming and overpriced, but they were way past caring. They got their key and slept for nine hours straight.

—Separate rooms? you try to say casually, but it comes out as more of an hysterical wail:—SEPARATE ROOMS?

—Separate beds, says Sally.

You weigh this up. Seems like a reasonable compromise, given their lack of funds. Before you can ask her about the sleeping arrangements in more detail, though, the blonde bombshell reappears.

—What can I get you, sir?

Sally has been talking for fully twenty minutes. You've been so engrossed you forgot you didn't have a drink. Where the hell has this girl been?

—I told you inside. Black coffee, please.

She writes this down carefully on her notepad. Which is reassuring; it's a long way back inside to the counter and she might easily forget such a complicated order.

—I wouldn't mind another coffee too, Sally calls after her.

But she's gone. Possibly forever.

Sally takes up her tale again without delving further into who slept where.

That evening they hit the nightclubs of Edinburgh. Sally and Nick took one half of the city, Danny and Carl the other. Both Nick and Carl had phones, so one pair could call the other if they turned up anything. Sally found it exciting at first, and slightly scary, but then ultimately rather dull. She'd never dealt Es at a club before. At first she was worried they'd get caught by the bouncers or robbed at knifepoint by the gangsters who owned the patch. But it soon became clear that as long as they were reasonably careful, they could do pretty much what they liked, talk to who they liked. She started getting into it after a while, the patter, the secrecy, the nods and winks. It was kind of like working the stall. Same buzz. She half wished she could stand outside the ladies, yelling:—ES FOR SALE! LARVELY ES! GET YOUR DISCO BISCUITS HERE LADIES AN GENTS! She had no luck with any of her questions, though. People just gave her funny looks when she started asking. She wondered if she was really cut out to be an investigator.

However, their luck was in. They hit the jackpot in the third place they went to. They'd done a couple of deals to no great effect and were standing at the bar, listening to the music for a bit. They'd pretty much decided they'd exhausted this place – in fact Sally was starting to lose heart with this scheme as a whole – and they were going to move on when this large skinhead came up to them. This really large skinhead.

—Hear you're looking for someone, he said.

Nick tried to look unfazed by this man's overwhelming bulk, but Sally could tell he was doing the same mental calculations as she was: nineteen stone? twenty? *more* than twenty?

—Yeah, Nick replied. —You the guy?

—No, said the man. —I'm just curious. Why would you be wantin to meet . . . my client.

—I see. It's like that, said Nick.

—It's like that.

—Well, we might be in a position to help, uh, your client. Help him a great deal, as it happens.

—Yeah? What kind of help?

—That I would have to discuss with your client in person.

The man moved forwards. Only an inch, but a very intimidating inch.

—I *am* his representative.

Nick stood his ground. —And you'll be welcome at our meeting. But I do need to speak to this gentleman in person.

The man stopped to consider this.

—Okay. We'll meet. Tomorrow morning.

He gave them a name of a café which he said was near the station.

—Oh, an just one more thing, he added. —Some of the other customers in this place tomorrow will be . . . business partners of mine. You won't know who they are unless there's any sign of trouble. Then you'll know exactly who they are pretty fuckin quickly. Get what I'm sayin?

Nick nodded and smiled. He held out a hand; the man refused it.

—I'll shake your hand when I know what the fuck you're up to, he said and walked away.

When he was gone, Nick turned to Sally and gave her a big hug. —We did it! We fuckin did it!

—Whoa, whoa! *Big hug?*

Sally rolls her eyes. —It was a *celebratory* hug. That's all. We'd just got out of a potentially dangerous situation. We found our guy. The thing was working.

You think about this for a moment.

—Okay. Carry on.

They went up to the chill-out to phone Danny and Carl and tell them the chase was over. It was a difficult conversation as they were fighting against a bad line and two lots of background music. Nick gave Carl the name of the place they were in.

—WHY DON'T YOU COME ON OVER? he shouted. —WE'RE JUST GONNA DO AN E AN HAVE A DANCE.

We are? thought Sally. Then she looked around nervously to see if anyone else had caught this rather loud declaration.

Danny and Carl were in full agreement, though. They came over and the four of them stayed until the place closed. The pills they'd managed to acquire between them were nothing special, but they were all high on the adventure anyway and had a good time.

Which meant that none of them was on top form when they went along to the meeting the following morning. They got to the place early and they sat in silence, eating their fry-ups, each of them looking around to see if they could work out which of these other people might be heavies in disguise.

He showed up late. A short, stocky man, maybe ten or fifteen years older than them. It was hard to tell, though; he had the kind of weatherbeaten face that could have been any age. He was wearing a bomber jacket and scuffed black Doctor Martens. He seemed to know exactly which table to come to. He eyed the four of them in turn, then pulled himself up a chair.

—Hi. I'm Alistair, he said.

—Alistair . . . ? asked Carl.

—Alistair.

—Right.

Through the window, Sally could see the Enormous Skinhead waiting outside.

—So, said Alistair, looking round at them all in turn again. —Are we just here for a pleasant chat or what?

Danny started talking. He told the whole story from his point of view – the cheap batch of pills, the threats, how Nick had tracked him down. He looked over at Alistair for signs of recognition. Alistair was shaking his head, though. This wasn't his experience at all. He'd bought this batch off a regular supplier, he said, and had no reason to suspect they might be dodgy.

—Shit, said Nick. —There's another middle man . . . Can you introduce us to him?

—Are you jokin, pal? said Alistair violently and it looked for a second as if he was going to lean over and thump Nick. —I'm pretty keen to speak to the bastard myself.

—Look, said Nick, and his voice sounded only partially terrified. — I don't want to tell you how to run your affairs . . .

—Too fuckin right you don't.

—. . . but go easy on this guy, okay? I'm sure he had no idea what he was selling you. If you want proof, see if he recognises this guy . . .

He dug out the pictures of the gang he had taken outside the house in Bradford, which Fat Cunt had had enlarged, and handed over the one of Macmillan. It was blurred and barely recognisable.

Alistair peered at it. —Who the fuck is this supposed to be, then?

Nick drew a deep breath and outlined the great conspiracy theory. As he did so, Sally suddenly realised just how ludicrous it sounded told in black and white like that and she wondered if this might just be the final straw for Alistair. She started strenuously backing Nick up, saying 'yeah' and 'exactly' whenever he paused for breath and nodding furiously. Carl and Danny joined in.

Alistair was unconvinced. —How can I be sure you're on the level?

Nick pointed round at them all. —Look at us, man. What the fuck else would we be doin here? We just want to nail these bastards an we need your help.

Alistair looked at them all again, then back at the photographs. —Okay, he said. —If what you're saying is true, I wanna get these cunts too. People dyin all over the shop isnae too good for business, know what I mean?

He laughed and the others laughed with him. Loudly.

After that the conversation settled down and Alistair started joking with them, always looking around for a reaction. Sally felt her nervous laugh sounded ridiculous and he would surely notice that she was faking it, but he didn't seem to.

Nervously Nick broached the subject of his newspaper article. He wanted permission to quote some of the stuff Alistair had said.

—Obviously I won't name you as my source, or make you identifiable in any way. I made the same promise to Danny here. I'll change your name, appearance, circumstances. I'll even change your fuckin colour if you like. Make you a black lesbian dwarf. How's that? No one'll know it's you. Swear on my mother's life.

Alistair nodded amiably. —You realise that's a literal promise you've just made, don't you?

When they'd finished talking, Alistair picked up the tab for the whole table.

—No, no, he said, waving away protests. —You guys have risked a lot to help me an I appreciate it.

He scribbled a telephone number on a piece of paper.

—It's not my number but you can get hold of me here. Gis a call in a couple of days and I'll tell you if my man knew the cunt with the moustache.

As they got up to leave, several men at other tables stood up also.

Sally felt like she was in a movie. Nick was visibly thrilled. They'd won over the gangster! They'd got his phone number!

When they got outside, things started to happen very quickly. A large black car pulled up outside the café and two men jumped out. One of them punched Danny and knocked him to the ground.

—Wait just a fuckin minute—Alistair said, but he was prevented from finishing the sentence by a sharp punch in the stomach from the other man.

The heavies gathered round. The Enormous Skinhead appeared. It looked like there was going to be a pitch battle in the street.

Then the man who had just hit Alistair produced a gun.

The stakes were raised. Everyone froze.

—Don't fuck with us! the man yelled. —Don't fuck with us an everythin'll be cool.

The whole street had gone silent.

—Get in the car! he barked at Alistair. The Enormous Skinhead moved towards him, but the man spun round waving his gun in the air. —Take another step and you're fuckin deid, got it?

Alistair motioned for his men to calm down and climbed into the car.

Then Sally realised what was going to happen. Once the car had driven off with Alistair inside, his men would come after them. They'd assume she and Nick had set this up in some way, or at the very least knew what was going on, and they'd want their man back.

Nick had worked out the exact same thing. —We gotta run, he whispered to her.

Sally nodded. She wasn't sure if she was going to be able to run, though. She felt paralysed with fear. Her legs didn't feel like they'd support her much longer, let alone take her anywhere.

But when she started moving, she was amazed at how fast she could run. Behind her, she heard the car moving off. That meant the others would be chasing them now. She ran even faster.

They ran without thinking about where they were running to. They ran up long, steep flights of steps, past startled pedestrians, across parks, trampling on flowers, up and down more steps. Still they were followed. Still they ran. Eventually they managed to lose their pursuers by ducking into a maze of little alleyways, twisting and turning, hoping to Christ they wouldn't double back on themselves. They emerged, wheezing and coughing, on to a wide, bright shopping street. A bus pulled up in front of them.

—Come on, Nick panted. —We're not out of this yet.

They jumped on the bus, not giving a shit where it was going. Just away from there, they hoped. They sat at the back in terrified silence, convinced that it would turn a corner any second and there would be Alistair's men waiting for them. Or its route would take it back past the station and they'd be recognised by one of the onlookers. The cops'd be there by now, for sure.

But it made only a few more stops in the city and then trundled off out to the suburbs. They sat there, breathing deeply like a couple of marathon runners. They rode it for about fifteen minutes until they were sure they were well away from danger, then they got off.

They found themselves in a quiet, well-to-do neighbourhood.

It seemed a different planet from gangsters waving guns outside railway stations a few minutes earlier. There was a little square of grass with a phone box, two swings and a bench. They sat down.

Sally started crying.

—HE HAD A GUN, NICK! HE HAD A FUCKING GUN!

—Yeah, I know, Nick said quietly.

—HE COULD'VE KILLED US!

—If they wanted to kill us they'd've done it then. Or taken us with them. They let us go; that's a good sign.

But he was only trying to convince himself.

190

—YOU DON'T KNOW THAT! she screamed. —YOU DON'T KNOW! YOU DON'T KNOW! YOU DON'T KNOW!

She started hitting him. He made only half-hearted attempts to stop her.

When she'd stopped and was sat there, blubbing softly to herself, he took out his phone.

—What you doing? she said through the tears.

—Gonna phone Carl. See if they got away okay.

She moved closer to listen. The phone was answered after several rings.

—Yeah? said a nervous voice.

—Carl. It's Nick.

—Nick! Where are you?

—Fuck knows. Away. Sally's with me. How bout you? You safe?

—Yeah, think so. Time being anyway. Reckon they got Danny, though. He didn't make it away with me. What the fuck was going on back there?

—Dunno. Looks like our polite and respectable psychopaths have got themselves some muscle up here.

—Yeah. Jesus . . . I suppose they were just after Danny and Alistair, they're the two who can link the gang to the deaths . . .

Carl was quiet for a moment.

Then he said:—What you think they're doing to Danny?

—Oh fuck, man, I don't even wanna think about it.

They both fell silent again.

—What you gonna do? asked Carl finally.

Nick sighed. —Dunno. Up to now I was just thinking bout getting away . . . I haven't a fucking clue, to be honest.

Carl seemed to have some kind of plan. —Listen, I'm not that far from the hotel, he said. —I thought I'd go back an pick our stuff up before they trace us back there. Then I was gonna hire a car. Get out of the city that way.

—Yeah?

—Train's too dangerous, I reckon. If Alistair's guys aren't waiting for us at the station, the cops will be.

—Yeah, that could be true . . . fuckin hell, this is a mess, isn't it? What we gonna do?

Nick held his head in his hands.

—What we gonna do? What we gonna do? he said over and over. He was holding the phone away from his mouth. Sally could hear Carl at the other end asking if Nick was still there. She took the phone from him.

—Carl, it's Sally. If we can find out where the fuck we are, can you come and pick us up on the way out?

—Yeah . . . that sounds okay. Call me back in half an hour or so . . .

A coffee arrives. A lukewarm, white coffee.

You've been left absolutely speechless by what Sally's been saying. You scarcely notice the drink.

—Aren't you gonna say anything? That's taken half a fuckin hour, she says, pointing at your cup.

—No. Finish the story. How'd you get back?

—Just that, she goes. —Carl hired a car an gave us a lift back to Leeds. Then we got a train down here this morning.

You hardly dare ask. —And what about Danny?

—He made it! she says, beaming. —He just got split up from the rest of us as we were trying to get away. Carl got a call from him shortly after he picked us up; he'd run as far as he could away from all the aggro an then managed to hitch a lift out of town.

—So they weren't after him after all?

—Well, I don't know . . . maybe not.

—So it could be nothing to do with your thing at all. It could've simply been a rival gang or something coming after Alistair.

You cling on to this. Otherwise, this is too close for you. It would mean your girlfriend was wanted by people who wave guns around on crowded pavements.

—And where's Nick?

—Hiding, she says, fishing herself out a cigarette. —He's in no doubt who those people were an what they want.

She looks at you pointedly as she says this and you hate yourself for even asking the question. Of course it was all tied in. And now your two best friends in the world are in some real fucking danger; and just because you don't want this to be the case won't make it go away.

Sally continues. —He said it was better if we stayed apart until this thing is out in the open. Safer for both of us that way.

You watch her blowing out smoke. You've just noticed, yet again, how beautiful she is. You can't believe she's this calm when she's in so much danger.

—How's it gonna come out in the open? you ask her.

—He's sending everything he's got to the cops. Anonymously. He's still got copies of all the photos, you see. I don't think the gang realise he's got them all on film. I mean, he's still gonna try an do an article, but you know, it's a different ball game now. The main thing is to get these fuckers arrested an stop them killing people. Otherwise we're just gonna be hiding from them for ever. By the way, that reminds me, Nick asked me to give you a set of the photos . . . you know, just in case.

—Just in case what?

You don't want to hear the answer to this.

—In case anything happens. To Nick an me.

—An if it does?

—I dunno . . . try again with the police, I guess.

Your first and strongest impulse is not to take the pictures. Surely just owning this set of pictures puts you in danger too? And this has stopped being even vaguely exciting.

But you can't just bugger off and leave your friends, can you? Not when they've risked so much and you've just doubted their word the whole way along.

—But you still haven't got any proof. What good is sending this to the police? It's just a bunch of pictures of people: respectable, upstanding people who I bet don't have a parking ticket between them.

Sally shrugs. She looks very tired all of a sudden. —There's circumstantial evidence. We'll just have to hope that's enough for them to piece together a case. There's also a couple of witnesses, if they can be persuaded to speak up.

—What, Alistair you mean? Don't suppose you ever found out what happened to him?

She reaches in her bag and produces one of yesterday's papers. She shows you an article headlined: UNDERWORLD MAN DISAPPEARS. Edinburgh businessman, Alistair McGovern, 43, who is strongly rumoured to have underworld connections, has been missing for over twenty-four hours, the paper says. There are fears that he may have been the victim of a gangland killing.

The story links McGovern with an 'incident' outside Waverley Station and is accompanied by a picture of a balding, rather weedy-looking man. Looks like Kevin Spacey in *The Usual Suspects*. Not how you imagined him at all.

—That's what I was looking for in today's paper, Sally says. —See if they'd found him yet. But there's nothing bout it at all. Seems like it's just been forgotten.

You both sit in silence for a long time.

Then Sally takes your hand.

—Listen, John, I think it'd be better if we didn't see each other until this shit blows over. I don't wanna put you in danger too.

You shake your head vigorously. —Uh-uh. I wanna stay with you. I'm just gonna worry to death bout you otherwise.

She's firm, though. —Honestly, I think it's for the best. It'll only be a week or so hopefully. Just . . . don't call me, okay? I probably won't be at my place anyway. I'll call you when I've got a clearer idea what's going on.

—Well . . . okay . . . if you're sure.

She's sure. She's already standing up, stubbing out her cigarette, putting her newspapers back in her bag.

You watch her go and feel longingly, achingly lonely.

Your coffee's now stone-cold. You haven't touched it and you're certainly not bloody well paying for it.

∫

After five days of deep space travel, the Midnight Patrol came upon the Ancients' mothership. They tried to cloak their craft, but it was too late. The Ancients' sophisticated scanners had detected them and they were already locked into their tractor beam.

Matrix was able to download details of the mothership layout from the on-board computer.

'Okay, this is what we'll have to *do*,' said Captain Midnight. 'As soon as we're within *range*, we'll each transport to a *different* part of the ship! Matrix has calculated the six *weak* areas of defence for the ship, so we'll take one *each*! It's important we stay in *contact* with each other!' There were nods around the room. 'If that's understood, everyone should study their *sectors* of the mothership! Oh . . . and *good luck!*'

The Captain himself took the engine room. It was the area of most strategic importance in the ship. If he could gain control of this small sector, he could hold the entire craft to ransom. He was determined to *try* and negotiate with these creatures, even though he knew in his heart of hearts that it would be futile. He had encountered so many alien tribes that he had learned to get a feeling for which ones would talk and which ones would battle blindly on to the death.

Matrix's readings told him there were four personnel in the engine room. If the Captain transported to the correct spot, there would be two to his left, one to his right and one straight in front of him, all with their backs turned, facing their instruments.

He came out blazing. Before he had even fully materialised, he shot a laser jet out to his left and then to his right. WHOOOSSH! This took out two of the four. They fell to the ground in agony and surprise. NNNNGGGGRRRHHHH!

The one in front of him turned round, but Captain Midnight was too quick for him. A third orangey-red laser jet issued forth from his weapon, hitting the creature full in the abdomen and sending him flying back on to his control deck. Sparks flew and the deck crackled and sizzled. SPTTTSSSSHHHH!

It was the second one on his left that caught the Captain out. He'd moved from his station, so the fourth laser jet, intended for him, simply ploughed into machinery, causing more sparks. PWCCCCHHHH! The first Captain Midnight knew about the fourth Ancient's position was when the strange beam of an unfamiliar weapon hit him on the shoulder and threw him to the floor. The pain was familiar enough, though, and he howled. AIEEEEEEE! He tried to make out where the beam had come from and was just able to avoid a second one which came hurtling towards him. There was a small explosion behind him. He heard an alien voice from above, although he could still see nothing; presumably the creature was calling for reinforcements. He didn't have much time. He aimed a laser jet at where he thought the voice was coming from. There was a flash of light as the laser hit a cable – WHAAMMM! – and a gangway on the second level gave way. The remaining Ancient tumbled to the floor at the Captain's feet. Captain Midnight laughed and blew him away with a bolt to the face.

The engines looked pretty straightforward. They were more advanced than any the Captain had seen before, but worked broadly along familiar principles. The damage caused by the fight was only superficial, but it would be easy to put them out of action permanently. A laserbolt in a couple of key places would do the trick; the only difficulty would be getting out of the room before the whole thing went up.

He never got time to figure out a way to do it, though. Before he could fire his first shot, an Ancients security team burst through the door and he was felled instantly.

$\int$

Friday passes in a haze. You wake up so worried you can't eat so you go to work without breakfast; at work you offer to do as many customers as possible because if you have any time to yourself you'll just worry; then when you get home you worry your nuts off until it's time to go to bed. You do try to keep your promise not to contact Sally, you really do, but at ten o'clock you give in. What are you supposed to do? You're in love with her, aren't you? So you phone her up. And she's not fucking there. So you phone Nick up. And he's not fucking there. So you try Sally again and then Nick and then Nick's mobile and then Sally and then Nick and you keep on like this for the whole evening. And they're Not. Fucking. There.

Bastards.

By Saturday morning Nick's mobile has been disconnected and the computerised woman tells you not to bother calling this number again.

Bastards.

What are they trying to do to you? They know you're their mate – rather more than that in Sally's case. What do you expect you to do apart from go out of your mind with worry? You had been trying to tell yourself that all the evidence was circumstantial, there could be nothing in it all: they hadn't actually *seen* Macmillan dealing any pills to anyone, McGovern *could* have been picked up by a rival gang in Edinburgh. But if that was the case, if they really were sitting safe and sound somewhere, they'd phone. They'd return these increasingly frantic messages of yours. Wouldn't they?

You buy all the papers you can lay your hands on and scan them for mentions of McGovern, but nothing. Then you have the terrifying thought that if things have come to the worst, you might read about Nick and Sally in one of them. Shit, you couldn't handle finding out like that. You scrunch up all the papers and throw them away and don't buy any more.

Now what?

Now you're in a blind panic permanently, that's what. You wander around the flat mumbling to yourself. Bollocks, bollocks, bollocks, bollocks . . .

Apart from anything else, it's exhausting being this scared.

You make up the extra hours at work on the Saturday as promised. You haven't slept a wink on the Friday night so your coiffuring skills are perhaps not at their sharpest but fuck it, you've got nothing else to do. You're certainly not hanging around the flat on your own all day. Louie now thinks you're in need of psychiatric help and gives you the name and address of a shrink, a Greek gentleman by a startling coincidence, who he tells you is very, very good.

—He gave a lot of help to my wife when she had a problem with the . . . you know . . .

No you don't know, you haven't got a fucking clue, but you've no intention of enquiring any further either.

You spend your overtime cleaning out the hair gel dispensers. Now Louie is convinced you've lost it. But when you get home, you wish you were still back at work, scraping crusty bits of bright blue jelly off the rusting containers. At least it kept you occupied. Here at home you can't do anything. You can't concentrate on the TV, you don't want to listen to music; it all seems so frivolous in your current situation. Tony and Laura are having a slagging match in the next room so you just sit and listen to them. Their troubles seem so petty compared with yours. You want to march in there, grab them both and shout, It doesn't matter! It's not important! Okay, so Laura may or may not have slept with some other blokes.

She's still alive, isn't she? She's still fucking here. That's what counts.

You try Nick again. Fourth time today. Still no answer at his home and his mobile's now completely dead. Fucking marvellous.

The Incredible Shagging Neighbours start up.

Grunt . . . grunt . . . grunt . . . grunt . . .

Right. That's it. That's fucking *enough*.

You march out of your flat and bang on their door.

Grunt . . . grunt . . . sigh.

There's some rustling, padding feet and the door is opened. It's Mr Incredible Shagging Neighbour, wearing nothing but a fluffy white dressing gown. Sticking out like a tent in the middle, you can't help noticing.

—Yes? he snaps.

—Uh . . . I was just wondering if you wouldn't mind keeping the noise down a little.

—I'm not making any noise, he says.

—Well, there is this sort of . . . grunting sound coming from your flat.

—That's the wife.

—I see. Well, perhaps you could ask her to keep it down a little.

—And why should she do that?

There's muffled yelling in the background. You can hear Tony and Laura even in this guy's flat.

—It's just that my flatmate and his girlfriend are trying to have a little domestic and I don't think it helps them, really, to have this amazing tantric sex going on next door.

—Tough.

—Who is it? calls Mrs Incredible Shagging Neighbour from the bedroom.

—Nothing, love. Won't be a second.

—Right, yeah. If you could just hurry it up a little, then?

—Fuck off, he says and slams the door in your face.

There. That's cheered you up a little.

You get back to your flat in time to see Laura leaving in tears. You go inside to find Tony standing in the kitchen with his head in his hands.

—She's left me, he says flatly. —She's gone an bloody left me.

You try and look concerned. You're upset for him obviously, he's a mate, but you can't help feeling relieved at the diversion from your own moping. And Laura *was* an annoying bitch who slept around a lot, so it's not exactly breaking up the romance of the century.

You put the kettle on and sit him down in the front room.

—What you gonna do? you ask him gently.

He thinks about this for a moment.

—I think I'm going to go out an get fuckin rat-arsed, he says.

Then he looks up at you.

—Wanna come?

You consider you options. A night down the boozer with Tony talking about his failed love life is not your absolute dream date. On the other hand, it doesn't look like Sally and Nick are going to call and you're not sure you can face trying to round up anyone else to go clubbing with. You're not even sure you want to go clubbing; you're hardly in the mood for it. So the alternative is Saturday evening TV. And you have this theory about Saturday evening TV. You can't prove it, not being a scientist, but you strongly suspect that the sugary combination of game shows, old sit-coms and useless drama series they put out actually destroys more brain cells than an E or several pints of lager. It's just a hunch, but you'd like to see some tests done.

—Okay, fuck it, why not.

—Thing is, says Tony, rolling up his sleeves, then placing his hands back comfortingly around his fourth pint of Krönenbourg.

Something about the way he rolls up those sleeves. You just know you're not going to get a word in edgeways for a couple of hours.

—Thing is, she says she left me cause I was too jealous of her. Jealous an . . . what's that other word she used? Possessive, that's it. Jealous and possessive. Now, the way I see it, that ain't really a crime. Cause what does it mean if you're jealous? All that means is you think someone's beautiful and special, so it stands to reason you're gonna think other people'll feel the same way too, and it's only natural to want to protect what's yours. Innit? I mean, that's what it is. It's not being possessive, it's being *protec-*

tive. Completely different fuckin thing. It's all part an parcel of going out with someone, being in love with them, far as I can see . . .

You drift off. This is one of those conversations you can take a break from and come back to later without missing too much of substance. An *EastEnders* kind of conversation. The pub is full to bursting. You've managed to slip into a couple of seats by the window; it's not exactly the height of comfort, but you're just glad to be sitting down. All around you people are pressed together like a rush-hour tube, desperately trying not to spill their drinks. It's about a hundred degrees. Is this fun? You wonder about some of these people: for many of them this will be the highlight of their week. Saturday night down the pub! The only time they let themselves get away from their jobs and their kids and their mortgages and their DIY . . . all the shit.

Tony's still droning on.

Your glass is empty. It's his round.

—You know, maybe she'd've preferred it if I hadn't shown any interest in her at all. Let her hang around with who she wanted, go where she wanted . . .

They're playing 'Rock The Casbah' on the jukebox. You drum your fingers on the table. You try and imagine what life would have been like if you'd been born Topper Headon.

You reckon you'd have changed that name for a start.

—. . . these are just natural urges, after all . . .

It's your round, you cunt!

—. . . an you know the final straw? She said I was being too suspicious cause I asked her if she was sleeping with that guy from the offie . . .

—She was, you interrupt.

—. . . you know, the one with the glasses an the ginger hair, looks about sixteen . . . you what?

—She was, you repeat.

—Was what?

—Sleeping with that guy from the offie.

—What do you mean?

You try and think of a simpler way of putting it. You can't. And your glass isn't getting any fuller.

—Laura was sleeping with the guy from the offie. The one who looks about sixteen, you tell him again.

—How the fuck do you know that?

You scratch your head. —Common knowledge, man. Think it was Richie told me.

Tony looks aghast. —The fuckin slut! Fuckin two-bit slut bitch!

—I shouldn't worry bout it, you try to reassure him.

—What do you mean, don't worry about it? She was my bird an she was shagging around.

—Yeah, but you're not with her now, are you? You've told her where to go . . .

—That's true, says Tony. Although it isn't true at all: she dumped him.

—Best off without her, if you ask me.

—Yeah. Too right.

—Cause, you know, she was even trying to go after Wide-Boy Wilson the other day.

—WHAT?

—You know, Wide-Boy, my . . .

—Your fuckin dealer! Christ!

You're just playing with him now. It's cruel, but then he should get his fucking round in, shouldn't he?

—Just forget her, man. That's my advice.

—Yeah . . . Anyway. Must be my round. What you havin?

Orchestras of angels fly through the pub singing the Hallelujah Chorus and praising Lord God On High.

Nine thirty. You're pissed. You've been here two and a half hours. You have suggested moving on at various points throughout the evening, but somehow you've never got round to it.

Empty glass. It's Tony's round again, but you're past caring now. You're not sure you could cram any more fizzy liquid into your body anyhow.

—So how bout you? he asks out of the blue.

—Eh?

You're taken aback. Tony's been talking about himself solidly since you got in here. Surely that wasn't an enquiry about *your* well-being?

—Where's your bit tonight? It's Saturday night, mate. You an her should be out having a bop. Doing some of your funny pills.

—I don't know where she is, you tell him.

—You what?

And you tell him the whole story. You've been listening for so long – or not listening, as the case may be – that it feels good to talk for a bit. And it feels really good to get this shit off your chest. You hadn't taken in how good it would feel just to talk about it. Doesn't solve any of the problems, doesn't even bring them closer to solution; it just makes them seem less overwhelming for being out in the open. You start at the beginning and tell him about Nick's trip to Leeds, then the trip to Scotland, all about Sally, Danny, McGovern, the guns. The whole bit.

And when you're done, he gives you his measured opinion.

—Fuckin bollocks, mate, he says.

—What?

—Pile of shite, he says, by way of contrast. —She's never in fuckin hiding. She's avoiding you. It's obvious.

—Is it?

—Course it is. Never heard such a pile of wank in my whole life. She's taking the piss, mate.

You can't believe this. Is he trying to be funny or something?

—She's not taking the piss. She's in grave danger.

—Look, mate, I'm sorry but this story just doesn't hold water. Even if the whole thing about gangsters running around in Edinburgh isn't completely made up, an I'm by no means sure about that, they're not in any danger down here are they? No one's got their names or addresses or anything. They just need to be a little bit careful, not lock themselves away like fuckin hermits.

—So what you saying?

—Well, I'm sorry to be the one to have to tell you, but it looks pretty obvious to me she's gone an left you for Nick. Now, I can't see why she would wanna do that personally, cause I think Nick's an oily little fucker as you know, but there you go. Those are the facts as far as I can see them. Sounds to me like she had the hots for him from the word go . . .

He drones on, but you've stopped listening. He's talking shit, isn't he? He just wants Sally to have left you because Laura's left him, so he can bond with you; so you can go out on the piss together and be Dumped Mates On The Pull. Well fuck that.

—Bollocks, you say when you notice he's finally stopped talking.

—No, I'm serious. I bet you any money if we go round to her gaff now, she's shaggin your so-called best mate. Or if they're not at her place they're at his.

Now he's just being offensive. —Fuck off, man. You don't know what you're talkin about.

—Come on then, says Tony. —Let's go check it out. I'm bored of this pub anyway.

It's a challenge you can't refuse without looking like you're scared he might be right. You're drunk and you're a bloke and drunken blokes never back down, ever. So you check it out. You get on a tube stuffed full of sweaty, pissed-up Saturday night people on the verge of throwing up and you ride ten stations in the opposite direction to your house. To check it out. Tony waits in the video shop at the end of Sally's road. You feel very lonely trudging up the empty street towards her block of flats. It's that hour of Saturday night when you really ought to *be* somewhere. You ought to have got wherever you're going by now. Even if it's only to a hundred degree pub already twice as full as fire regulations allow. Or else you should be at home, mug of steaming tea or large gin and tonic in hand, settling down to the Blockbuster Movie on TV. Not here, though. Not trudging on your own up your girlfriend's street trying to settle a drunken, illogical bet.

You enter the code and push through the front door into what Sally laughingly refers to as the foyer of her block: a small, damp, piss-stinking room with a dead plant in the corner. There's a desk where a concierge could sit and make sure the residents were not pestered by undesirables. But no one's worked here for years. Rents are high enough as it is. The lift's not working so you clamber wearily up the three flights of stairs to her flat. Trudge, trudge, fucking trudge.

You stop outside her door and compose yourself. Compose yourself as best you can for a drunken idiot. Then you knock once . . .

No answer. There. She's not in. That proves your point. She's hiding out somewhere in fear of her life. How could you have doubted her? You turn to leave, to go and give Tony a piece of your mind for wasting your time like this, when you think you hear a faint rustling from within.

You knock again, more tentatively this time.

Footsteps. Definitely footsteps. Shit . . . there is someone there.

Sally opens the door wearing nothing but a large, bright white T-shirt. She doesn't even put the safety chain on. How scared is that?

—John! she says, startled.

—Hi, you mumble. —I . . . uh, I just thought I'd come an see how you were . . . I tried calling . . .

—Yeah . . . nothing's sorted out yet. I've been too scared to answer the phone.

You stand there in cold, uncomfortable silence. Doesn't look like she's going to ask you in.

—Seen Nick? you ask.

She thinks for a moment.

—No . . . no news at all.

Then, with the timing of a Swiss watch, there comes a voice from the bedroom. A very familiar voice. —Hey babe, what's goin on?

Well. No news at all apart from the fact that he's lying in her bed right at the very moment.

Sally looks like someone's just died. Maybe they have.

—John . . . I can explain . . .

You think of Mrs Incredible Shagging Neighbour earlier this evening, cooing,—Who is it?

Got it now, arsehole?

Sally is fucking Nick.

Nick is fucking Sally.

Sally and Nick are fucking each other.

See . . . ?

SALLY IS FUCKING NICK.

SALLY . . . IS . . . FUCKING . . . NICK.

SALLY

IS

FUCKING

NICK

!

Got it now? *Arsehole?*

—John . . . I can explain. Why don't you come in for a bit?

—No, I've, uh . . . gotta meet someone.

—We were in a dangerous situation! That's all it was. We still are in danger. And it's only natural in these circumstances . . . I've read about it . . .

Her voice drops to a whisper. —It's you I want. Not him. It's just . . . I wanted to keep you out of this . . .

You walk away, leaving her talking. Why is she bothering to do this? Can't she have the courage of her own fucking convictions? Even now?

—John, come back! John! Can I call you?

From the end of the corridor, you turn to say goodbye. To look at her for the last time.

Jesus . . . she's *gorgeous*.

And you never told her . . . Did you?

—Have a nice life, you say. —Oh an try not to get killed by any gangsters with guns.

Hey babe. What a fucking tosser.

—So which you reckon is better, *Ace Ventura* or *The Mask?* Tony's asking the guy in the video shop.

—You win, you shout at him from the door.

You make him jump. He spins round.

—What?

—I said you fucking win. She's there with Nick Jones.

He doesn't look like he's just won a bet. —Shit . . . I'm sorry mate.

You shrug it off. It hasn't really hit you yet.

—So what you wanna do now? he says.

Another shrug. —Dunno.

He holds up the two boxes, one in each hand. —Jim Carrey movie?

—Fuck off.

He thinks. —Okay, I've got another idea.

—Yeah?

—We need to go outside.

He puts the boxes down and ushers you towards the door.

Outside he says:—How bout we go dancing? You an me. You got any of your funny little pills?

—Yeah, but . . . honestly, Tone, it's no fun if everyone else is off their tits an you're not.

—So? I'll do one as well then.

—But you don't . . .

He holds up a hand. —Bout time I tried then, innit? I'm always mouthing off about this shit, but I don't know the first thing about it. I should do it at least once so I know what I'm talkin about. Shouldn't I?

You look at him warily. You hate this. You hate initiating new people into the brotherhood. Makes you feel like a tobacco rep hanging around outside a school. The way you see it, people have had ten years to get into this shit. If they haven't got the picture by now, that's too bad.

On the other hand, you really could do with getting off on one and dancing tonight.

—My only concern, Tony adds,—is that shite music you play the whole time. Now, if I take one of these little doo-dahs, am I gonna start liking all that techno bollocks?

You smile. It feels weird to smile.

—Oh yeah, you say happily. —It's not just a Saturday night out. This is a major lifestyle choice you're making here.

He looks unsure.

—But it's okay. You'll still like your Madness records just as much. This is addition to your musical taste, not a replacement.

This seems to reassure him. It's agreed then.

But where can you take him? Nowhere too trendy, obviously. Nowhere too expensive. And most importantly, nowhere where there's the remotest chance of running into Sally and Nick. Because no doubt *they'll* be hitting the town tonight.

Eventually you decide on a tiny place just off Trafalgar Square. You came here with Nick about a year ago and he hated it, so you reckon you should be pretty safe.

This is a hardcore church of dance music. A small floor with a balcony and a chill-out the size of your bathroom. There's nothing in the way of decor, no distractions at all. There's just music. Loud, in your face music. And nothing to do but dance to it.

Tony looks bewildered when you first get there. You buy him a Coke and slip him his pill. You take them immediately. It's late and people around you are already starting to come up. He grimaces and washes it down with some Coke. Then he looks around, waiting for things to happen.

—It'll take a while, you tell him.

He starts asking you about Sally again, but you don't want to talk about her. At some point you'll have to deal with how you feel about that, but not now. Not tonight. So then he asks you about your comics. The other aspect of your life he doesn't begin to understand.

—They're very real for you, aren't they? he goes.

—What d'you mean?

—The characters an that. They're real for you. It's easy to forget that it's all made up, just cartoons . . .

What's this all about?

—No! you say. —It's a fantasy world. It's an *escape* from reality. It's nothing to do with reality itself.

—Okay, it's a fantasy world. But a world you'd like to escape into . . . ? Sometimes . . . ?

—Yeah . . . I guess.

—And don't you think you occasionally want to escape into this world so much . . . I mean *so much* . . . that you can get a bit muddled up as to which world is which?

—What are you getting at?

—I was just thinking bout the other night. What you were saying to yourself in front of the mirror . . .

Bastard. He had to bring that up.

—Told you, man. I was stoned. Totally bonced.

—Yeah. See, this is what worries me. These drugs, they do funny things to your brain, don't they? An I'm thinking, I'm already a bit fucked up, my girlfriend's left me, the real world's not looking too clever at the moment . . . now I've taken this little doo-dah, will I start thinking I'm Judge Dredd? An will I wake up tomorrow morning and still think I'm Judge Dredd?

You laugh at him. —Nah. Don't worry, you'll be okay.

—But you did! You thought you were Captain Midnight or one of his men or whatever . . .

You're starting to feel very uncomfortable with this.

Deep breath. —Okay, maybe while you're under the influence, you try to explain to him. —While you're under the influence your brain can do weird stuff to you. But you don't really believe it, even then . . . not *really*. You just kinda go with it so you can have a good time. An you certainly know what's going on the next morning when they've all worn off.

He doesn't look convinced. It's too late for him to be having second thoughts about this now.

—So you've never seriously believed you were a member of the Midnight Patrol?

—No!

What are you going to tell him? That, yes, you have sometimes felt deep down that things aren't quite what they seem, but you really don't think this has anything to do with the drugs? You don't want to freak him out completely. You want him to have a good time with this.

—Come on, let's go in the main room, you say. —It'll come on quicker if we start to dance.

You find a good spot up on the balcony where you can watch the other people. It's deep, hard trancey stuff they're playing and you get into it immediately. You can feel the rush coming.

Tony's not sure what to do. He holds on to the railing and taps his toe. He comes up slowly. The MDMA has to fight its way through all the alcohol sloshing around in his blood. But when he's there, you can see it straight away. He gives up on the dancing and wanders off, and he spends his evening quite happily walking around the place, slowly and steadily, looking people in the eye to see if they're there with him. Most of them are. He gives them a nod and a wink and moves on.

You lose track of him. You're too busy dancing. Dancing with an empty head. Every so often Sally and Nick encroach on the periphery of your thoughts, but you shoo them away again. You can't quite shake them off completely; you know they'll be waiting for you tomorrow morning. But not now. Not tonight.

You find Tony sitting against the back wall, eyes wide, toe still tapping, looking around rapidly, checking everybody and everything out.

—Havin a good time? you ask him.

He grins and sticks his thumb up, Paul McCartney style.

—Like the music?

He does it again.

You put your hands on his shoulders. —So you can understand? You can hear the music?

—YES! he shouts.

—CAN YOU HEAR THE MUSIC? you shout.

—YES! he shouts again.

And he stands up and starts dancing. It's a cumbersome, oafish dance, a ridiculous dance. But it's a totally brilliant dance. You give him a hug.

A record you know very well comes on. You get a second wave of hot rushiness. You start to sing along:

—My house is your housey.

—My house is your housey.

You tap Tony on the shoulder and try and get him to join you.

—My house is your housey.

—My house is your housey.

You point at yourself, then at Tony, still singing along.

—My house is your housey.

The music rises to a crescendo, the drums getting louder and faster and harder.

—My house is your housey.

Suddenly Tony puts his hands in the air and throws his head back.

—YOUR HOUSE IS MINE! he yells.

Bang.

—I HAD A FUCKIN BRILLIANT TIME! NO, I MEAN IT. THAT WAS BLINDING, MAN, FUCKING BLINDING!

Tony's still yelling. He hasn't stopped for what seems like days.

—I DON'T FUCKIN BELIEVE HOW GREAT THAT WAS. I FUCKIN LOVE YOU.

You brace yourself; you can feel a hug coming.

—I FUCKIN LOVE YOU, MAN.

You're walking down the road to the night bus, arm in arm, both as wired as each other. You've taken every pill you had on you, the whole batch Wide-Boy sold you other day; anything to ward off the onset of reality. Tony's just had his one, but he's still flying from that.

—Totally left all my worries behind, he goes on, lowering his voice as you approach the bus top, although most of the people here look as mashed as you two are. —I mean, fuckin birds, eh? Who needs em?

—Yeah. Who fuckin needs em! you agree.

—Who fuckin needs em! he says again.

—WHO FUCKIN NEEDS EM!

Then you remember. You need them. Or at least you need one of them, and quite badly. Shit, what do you have to take to keep this stuff at bay?

—So you really reckon Nick is an oily little fucker, eh?

—Yeah, says Tony. —Never liked him. This little stunt doesn't surprise me at all. I never trust a bloke who doesn't get his round in.

—Yeah . . . I feel like such a dickhead for not noticing.

—See, you should listen to your Uncle Tone when he tells you your mate is a cunt.

He wags a finger at you sternly and you laugh. The way he does it reminds you of Louie the Greek.

—Yeah. I do love Sally, though.

And you stop laughing immediately as you realise how true this is.

Tony looks disappointed. —Shit, man, I thought we had an agreement. FUCKIN BIRDS, WHO NEEDS EM!

He nudges your shoulder to egg you on.

—Yeah, I *wanna* believe it, you go. —Honest.

Tony books despondent for a moment, then snaps out of it with the surefire resolution of a bloke who's completely off his head. —Right then. We got to get her back for you.

As loved up as you are, you're in no mood for him taking the piss. —Fuck off, Tony.

—No mate, I'm serious. You can't let yourself be beaten by an Oily Fucker! Where's your self-respect? You let one Oily Fucker walk all over you like this, before you know it your whole life'll be overrun by Oily Fuckers.

He's not taking the piss, he's enjoying himself; you might as well go with it.

—Yeah? So how'd I go bout getting her back then?

He pauses to consider this for a very brief moment. —Well. Like I say, far as I can see, the only reason she went off with him in the first place was she thought it was kinda cool the way he was chasing this story of his. So what you got to do is get in there, do a bit of digging around yourself. Get up to Leeds, check out these Mad Old Dears . . .

This already sounds like a shit idea to you. Much as you want to win Sally back, much as you want her to admire and respect you, chasing psychopathic vigilante action groups around the north of England is not your idea of the height of romance. Tony makes them sound all cute and safe, calling them Mad Old Dears, but at the end of the day they're also *Murdering* Mad Old Dears. It's an important distinction as far as you're concerned.

—I don't know, you begin to say.

But he holds up a hand to stop you; he's on a roll. —No, listen mate, you can't lose. I mean, you can't do any worse than Nick did, can you? He's found out fuck all when you think about it. You don't have to put yourself at any risk – well, not too much anyway – you just got to get some proof one way or the other. Then either you go to the cops an get these people arrested an save your girlfriend from danger, in which case she'll want to sleep with you; or else you'll prove the whole thing's a crock of shit, in which case Nick will look really stupid, your girlfriend will be saved from danger and she'll want to sleep with you. Trust me on this, it's a win-win deal.

The bus pulls up and you clamber aboard.

—I don't know, you mutter as you count out your change for the driver. —I don't know . . .

—Come on, man. What else you gonna do? Lie back an give it all up?

You go upstairs. Some bastards have already got the front seats so you sit about halfway down.

—How bout you come with me? you ask him.

He shakes his head. —Nah, mate. It's your thing. You got to do it by yourself or it won't look so good. Anyway, I got my life, my job . . . I'm young, free an single now!

—*And*, he adds, and you think he's trying to give you a wink here. —And I got some catching up to do.

—Eh?

He attempts another wink. —You got Wide-Boy's number?

—Serious? you ask him.

—Fuck, yeah!

Of course you could tell him that it'll never be as good as this first time, the whole thing is dying on its feet anyway, now is an *especially* bad time to be getting into this shit . . . but what's the point? He'll find out for himself soon enough. So you smile and look out of the window. Who'd've thought it.

The bus takes a long while to fill up. When it does eventually start moving, you begin to drift off. As you watch the lights of the city fade into the first rays of dawn, you think about Captain Midnight chasing evil aliens across the galaxy to protect the innocent and avenge the death of his son.

You think of Sally, sitting on her sofa, urgently telling you: I wanna *do* something.

You think of a bloke waving a gun around on the streets of Edinburgh.

You think of those insane bastards cooking up fatal pills, killing people off one by one until they've destroyed an entire way of life. A way of life you're still, despite it all, very attached to.

You think of Harry, shrugging his shoulders in the café, saying: well, it had to end somewhere.

Those words in particular won't leave you alone. Had to end somewhere . . .

It's about six thirty when you get home. Tony's coming down finally, his eyes are more or less back to normal size, and he hits the sack immediately. You're still buzzing like a fly, though. You go into your room and look at your bed. You dig out your battered black sports bag and put it on the bed.

Now what?

It's a clear, stark choice in front of you. Either you kick the bag off the bed, climb in, go to sleep, get up sometime tomorrow afternoon and carry on your life in exactly the same vein, only without your girlfriend and your best friend and with the possibility of reading about somebody dying every few weeks and knowing you could have done something about it.

Or you pack it full of a few things and go up to Yorkshire on a wild goose chase, giving up your job and your friends and risking capture and torture and stuff you don't really want to think about.

Next door, Tony has begun to snore. You put a record on and whack it up. It's an unsociable hour and will no doubt lead to knocking on the wall from the Incredible Shagging Neighbours. But do you look like you give a fuck?

You get out your little tin of draw and try to skin up, but your hands are shaking too much.

Come on. Think. *Think* . . .

∫

The rest of the Midnight Patrol fared little better than their Captain. Matrix tried to infiltrate the ship's computer from a terminal in the Captain's quarters and instigate a self-destruct programme. But the ship's computer was wise to this. It had already detected that information had been downloaded from its memory bank and was ready and waiting. It had a virus prepared which closed down Matrix's vital functions within seconds.

Karlax was transported into the galley area of the ship. According to Matrix, there was a terminal here which could short-circuit the ship's life-support systems. There were only two unarmed Ancients in the room, silently eating their rations of baby stew. Karlax's superior strength saw off both of them easily. The first came at him with a strange-shaped eating implement and was dispatched with a kick in the stomach. OOUUFFFF!!

The second offered no resistance at all. Karlax grabbed him around what looked like his neck and demanded to know where the terminal was. They had no common language and the Ancient pretended not to understand. There was only one reason why an intruder would come to this room, though. Karlax tightened his grip until he heard a soft KRRAACCKKK! Suddenly the Ancient was pointing desperately at a console in the far corner of the room. Karlax noted the console and carried on squeezing.

KRA-A-A-A-C-C-C-K-K-K . . . !

Dropping the lifeless alien, he ran over to the terminal and punched in the formula Matrix had given him. Once again, though, the ship's computer had primed itself against interference and the formula was useless.

In fact, it seemed as though the whole attack had been foreseen by the Ancients. Each member of the Patrol's special powers seemed to have been anticipated in advance. Roltan's invisibility screen was easily penetrated by their scanners; Zanzi's lasers were neutralised as soon as she tried to use them.

Karlax eventually succumbed to an armed security team, which found him smashing up the console in front of him in frustration. When the strong man was marched into the hold, he found his Captain and the rest of the Patrol waiting for him. He howled with despair.

'So,' said the head of the Ancients' security team through a translation device, 'Captain Achten will be here to *see* you *shortly*. And then . . . you will be taken to the *Reduction Rays!*'

The members of the Midnight Patrol looked uneasily at each other. After all they'd been through together, was this how it would end? Stripped by a diabolical alien machine of the will to live . . .

Down on the planet, Machtbar had encountered her first setback. It appeared the people of this world had not yet developed methods of transportation. The only way to get to the other side of the planet was by loud, cumbersome flying machines which could take several hours or even days. The plan had been for the team to split up on arrival and each concentrate on one land mass and identify the centre of power for that region. Clearly that would now take longer than they had bargained for.

There was one good sign, though. These creatures really were going to be a pushover as far as their emotional gullibility was concerned. Machtbar began to frequent nightclubs as she found these by far the best source of positive emotions. Here people seemed to know only happiness. It was pathetic really. These creatures would ingest chemicals to empty their heads of all their worries and pains and fill themselves up with joy and love. It was playing right into her hands.

She had never encountered a more immature race masquerading as intelligent life. Their culture, their conversations, their sense of humour, all suggested a people barely out of the slime. She was greatly looking forward to destroying the lot of them.

∫

You come to and you're propping up a bar, head slumped over a warm, half full glass of beer with a cigarette butt floating in it. Wearily you open your eyes and look around. It looks like the bar of your local has been dropped into some place that looks very much like that club you went to in Brighton. You've no idea what the time is, but you reckon it must be kicking out time. Either that or this place is the biggest shit hole you've ever been in. The lights are on full blast, the music's turned down low and the few people left in here look the worse for wear. You call over to the barmaid to see if you can get another beer before last orders.

As she comes over, though, you get the shock of your life when you see it's Sally. She's shaking her head and wagging a finger at you; doesn't look like you're going to get served in a hurry. Only it's not Sally as you know her, it's Sally as she will be in twenty years time, all rolled up with your mother. And all of a sudden Nick is standing next to her, only it's Nick hideously mutated into your dad. And they're both wagging fingers, telling you you've had enough, it's time for you to go home, you've got work in the morning. You can't handle this. You pick up your existing drink – well, you can fish that butt out, can't you? – and walk away from the bar.

Over in the corner you spot a familiar face. You can't quite place him yet; Christ, doesn't it piss you off when that happens? But you know he's a mate of yours, and he's signalling you with a smile, so you go over.

'All right John?' he says as you sit down.

Shit, this is driving you nuts. Who is this guy?

'Uh . . . yeah . . . yeah, fine.'

Big muscley bloke, serious-looking face, heavy black mask, bright blue skin-tight uniform . . . no, still not ringing any bells.

'How bout you?' you ask him politely.

'Yeah. Bangin, mate.'

And you both fall silent again. What can you ask him? What can you ask him without giving it away that you don't know who the fuck he is? A vaguely familiar record comes on. You reckon this must be some geezer you've met out clubbing, why else would he be here? So you reckon it's got to be safe to talk about music.

'Top tune, this,' you try.

He turns and looks at you as if you're mad.

'Fuckin handbag shite,' he says.

Now you've got him! It's Captain Midnight! It's only Captain Bleeding Midnight sitting in a club talking to you, telling you how crap the music is! You knew the saviour of the universe would have great taste in music – because he's right, this is noncey handbag bollocks and not a 'top tune' at all – but it's pleasing to have your theories confirmed.

'So you here on a mission, then?' you ask him.

He puts a finger to his lips to shush you. 'Last of the Ancients spies,' he whispers, pointing to the floor, '*in this club!*'

Fuck! This is more exciting than you can possibly imagine. You're actually going to see the Captain in action, catching baddies and saving the Galaxy. You follow the faraway gaze in his eyes and find it resting on Nick and Sally, still squabbling with customers at the bar. You sit and wait for things to happen, barely able to contain yourself.

'Hey John, got pills?' says the Captain after a pause.

'You what?'

'Got pills, mate? I'm all out an I could do with another little buzz before I . . . you know . . . start saving people an shit . . .'

Hang on. Captain Midnight doesn't do pills. Or go to night-clubs. Or use words like Fuckin and Handbag and Shite. It must be someone else, it must be . . . of *course!* Now you've got it – how fucking stupid of you not to see it before . . . It's Fat Cunt! It's Fat Cunt in fancy dress! He gives you a big grin once he realises you've rumbled his disguise and produces a humongous spliff which makes the Camberwell Carrot in *Withnail & I* look like a matchstick. When he lights it, however, fireworks start shooting out of the end of it, the floor gives way beneath you and you can feel yourself falling . . . shit . . .

You come to and you're sitting in a stranger's car in the car park of some place called the White Horse Hotel. It's freezing cold and barely light outside. You've no idea where you are or how you got here. In the container between your seat and the driver's seat there's a row of cassette cases . . . The Grateful Dead, Hawkwind, Uriah Heep . . . oh God, now it's coming back . . . you drift off again . . .

You come to and the clock on the dashboard is flashing 8:45 at you. The sun is now up, it's not cold any more and you're feeling a whole lot better. Bit of a thumping head, but otherwise fine. You've more or less pieced together what happened yesterday, although you're still not quite sure how you ended up in this car in this car park at this time in the morning.

You left your flat about eleven. You knew you had to get out and on the road before the Es wore off, otherwise you'd just have gone to bed and that would have been the end of it. You went into Tony's room to let him know that you were off, that you were taking his advice and that you'd call every so often to let him know you were okay and to tell him what you'd found out. What you really wanted was for someone to wish you good luck before you set off, but Tony was still dead to the world.

You caught the bus up to Brent Cross and then walked to the end of the M1. It was now a bright, sunny day and you were squinting into the sun as the cars sped past you. You'd decided to hitch because you reckoned this little jaunt, even if it only took a few days, was going to cost you your job, so money was going to be tight for a while. Also, it would sound even cooler if you told Sally you *hitched* up to Leeds and cracked the case while sleeping rough.

The first lift came along in no time at all. This was going to be a piece of piss! It was a youngish, stern-looking woman who barked at you to jump in like she was giving orders in the army. You threw your bag on the back seat and got into the passenger seat next to her.

—You look a bit rough, mate. Heavy night? she said by way of opening gambit.

You looked over to see if she was smiling at this. She wasn't.

—Uh . . . yeah, I was totally out of my head—

—Actually, before you give me the details, she interrupted, and she reached into the glovebox by your knees and produced a police badge. —Off-duty copper. Careful what you tell me, eh?

—Oh, yeah . . . uh, right, you mumbled, feeling unspecifically guilty. —Yeah, I stayed in last night an watched *Casualty* . . . very traumatic episode . . .

You looked over again. *Almost* a smile. You didn't bother trying too much with conversation after that and neither did she.

She was only going as far as Northampton and let you off at the Watford Gap services. Now you were on the road you were buzzing again and feeling up for the whole adventure. You had a wash and a piss and a couple of games of pinball and then realised you hadn't eaten for a while so, forgetting for a moment that you were supposed to be on a budget, you ventured into the wildly overpriced food hall and spent fully twenty minutes building a salad that defied the laws of gravity. After you'd finished this, you got a piece of cardboard from a pile of broken-down boxes outside the garage, bought a marker pen from the shop and made yourself a sign that said LEEDS!

Now you felt like a proper hitch-hiker.

If you'd know just how long it was going to take you to leave this shit hole in the middle of nowhere, though, you wouldn't have spent so long arsing around at the salad bar. No fucker, it quickly transpired, was going to Leeds. After an hour of watching cars zoom past you, you began to get paranoid. Maybe you were now starting to look, and smell, as shit as you felt; maybe you'd become invisible; maybe all of a sudden you'd taken on the appearance of Rutger Hauer. As an experiment you tried adding the word PLEASE to the bottom of your sign. Made no difference. So after another hour of fuck all, you added above the word LEEDS: STOP YOU BASTARDS AND TAKE ME TO . . . Still nothing. You tried catching the eyes of the drivers as they whizzed by you, you tried smiling, you tried looking forlorn and desperate. Eventually, as the sun was beginning to set, you wrote on the back of your sign I FUCKING HATE YOU ALL and waved that at the cars instead while throwing V-signs with your other hand.

The second car stopped.

—God, yeah, man, love that sign. It's really, like . . . conceptual.

Young, dishevelled guy, Australian accent, beat up old Fiat with the engine making farty noises. Normally you wouldn't have touched this lift with a barge pole, but you didn't fancy spending the night on this slip-road.

—Where you goin, mate? the hippie asked.

You flipped over your sign to show him.

—Leeds. Yeah, cool, I could go for that. I'll have to make a few stops along the way, but yeah . . . I could stop in Leeds tonight . . . why not?

You climbed in reluctantly. The guy's name was Bryn. He made his own jewellery and was currently doing the rounds of small craft shops, selling what he optimistically described as his autumn collection. —So I could go to Leeds if I want, he explained. —That's the beauty of this job, I can go where I want. I mean, they have jewellery shops in Leeds, yeah?

He explained further about the beauty of his job, how there was no timetable to it, how he could come and go as he pleased. —I'm as free as a bi-ird, he started singing. You considered demanding he stop the car right there and let you out on the hard shoulder.

Then he talked some more about his job, and then he talked some more about it. It was breathtakingly dull, but after a while you found yourself dozing off. You became aware of how tired you were . . . finally being on the move again . . . his soft, rolling voice telling you nothing you wanted to know . . . songs on the stereo with guitar solos longer than some of your relationships . . . you weren't planning on falling asleep, you just thought you'd close your eyes for a moment . . .

And then . . .

And then now. If he made those stops he was talking about, you don't remember them. The next thing you remember, after some fitful and weird dreams, is coming to and still being in this beat up old Fiat. Bryn seems to have left you alone, all night, in his car. Even for a hippie, this seems remarkably trusting. You look around. There's a note stuck to the steering wheel.

Hey John

Man, you know how to sleep! I eventually holed up in this little ole place. I didn't see any point in you paying for a room when you were out like a baby anyways. I locked you in for safety's sake – just pop up the little fellers on the door when you want to go. And when you do, please lock the doors behind you by holding down the handle. I don't know if I trust the natives!

Hang loose buddy

Bryn

You pick your bag off the back seat and wander over to the hotel – having been *very* careful to lock the car behind you. On closer inspection it turns out that 'hotel' is a bit of a grand name for this place; it's more like somebody's house with an ad-hoc reception desk in what ought to be the hallway. And behind the reception desk sits a very large woman in a flowery dress who looks like she's wearing her make-up for a bet. She smiles at you as you walk in and you're scared her face is going to break.

—Good morning, sir. How may I help you?

—Uh . . . yeah. I was wondering if I could leave my bag here for a few hours . . .

Is this a cheeky thing to ask? Given that you've no real intention of staying here?

She doesn't think so. —Certainly, sir. I'll just pop it behind reception for you . . . Is there anything else I can do to help?

—Yeah . . . do you have a phone book?

Her voice and very nature is spooking you just a little, but she is being very helpful.

—Yes we do, sir.

She lifts up a large residential phone book from under the desk.

—Can I look something up for you, sir?

—Uh, no, it's okay. I'll do it.

You take the book from her and flick through to the Ms. There's only one Macmillan, R. Must be the guy; you know he's listed. You show the woman the address.

—Can you tell me where this is and how I get there?

It turns out there's nothing she'd like better than to tell you where that is and how you get there. With great enthusiasm she tells you which bus to get and where you need to get off and scribbles down exact directions to the road. Then she gives you another one of her precarious smiles.

Despite yourself, you're greatly cheered by this pathologically helpful woman. You walk down to the bus stop with something approaching a spring in your step. You're feeling young and intrepid and free. You're on an adventure! Get the baddies, win the girl. It's something you'll be able to tell people about in years to come. When they ask how you and Sally met, you'll be able to nod sagely and say, Ah, you see it all goes back to the Case of the Deadly Es.

At last, you're *doing* something.

The bus comes along quickly and you resist the temptation to ask the driver for a single to the Ecstasy Murderer's house, please. You sit in the back row and whistle softly to yourself.

It's Monday morning! Right about now Louie'll be phoning you at home to say he's had enough and you're fired. No doubt Harry'll be sorry to see you go, but he'll be pleased for you as well. Pleased, that is, until Mr Noggin shows up in a few minutes time and he realises there's no one else to do him. You start making a list of all the other awkward bastards who used to come in regularly who you'll never have to see again. You didn't realise this could be so much fun.

You're still well away in cloud cuckoo land when you notice the bus has stopped and the driver's waving at you.

—Here, mate, this is where you wanna get off.

—Oh yeah . . . cheers.

Macmillan's house is about two streets away from the bus stop, but with your helpful instructions you find it no trouble. And it's every bit as posh as Nick said. Hidden away behind a row of trees there's a well-kept garden and a large car park out the front and just a quick count of the windows shows there must be at least a dozen rooms inside. The guy runs an off licence doesn't he? You never knew you could get so rich selling booze: people round here must like a drink or two.

You sneak in through the gate and have a poke about in the garden. You're just about to go up to the house and start peering in through the windows when you notice a neighbour staring at you over the hedge.

—Uh, hello! you call over to her, trying to look as unsuspicious as possible. —I'm looking for Mr Macmillan.

—Well, you've got the right house . . .

Yes, you knew that.

—. . . But there's no one in right now. Mr Macmillan will be at his shop.

—Oh yes . . . yes, of course. Actually, I was here to see him on a business matter . . .

You regret this lie immediately. You're dirty, unshaven and you're wearing some of the shabbiest clothes from a particularly shabby wardrobe. To what extent do you look like you're here to see anyone on a business matter?

She doesn't laugh in your face, though, so you press on. —I was wondering if you could tell me where his off licence is.

She gives you some simple directions and you nod. Then, feeling suddenly bold, you start fishing. Well, you *are* supposed to be here on an investigation.

—So, this Macmillan guy, he's . . . he's all right, is he?

She looks puzzled. —Yes, he's fine as far as I know.

—No, I mean . . . you know . . .

She doesn't know. You're going to have to spell it out.

—What I mean is . . . I'm thinking of doing some business with the man, what I need to know is . . . you know . . . you're his neighbour an that . . . is he an upstanding kind of bloke?

She doesn't look as surprised as she ought to by this question. In fact, she looks almost pleased to be asked. —Oh no, he's a very nice chap, they keep themselves to themselves pretty much. Of course, he has his . . . peculiarities.

This sounds good. —Yes?

—Well, you may have heard about his, um, *meetings*, she says cautiously.

Meetings! Fucking hell! She knows!

—What meetings? you ask her, barely able to contain the excitement in your voice.

Then, infuriatingly, she starts backpedalling rapidly. —Oh, him and his wife just have a few strange friends and they get together from time to time, that's all, she says quickly. —It's really nothing. It's just that people round here, you know how it is . . . they do like to gossip.

Not her, though, obviously.

—What do they say about these meetings, then? you ask hopefully.

She shakes her head. —No, love, it wouldn't be fair of me to say. Honestly, there's nothing you need to worry about. He's a very good businessman is Mr Macmillan and that's all you need to know. You've no need to trouble yourself with old wives' chatter.

You could throttle her. But you restrain yourself and decide to let it be. You'll be back to talk to her again, though.

Your head's spinning as you walk up the road to Macmillan's place of work. It's true, then. These meetings happen and the neighbours know about them, or at least they suspect what's going on. How much do they know, you wonder. And does that make them accessories, if they keep quiet about it?

Shit, what if they're all in on it?

Suppose the old witch has phoned Macmillan to tell him you've been snooping around his house and now you're on your way down to his shop. Suppose he's waiting for you there with a club or a gun or something . . .

Your knees go trembly.

Fuck, don't even think about it. You're letting your paranoia run away with you. This is Yorkshire, not Twin fucking Peaks. Pull yourself together. Jesus . . .

The off licence is on a small parade of shops about ten minutes walk from Macmillan's house. You peer in through the window. Macmillan's there behind the counter; he's hardly recognisable from Nick's shaky photo, which you still have locked away at home, but it must be him. Podgy face, dark hair, perfectly groomed moustache . . . is this the face of a vigilante serial killer? He doesn't *look* too dangerous; he's not wielding a club or a gun at the moment, at least. Your plan, such as it is, is to go in, buy a couple of beers and try and get him talking. Even in your hyped-up state you're aware that this isn't the greatest plan ever, but it's all you can think of right now.

All you can think of until you notice the small handwritten sign stuck to the window. The sign that *almost* makes you suspect, just for a fleeting moment, that there might be a God. The sign that reads: FULL-TIME ASSISTANT REQUIRED. APPLY WITHIN.

You walk on up the street a bit to let this sink in. You don't believe your luck. This could get you close to Macmillan *and* sort out your money worries at the same time. By your reckoning you've got about three hundred quid in your bank account, which is loads more than you usually have and would normally be an excuse to go absolutely mental for a weekend, but it's been at the back of your mind all trip that it's not going to last you too long without a job.

And of course you're going to walk right into this job, aren't you? A dirty, unshaven, unkempt weird bloke of no fixed abode and with no experience whatsoever. It's going to be a piece of piss.

Fuck.

You check into a pub to get a Jack Daniels to calm your nerves and take stock of the situation. Which is this: you have just been handed a piece of unbelievable good fortune, but unfortunately, due to your circumstances you are unable to take advantage of it. *Fuck!* It's the kind of thing that could drive a man to drink, if you weren't there already.

You nip into the gents to see how bad the sartorial situation really is. It's bad. Your hair has started to go wispy in that unruly way that is supposed to look sexy on Hugh Grant but very definitely looks shite on you, especially as you haven't washed it in a week; you've got about three days' growth on your chin; your shirt has never seen an iron in its life; and your jeans have got a hole in one of the knees.

FUCK! You don't believe what a bastard your luck can be sometimes. You wonder if you ought to go and pick your bag up and have a proper wash and brush up somewhere. But that's going to take a while; what if someone else comes along and takes the job in the meantime? If you fuck up on this quest and you haven't taken advantage of this opportunity, you'll never forgive yourself. No, you're going to have to go for it as you are.

You run a sinkful of cold water and splash some on your face. It feels wonderful, and also unfamiliar. Jesus, when was the last time you had a wash? You shake your head and make a loud, neanderthal noise as you exhale. There, that feels better already. You're reminded, and somewhat cheered, by that scene in *The Hustler*. Minnesota Fats, looking a bit the worse for wear after shooting pool for twenty-four hours straight, goes into the bathroom for ten minutes and comes out fresh as a daisy while Fast Eddie keeps on drinking and loses the game. You and Nick once had a huge stand-up row about this scene.

—Well, it's bleedin obvious innit, he was saying. —He goes in there an does a couple of quick lines of whizz. No wonder he comes out so fuckin chirpy.

—Jesus, do you have to find drug references in absolutely *everything*, you'd shouted at him. —You'll be tellin me there's druggy overtones to Peter Pan next . . .

—Oh man, don't even start me on Peter Pan. A boy who flies? An never grows up?

Shit, you're going to miss Nick, it dawns on you. Because whichever way this goes, you can't see you and him being big mates again. You're going to miss having someone to talk to who's done all the same stuff as you. With Nick you never had to ask, Have you seen—? or Have you heard—? You could just plough straight in telling him what you thought about it.

You splash some water over your hair and tease it into some sort of shape. See, it's amazing what a bit of cold water can achieve. You're starting to feel a bit more confident about this now. You smooth down your stubble with some water and kid yourself it looks designer-ish and cool. A lot of the problems with your shirt are solved by simply tucking it in. Hey, at least you're wearing a shirt and not one of your Freak Brothers T-shirts. And your jeans . . . well, fuck the jeans; nobody's perfect.

You catch yourself one last time in the mirror before you go. Looking good, feeling good.

Actually you look like a twat with wet hair, but you can't afford any self-doubt right now.

You order up another Jack for courage, down it in one and walk back up to the off licence. Positive mental thinking, you keep telling yourself, that's all that's needed.

—Hi, I'm, uh, here about the job, you say as you walk through the door. Purposefully. Confidently. Yeah!

Macmillan looks surprised. —Oh. Uh . . . really? Jolly good. I thought I was being a bit hopeful putting that sign up. Well . . . I suppose we'd better have a little chat. We'll have to do it here at the till, I'm afraid. The lad who used to work here didn't show up this morning, got a new job you see, hence the vacancy. Course he didn't see any need to give me any notice or anything so I'm just here on my own today. Now . . . what's your name?

—Santini. John Santini.

Steady on. You're applying for a job at an offie, not the Secret Service.

—Roger Macmillan, he says, smiling and holding out a hand. Is that the smile of a killer? Are you about to shake the hand of a killer? Actually, he looks and sounds completely normal but you can't help feeling a sense of dread as you take his hand. You've never touched a real live psychopath before.

—You're a Londoner too, aren't you? he says.

—Am I? you blurt out before you can stop yourself. You cunt. —I mean, yes I am. Course I am.

What you meant was you hadn't noticed he was a Londoner. You haven't been up here long enough for a Southern accent to stand out.

—Whereabouts in London? he asks, still smiling.

—Oh, all over really. Last place I lived in was just off the Holloway Road. Highbury.

He nods. —And when did you move up here?

—Uh . . . recently. This weekend, in fact . . .

—This weekend?

—Yeah . . . I had a bust up with my girlfriend . . . you know . . .

You steel yourself for some heavy-duty lying if he probes any further, but all he's interested in is how long you're staying. —You are looking for a permanent job, aren't you? I can't afford someone else who's going to vanish at a moment's notice.

—Oh yeah, yeah! you say quickly. —We were thinking of

movin up here anyway, me girlfriend an me. In fact that was one of the reasons we split up, she kept wanting to delay the move. So if we get back together, which is pretty unlikely to be honest, it'll be up here, not down there.

Fantastic bullshit. You're so proud of yourself. Macmillan seems to buy every word of it.

—So, have you got any experience of the wine trade, John?

—Uh, no . . . not exactly. I'm just looking for a job really. But I do know a lot about drinking . . .

This didn't come out exactly the way you wanted it to.

—What I mean is, I know a lot about alcohol . . . no, I mean . . . Shit, how *do* you say this?

Macmillan starts to laugh. There's no way out of the hole you've dug for yourself so you join him in laughing. And as you do so, you notice the whisky on your breath.

There are a few more mundane questions, a brief description of the job, which also sounds pretty mundane, and then Macmillan holds out his hand again.

—Well, thanks for coming in to see me, John. The Job Centre is sending a couple of people over this afternoon so I'll see them and then I'll call you this evening, okay? Now, what's your number?

—Uh, I don't have a place to stay just yet.

—Of course, you've only just come up, haven't you. Which hotel are you staying in, then? I'll call you there.

You feel it probably wouldn't look too good if you told him that actually you'd been staying in a hippie's rusty old Fiat up to now, so you give him the name of the White Horse. You just hope they still have a room free when you get back there.

They do. In fact, the Stepford Receptionist seems completely enthralled by the fact you want to take a room there. She asks you to fill out a form *sir*, and gives you a key *sir*, and shows you where the bar is *sir*, and wishes you a pleasant stay *sir*. You could get used to this.

You go up to your room and, having nothing better to do, go straight to bed.

You wake up around five. You could actually do with a couple more hours sleep, but you reckon Macmillan might call soon so you struggle out of the sheets. You go downstairs and go to leave a message at reception that you're expecting a phone call.

Sadly your friend in the flowery dress is off duty and has been replaced by her diametric opposite, a bored-looking bloke, probably a few years younger than you, wearing a faded Nirvana T-shirt over the top of a dirty-white long-sleeved sweatshirt. You fucking hate people who do that.

—Uh, my name's Santini. I'm in Room 12. Listen, I'm expecting a phone call this evening . . .

—Yeah? he says, yawning.

—I'll be in the bar, so can you let me know when it comes through?

—We-ell . . . whereabouts in the bar?

—I don't know.

How big is the fucking bar?

—I'll make sure I'm easy to find, okay? Just put the call through.

You walk away before he has time to protest. When you get through to the bar, it turns out to be big enough to hold about half a dozen people.

And one of the ones already there is Bryn.

—John! How are you, mate?

—Yeah, good.

—Man, you look like you just got out of bed, he says.

—Uh, yeah . . . yeah, I did.

He's impressed. —Shit. How do you do that? I wish I could sleep like that. Man, I like to sleep . . .

—Yeah . . . I hadn't slept for a couple of days when I got in your car. Sorry, I guess that's kinda rude if you're hitch-hiking, to fall asleep straight away.

You get yourself a pint and sit down at the table opposite Bryn.

—So tell me about yourself, mate, he goes. —I told you all about my job yesterday an it thrilled you so much you fell asleep. So what do you do?

—Just been for an interview today, you tell him. —Waiting to hear back from them now, as it happens

You elaborate a bit on the story you started to tell Macmillan about leaving your girlfriend because she wouldn't move North with you. The more you say, the more wildly implausible it sounds, but what the fuck, you're never going to see this guy again. When you start to tell him about the interview, though, you realise just how unlikely it is that you're going to get this job. God, you fucked that interview up, didn't you? You dressed like a tramp, you were drinking beforehand, you gave some ridiculous answers ('Oh, am I from London?' You gormless wanker) and you let on that you're staying at a hotel, so he'll worry about whether you're going to stick at the job.

Shit.

You don't have time to dwell on this, though, because Bryn has decided that he's bored of talking about you and wants to talk about himself again. It turns out that he's had a great day. Not only are there loads of jewellery shops in Leeds but they nearly all liked his stuff. Oh good. You're so pleased. He goes into details about one of his favourite pieces and you start to drift off.

You stare glumly at your warm, flat beer and wonder how Bryn would take it if you dozed off on him again. You're snapped out of it, though, by Kurt Cobain from reception.

—Hey you, number 12. That call's come through for you.

Bryn pauses mid-sentence. —Fuckin hell, mate. That must be it.

He gives you a thumbs-up and wishes you good luck.

As you walk through to the phone, knowing the inevitable outcome, you wonder how you're going to take it from here. You can't very well go hanging around Macmillan's off licence, or his house, now he knows your face. What were you thinking of, walking in there like that and giving him your real name? All you've done now is blow your cover. Shit, you didn't really think this through, did you?

You pick up the phone with trepidation.

Macmillan sounds cheerful at the other end. —John, I have some good news for you . . .

Fucking hell. You don't believe it.

—I'm pleased to say I'm able to offer you the job . . .

Wow, maybe the interview wasn't so bad after all. Actually, looking back on it, you can see how he might have been swayed by your happy-go-lucky naïvety, and just maybe he thought some of your answers were supposed to be jokes.

—The candidates from the Job Centre didn't show up in the end, so it had to be you . . .

Okay. Whatever

—Now, do tell me you're going to stay with us long term.

—Oh yeah, yeah, sure, you splutter. —Course. No problem.

—Good. Well, shall I see you tomorrow then, about ten thirty?

You agree. This sounds like a very civilised time to start work to you.

—Oh, and John . . .

—Yes?

—No need for a shirt and tie or anything, but, you know, a little smartness wouldn't go amiss.

—Oh, uh, yeah . . . fine. See you tomorrow, then.

You go back into the bar with a grin so big Bryn doesn't have to ask you how it went. He suggests getting a few drinks in to celebrate, but you remind him that you're celebrating the fact that you have to get up and go to work tomorrow morning. Instead you go find a McDonald's where you feel flush enough to buy the two of you two Big Mac's each.

Later on you phone Sally for a little gloat. She's not in; round at Nick's no doubt. But it's her you want to speak to, not that bastard journalist ex-friend of yours, so you hang up and phone back when you've prepared a message. A very well-prepared message as it turns out. You even end up writing it down before you call, for Christ's sake. You tell her that out of concern for her safety you've decided that it's high time someone did some proper investigation on this case. Otherwise she and Nick are going to be running for the rest of their lives. So you've come up here, you're now working undercover at Macmillan's shop and you'll let her know when the whole thing's wrapped up. Should be in a few days, all being well.

As you hang up, you burst out laughing. You can't remember feeling this good in years. You imagine her coming home from Nick's, playing the message and realising the hideous mistake she's made. Oh yeah, she's going to be feeling pretty fucking stupid the next few days. Who's the brave and glamorous one now? Eh?

And deluding yourself into near-ecstasy, you drift back off into what has become your natural state just recently. Sleep.

∫

After a satisfying meal of two of his baby nieces roasted with seasonal vegetables – seasonal, that is, to the planet of the Ancients on the other side of the Galaxy and lovingly recreated by the ship's computer – Captain Achten went to visit his prisoners.

The procedure to remove their positive emotions was already under way. The one who appeared to be their leader was strapped into a chair and Reduction Rays were being passed over him. Later, these rays would be passed over the whole planet below them and an entire population would be subjected to the same process.

This was good: the crew had enjoyed no fresh emotions to feed on since they had left the Serpicus Six system. Young were all right as far as they went, but nothing could beat the taste of someone else's happiness.

The officer who was operating the ray looked concerned, though.

'It doesn't seem to be *extracting* anything, Captain!'

Achten approached the man in the chair. 'Tell me, what is your *name?*' he asked through the translator.

Captain Midnight told him.

'Ah, so you share the same *rank* as me!'

'We have *nothing* in common!' said Captain Midnight through gritted teeth.

'Well Captain, it seems as though you are *resisting* our Reduction Ray. At the moment you are being *successful*. But I warn you, they will *penetrate* eventually, nothing can resist them *forever*, and the less you resist, the less *painful* it will be!'

'I am resisting *nothing*! I am too *weary* to resist!'

Achten turned to his officer. 'What, then, is the *problem*?'

The officer shook his head. 'According to the readings, the rays are extracting *nothing* from this man because he has *nothing* to extract. He possesses *no positive emotions*!'

'The readings must be *incorrect*! No one can *block* their emotions so successfully!'

While this exchange had been taking place, Zanzi had been working on the Captain's bonds with her laser eyes. As Achten and his officer peered at their machinery, trying to make some sense of its readings, Captain Midnight broke free. Achten received a sharp kick to the stomach. OUFFF! The officer got a smack on the head. KRRACCKKK! Then Captain Midnight grabbed Achten's weapon and blasted both the Ancients before they could come round. WHOOOSSSSSHHHH!

Without delay, he released the force field that was holding his colleagues prisoner and barked instructions to them. 'Okay, we've got to move *quickly* before they find out we've bumped off their *Captain*! We're going down to the engine room again! I think it's better if we travel as a *team* from now on!'

There were four new Ancients working in the engine room in exactly the same positions as the previous ones. The alarms were just going off as the Midnight Patrol burst through the engine-room doors and made quick work of the four unsuspecting aliens.

'Come on, we don't have much *time*!' muttered Captain Midnight as he punched a self-destruct sequence into the computer. The computer wouldn't accept it. Not without Captain Achten's personal authorisation.

'Okay, we're just going to have to *blast* the engines! Matrix, I reckon we'll have about *six minutes* once we start firing! Can you transport us back to the shuttle and pull us *away* in that time?'

'It'll be tight, but I think so, Captain!'

'Okay, let's *do it*!'

'But Captain,' Matrix continued, 'I think there's one thing you should know . . .'

'What is it, Matrix? We don't have much *time!*'

'According to the ship's computer records, a *pod* has already been *released*. There are apparently five crew members on the *planet surface.*'

Captain Midnight said nothing. There was a look of grim determination on his face. No one had said this mission would be easy.

They began firing.

PWCHHWCCHHHWWCCCHHHHWWWCCCCHHH-HHSSSTTTTT!

KRACK.

BOOOOOOOMMMM!

Back on their shuttle, the Midnight Patrol watched the mothership as they raced away.

BOOOOMMM!

PPOOOOWWWWW!

SPLAAAAAAMMMMM!

The fallout from the explosion was visible in the Earth's atmosphere. The five Ancients on the surface certainly saw it. The *X-Files* creeps went beserk.

∫

You settle into the new job without too much bother. Of course you're slightly nervous about working for someone you suspect to be a murdering psychopath, but apart from that it's a piece of piss. As with all the other shitty, menial, dead-end jobs you've done, this one has its good points (discounted alcohol: mmm, don't those two words sound good together) and its bad points (that civilised starting time is balanced by some late nights; three times a week you have to work until eleven and you're surprised to discover that even a nice neighbourhood like this has its share of nutters who hang around outside offies at night).

Roger – oh yes, it's Roger now – helps you find a flat. At first you think this is unreasonably kind of him, but then you figure he has his own motives. If you've put down a month's deposit on a place, you're less likely to piss off back to London at a moment's notice. You're reluctant initially to fork out such a big wedge; after all, you're still supposed to be paying rent on your place with Richie and Tony. But when you find out what a laughably small amount they're asking for, and when Macmillan offers to lend you some for the deposit, it seems churlish to refuse. You may be up here for a few weeks and it'll be cheaper in the long run than staying in a hotel. And if you end up losing your deposit, it'll be worth it to get Sally back. Just about.

So you move into a small room in a flat owned by a friend of his, a woman called Angela Swaine. You wonder how you're going to get on here. Living with a woman in her early fifties – your best guess – is going to be very different to living with your previous flatmates. In the end, however, it proves to be academic. Angela is hardly ever there and if she is, she tends to be slumped in her favourite armchair with a bottle of white wine and Billie Holliday on the stereo and not really looking for conversation. She seems to be too rich to work and spends her days in cafés and museums and lunching with gentleman friends and sometimes visiting them in their houses. All this she tells you about briefly over breakfast or just before going out again in the evening, skirting mercifully over the juicy bits with an elaborate wink. And she's your mother's age! It strikes you that she's the coolest woman you've ever met.

Towards the end of the week you're beginning to wonder if anything is going to turn up. You're bored already by your job and you miss having someone like Harry to piss about with during the quiet moments. The rest of the staff are all part-time and seem to do one shift a week each, so it's going to take a while to get to know them. You'd do your nut if you thought you were going to do this job for very long, if you thought you'd ended up in yet another shit job with no prospects. So you have to keep reminding yourself that you're not *really* working in an offie; really you're an undercover investigator. On the Thursday night you follow Macmillan home and hang around outside his house for a bit, but you can see all he's doing is watching TV with his wife and you're scared that neighbour of his will spot you again. So you go home after about twenty minutes feeling foolish and depressed and, not having anything else to do, you have a rake through Angela's cupboards and drawers while she's out.

Then, the following morning you get a break. While Macmillan is out at the bank there's a phone call for him. An angry-sounding Scottish woman called Maggie says she's calling about this weekend and demands that Roger call her back immediately.

—Can I just take a note of your number . . . ? you start to ask.

—He's got my bloody number, she snaps.

When you tell Macmillan about this, he looks anxious. —Oh

yes, there's a, uh, trade fair up in Scotland this weekend that I'm supposed to be going to . . .

You look at him sympathetically. This is one of the worst lies you've ever heard.

He knows it. He sits down heavily and lets out a deep sigh. —No there isn't, there's no trade fair . . .

No. Really?

—I kept telling Ralph, the chap who used to have your job, I kept telling him lots of lies, but I don't think I can be bothered any more. John . . . can you keep a secret?

You nod, although it's irrelevant now. You know what his secret is.

—No, I mean *really* keep a secret. I need to be able to trust you. Even once you've met my wife, who's a lovely woman who I'm sure you'll get on with, I need to be able to trust you to keep this secret.

He seems so wound up you get a glimmer of hope. Maybe he's about to confess to the whole thing: the Meetings, the murders, the pills, the whole lot. Maybe the stress on his conscience has just been too much and now he's cracked and is about to open his soul to a relative stranger . . .

You nod some more. —Yeah, I can keep a secret, you say eagerly.

—I'm having an affair, he says.

You can't help but look a little disappointed. Oh yeah, that. You knew *that*.

—She calls me at work, obviously, so Pat, my wife, won't find out. So I'm sorry, you may have to field a few of these calls. She's a charming woman and I love her very much, but she can be quite demanding. And it's not easy, you know, her being up there, me being down here . . .

Stop. You can feel your heart breaking.

—But she's married too, you know. And she's got a job up there, she's a lawyer, so she's got her other commitments. I don't get to see her every time I want to and I don't complain. She's even got a little kid, Shona; she's about two and a half now . . .

You don't care!

Thankfully a customer comes in and he shuts the fuck up. You go to serve the bloke, while Macmillan shuffles into the back to phone his angry lover. When the customer's gone you stack some shelves near the store room so you can hear what's going on. Macmillan's getting a hard time, but he's staying firm.

—No, I can't come up this weekend . . . no, you can't come down . . . I told you . . . you *know* why . . . no, not next weekend either, I've already told you . . . look, Maggie, these meetings are important to me . . . yes, of course you're important too . . . it's not a question of more or less important . . . no it isn't . . . no it isn't . . . no it—

There. That's what you've been waiting to hear. There's a meeting this weekend and then another one next weekend. Fucking hell, they must be stepping up their activity.

A couple of hours later Macmillan gets another call which he looks kind of shady about. While restacking the already amazingly well-stacked bottled lager shelves, you distinctly hear him saying:—Yeah, okay, Howard, tomorrow seven thirty, see you there . . .

There it is on a plate. Tomorrow, Saturday. Seven thirty. The only thing you don't know is exactly where. Your heart starts pounding, you've got butterflies in your stomach. You're *this* close now. *This* close to finding out what all this shit is about.

You and Macmillan both knock off at five o'clock on Saturday, leaving two part-timers for the evening. You get straight on a bus into town and head for a mini-cab place you noticed on your first night here. Looking as official as you can, you stroll in and ask how much it would be to 'hire a man' for the evening.

The guy behind the desk shoots you a 'don't fuck with me' look.

Perhaps 'hire a man' wasn't exactly the phrase you were looking for. It sounded good when you were practising it earlier on.

—Look, mate, I'm doing some surveillance work, yeah? An I need a car an a driver I can trust, someone discreet, who won't ask any questions. Can you help or not?

You imagined that this would sound impossibly cool, but the guy looks like he's about to piss himself laughing.

—Hey Sammy, he calls over to his mate in a lazy drawl. —Guy here needs a car for the evening for some . . . ?

—Surveillance work, you say.

—Yeah. Surveillance work. You up for that?

Sammy's laid spread out on the threadbare sofa the other side of the room. His face is entirely hidden by a turban, shades, a big, bushy beard and a pair of enormous headphones, through which you can hear a rapid, jittery clickety-click of drums even at this distance. Fuck knows how loud that sounds in his head.

Of course he can't hear his mate calling to him, so the guy starts waving his hands and, when that fails, picks up an apple core and throws it at him.

Sammy peels off the headphones and shades. Underneath, and despite that beard, you reckon he looks about twenty years old. The guy behind the desk gives him the request again and he nods okay. They quote you a mileage rate and a waiting rate which sound pretty reasonable.

—I got a maximum of sixty quid, you tell them. —So you got to tell me when we get near that an take me home.

Sammy nods again and leads you out to the car. You thought your driver would be kind of excited by this prospect; they can't get many requests like this, surely? But this guy looks like he's having a tough time staying awake.

He drives you up to Macmillan's house and you park up the street, where you'll have a good view when he leaves. It's shortly before six, so you reckon you'll have quite a wait yet. Sammy settles back and puts on his shades again. You follow suit. And the two of you sit there, in silence, looking like comedy spies from a sixties caper movie. You think of Nick and Carl sitting outside this house for the best part of a week. Christ, they must have gone out of their minds.

Once again, this isn't going exactly as you thought it would. You figured your driver would be intrigued and ask you all sorts of stuff about who you were trailing and why, to which you would have to shake your head and say sternly:—Hey, no questions, that was part of the deal.

But Sammy's just sitting there, staring out in his own private world. Bastard. He's spoiling your fun. Eventually, you're the first one to break. Inevitable really; you have the attention span of a goldfish on speed and are completely unable to cope with your own company unless there's a TV, a comic or some music involved.

—So, you been driving for long, Sammy? you ask him.

—Coupla years, he says, without looking over at you.

—Must be interesting, yeah?

He frowns. —No, not really.

—But jobs like this, you go on. —They must be kinda interesting . . .

Now he looks over to you. —What, sitting outside a bloke's house, doing nothing? Yeah, fuckin riveting.

—But *anything* could happen.

—Yeah. Or nothing could.

Jesus, what's the matter with this guy? There were more positive vibes knocking around on the *Titanic*.

—So who is it we're supposed to be watching? he asks at long last.

—Hey, no questions, you say triumphantly. —That was part of the deal.

—Okay, he shrugs and turns back to staring out of the windscreen.

Bollocks. This guy is *so* frustrating.

—Look, these people are dangerous an anything could happen, okay? you say irritably.

—Yeah, whatever, he says. —But if they're who I think they are, not much is gonna happen.

You're taken aback by this so you get him to repeat it.

—I said, if they're who I think they are—

—What do you mean, if they're who you think they are? Who the fuck do you think we're watching? The fuckin Rotary Club?

—Well, I dunno . . . I just kinda assumed it was that Satanist group that meets round here somewhere.

What? What fucking Satanist group?

Okay, okay, calm down. Play it cool, you'll get more out of him that way.

—Uh, yeah . . . yeah, it could be, you say, trying to compose yourself. —What do you know about them, then?

—You know, just what was in the papers whenever it was, last year sometime. There was this group of middle-aged people who met up somewhere round here an' they were into some kind of devil worship or something. I didn't think anyone gave a fuck about it any more. You know, whatever it is they do, they do it behind closed doors

—What you saying? Course we give a fuck, you tell him, winging it madly. —It's fuckin devil worship, isn't it?

—Okay, whatever, Sammy says wearily, and the bastard hunches down in his seat again to show you just how uninterested he is in your conversation.

You're going to have to press him. —So what's your problem then?

—Look, man, I can tell you're not from up here, he says. —People up here, we don't give a shit bout this kind of stuff. There's so many religious fuckin headcases around, people have learned to be tolerant. An you should too. Even the papers were forced to admit, these were nice, ordinary people who just had a weird kind of hobby. No bother to no one, though. So, you know, just leave em alone, man.

—Actually, it's more serious than you think, you tell him in what you hope is an air of mysterious authority. Although, as is so often the case, you merely end up sounding like a pompous twat. Don't kid yourself: this guy's got your number.

Shortly before seven thirty, the Macmillans leave their house. Immediately your heart starts pumping again. You forget things haven't been going entirely to plan with Sammy and let yourself get carried away with excitement.

—Okay, you whisper to him. —Follow them ve-ery carefully.

Sammy perks up a bit now he's got something to do. He takes pride in his driving, staying unobtrusively two or three cars behind the Macmillans and jumping red lights and roundabouts when he has to. They drive about eight miles further out of town and stop outside a large house. The house has its own parking but it's already full of cars, so they have to park on the street. Expertly, Sammy drives by and stops further on up the street, where you're relatively inconspicuous but can still see what's going on.

—Okay. What now? he says, switching off the engine.

What now indeed? You haven't got a fucking clue. You didn't plan this out beyond here. You just kind of hoped that if and when you got to this stage, it would become obvious what to do. But it isn't. It isn't obvious at all.

—Uh . . . we're just gonna wait awhile. See if anyone else shows up, you tell him unconvincingly.

Sure enough, a few minutes later another car pulls up and a large man gets out. After that, though, nothing.

Half an hour drips by and you're both starting to get itchy feet. Sammy's stroking his beard, looking deeply unimpressed. Shit, you can't just sit here all fucking night. You've got to do *something*. But what exactly? You've no idea and you can't concentrate with this cunt just sitting there like that.

—Okay, you stay here, I'm gonna check it out, you say, just for an excuse to get out of the car. —An be ready to make a quick getaway if necessary, you add dramatically.

You walk up to the house, madly thinking things over. You're not sure what to make of this devil-worship crap. Your new boss doesn't stike you as a follower of Beelzebub. But then neither does he strike you as a psychotic mass murderer. And there's *something* going on here.

As quietly as you can, you creep around the garden. You can't see anything that's going on inside; the curtains have all been drawn even though it's still just about light. Still, that's okay. Means they won't be able to see you either. Now, if you could just *hear* something going on inside, that would be enough, wouldn't it? If you could hear some kind of diabolical chanting, or black mass being said, or the happy sound of a virgin being slaughtered . . . who are you trying to kid? Whatever they're doing in there, they're not going to make it audible to the outside world. No, somehow you've got to get yourself into that house and see what's going down with your own eyes.

Of course, what a great plan. All you do is knock on the door, pretending to be a Jehovah's Witness or encyclopedia salesman or pizza delivery boy or something and they're bound to let you in and show you around, aren't they? And if they're dressed in robes and splattered with sacrificial blood, you'll know they're Satanists; and if they're dressed in white coats and surrounded by evil-smelling chemistry apparatus, you'll know they're concocting their latest deadly pill. Simple.

You fucking shit-for-brains.

You sit down on the patio steps in this huge garden, exhausted by the futility of all this. Why didn't you think of some kind of plan before you came all the way out here?

But what kind of plan could you have thought of? You're a fucking hairdresser, after all, not a private investigator. How many devious plans were you likely to come up with?

Just as you're hitting the depths of despair, you look up and catch the eye of an old geezer passing by on the pavement who's looking at you suspiciously. He looks away quickly and walks on. Fuck! You forgot for a moment that not only is this a completely futile situation, it's also an extremely dangerous one. Glancing behind you to see if there's any movement, you march out through the front gates and back up to the car.

—So, we need to make a quick getaway or what? asks Sammy.

—No, you sigh, getting in beside him. —Just, uh . . .

You have no idea what you want to do now.

—How much we got on the clock so far? you ask him.

There isn't a 'clock' as such so he just plucks a number at random. —Thirty, he says.

So, big shot. What are you going to do now?

—Fuck it, Sammy, it's Saturday night. You know any good clubs?

—Yeah, sure, he says, brightening up. —I'm your man. What kind of place you wanna go to?

You think for a moment. —Drum an bass, you decide. —But, you know, some cool, mellow drum an bass.

—Okay, I got the picture, he says.

And freed suddenly from stealth and discretion, he slams the car into gear, spins it round a hundred and eighty degrees, burning rubber and screeching, and shoots off back into town.

You're surprised, but pleased, when he parks the cab in a dingy backstreet and you realise he's planning to come in with you.

—Fuck it, he says. —Boss ain't expectin me back till the early hours. I got a couple of hours. I can enjoy myself.

Once inside the place, however, he loses you pretty quickly. He seems to know a lot of people here and you don't try to keep up with him. You don't mind. This place fits the bill you gave him exactly so you're happy to wander around on your own.

There's a permanent waft of dry ice which mixes with the

cigarette and reefer smoke to make you feel like you're standing in the middle of a cloud and the combination gives off a heady smell. The place is unlit apart from a row of piercing blue lights at either end of the room and an occasional strobe which gets busy when the music does. It's precisely the kind of laid-back jungle you felt would be so good for your soul right now: something about the way those gentle melodies are offset by the insistent madcap rhythms. It is, in its own perverse way, soothing. You get a beer and stand at the back of the hall, nodding your head and watching the other people in here throwing their strange shapes, and pretty soon you've shaken off your sense of failure from the evening. It's okay, you tell yourself, you made some progress. You now know for sure that Macmillan, for all his pleasant, normal outward appearance, is up to something dodgy. And you know that common knowledge has it that he's taking part in some kind of Satanic rite at these meetings of his. All you need is some shred of tangible evidence, something you can take back to Sally and say:—Look, there you are, there's nothing to worry about, you stupid bitch. Now come home with me.

At the other end of the hall is a small stage and shortly after you get there, a small group of people dressed in black shuffle on to it. The DJ cuts the music out, there's a huge roar from the crowd and then the band strikes up. It's a similar kind of vibe: what Nick used to refer to, with a straight face so far as you could tell, as 'intelligent' drum and bass. The crowd loves it. The whole room has shifted up a gear, throwing hands in the air, whooping and yelling during the breaks in the beat. You get carried along with it, your legs and feet lock into the groove and before you know it, you find yourself with your hands above your head, pointing at the stage. The band themselves are hidden behind their banks of machines and perhaps it's just as well: people in dance bands can look kind of uncomfortable on stage. It's hard to make flicking a few switches on a mixing desk look as dramatic as playing a screaming lead guitar solo or scrunching up your eyes and belting out a soul classic from the heart. You can't really start playing a sampler with your teeth, or smashing up a synth, setting fire to it and tossing the remains out into the audience. There's not that sense of theatre you get at rock gigs. All you can see here are a few heads rocking behind their keyboards and the occasional arm raised aloft, which is always greeted by a cheer from the crowd. But you don't need stuff to look at with music as intense as this; the tension's all there in the way the drums crash in and out and the samples repeat and repeat until you feel like they've been hammered into your brain. Then, just when you think you can't take it any more it all cuts out and you're left with a piano pattern, or a flute solo, or maybe just the simple sound of birds singing, that sounds impossibly beautiful.

After what seems to you like a ridiculously short set, the band shuffle off in much the same way they shuffled on, as if they're embarrassed to be there and are desperately trying to sneak off before anyone notices them. All apart from one guy, who comes to the front of the stage and starts applauding the audience the way footballers do at the end of a match, acknowledging the audience's contribution to the event. That's something else you don't get at rock gigs. There's a moment's respite while people move about and take stock of what they've just seen and heard. Then there's an announcement that the club has a special guest tonight, a top-name female drum and bass DJ from London. You've heard this woman play before and she's fucking awesome. This is some place your cabbie has brought you to.

On your way back to the dancefloor you spot him standing up against a wall and go over.

—Fuckin top place, this, you tell him.

He smiles and hands you a toke of his spliff.

—You heard this DJ before? She's somethin else, you say.

He shrugs. He doesn't seem too interested in who the DJ is. It's all one big groove to him.

—Listen man, he leans over and shouts into your ear. —You planning on being up here for a while?

You nod. —Yeah. Few weeks probably.

—Okay. You need anything, you come to me . . .

You look puzzled.

—You need some draw?

Right, that's what he means. You think about it. —Yeah, I guess I could use some.

You left your tiny stash back in London and right now cannabis seems like an entirely wonderful thing.

—Es? he asks.

—Nah, don't do Es no more, you hear yourself saying. When did you decide that? Which part of your brain made the decision?

—Okay, I'll drop by this week, he says and he drifts back off to talk to some of his friends.

You spend the rest of the evening on your own, but you stay late and have a cool time. You could get used to this place. You're not at all worried by the fact you've achieved exactly sweet fuck all with your little adventure tonight. In fact you feel quite good about yourself.

But then sometimes you have such low expectations of yourself, it would be impossible *not* to feel good.

By Monday afternoon the feeling has long worn off. You're tired, depressed, bored and your worst nightmare has just walked in through the door.

—I see. So this is what you call 'doing business', is it? comes a sneering voice.

Macmillan is out somewhere. He seems to have even more unspecified Errands than Louie did. You're sitting with your feet up on the counter, reading a Spider-man comic and drinking a bottle of Rolling Rock, which, naturally, you'll depreciate when you do your stock count later today.

—I'm sorry. Do I know you?

You know damn well who it is, but you're going to see if you can get away with it.

—You know exactly who I am, she says firmly.

You're not going to get away with it.

—I saw you last week poking around in Mr Macmillan's garden and you told me you were about to 'do business' with him. Now I find that you were merely looking for a job as his sales boy.

Sales boy. Fuck off. You're a Retail Executive; says so on your contract.

—I suppose I should have known from your general demeanour that you weren't a serious businessman, she continues hoity-toitily.

Well fuck you, saggy-tits, is what you want to tell her, but somehow you've got to bring this old bag round on to your side.

You start to protest that you were making perfectly reasonable enquiries, but she interrupts:

—*And* I saw you again yesterday afternoon, knocking on doors up and down our street, no doubt asking some more of your fanciful questions.

Bollocks. You *were* knocking on doors yesterday, mainly so you could feel you were doing *something* to build on the escapades of Saturday night. You didn't turn up much, certainly nothing concrete, but it was interesting to hear how many of them came out with the 'Oh yeah, I believe they're devil-worshippers actually' line. You'd've thought people would have objected a little more strongly to their near-neighbours summoning up the Lord of Darkness on a regular basis, but these folk – all middle-aged, well-to-do like the Macmillans – seemed to think it was funny more than anything. Maybe Sammy was right; maybe people round here simply are super-tolerant. Whatever, you'd felt pleased with your efforts. Nick and Carl had talked to some of the Macmillans' neighbours, hadn't they? And they hadn't uncovered any of this stuff.

You didn't realise the Old Witch had seen you, though. Now you've got a real headache. If she lets on to Macmillan that you've been asking questions about him, what excuse are you going to give?

—Well, surely I got a right to find out a bit about an employer, you begin unconvincingly. —Specially when there's as many weird stories floating around as there are bout this guy . . .

—I don't mind you asking the questions. What I object to is the fact you lied to *me*.

You shrug. If that's really all she's worried about, that's cool. —Sorry, you say. —I guess I'm just embarrassed bout being a lowly sales boy.

She stops rabbiting. Perhaps the mad old bat has accepted this.

—So are they true then? you ask her, pushing your luck just slightly.

—Are what true?

—These stories bout the Macmillans. You know . . . the weird ones.

She takes a long, deep breath. —Well, as you know I don't like to gossip . . .

Course not. Heaven forbid.

—. . . but have you seen the film *Rosemary's Baby?*

What? They've got a pregnant Mia Farrow held hostage up there?

—I, uh, dunno. What do you mean? you ask.

She leans towards you. —People say . . . there's a *child* up there.

Right, that's it. She's off her fucking head.

—But as I say, she carries on breezily. —It's really nothing you need worry too much about. They keep themselves very much to themselves.

Oh, so *apart* from the fact they're rearing the spawn of Lucifer, they're essentially decent people . . .

—Can I get you anything? you ask her, smiling sweetly. Now that you've noticed that she's clinically insane, and therefore presumably Macmillan wouldn't believe anything she told him anyway, you want her the fuck out of here as quickly as possible. She's giving you the creeps.

Rosemary's fucking Baby . . .

—Actually, I came in for a bottle of Gordon's.

You reach it down immediately. She takes out her purse but you wave it away.

—On the house, you say, winking at her smarmily. —Just not a word to the boss bout yesterday afternoon, yeah?

Now you're tapping your nose with your finger.

—Okie doke, she says, and now she's tapping her nose too. —You won't tell me any more lies, though?

—Promise, you say solemnly.

You reckon you've won her over.

It's an interesting theft you've got to report later, however: one bottle of Gordon's and one bottle of Rolling Rock. That's precision shoplifting; will Macmillan buy it? Perhaps you need to sink a few more bottles while he's out to make the whole thing seem credible.

So where exactly have you got to with this great investigation of yours? The one that's going so well?

Absolutely fucking nowhere, if you're honest with yourself. Your new boss is up to something dodgy, but you've got nothing you can actually pin on him, beyond the fact he's having a bit of how's your father behind his wife's back. The bottom line is you've got to get into the next meeting this Saturday, otherwise you'll just have a repeat of last Saturday night and you'll never find out what's going on.

But how do you do it? How do you go about getting yourself into a meeting like this?

A couple of days after your run-in with the Old Witch, the break comes. A large, bearded man comes into the shop. You recognise him immediately as the man you saw going into the meeting on Saturday night. Your heart leaps.

It's clear he's not come in here to buy alcohol. He comes straight up to the counter. —Is Rog about? he goes.

Macmillan hears him and comes out of the store room. —George! he half-shouts and the two men exchange a handshake in which you're sure you can hear their bones crack.

—So how's, uh . . . what's this week's one called? asks Macmillan.

—Rachel, says George, pretending to be more pissed off than he really is. —And it's been two months I'll have you know.

He gives Macmillan a playful punch on the shoulder. Macmillan punches him back. This is male bonding gone into orbit. You're terrified they're suddenly going to get naked and wrestle.

George is quite an intimidating bloke. He's huge, but flabby rather than seriously fat; there's muscle underneath there somewhere. And pretty much every visible piece of flesh is covered with hair, greasy wet hair that sticks to his skin. He reminds you of Oliver Reed in *Castaway*.

—Actually it's Rachel I want to talk about, he says. —Wondering if I might bring her along on Saturday night?

You look over at Macmillan. He's giving George an alarmed, 'not in front of the lad' stare.

George blunders on regardless. —I've spoken to her about it and she's fine, she shares our, er . . . philosophy.

This is it, you suddenly realise, this is your chance.

—I don't know, says Macmillan uneasily. —I don't know what the others would think . . .

This is your chance! Say something now!

—Come on Rog, I can't ask everybody in turn. It's your party, if you say it's okay, I'm sure everyone will accept that. And she's a very nice girl . . .

Say something now, or you'll never sleep with Sally again!

—Well, I suppose it would be okay . . . Uh, John, could you go out back—

—I wanna come too! you blurt out.

Macmillan stares at you in horror. —You *what?*

Shit. No turning back now.

—Your meeting . . . I wanna come.

There's no answer.

—Please, you add.

—Do you know what we do at these meetings? George says finally.

—Yeah, you say confidently.

—John . . . *how* do you know?

Only one thing you can say to this. —Uh . . . your neighbour. She told me.

They both look horrified.

—Oh my God, says George. —She's been looking through the bloody window . . .

Macmillan shakes his head. —She can't have been, I don't see how . . . Look, John, I really don't think it's a good idea—

You can't let him refuse now.

—You just said this Rachel could go an she's never been before.

—He's got a point, says George. Suddenly you're warming to him. —It'd be easier on both of them if there were two new people at once.

Macmillan still looks unhappy.

—You are broadminded, aren't you John? George asks you directly.

—Yeah. Course I am. Wouldn't be asking otherwise, would I? An I totally share your philosophy too.

Whatever the fuck that philosophy is.

Macmillan still looks unhappy, but you think he may be about to break.

—Okayyy, he says unhappily. —If you're sure you want to come.

Bingo.

—Yeah, I'm sure . . . thanks.

—Right, well, seven thirty, Saturday night at our house then.

Yes! You want to punch the air and dance round the room. But you manage to stop yourself.

Well done. You just got yourself invited to a party that's *either* a group of moral psychopaths planning their next murder, *or* it's a group of Children of the Devil meeting for prayer. Have a great Saturday night.

None of this bothers you right now, though. Right now you feel on top of the fucking world. You've done it! You've been accepted into their group. Now you're going to find out what the fuck is going on.

You can't wait to call Sally tonight. She's going to go crazy when she hears about this. She's going to be so fucking proud of you! If she doesn't leave Nick and come back to you after this . . . well, you'll be pretty pissed off about it. As it happens, though, you don't have to call her. As it happens she's waiting for you outside the offie when you finish work, leaning up against a lamp-post, smoking.

At first you don't even realise it's her. For a moment all you see is an astonishingly attractive girl eyeing you up outside your place of work.

—Sally . . . ?

—Hi, she smiles.

—What you doin . . . ?

—I thought I ought to come an check how you were . . . you know, we need to talk.

A shot of adrenalin surges through your body. This is better than you could have dared hope for. She's *here*. In person. You're going to get to tell her all your shit face to face. And then, obviously, she's going to sleep with you. She'll demand it.

Oh yeah, hold that thought: tonight, you're going to sleep with Sally again.

You break out into goosebumps, you start to sweat a little, you can feel your hair sticking to your skin, your skin feels like it's about to jump off your body. It's pathetic really.

—Oh, uh, yeah . . . yeah, great, you stammer, still trying to come to terms with your outrageous good fortune. She's here!—You, uh, wanna get a drink or something?

She doesn't look sure. You've got to be careful now, play it cool; you don't want to tell her everything all at once. It'll have more impact if you let it out little by little.

—Or we could go back to my place?

She smiles again. —Your place?

—Yeah, it's not too far . . .

—What, you've got your own flat? she says as you walk up to the front door and she realises you haven't taken her to a hotel room.

—Yeah . . . well, I'm just renting out a room . . .

—Shit, John, how long you planning on staying here?

—I dunno. Long as it takes.

You slip unwisely into your Inspector Clouseau impression. —Until the case is solv-ed, you tell her in a voice that sounds more like Charlie Chan.

—But what about your place with Tony and Richie?

—Well, Tone's cool about it . . . Fact, it was his idea I come up here in the first place an I talk to him pretty regularly. He's got a mate of his moving in tomorrow for a week or so, but I still got the option to move back when I want.

She shakes her head. —I can't believe you're doing this . . .

You unlock the door and show her in. —*Et voilà*, you say, unable to shake off this Clouseau thing now you've started.

The door opens straight on to the kitchen and, tonight, straight on to an empty bottle of wine and a packet of Pringles on the table; Angela's obviously started early. From the bathroom you can hear her warbling 'God Bless The Child'.

—Landlady, you mouth to Sally by way of explanation.

You walk over to the bathroom and knock on the door. The warbling stops abruptly.

—Angela, I'm back, you shout through the door. —I've brought a friend with me, I hope that's okay.

—Boy or girl?

—Girl.

—You lucky devil, you. Well, don't mind me, I'm going out in five minutes, just as soon as I'm finished in here. So I'll leave you two to your . . . fun!

She can't quite spit this last word out for hysterical giggling.

You smile back at Sally. Good job you're on for a guaranteed shag tonight, otherwise you'd have found this little exchange with your drunken landlady kind of embarrassing.

Sally seems uncomfortable talking about serious stuff with this other woman here, so while Angela fusses around you, clearing up and dousing herself in perfume, you try and make small talk. You ask her about Petra and the market and which clubs she's been to the last couple of weeks. She says she hasn't been out just recently, you know, what with everything going on.

As soon as Angela's out of the door, though, she loosens up.

—So what do you mean, you don't believe I'm doing this?

—I mean I don't fuckin believe you're doing this! she says. —I don't believe that while me an Nick are hiding out in fear for our lives from this gang of psychopaths, you've come up here an got a job with the fuckin ringleader! I couldn't believe it when Tony told me. Are you mad?

—I just wanted to help, you say casually. —I couldn't just sit on my arse while you two were going out of your minds.

—But this doesn't help! This just makes it worse. Now *you're* in danger too. An Nick an me are probably in more danger . . .

You put up a hand to calm her down. —It's okay.

—It's not okay!

—No. It *is* okay, you tell her firmly. —You're not in any danger.

—What do you mean?

—This gang. They're not psychopaths. They're not killing people. There's no deadly Es. No conspiracy.

There. Now you've said it.

She's not buying it, though. —But what about the meetings? Nick's seen their meetings. He's taken photographs.

—I've seen their meetings, you tell her, racking up brownie points. —They're just meetings. They could be meetings about anything.

—Yeah? So what do you reckon they're about then?

Okay, time to play your first ace. Deep breath. Choose your words carefully.

—I think they're some kind of devil worship group . . .

—Oh, for fuck's sake John! she shouts. —Where the hell did you get that from?

There's been an aggressive, confrontational edge to this conversation ever since Angela left the room. Knowing you have all the cards up your sleeve, it excites you to see Sally getting so worked up. Damn, you're going to get a good seeing to tonight.

—It's common knowledge round here, you tell her. —But people just leave em to it.

—Common knowledge as in idle gossip, you mean. I bet no one's actually seen what goes on. In fact, I bet they started the rumour themselves as a cover. Course, that must be it. You stupid dickhead, you just accepted this story without thinking bout it for a second . . .

God, you love her when she gets angry.

—I mean, how fucking likely is it that these people are devil worshippers? she continues at the same volume. —*Devil fucking worshippers!* How likely is that?

You're just about to concede that okay, it's not very likely at all, but then neither is the idea that they're operating some kind of poison drug factory particularly plausible, when the front door bell goes.

It's Sammy. What the . . . ?

Oh yeah. You vaguely remember him saying Saturday night he'd come round.

—Sammy . . . how'd you find . . . ?

—My job to know stuff, he goes. —So can I come in or what?

You show him in.

—All right, love? he says to Sally.

Sally smiles back through gritted teeth. She's still all wound up from your argument and she fucking hates being called love.

You remember all over again why you fell for her.

—So what you want? Sammy asks, sitting down in the largest chair in the room.

—Uh, I dunno . . . let me see . . .

—Some draw an some Es, wasn't it? he says. —Maybe some whizz.

—Yeah, I think it was just the draw . . .

—Oh yeah, that's right, cause you don't do Es no more, yeah?

He shoots a wink at Sally and you know immediately what she's thinking: can she reach his bollocks with her boot without getting up?

—How much you need then? Ounce?

Shit, this guy's good. He should be selling stocks and shares or something, not driving a mini-cab round Leeds and doing small-time deals on the side.

—You got any ten deals?

—What, ten-pound deals? he says incredulously.

No, ten zloty deals.

—Yeah, course . . . ten deals, you say pathetically, feeling as thoroughly ashamed of yourself as all good salesmen make their buyers feel.

He draws in breath. —Don't really do ten pound bags, he says, furrowing his brow to show you he's *really* thinking hard to try and find a way of helping you out here. —Could do you an eighth for twelve fifty . . . ?

He reaches into one of the many pockets of his impossibly large anorak and takes out a small bag which he passes over to you. You take out the lump of resin and examine it. You're not quite sure what this is an eighth of; some little-known Yorkshire system of weights and measures maybe; it's certainly not an eighth of a fucking ounce. But it smells and crumbles okay, and you've had worse deals for twelve fifty, and you're not sure you can be bothered arguing with this bloke. You really want him out of your face as quickly as possible so you can get back to arguing with Sally.

—Can we call it twelve? you say, just to make a token effort.

—You can call it what you want, mate, says Sammy. —Long as you give me twelve pound fifty for it.

You smile weakly and make up the fifty in the smallest bits of loose change you can find.

He leaves a calling card for the taxi firm on the coffee table as he gets up to leave. What a wanker this bloke is; how the hell did you not notice this on Saturday night?

—Have a good evening, kids, he says on the way out.

Kids? This guy's at least five years younger than you. Fuck off, you beardy little whippersnapper.

—So you wanna get stoned then? you ask Sally when he's finally out of the door.

—Yeah, why not? she says, but she makes no move to get it together herself, so it looks like it's up to you.

Uh-oh.

You skin up in much the same way as Tommy Cooper might have done if he'd ever done a Rolling A Joint routine. You blag some skins off Sally, but you can't get them to stick together. You open up one of her cigarettes, but it seems to explode in your hands, sending tobacco everywhere. You burn your thumb trying to heat the blow. While you're trying to squeeze the roach in one end, the stuff all falls out of the other.

Forgetting that she's supposed to be mad at you, Sally bursts out laughing. —Here, let me have a go, she says.

The mood appears to be lightening. You think it may be time to move in for the kill.

—It was really sweet of you to come an check up on me, you say softly.

She looks pained. She lets the joint fall apart in her hands. It's not funny when she does it, though.

—I just wanted to make sure . . . you know, I thought you might be going off the rails a bit . . .

She puts the thing down altogether.

—Actually I didn't really come to check up on you, she says. —I came to tell you . . . I thought we ought to talk.

—Yeah . . . Okay. Talk bout what?

She pauses. She's thinking hard about how to say this.

—You know what I said to you that night you came round . . . bout me an Nick? How it was all to do with us being in a dangerous situation?

—Let me guess, you say. —Now you think it was nothing to do with that at all. You reckon you just shagged him cause you fancied him.

—Well . . . yeah, I guess . . .

—An now you think you wanna carry on shaggin him . . .

—John, I love him . . . I thought I owed it to you to tell you in person.

Ah, isn't that sweet of her?

Actually you can't help smiling. Poor misguided sweetheart. Oh yeah, she may *think* she loves him. But wait till she hears what you've got to tell her . . .

—Look, what's the only way of finding out what this group are *really* up to? you say, abruptly changing the subject to get back to business. The time has come to move.

—What do you mean?

—The only way we're ever gonna know for sure, I mean *really* know what they're doing, is to go to one of their meetings, yeah?

—I don't . . . ?

Okay. Time for your big triumph.

—They're having their next meeting Saturday night an I'm going along, you tell her, practically stumbling over the words in your excitement.

Oh John, that's marvellous. You're so brave. It's you I love, not Nick. Fuck me now, is what you expect her to reply.

It's a perfectly reasonable expectation. You worked on this, you planned it all out, you waited for your moment and you struck with precision. What other response could she possibly have?

You silly cunt.

—YOU'RE FUCKIN KIDDING ME! is what she actually says. Very loudly. Standing up, as she does so, and walking over to the other side of the room. —ARE YOU OUT OF YOUR FUCKIN MIND?

Not quite the result you were expecting.

—They'll kill you. They'll know you're an imposter an they'll fuckin kill you, John. An if they know you're an imposter, they probably know I'm here by now an . . . oh shit, what have you done?

She clasps her hand to her mouth, pacing up and down the room. She's gone through angry to just plain scared now. At least she's stopped shouting.

You try and calm her down. —It's not that dangerous, honest. Like I told you, I don't think this group are who you think they are. I think they're into some kind of occult thing . . .

—John, *think* for a minute. Who phoned Danny to warn him off going to the police? That's how we tracked these bastards down in the first place. Of course they're who we think they are.

—Well, if I go to the meeting, then we'll know for sure . . .

—What's the point of knowing if you're fucking dead?

Sally's on the verge of tears. You're all confused now.

—John, she says quietly. —Please don't go.

Fuck, what did she have to say that for? You can't not go. You're left with nothing if you don't go to this meeting.

You try and pick yourself up a bit. It's okay. This is just a minor setback. Once you've been to Macmillan's house and proved her wrong she'll come round.

—I've got to go, you tell her. —For you an Nick.

—We'll be fine, she urges you. —We've sent everything we have to the police, we'll lay low till these people forget who we are, whatever . . . John, *please*.

You shake your head. —I have to, you say firmly.

—Well, fuck you then, she snaps suddenly. —What is this, some kind of revenge thing? You think by going out an getting yourself killed by a bunch of psychos, you're gonna make me feel bad bout leaving you for your friend? Is that your twisted, fucked-up plan? Cause it's bollocks, John, it's fuckin bollocks. Go ahead, be a fuckin martyr if you want, but don't expect me to feel guilty bout it . . .

She's pacing towards the door now, picking up her bag on the way. Wake up, man, she's in the middle of storming out on you.

—Sally, wait—

—This was always you, wasn't it, she goes on. —Just a macho fuckin dickhead at the end of the day. I should've known . . . I should've known when you started picking on that bloke in the pub in Hackney . . .

What? What the fuck has that got to do with anything?

She opens the door. You try to shut it again, but she's too strong for you. Now she's out in the corridor. She's on her way out of your life.

—Sally, come back—

—Sort yourself out, John. There's more to being a man than taking stupid risks. Specially when they put your friends in danger too.

—Sally, come back . . . We can talk about this . . . I'm doing this for you, I only wanna help . . . I'M DOING THIS FOR YOU . . . I'M DOING THIS FOR YOU, YOU FUCKING BITCH!

—Sally, I love you, you tell her once she's well out of earshot.

Well, that's that fucked then.

You go back inside and sit down heavily on the couch. The half-made joint is still sitting on the coffee table. You pick it up and throw it across the room.

What happened there? How did you misjudge that so completely? The plan seemed simple and foolproof. You solve the case; she wants to sleep with you again. What could possibly go wrong with that?

Actually, the sad fact is, you pathetic lump of shit, that there are any number of reasons why she might prefer to go out with Nick rather than you. Your complete lack of ambition for one thing, your childish sense of humour, your obsession with comic books, your underwhelming genitals, your inability to roll a decent spliff, your failure to tell her at any point during your brief relationship how you felt about her . . . the list is fucking endless.

Face the facts. You're a twat and a loser: she's gorgeous and attractive. What did you think was going to happen?

∫

Captain Midnight sat at another bar with another drink. The bar was a neon-lit hell-hole in a city called London. It made Misty's look like a class joint. The drink was fizzy and too cold to taste.

When the rendezvous time came, he left the bar and made his way to the appointed place to meet the rest of the Patrol. He had arranged to meet them at a square in the centre of the city, which he believed would be easy for them all to find. He was glad to see the square was busy. The more people there were, the less he and his friends would stand out. In fact, no one gave him a second glance despite his alien appearance. They were obviously used to strange-looking creatures in this part of town.

While he waited for his colleagues, he looked around the square. It was brash and ugly. Large neon signs advertised COCA-COLA and FOSTER'S, both of which he had tried during his stay and found repulsive, and also TDK and SANYO, which he presumed were yet more disgusting fizzy liquids. He really couldn't wait to leave this place.

The mop-up operation on Planet Earth had been partially successful. Four of the five Ancients had been uncovered and eliminated. Four of them, in four different continents, by four different members of Midnight Patrol. A proper team effort.

The Captain, in fact, was the only one who had not been able to track down his quarry. In truth, he hadn't really tried. He had lost the thrill of the chase; whatever remnants of a sense of action lurked within him had been sucked out by the Ancients' Reduction Rays. And once he learned of the successes of the other four . . . well, what damage could one alien do on its own?

So he reconvened the Patrol and told them the mission was over. They were upset. Chaymar in particular was concerned at leaving a job unfinished. But Captain Midnight was adamant. There was no real harm one lone Ancient could cause and he had tired of this planet and its dismal, primitive people. They had been here for over one terrestrial month now and he wanted to go home.

Reluctantly the others agreed. They had no choice: for as long as they were Midnight Patrol, Captain Midnight was their leader. It was just sad that what would probably turn out to be their last adventure together had ended with a bang and then a whimper . . .

. . . and somewhere out in that heaving city, a brave, lonely alien was integrating herself so successfully into the local culture that she would never be suspected, feeding cautiously on the ample supply of underdeveloped host emotion, and dreaming of her proud parents many distant galaxies away and new-fangled buildings with escalators on the outside . . .

∫

So what do you do? Do you go to this fucking meeting or not? Now that you know that it's not going to make any difference with Sally, is there any point?

Do you take her word for it that you're bound to be trussed up and whacked on the head as soon as you walk through the door? On the face of it, it seems unlikely. You've got to know Macmillan pretty well over the last couple of weeks and he just doesn't strike you as a trussing up and whacking over the head kind of bloke. Or, for that matter, a manufacturing deadly pills and killing lots of people kind of bloke. Okay, as an investigator you've got to be able to keep an open mind, and there is the small question of his threatening calls to Danny to be cleared up, but on the whole you reckon you've got your new boss sussed.

So is there any point in going? Or maybe the question should be, what the fuck are you going to do if you don't go? Go back to Louie's and plead for your old job back? Fuck that. On the other hand . . . what the fuck are you going to do? Whatever happens, if you go along to that meeting on Saturday night you can't see yourself going in to work for Macmillan again on Monday morning. So then what? Where *do* you go?

Perhaps you should just cut your losses, stay at home Saturday and keep your job at the offie. It's no worse than cutting hair at the end of the day.

But then you've just got another dead-end job, only now you've got no girlfriend and no mates and you're not living in London any more. Fuck that too.

Fuck that. Fuck everything.

You're not sleeping too well just now. You're absolutely knackered at work, you get home and you drink a bottle of beer and smoke a spliff before bed to help you sleep, and then you toss and turn half the fucking night with all these ridiculous questions.

Only they're not ridiculous questions, are they? They're questions fundamental to your life and somehow you've got to find some answers to them.

Friday night you have another one of your headfuck dreams. You're back working at Louie the Greek's, only it's not Louie in the office, it's Captain Midnight again. You're doing a particularly difficult mohican on this old guy who looks horribly like Mr Noggin and you can hear the Captain muttering away, counting his money. Suddenly he comes marching out.

'What in hell's name do you think you're doing?' he barks at you sternly. 'You've got much more important things than this to be getting on with!'

You start to panic. You've no idea what he can be referring to.

'The last of the Ancients is still at large!' he bellows, so everyone in the room can hear. 'AND YOU KNOW WHERE SHE IS, DON'T YOU? YOU KNOW WHERE SHE IS, SANTINI!'

—You know where she is . . . you know where she is . . .

You wake up in a sweat. You peer over at the clock; it's nine fifteen. No point in trying to go back to sleep then.

You crawl through to the shower and the cold water slowly brings you round. What the fuck was that all about then? The shit that goes on in your head scares you sometimes.

You still haven't decided what to do about this meeting tonight. Shit, you can't even decide what to have for breakfast. Dripping water everywhere from your soaking-wet hair, you go through to the kitchen and lay out on the side Frosties, eggs, bread, marmalade and bacon and then you touch them all thoughtfully in turn. One thing about living with Angela, she sure knows how to keep a well-stocked cupboard. Still deep in thought you go over to check the mail. None of it's for you: of course none of it's for you, no one knows you're living here apart from Sally. But you still can't help checking. You weed out a couple of things that look like they might be bills for Angela, throw all the junk shit away and have a flick through the local paper for a laugh.

The headline reads: LOCAL MAN COMES THIRD IN FIFTEEN-TO-ONE!

Jesus . . .

Something at the bottom of the front page catches your eye, though: PETER IS STILL OUR BABY: Howard and Melinda Bartlett four months after their son's tragic death from drug abuse, by Gavin Armstrong. See page 5.

You turn to page five and there is a short, unrevealing interview with Mr and Mrs Bartlett, who apparently still don't think ecstasy is a very good thing, and a picture of them taken around the time of their son's death.

You read the article through several times, searching for clues. There are none, nor is there any mention of the Macmillans or the meetings or anything. But it does give you an idea for someone you should go and see before you decide whether or not to go to this thing tonight.

Gavin Armstrong is already pissed by the time you get to the paper's offices, which is quite impressive as the pubs haven't even opened yet. You weren't sure if he'd be at work on a Saturday. But he is; and he's pissed. He's sitting, tapping away at a keyboard, half-singing to himself:—Blah, blah . . . bollocks, bollocks . . . blah di blah . . .

—Uh, Mr Armstrong . . . ?

He spins round on his chair. —Young man, I trust you've brought me the scoop of the century!

—Uh, no . . . well, maybe . . .

—Maybe! I'm interested, come in and sit down.

—It's about this piece in today's paper about the Bartletts, you say, entering his domain nervously. It was kind of him to ask you to sit down, but there's nowhere to actually sit that isn't covered with bottles or bits of paper, so you stand self-consciously in front of him.

—Oh bugger, he says, turning away from you. —I knew someone'd bloody rumble it. Okay, I made the thing up. We had a page to fill and everyone had run out of ideas. But, you know, it *was* a good story at the time, and I was nice about them and everything . . . It's just we haven't had a decent drug story for a while now . . .

He looks ashamed for a moment, then suddenly he becomes animated again. —You know, for a time I thought we had a real epidemic on our hands, he says wistfully. —Looked like we were gonna get one of these ecstasy kids every other week. Bloody marvellous for sales, I can tell you. But now they all seem to have dried up . . .

—Yeah, it was that I wanted to talk to you about.

Now he does look interested. —Go on.

—I'm a friend of Nick Jones's . . .

Friend! Ha!

Armstrong looks puzzled.

—Uh, I think he told you his name was Hales, or something. You met him when that last kid died of E, David Samuels . . .

—Oh yes, I remember . . . had some kind of strange theory, didn't he?

—Yeah, I'm helping him do some research on it. We believe that an off-licence owner called Roger Macmillan may be involved.

You study his face for a hint of recognition of this name. There is none. Mind you, in his current state he looks like he'd be struggling to remember anyone's name apart from Jack Daniels'.

—And . . . ?

You go on. —Macmillan and his group are having a meeting tonight an I've managed to blag my way in. I just wanna know if it's safe or not. Local gossip says they're all a bunch of devil-worshippers—

Something clicks. —What did you say?

—I dunno, they're some kind of Satanists or something—

—Ah yes! Macmillan. The Satanist. Of course, I remember now . . .

He drifts off into gentle thought.

—So what's the deal? Should I go to this thing tonight or what?

—You've been invited to one of their, uh, sessions?

—Yeah.

—And you don't know what to expect?

—I haven't a fucking clue.

Suddenly he roars with laughter. You jump out of your skin.
What's so fucking funny?

—Oh well, yes, you should definitely go along then.

—So tell me, what goes on at these sessions?

—Oh no, he says, shaking his head and still smiling. —It'll be
much more interesting for you to find out when you get there.

Bastard.

—But I'm shittin myself here, you point out to him.

—Oh, don't worry. There's no danger involved. Just . . . keep
an open mind, that's all.

You stare at him, but he's obviously decided that's all he's going
to give you.

Fat drunken bastard.

You walk out of his office, feeling your face getting redder.

So, was that any use? Do you trust the mad ramblings of a man
who's drunk by eleven o'clock on a Saturday morning?

If not, who do you trust?

Fuck.

Fuck fuck fuck fuck fuckfuckfuckfuck . . .

Fuck. It's quarter to eight, you're standing on Macmillan's
doorstep. And you still haven't decided for sure whether you're
going to this meeting. Meeting, session, party, whatever. Your
shaking index finger is poised in front of the doorbell. It's getting
pretty close to the time when you're simply going to have to make
your mind up.

You've listened at the window, you've had a nose round back,
you've peered in all the cars in the driveway. No clues. What to do?

What to *do?*

Fuck.

Time stops. You're taken back to a particularly important
school football match when you were eleven when you were called
upon to take a particularly important eighty-eighth minute penalty.
As you stood at the edge of the area, waiting for the ref's whistle,

listening to your older and larger team mates hissing at you to let you know exactly what they were going to do to you if you missed, you were suddenly hit by a comforting and reassuring thought: in a minute this'll all be over. One way or another, one minute from now, I'll know what's happened. Either I'll have scored or I'll have missed and it won't matter any more . . .

You watch your finger creep towards the bell, millimetre by millimetre. Finally, agonisingly, it makes contact with the cold, shiny, round button. It's quiet now; very, very quiet. The button goes slowly in, further and further in until it's completely out of sight.

BBBBRRRRRRRRRRRRIIIIIIIIII-INNNNNNNNNNGGGGGGGGG!!!!

BBBBRRRRRRRRRRRRIIIIIIIIII-INNNNNNNNNNGGGGGGGGG!!!!

JESUS FUCKING CHRIST ON A BIKE!

You leap away from the door. That is the loudest fucking doorbell you have ever heard in your life. In fact, it can't be a doorbell. Somehow, by mistake you must have pressed that red button that the President of the United States always carries around with him, the one that sets off all the nuclear bombs in the world. Oh God . . .

And then snap, it suddenly goes very, very quiet again.

There's footsteps, someone's coming to the door. The handle turns, the door opens . . . and there stands your boss, smiling uneasily at you, dressed in nothing but a white dressing gown.

—Uh, John, he says nervously. —So glad you could make it. Do come on in.

Immediately you're straining to see past him to see if you can catch a glimpse of Satanic abuse. It's not too late to turn and run away.

But there's nothing visible apart from a tastelessly decorated hallway. Macmillan stands to one side to let you in. He doesn't look so glad you came at all. In fact exactly the opposite: he looks like he was kind of hoping you might have contracted meningitis and been forced to cancel. You walk past him feeling as nervous as he looks. He leads you to a door at the end of the hall. You brace yourself, this is it. The whistle's gone, you're stepping up to the ball. One minute from now you're going to know. One way or the other, you're going to know. You're prepared for anything, you're prepared for anything, you're prepared for anything. The door opens. Oh shit . . .

You're not prepared for *this* . . .

What happened? You'd almost forgotten. The trauma was so severe you'd buried the memory deep down in your psyche, not to be touched except in times of extreme emotional stress. Almost forgotten, but not quite. It's still there, it's always been there and now, as you stand gaping at the appalling sight in front of you, the memories come thundering back, flooding your entire consciousness.

What happened? You missed the fucking penalty of course. Your foot hit the ground before it hit the ball and the shot barely limped into the six yard box. It was more like a golf putt than a penalty. The goalie scooped the ball up with one hand while giving you the finger with the other and after the game the rest of your team played headers and volleys with your newly-dropped bollocks in the shower.

It was the *girls*, though, that really screwed you up over this. For weeks afterwards girls who didn't even like football, who didn't understand the offside rule or anything, were taking the piss out of you for missing that penalty and asking how your balls were. That hurt. That hurt more than the kicking.

But as soon as your foot hit the ground, you knew.

What you see before you could be a painting; it could be a scene from a Peter Greenaway film.

What you see before you, put very simply – and you need to put it simply so your poor fried brain can make some kind of sense of this barrage of images assaulting it – is a hideously decorated, blue-themed living room full of naked people. One, two, three, four, five, six, seven, eight, nine, ten naked people.

No, it still doesn't make any sense, does it? Try again. What you see before you is a hideously decorated living room full of naked people.

Only these are not like any naked people you have seen before.

True, you haven't seen many naked people before, not since you stopped taking communal showers at school anyway. There have been the miserable handful of people you've slept with, plus the increasing number you get to see in films and on the box, and they all looked pretty much the same. All in their twenties and thirties and all fairly pleased with themselves. Not these folk, though. These are the Naked People From Another Planet. They're middle aged with flabby bits; the men have beer guts and an astonishing amount of body hair; the women have stretch marks and enormous breasts which lie on their stomachs when they sit down the way you lie on a sofa to watch TV. You feel like you've wandered into a Victorian circus of grotesques.

Nor are they acting like normal naked people. There ought to be very few things that naked people do: they have sex, they wash, they go to bed and occasionally, for some perverse reason, they seem to play volleyball in the countryside. They don't as a rule sit around drinking gin and tonic, eating twiglets and talking about the fucking weather.

Check these three on the window seat to your immediate right. Two men and a woman. The men are deep in discussion, the woman looks bored shitless. You catch little fragments of what they're saying:

—Oh yeah, the A657 can be a bloody nightmare, can't it?

—Stuck for half an hour tonight. Couldn't get out of second gear.

—Have you tried cutting through Farsley?

Have you tried getting a life, mate?

Over on the other side of the room a slightly younger couple are sharing an armchair, sucking face. You wonder if they even know each other. And there are three people sitting with their feet up on each other on a very large sofa, one man and two women and . . . oh God, the woman at the far end is Angela Swaine, your landlady. Naked. Smiling at you.

—Let me introduce you to one or two people, Macmillan says, pointing towards the small group on the window seat. He's lost the dressing gown.

Of course. Introductions. Just because everyone is lounging around in their birthday suits, no reason to let social standards slip.

—John Santini, this is Bob Langley, Howard and Melinda Bartlett . . .

Bartlett . . . Shit, these are the parents of Peter Bartlett. You didn't recognise them with their bits hanging out, but now he mentions it their faces do look familiar from the pictures in the local paper. And from the blurred photographs Nick took. In fact, looking around the room again, you realise you know all these faces.

A short, dark-haired woman comes into the room behind you carrying a tray of celery sticks and dip.

—And this is Pat, my wife.

Mrs Macmillan puts the tray down and holds out her hand. You take it. You have now lost all sense of proportion. You are shaking hands with the naked wife of your boss in their own living room while 'Copacabana' by Barry Manilow plays softly in the background.

—Come through with me, John; you can leave your clothes in the study, Mrs Macmillan says cheerily.

Excuse me?

Before you can think clearly, she's already ushering you out of the living room and towards a smaller room off the hallway full of neat piles of clothes.

Okay, Okay, rational thought. You *mustn't* go into this room. If you go into this room, you will have to get undressed and all will be lost. You can't really make a quick getaway once you're stark bollock naked. And that was your landlady in there. Your fifty-year-old landlady, wearing nothing but a predatory smile.

What you need is time. Time to get your head together and work out what the fuck is going on here.

—Uh, could I use your toilet for a moment?

—Certainly, love, it's just behind . . . oh no, I've just remembered, George and Rachel have gone in there, haven't they . . .

You close your eyes and try and wish your way out of this.

—They've just started going out together, she adds with a wink. Like this explains everything.

Indeed, now you listen closely, there are vaguely frantic grunting noises coming from behind the door at the end of the hallway. You're immediately transported back to your flat in North London with the paper-thin walls. Oh sweet Jesus . . .

—Don't worry, Mrs M says brightly. —There's another one upstairs. Our little en suite, just off the master bedroom. Upstairs and to your right.

You thank her profusely while backing away from her and practically run up the stairs.

Upstairs continues the blind-person-in-a-hurry design theme: fluffy carpet that almost covers your ankles, wallpaper that veers between blue and sickly yellow, fucking knick-knacks everywhere. You poke your head into two or three rooms before eventually finding the master bedroom. This is the Grand Chamber of Tackiness. A vast four-poster bed with heart-shaped cushions scattered across it, a vanity table laden down with Body Shop tat, two giant photographs of two boys you take to be the Macmillans' sons. It's the kind of room Elton John would complain was too vulgar. It occurs to you on the way past that one of these boys looks eerily familiar. However, you don't want to linger. You're terrified that one of these fucking psychos will decide they want to watch and follow you upstairs. You go into the bathroom and quickly lock the door behind you.

Then you sit down on the toilet with your head in your hands and try to stop yourself bursting into tears. What the fuck is going on here? Who are these people? What are they doing?

This must be part of their rite or something. They start by stripping off and sharing drink and food before getting down to the serious business of summoning up the Horned One. Yeah, that's it, they're just preparing for their Black Mass, this is some kind of pre-Service celebration. Of course it is. Of course it is.

Of course it fucking isn't. This isn't a Black Mass, you bloody idiot, it's old people trying to have an orgy. There's two of them shagging in the toilet downstairs, for Christ's sake. It's old people trying to have an orgy, and they want you to be a part of it. Shit, you *asked* to be a part of it.

You silly twat. What have you done?

You've no idea how long you've been sitting with your head in your hands, when there's a rap on the door and a concerned voice:

—John, are you okay in there, love?

It's Mrs Macmillan.

—You're not climbing out of the window are you?

Climb out of the window! Fantastic idea!

The only window in the room is a narrow slit, blocked by an extractor fan; an Action Man couldn't squeeze out through it. The bitch. She was just trying to get your hopes up.

Another rap on the door. —John . . . ?

No way out, man. You're going to have to face the music.

Reluctantly, you unlock the sliding door and pull it open.

—Are you okay? says Mrs Macmillan again.

—Uh yeah . . . just thinking a bit, you mumble apologetically, looking up at her. You wish she'd put some clothes on.

—Oh dear, all a bit overwhelming for you, is it? she says mumsily. —Come over here and sit down, love, and let's have a little chat about it.

She leads you over to sit on the edge of the bed, while she goes into the bathroom to fetch her dressing gown.

Thank you, God.

—There's nothing to worry about, she says, coming out again and sitting down next to you.

Well, that's reassuring. You're not *worried* anyway; you're fucking appalled.

—It's just not . . ., you start to explain, and then change tack:—What exactly do you all do here?

—Oh, you don't have to *do* anything, she says. —We just sit around and chat and get relaxed and then later one or two of us might get . . . er, intimate . . . We don't mind at all if you just want to watch for your first time, though . . .

Great, thanks.

—I thought Roger said you knew what happened at our parties . . . ? she continues, sounding nervous now.

—Uh . . . yeah . . . I did know, I mean I do know, I mean . . . well, I was expecting something different to be honest with you. I was going by what some of the neighbours had said.

She looks at you hard. —Which neighbours?

—You know, the woman that lives next door . . .

—Mrs Peabody, I might've known it. Did she tell you . . . ?

Her voice trails off. She doesn't want to say it and neither do you.

—Yeah . . . she said there might be a, uh, religious element to the meeting.

Suddenly she turns angry. —Nosey old cow. I thought that'd all died off, but I guess people don't forget . . .

—Forget what?

She stands up and walks over to the window, where she stares out. Stares back out at the nosey old cows that watch over her.

—About a year ago there was a piece in the local paper, not naming us or anything but identifying us clear as day for them that knew us, claiming we were into some kind of devil-worship or summat. I tell you, we were all right peed off at the time cause there was nothing to it, the guy had just made it up for something to write. But we couldn't sue, or complain even, in case the real truth came out, so we've just had to live with it . . . Neighbours have had a bloody field day . . .

You let this sink in; it seems to make sense. A penny has dropped with Mrs Macmillan, though.

—So you thought we . . . ? But that must mean *you* . . . ?

You stare back at her in horror.

Congratulations, motherfucker. Dig yourself out of this one.

—Yeah . . ., you say hesitantly. —I thought there was gonna be a, uh, ceremony here tonight.

—Oh my God!

She moves away from you, grasping for the crucifix around her neck. Which isn't there, because she took it off earlier on so she could have group sex with relative strangers. She is now more repelled by you, though, than you are by her.

You stand up. —Look, I think I better go . . .

She nods readily.

—I'm sorry bout the mix-up an everything . . . My fault, I guess, for jumping to conclusions . . .

Your voice tails off as you catch sight again of the two enormous photos on the wall. Yes, you definitely know one of these kids.

—These your boys? you ask her, going to have a closer look. You don't believe your eyes.

—Yes, she says, and it sounds from her voice like she's starting to cry. —Jason and Rupert. Both live down South now.

You peer at the boy on the left. Rupert. It's a picture of a fresh-faced, smiling, thirteen- or fourteen-year-old, alarmingly different from the man you know today. But it is him, you're sure of it. Those piercing eyes, those podgy cheeks, you'd know them anywhere.

Something clicks. At last this shit is starting to make some sense.

You turn round, beaming. —Thanks for a great party, Mrs M.

This feels good. For the first time in a long time you know where you're going and why you're going there. You got the address off Mrs Macmillan, who'd have told you anything to get you out of her house; although you're pretty sure, being the hotshot dogs-bollocks investigator you are, that you could have found him yourself. How many Rupert Macmillans can there be in the world? You left the party without saying goodbye, you packed up your stuff and moved out of Angela's without leaving a note. It was time to move back to London and you didn't want to leave any trace of yourself up there.

And now here you are, outside the address Mrs M gave you, and it feels good. It's a broken-down, high-rise estate in Hackney. It's been painted pink to try and cheer the place up a bit, but the paint has faded and is peeling away, which makes it look even sadder and shabbier somehow. There are various signs dotted about telling the children not to play ball games. What a waste of time: kids round here don't want to play fucking ball games, they want to shoot up, torture stray cats and mug old ladies. It stinks of sick and piss and despair and you wonder what the hell the young Macmillan is doing living here. Anyone called Rupert living in a place like this has got to be doing it out of perverted choice.

You climb up a couple of dark stairwells, past the tired, obvious graffiti, to number 47. A white door with a variety of bizarre symbols, including an upside-down cross and a back-to-front swastika, scrawled on it. This must be the place.

Taking a deep breath, you knock on the door.

No reply.

It's Sunday lunchtime; he'll be sleeping off the night before; you try again, a little louder this time.

Still no reply. Where is the bastard? Not at fucking church, that's for sure.

You bang as loudly as you can on the door.

Then you do something very brave and very stupid. You start singing – tentatively at first, then getting louder.

—Roo-pert. Rupert the Cunt. Everyone sing his name.

You start singing louder still. It's the only way you're going to get the fucker's attention.

—ROO-PERT! RUPERT THE CUNT! EVERYONE SING HIS NAME!

You don't hear the footsteps coming to the door. It just opens all of a sudden and there, in a huge black T-shirt and boxer shorts and already with a big, fat one wedged between his stubby fingers, despite the fact it's clear from the sleep in his eyes he's only just woken up, is Rupert Macmillan.

He looks pissed off.

—Fat Cunt! you say as confidently as you can. —How's it hangin?

He steps back from the door in surprise. Whoever he was expecting at this time on a Sunday morning, it wasn't you in a good mood. You take the opportunity to march past him into his flat.

What in the name of fuck do you think you're doing? Okay, you're all fired up by self-confidence, but aren't you taking a bit of a chance here? This is the guy, remember, you once saw open a beer bottle with his teeth and then eat the top.

And he still looks pissed off.

—How'd you find out where I live? I don't tell no one where I live, he growls.

—I, uh . . . someone told me.

Fuck it, man, there's no point in being cagey now. You've just burst through the guy's door; you've got to go through with it.

—Yeah, well they can fuckin well untell you again. I don't like people coming round here. My place, my fuckin space, all right?

You look around. He's fucking welcome to his fucking space. It's a shit-hole. Useless, falling-apart furniture, crap all over the floor, books and magazines and records everywhere. The only thing that looks like it receives any degree of tender loving care is the computer in the corner, where no doubt Fat Cunt spends many a happy hour talking shite on the Internet to like-minded nutcases around the world. Oh, and the life-size poster of Gillian Anderson in the nude, that looks in pretty good nick too.

—What you want anyway? he says, waving the spliff around threateningly. —You come here for some gear, I suppose? What can I get you: pills? grass?

—No. Don't do that stuff no more.

There you go again. Who *is* making these decisions for you? There's nothing big or clever about not taking drugs, you know.

—What then?

Okay, this is the moment. This is the moment when he either beats the living shit out of you, or he sits down and listens to what you have to say.

—I wanna talk to you bout your parents.

—My parents?

—Yeah . . . Fact it was your mum told me where I could find you.

He moves towards you. Looks like it could turn nasty.

—My *mother?*

Obviously he's not going to offer you a seat, so you decide to take one anyway. Maybe it'll help to diffuse the situation slightly. You clear a small space on the sofa by pushing a pile of clothes on to the floor and sit down.

At least this stops his advance. The non spliff-holding hand is still clenched ominously into a fist, though.

—What you been talking to my mother for?

—It's this thing you sent Nick to look into . . . you know, the kid that died? I've been helping him out a bit.

—Yeah?

You've got his attention; he sounds calmer now.

—I thought he was shaggin your bird, he goes on.

—Uh, yeah . . . yeah, I think he is.

Now he's interested. He even pushes some shit off the armchair and sits down opposite you. This is almost getting cosy.

—So what you doin helping him out, man? You should be punching his fuckin lights out.

Yeah. Maybe you should. Maybe instead of risking your life on a wild goose chase, you should simply have decked the cunt. Would've been a whole lot easier.

—I dunno . . . I guess I'm just intrigued, you say. —What I wanna know . . .

He leans in closer towards you.

—What I wanna know is why you told him those lies bout your parents.

Whoops. Wrong word.

—LIES! I DIDN'T TELL HIM NO FUCKIN LIES! he screams, jumping out of his chair. The whole situation's turned around again.

—It was my parents told the fuckin lies. Whatever they told you was a load of bullshit, man. All right? They're killing people. They're all tied up with some government plan an they're killing people. I got the proof.

—You've got proof?

—Yeah! he says and he starts pacing up and down the room. —For several months my parents have been holding secret meetings with a Mr and Mrs Howard and Melinda Bartlett, the parents of Peter Bartlett, a young kid who died from takin E in Bradford a few months ago. Now, these two are fuckin crazy . . .

He points at his temple to show you just how crazy they are.

—Complete fuckin headcases. An so are my mum an dad, total anti-drug fuckin psychos, mad as you like. An I reckon the government must be involved somehow cause otherwise these people wouldn't have the technical knowledge to do this. See, what they're doin is making little pills that *look* like ecstasy—

—Yeah, but you said you had proof?

—I got the photos, man! I got the photos!

He stops the pacing, quickly rummages through a pile of papers on a table by the door and his fingers go straight to a set of familiar black and white photographs. He knew exactly where they were; obviously this isn't a disgusting mess at all, but a fiendishly complicated and highly efficient filing system.

—Look! Nick took these pictures at a house on the outskirts of Bradford. There's a whole fuckin gang of them.

It's the same bunch of photos Sally gave you. It proves fuck all.

—Look, man, this isn't proof, you try and tell him gently. —All this shows is a group of people met up one night. They could've been doing anything . . .

He shakes his head like you're talking the biggest load of shite he's ever heard. —Come on, man, what *else* could they be doing?

Oh God, he has no idea. He's got no fucking idea at all. How do you tell him? How do you tell a guy something like that about his parents. *Should* you tell him? What's his reaction going to be? And is it going to hurt? On the other hand, what do you tell him if you don't tell him?

You tell him.

He freezes for a moment, then takes a step towards you. Is this it? Is this where you finally get the kicking you deserve?

No. This is where Fat Cunt points at you and starts to piss himself laughing.

—Yeah, right . . . that's really funny, man, that's fuckin hilarious . . . my old man . . . an his fuckin friends . . .

—No, seriously, you try and tell him. —They're not doing weird stuff or nothin, but that's what happens when they get together . . .

Without warning he stops laughing and fixes you a stare. —Look, my mum an dad never had sex, right? Ever.

Okay, so you're talking to Jesus Christ all of a sudden. This is going to upset some of His followers a bit, that He's decided to come back as an overweight, paranoid drug abuser who likes kicking people.

He goes on. —They're all involved in this plot, man. I *know* it's true. I know my mum an dad. I know the fuckin headcases they hang out with . . . I never thought *I'd* be so close to something like this, though. Know what I mean? It's a fuckin responsibility, man. I got to get the truth out to people . . . Ask Nick, he knows the fuckin score . . .

Shit, what's the point? What's the point in arguing with him? If the silly fat fucker really wants to believe that he was born by immaculate conception to a pair of psychopathic mass-murderers, who are you to tell him that he wasn't?

There's only one more thing that you want to get cleared up. And then your best strategy is probably to get the hell out of here as soon as possible before his tenuous grip on reality finally slips away altogether and he starts breaking your limbs for fun.

—It was you that called Danny from your old man's house,

wasn't it? you ask him bluntly. —Threatening him an making him believe that it was your old man sold him the dodgy pills . . .

Okay. Is *this* where it happens?

Still no. Fat Cunt seems unfazed by the question. —Yeah, well I was just testing Nick out, really, he goes. —See how good he was at digging things up. So I got this guy Danny's number off him, went home for a weekend an started calling the bloke up. It was a bit of a laugh to tell you the truth, you know, hearing this guy shittin himself at the other end. An it took longer than I expected, couple of visits. But the point of it was to see if Nick had the nous to trace the call back to my old man . . . cause otherwise I was afraid he wouldn't make the connection.

Because there's no fucking connection to be made, you insane freak of nature.

—An it worked! he says, beaming at you proudly.

Worked? In what sense has this ridiculous plan of his *worked*? He's not even got the wrong end of the stick, he's got the wrong fucking stick altogether. Meanwhile, Nick and Sally are cowering at home in fear for their lives from a gang of murderers that doesn't even exist.

Yeah, if it wasn't for Fat Cunt and his overactive imagination, you'd still have your girlfriend.

In your dreams.

He starts the pacing again. He's still waving what's left of his spliff around, explaining the whole conspiracy as he sees it, in ever more paranoid circles. You've had enough of this.

—Yeah, maybe you're right, you say, trying to sound like he's convinced you.

You sound pathetic. He's never going to believe that you've just changed your mind like that.

—Course I'm right! he says, believing you immediately. —I knew you'd see sense. I mean, obviously it's good to have your ideas challenged to see how they stand up, but you can't argue with physical evidence . . .

And you can't be bothered to argue any longer with a raving maniac. You get up off the sofa. —Yeah, man, look, I got to go . . . see you round, yeah?

Now his intellectual rigour has triumphed, he seems genuinely disappointed that you're leaving. —Yeah . . . yeah, right . . . good to see you, man. Listen, you need anything? Bit of whizz?

—Nah. You're all right.

—Yeah, course, he says. —See you round then.

He starts reeling off a list of parties and clubs he'll be going to over the next couple of weeks. You nod and pretend to be interested. Not that long ago you'd have been standing here with a pen and paper, scribbling this stuff down. But not now. Now, apparently, you don't do this shit no more. So you just give him a little salute and turn to leave.

You give Gillian Anderson one last look before you go; seems rude not to. On closer inspection you can see it's not her at all, though. It's her head grafted clumsily on to someone else's body. Fat Cunt's mother has a giant photograph of him on the wall; he has a giant photograph of Agent Scully in the buff. How fucking sad is that?

Outside it's turned into a gorgeous, sunny day, so you decide to walk a bit. You've got shit you need to sort out in your head.

Your first thought is: this is it. You've fucking done it. You risked it all and you won. You went up to Leeds with all the odds stacked against you and through your courage and ingenuity and, okay, a little bit of luck, you found out exactly what was going on and you've saved the day. For someone like you who's been a complete fuck-up his whole life, this is pretty good going. You don't know how you should be reacting; you've never actually *achieved* anything before. Slowly it dawns on you that this weird kind of glowing sensation you can feel all over your body must be pride.

You stop walking and take a deep breath. Everything everywhere is perfect. You've sorted it all out and now Sally will come back to you and Nick probably won't mind too much. Maybe he'll be a bit fucked off to begin with, but he'll soon get over it. There's certainly no reason why this should interfere with your friendship any longer.

Your next thought is: so fucking what? Do you really want her back? Do you give a toss any more whether Nick's your mate? What were these friendships based on anyway? Clubbing and Es and music and not giving a fuck. And, as you keep reminding yourself, you don't do that shit no more. It's become a mantra inside your head – don't do that shit no more, don't do that shit no more, dontdothatshitnomore, dontdothatshitnomore, dontdothatshitnomore . . .

And maybe it's no bad thing. Maybe it's time to sort your life out, grow up a little. This would be a good time to knock the comics on the head as well. You can't go through your whole adult life being obsessed with super-heroes, can you? Maybe now you've had a little adventure of your own, and even achieved something almost worthy of Midnight Patrol, maybe now's the time to kiss the Captain goodbye.

So that's that then. No more clubs, no more drugs, no more comics. It's time to open your arms and embrace the heady, grown-up world of early nights, Saturday evening TV, IKEA and Everything But The Girl albums.

You're twenty-eight years old and you've never been to IKEA in your life. Do they sell Everything But The Girl albums at IKEA? Probably they do.

Walking across London Fields, watching the children play in the sunshine, thinking about that warehouse party you went to just up the road from here – Jesus, was that only three weeks ago? – and whistling a happy tune, you suddenly stop in your tracks, look up to the sky and holler as loudly as you can:—FUCK THAT!

Wow, that felt good.

—FUCK THAT! FUCK THAT! FUCK THAT! FUCK THAT!

Time to go get your girlfriend back.

There's no one in at Sally's and no reply at Nick's, although here you can tell the place is occupied because there's a window open and you can hear music. You bang louder on the door. Come on you bastard, open up. Still no answer, though. Christ, even Fat Cunt was easier to rouse than this. Eventually you resort to kneeling down and yelling through the letter box:—NICK, IT'S ME . . . JOHN! OPEN UP!

At long last there's some movement inside. Nick opens the door on the chain and peers suspiciously out at you. Even through this small crack you can tell he looks like shit. Pale, drawn face, dark rings around his eyes from lack of sleep, faraway look. In the early eighties there were people who paid good money to look this fucked-up.

—Come on, man, let me in. We need to talk.

—You're not still pissed off at me? he asks nervously.

—Course I am, you tell him. There really is no point in not being honest, not now. —But I'm cool about it. I'm not about to fly off the handle. Just let me in so we can talk, yeah?

He thinks about it a moment longer. Then reluctantly he closes the door to take the chain off, then re-opens it. You walk past him into the cramped hallway. You notice the door to the bathroom is shut and the music you could hear is coming from in there: an old Charlatans album being played loudly through a tinny speaker. You guess Sally is in there.

You go through to the front room, which is unusually tidy for Nick, the absolute opposite to the tip you've just come from. The terrible thought strikes you that Sally must have already moved in. Fuck, that was a bit quick, wasn't it? Mortal danger or no mortal danger.

Nick sits down on the sofa with a tired thump and relights the half-smoked spliff in the ashtray. The ashtray, you notice, is already full of roaches and right next to it is a compact mirror with tiny white speckles on it. Things don't look too clever.

—So how's it goin? you ask him, although you can see perfectly well.

—Fuckin police, man, he says, shaking his head sadly. —Can you believe what they did?

You shrug and refuse the joint he offers you.

—Well, I sent em all me stuff, right? All the photos an a long report on everything I'd uncovered, sent it all off to Scotland Yard in a brown envelope. Completely anonymously. Somehow they manage to figure out where it's come from, though; some cunt must've grassed me up . . .

He looks at you accusingly, but doesn't actually threaten you.

—Couple of weeks later these two coppers come round, he goes on. —Plain clothes coppers. They thank me for the information I gave em an take this fuckin great long statement from me an then they tell me they won't be taking any action against this gang cause there's no hard evidence against them. And – get this, right – their colleagues in Yorkshire have told them that all the people I've accused are upstanding citizens with no criminal connections whatsoever. So they're very sorry, blah blah blah, but there's fuck all they can do . . .

He's staring fixedly at something on the wall behind your back while he's speaking.

—Well I'm sorry, he explodes, still keeping his gaze fixed. —But aren't the Yorkshire police only completely the most fucking corrupt police force in the whole fuckin country? Who gives a fuck what they think?

You turn around to see what's holding his attention. There's a new poster stuck up on the wall.

Or rather it's an old poster he's dug out again. He showed you it once, shortly after you met, to show you what a misguided wanker he'd been in his youth, and therefore by implication how sussed and sorted he was now. For about eighteen months in his late teens, apparently, he'd been a fully-fledged anarchist, mohican, combat trousers, the whole bit. And among his Crass records and *Class War* back issues he had this giant poster of a policeman at Wapping beating a striking printworker with a truncheon. And the copper had a speech bubble coming out of his mouth with the slogan, 'I'M NOT POLITICAL, I'M ONLY DOING ME JOB!' And now here it is again, staring you in the face, only somehow it's more shocking than you remember. The printworker doesn't look heroic at all, he looks cowed, undignified and utterly terrified. The policeman looks calm, dehumanised, robotic. And there's one very real, physical change to the poster: at the bottom someone has added a new slogan in black marker pen, 'THE OLD BILL ARE A BUNCH OF CUNTS!'

You turn back to Nick. He's a fucking mess. You suddenly notice how old he looks now compared to the wide-eyed, idealistic twenty-year-old who first showed you this poster and encouraged you to laugh along with him at it. All you've got to do is tell him, though. All you've got to do is tell him what you know and the nightmare will be over for him.

All you've got to do is tell him . . . but you don't want to. Not yet. It would spoil the impact to tell him now, without Sally here. You have this whole thing worked out, but it involves telling them both together. The plan is this: you tell them the whole story, modestly playing down your part in it but giving them enough facts to draw their own conclusions. Then Sally comes over to you and gives you a big hug of thanks and in doing so realises just how much she's missed the closeness of your body and the gentle strength of your touch. She turns to Nick with tears in her eyes and tells him that she's terribly sorry but she's made a horrible mistake and she has to put it right now. Nick, also fighting back the tears, is so relieved that the danger is finally over, and so grateful to you for succeeding where he had failed, that he says it's probably for the best and he's just glad the three of you can all be friends again. He opens a bottle of wine and you all toast an everlasting friendship. Oh, and a stirring version of 'Love Is A Many Splendored Thing' plays somewhere off screen. It's a tender, beautiful scene. But sadly it involves Sally being present, so you can't put Nick out of his misery just yet. You selfish bastard.

In the end, however, he forces it out of you.

—Can't believe that fuckin stunt you pulled in Leeds, he goes.

—What do you mean?

—Going up there, putting yourself in all sorts of danger. You must've been out of your fuckin mind. Sally was well pissed off, I can tell you. She kept saying, as if it wasn't enough that we were hiding out down here, now she had to worry bout you an all . . .

Sally was worried about you. It still makes you feel good to hear that.

—And all that bullshit you gave her bout them being Satanists an you going to one of their meetings . . .

You can't help yourself. You blurt it out. —But it's true! I did go to one of their meetings, only they're not meetings really . . .

There. Now you'll have to fucking tell him and bollocks to your plan.

You sit down next to him on the sofa and refuse the spliff a second time. You tell him everything you can remember about last night, with as many of the grisly details as you think you can both stomach. The more details, the more convinced he'll be. He looks like he wants to believe you. Of course he *wants* to believe you; if he can only believe what you're telling him, the terror's over. But it's as though he's afraid that because he wants to believe it so much, it can't be true. He asks about Macmillan's phone calls to Danny and you tell him about your visit to Fat Cunt this morning. That clinches it.

—The fuckin bastard! he says, standing up. —The fuckin bastard was playing games with me.

—No, I think he genuinely believes it, you say to try and console him. You don't mind at all that you've told him now; you've got your mate back. —He's fucked up, man.

—Yeah, but me an Sally have been doing our nuts the last couple of weeks. An what bout poor Danny? What the fuck gave him the right to phone Danny up an fuckin terrorise the poor bastard? He's fuckin insane.

—Just trying to live up to his name, you say in a lame attempt at a joke.

—Bullshit John.

The two of you look up. You hadn't noticed Sally come in from the bathroom. You're not sure how much of the conversation she's heard. She's got a towel wrapped around her and her soaking-wet hair is dripping on to her shoulders; God, how you love her shoulders. As soon as she catches you staring at her, though, she pulls the towel tighter around her. It just reminds you how far you've come since she was waving her tits around in front of you in that hotel in Brighton.

—What you saying? Nick starts.

Sally marches into the room. —I don't know what his fuckin agenda is, but this is bullshit. He tried to spin me the same line when I was up in Leeds. Only then he said they were all devil-worshippers.

You look at her pleadingly. It was all going so well. —It's true! you say.

She catches your look and softens her approach a little, but not her position.

—John, we're your friends, or at least we used to be your friends. Don't do this to us.

—Do what?

—Whatever it is you're trying to do . . . I don't understand you any more, I don't know what's happening . . . You jack in your job all of a sudden and piss off without even saying goodbye or telling anyone what you're doing . . . an now you come back with all these ridiculous stories—

—They're not ridiculous . . .

You stand up. All three of you are now standing up, in a very close triangle. And you're all now shouting.

—But why would you do this? Sally wails. —Why would you give up your whole life an put yourself in all that danger? It doesn't make any sense. You must be on their side—

—BECAUSE I LOVE YOU!

Fuck. Did you just say that?

There's an icy pause in the room. You must have done.

You lower your voice slightly, and lower your head so you're talking to the floor. —I thought that if I found out what was going on an made everything safe for you, you'd leave Nick an come back to me.

Spelt out like that, it sounds pathetic and transparent. You suddenly remember that this whole plan was dreamed up by Tony when he was out of his head on his first E. You feel ashamed. You look from Sally to Nick and back again to see how they're taking this.

Nick speaks first. —So you made the whole fuckin thing up just so you could get it on with Sally again? I don't believe it—

—No! I didn't make it up—

—John, how could you? Sally says.

—I didn't do anything—

—You're a fuckin bastard, Santini, Nick says. —I think you better leave.

You look back to Sally. She's got to be your best chance. —Sally, please, I love you, you whine miserably. —It's taken all this shit happening to show me just how much . . .

But you don't get to tell her how much because Nick suddenly punches you in the jaw. The shock rather than the force of the blow sends you toppling backwards over the sofa.

—NICK, NO! Sally screams.

But Nick rushes round behind the sofa and starts kicking you, calling you a cunt, accusing you of betraying him, of working for the other side. Sally grabs him around the neck and pulls him away from you. —This isn't the way to sort this out, she says, straining to hold him back.

—Fuckin hell, man, let me explain, you start to say from the floor.

But this looks like it's only going to provoke Nick further. Sally's struggling to keep hold of him. —Look, John, fuck off will you? she says.

You pick yourself up and look around. All things considered, you can't think of a better idea. Trying to summon up some authority in your voice, you tell Nick sternly that you'll be back to talk about this properly.

And you run out of the door and down on to the street and you burst into tears.

Two hours later. You're in a phone booth on a small road off Regent Street. Drunk.

—WIDE-BOY! you bellow down the receiver. —IT'S ME, JOHN.

It's taken you about twenty minutes to get it together to dial his number correctly. There's a couple of irate people waiting to use the phone, but you can tell from their clothes they're tourists so they can fuck off.

—Listen, mate, I wanna get hold of some smack . . .

There's silence at the other end. Then Wide-Boy says nervously:—Uh, I beg your pardon?

—I need some smack, man. I've had a fuckin hell of a time, I need to get out of it.

—I'm sorry, sir, I think you have the wrong number.

—I HAVEN'T GOT THE WRONG FUCKIN NUMBER YOU CUNT! I NEED SOME SMACK! GET ME SOME FUCKIN SMACK NOW!

But he's already hung up. You dial his number again. It's engaged.

Bastard.

You start whacking the phone with the hand piece. You bring it down again and again, making a loud clanging sound each time, but not actually breaking anything. Come on you fucker, smash. You're going to look a prize fucking twat in front of the tourists outside if you try and smash the phone up and can't do it. A sense of national pride takes over: you're doing this for England now.

It's not happening, though. You're in more danger of breaking your arm than the phone. So you turn your attention to the window and start smashing the hand piece against that instead. But it's made out some kind of reinforced, IRA-proof fucking glass and the bloody thing just bounces off it. Even more angry than when you started this charade, you throw the hand piece down so it dangles by your knees and storm out of the booth.

The woman outside gives you a startled look. She's got dark hair and is wearing purple jeans with a hole in the knee and a lime-green sweatshirt with the words NAF-NAF written across it. She might as well have I'M A FUCKING TOURIST, PLEASE ROB ME tattooed across her forehead. —Is free? she asks you in a thick accent, pointing at the resolutely undamaged phone.

—No, it's very fuckin expensive, you say, a retort you imagine to be worthy of Oscar Wilde.

And feeling very clever you saunter away from her, slip on a piece of newspaper and fall arse over tit into a doorway.

You're way out there now. Picking yourself up out of the gutter, your first reaction is to check your half-bottle of whisky is okay. It is, you're safe. You take it out of your jacket pocket and take a good, long swig. Then, blissfully unaware of how much of a dick you look, you stagger up towards the lights of Piccadilly Circus.

At this stage of drunkenness, London looks like the opening credits of *Taxi Driver*. The lights melt hazily into one another, you can hear that strange, atonal Bernard Herrmann score inside your head and you get the distinct impression the lid could be blown off the whole rotten, stinking mess at any moment. Your plan is simple: you're going to get wasted. You're not going to worry about Sally or Nick or Fat Cunt or your job or your flat. You're going to go on the biggest almighty fucking bender the world has ever seen, and then you have a feeling the future will take care of itself.

There's a large group of people sitting underneath the statue of Eros, hanging out. More fucking tourists in their ridiculous almost-but-not-quite-right clothes. One of them, however, is wearing an outfit that even in this company stands out. And he's waving to you and beckoning you over.

'Here, John, give us a swig of your whisky, mate,' he goes.

'Uh, Captain . . .,' you stutter, and then compelled by the authority in his voice, you hand over the bottle.

'Damn, that feels good,' he says, guzzling. 'Haven't had a decent drink since we started this fucking mission . . . I'd developed quite a taste for the hard stuff, I can tell you.' When the bottle's drained, he hands it back to you. 'Now. John, I have to say, frankly I'm disappointed in you . . .'

'How come?'

'You had a chance to help me out, to really make a contribution to this mission, and you didn't take it.' he says sternly.

'I . . . I don't understand.'

'That friend of yours . . . what's her name?'

'Sally?'

'Yeah, Sally, whatever she's calling herself . . . you know who she is really, don't you? Deep down, you know.'

You think hard about it.

'I mean, look at the facts,' the Captain goes on. 'It's always been her who's stood in your way, hasn't it? You'd just about persuaded Nick that everything was okay, when she came marching in and ruined it all. She goaded Nick into punching you. She may have pretended to be all upset afterwards, but it was her that caused it to happen . . . Wasn't it?'

Yes . . . so what exactly?

'Now, what do you think her motive for doing that was?'

You don't know.

'Come on, John. Think! *You know who she is!*'

You don't . . . hang on a second.

The scales fall away from in front of your eyes. 'Of course. Christ . . . I've been so fucking stupid.'

'The clues were all there,' he says accusingly.

'Yeah, I'm sorry . . . I'm really sorry.'

'Never mind sorry!' he shouts, staggering to his feet. Whatever he says, he's been drinking more than your little nip of whisky. 'Never mind fucking sorry! What are you gonna do about it? How are you gonna make *amends?*'

'I, uh . . . I dunno . . .'

He lowers his voice, but it retains its menace. 'Oh, I think you do know,' he says.

Surely he doesn't mean . . . ?

'Oh yes,' he says, smiling.

Shit, is he reading your mind or what?

'Yes, I am.'

So he wants you to . . .

'Yes. That's right.'

Shit . . .

'SO ARE YOU GONNA DO IT?' he shouts suddenly, like a football coach trying to fire up his team.

What can you say? It *is* your responsibility.

'Yes,' you reply.

Not loud enough.

'I SAID ARE YOU GONNA DO IT?'

'YES . . . !YES!YES!YES!'

He grabs your hand and pumps it manfully. You're sure you can hear your fingers cracking. 'I always knew you were a good guy to have on the team, John,' he says.

And with that he's gone. Just like that, whoosh, into the ether.

People are starting to stare at you. You're standing in the middle of Piccadilly Circus, screaming bullshit to yourself at the top of your voice.

Well, fuck them. They don't understand. You have important work to do. Your mentor has entrusted you with the job of saving the Earth from evil outside marauders and you're not going to let him down. You're going to fucking do it.

You hail a cab and give the driver an address in East London. There's a fire in your belly; you feel invincible.

Death to the alien. Death to the Ancients.

You insane fucking bastard.

Part Three

∫

Christ, you feel old. You're standing in the corner of a large room, drinking a Coke. Music is playing and lights are flashing on your face. All around you people much younger than yourself are getting off on the record. And it *is* a good record; or rather it's a good seamless mix of two or more records, coming and going, overlapping. Although this is the first time you've been to a club in a long, long time, you've never stopped loving this music. You've still been finding yourself, alone in your room, tuning into underground radio, making tapes when things got especially intense, taking yourself to the places ecstasy used to take you. You've still been buying the odd twelve-inch and loads and loads of compilation CDs. Fuck, you used to *hate* those compilation CDs. You remember you and Nick once had a heated conversation on the way back from some club or other where you both agreed that if you were in the government, it would be *outlawed* for dance music to appear on any format other than vinyl. Techno CDs were nothing less than sacrilege. And now look at you: buying them by the truckload every weekend and spending your evenings through the week listening to them, on your own,through the very expensive headphones which are your latest pride and joy. But you have to admit, it is good to hear this shit mixed live again and pumped-out at awesome volume through speakers the size of your wardrobe. Good as your poncey headphones sound, they don't sound *this* good. You're not quite ready to dance yet, but you do move your feet a little and tap your finger against your Coke bottle.

Not that you're the oldest person in here. Not by a long way. There's a middle-aged mod couple talking and laughing privately with each other at the bar. On the dancefloor there's a group of serious-looking blokes, heads shaven to disguise their impending baldness, dancing as though they'd learned it out of a book; record company executives, probably, or music journalists or something. Chill out guys, you're here to enjoy yourselves. And over the other side of the room is a guy old enough to be your grandad, wearing a multicoloured waistcoat, beach shorts and odd socks. And nothing else. He hardly seems to count, though, not being from this planet.

You can't help sniggering to yourself. You're glad you came now. You really only came out of a sense of obligation, but now you're glad you did. The music's good, the vibe's good. Maybe you should start getting out a bit more again.

You take a wander for a change of scene. The chill-out in this place is something else; it's as big as the main room and decked out like some kind of Middle Eastern bazaar. There's a row of stalls selling all kinds of stuff from home-made jewellery to ganja accessories to hippy and crusty clothing to fluorescent things that seem to have no purpose at all other than being fluorescent. You can even get a massage here: at the end of the stalls a large, muscular crusty with an enormous tattoo of a snake on his back is having his torso pummelled mercilessly by a lunatic with cropped hair who looks like an army sergeant. And behind the row of stalls is something called a Smart Bar, which seems to sell nothing but Ribena and enormous slices of watermelon, and several small round tables with chairs, set out to look like a French terrace café. And sitting at one of these tables, sporting a goatee beard and a daft woolly hat is someone you haven't seen for a long time.

Nick Jones.

In fact you haven't seen Nick since he tried to beat you up last summer. You did catch him on the telly earlier in the year and he was well on the way to cultivating this pseudo-anarcho look then, so it doesn't come as a complete shock to you now. It was a late-night discussion programme about the legalisation of drugs and Nick had been roped in as a supposed expert from the Legalise Cannabis campaign. He sat there, stoned out of his brain, in all his trampy get-up with a large, red cannabis-leaf badge and came on like the greatest piece of anti-drug propaganda you've ever seen. He slurred his words, he rambled incoherently, he forgot questions he had just been asked and when he realised how badly it was going he resorted to hurling insults and accusations at the other members of the panel. It was embarrassing.

You're not sure you're ready to see him again. Apart from the unhealed wounds, he seems to have changed so much: are you actually going to like this version of him? You decide to leave him to his fruit and his scary-looking friends, but you decide this just too late; your eyes meet and his light up. He waves down to you. You can't avoid him now without making a run for it. Maybe this will do, though. Maybe if you just wave back and give him a smile, that will be enough.

Maybe not. He's getting up from his chair. He's coming down to the impromptu marketplace. You stay rooted to the spot, you don't know what you want to do. He comes up to you and holds out his hand. What are you going to do, refuse it? You shake it stiffly, formally, like you're a couple of businessmen meeting for high-level talks.

—John, man, he goes. —Good to see you.

—Yeah . . . me too, you say awkwardly.

—Thought you were still living up North.

—No. Came back bout a month ago. Got a job in a salon up in Covent Garden. Bit poncey, like, but good money . . .

There you go, you're always having to justify it. Ever since you started working in this place, you've had an underlying problem with it. You seem to think that just because you're working somewhere without the pole outside, somewhere where customers make appointments and have a fighting chance of actually getting the cut they asked for, somewhere where minor celebrities have been known to show up, this somehow calls your sexuality into question. Just accept it: you cut people's hair for a living and now, finally, you're getting to be quite good at it.

—Oh right, Nick says. —So you stayed with the hair cutting? I thought you'd gone back up to Leeds to carry on working in that offie.

—Nah, didn't really fancy it, you tell him, not really giving him the whole story. —I only went back to Leeds to be honest, cause I wanted to get out of London an I couldn't think where else to go. So I picked up another barber's job.

How could you have gone back to the offie? You'd seen Macmillan's bits. You'd seen his missus' bits. You'd cheerily admitted to both of them you were a disciple of the devil. How would that have worked?

—So if you been back a month, how come I haven't seen you round?

You give him a little smile. —Don't go out as much as I used to, you tell him. —Fact, I think this is the first time I've been clubbing in about a year.

—Yeah? Who you here with?

—Just on me own.

He looks at you sympathetically.

—Got in on the guest list, you tell him, knowing the effect this will have. He may be a campaigner rather than a fully-fledged journo these days, but you suspect these two magic words will still impress him. His eyebrows shoot up into his head.

—Yeah? How come? he asks with a pathetic attempt at non-chalance.

You check your watch; it must be about time. —Come on an I'll show you.

You go back to the main room. There's a new DJ on and the atmosphere has changed slightly. This music is much harder, much faster and the crowd respond accordingly. It's not drum and bass, although the drums jitter in a vaguely jungly way, and it's not quite techno either. There are great slabs of cheesy, handbaggy piano that keep breaking in, which ought to sound terrible, but somehow seem to make perfect sense.

Nick looks perplexed. —Who's this? he asks. —Don't think he's played here before.

You point up at the DJ booth. —Have a look, man.

Nick peers up at the man with an even more laughable beard

than his own. He's dressed all in black with a large coat, despite the heat in here, and a hat with the words DANCE TERRORIST sewn on it. Never has a white guy wanted so much to be black. You can see Nick's doing his nut; he knows he knows this guy, but he can't place him.

You take pity on him. —It's Tony, you say.

He looks puzzled. He still hasn't figured it out.

You tell him again. —Tony . . . Guy I used to live with.

Suddenly it clicks. —You're fuckin kiddin me!

He looks even more closely at the dance terrorist and then back at you, to make sure you're not taking the piss.

No. It really it is him.

—Phoned me up bout a week ago, you say. —Said he was doing his first major gig tonight an did I want to come along.

—But he wasn't into this shit, says Nick, still unable to believe his eyes.

—Yeah . . . late developer, I guess. I heard he lost his job last year an I think he splashed out the redundancy money on a second-hand Technics an a bunch of records.

Nick shakes his head. —Well, fuck me.

You both go over to the booth to watch Tony at work. He's hunched over his headphones, clenching them like a telephone between his right cheek and shoulder, eyes closed in concentration. This doesn't come easily to him yet. He spins the second record back and forth, trying to lock the beat in with the tune playing over the speakers. It takes him several attempts but eventually he does it and lets the headphones drop with a smile. He moves over to the fader and brings it up slowly and sure enough, you can hear the new record running alongside the original one and taking the baton. That was pretty good, if unspectacular, but Tony's not done yet. Instead of just letting the first record fade out gracefully he goes back to it and starts scratching it on the vocal sample. Then he cuts it out altogether and lets the piano riff from the second record play alone. Then as the drums come crashing back in, he whacks the first record back up again and they pump out in perfect synchronicity.

—Shit, he's not bad, says Nick.

Yeah. It's not the best you've ever heard, but for a bloke who a year ago thought lager was the final proof of the existence of God, it's not bad at all.

You turn and look out at the dancefloor. They're going mental for it. Where the fuck is Tony getting these records? They're mad. The drums fizz and spit and sound like they might take off and spin out of control at any moment. He doesn't do himself any favours spinning tunes like this; they must be bastards to mix.

Nick points towards the floor. —Fancy a dance then?

—You askin? you say, grinning.

You make yourselves some space and start moving. It takes you a while to get into it and find a rhythm. The drums are going like an express train, boing boing boing boing boing. You can't possibly try and dance on the beat, or else you'll end up pogoing and be out of breath in a couple of minutes. So you nod your head a bit and try and find some space around the beat to move to. Out of the corner of your eye you can see the Serious Slapheads still shaking their stuff. They seem to have found a way of dealing with it so you follow them.

Eventually you get into it and begin to lose yourself in the music. The banging, boinging of the drums becomes hypnotic, the swirling piano becomes uplifting and underneath it all a sinister voice growls:

—Get ready for some fireworks!

Louder drums. Faster piano. The voice comes back, slowed down slightly.

—Get ready for some f-i-r-e-w-o-r-k-s . . .

Everything cuts out. You're left with nothing but huge, open, white synthesizer chords filling the whole room. They don't have long, though. Faintly, ominously, underneath them you can hear the vocal picking up speed.

It ought to be a rallying cry for a party, a promise of good times, a celebration, a triumph. It sounds more like a prediction for the apocalypse.

—GET READY FOR SOME FIREWORKS!

The drums thunder back in like Zebedee on hot coals: BOING! BOING! BOING! BOING!

You do start pogoing, you can't help yourself. You wave your hands in the air and start jumping up and down. It's okay, Nick's doing the same thing. Even the Serious Slapheads are doing it. The whole fucking room is pogoing. There's a lot of people with their own drums here – mainly crusty blokes, stripped to the waist, living out some kind of Zulu War fantasy in their heads – and they bang these for all their lives are worth. Other people blow whistles or whoop and holler. There's even one bloke with a fucking didgeridoo. It's a huge colourful mess of sound. It sounds the way fireworks look.

One thing about this music, though, it doesn't half wear you out. Four or five records later and you and Nick need to rest up a little. You go back through to the Smart Bar (you still don't get this; what's so fucking smart about watermelons?) and Nick says a very strange thing to you.

He says:—You want a drink?

Fucking hell, he has changed. He means it, though. Look, he's got his wallet out and everything.

Seems churlish to refuse, even if you do suspect he's only doing it because he feels belatedly guilty about the way he treated you. —Yeah . . . I'll have a Coke . . . thanks.

You sit down at one of the tables and he introduces you to some of his friends. As far as you can tell they're all from the Legalise It! campaign; there's certainly a lot of cannabis-leaf earrings and T-shirts and badges about.

—So how've you been? you ask him.

—Yeah . . . good, he says. —I've been a lot more focussed since I got involved in this campaign. You know, it was really good being a journo an everything, but at the end of the day if you're a journo your ultimate aim is simply to get published, not to actually change things. It's been good for me to have something concrete to work towards . . . I was on telly a few months back . . .

—Yeah, I saw.

—You saw it, yeah? What did you think?

What did you think? You thought it was shameful. You thought it put the cause of legalisation back about ten years. —Could've been better, you tell him.

—Yeah, the fuckin audience was against me from the start.

—How's Sally? you ask to change the subject. And because you're dying to know.

He shrugs. —Dunno. She fucked off not long after we had that little spat. Haven't seen her since. I did try an track her down at the market a few weeks later – not cause I wanted her back or nothin, I just wanted to say goodbye properly – an I found that friend of hers . . . you know, the one she ran the stall with . . .

—Petra.

See. You remember shit like that, he doesn't. You knew your relationship with Sally meant more to you than Nick's did to him.

—Yeah, that's right. Petra. I found her, but there was no sign of Sally. An Petra hadn't seen her for ages either. She just disappeared off somewhere.

So that's that then. You'll probably never see her again. You feel empty in your stomach; it feels like something's been wrenched out.

—I wanted to kill her, you tell him in a matter of fact way.

—Yeah, I'll bet you did.

—No, I really wanted to kill her, you say firmly. —That night, after we had that fight, I went out an got blind fuckin drunk, I mean really steamin, an I managed to convince myself that she was an alien sent here to destroy Earth. And therefore I had to kill her. Not for me, not for any petty reasons of jealousy, but for the sake of the planet . . .

He's staring at you. Okay, it must sound like a pretty stupid story.

—So I got a cab, you go on. —An I came back to your place, but you'd both gone out. I tried to break down the door, I must've been there bout half an hour hammering away on the fuckin thing, but I couldn't do it. Too pissed probably.

—We hadn't gone out, Nick says quietly.

—You what?

—We hadn't gone out. We were huddled together, cowering in the kitchen. I thought they'd come for us. I've never been so fuckin scared in my life . . . You fuckin *hammered* on that door, man. I really thought we were gonna get it.

He gazes at you severely. It looks like his blood is boiling. Oh fuck, he's not going to hit you again, is he?

Then a smile breaks out across his face and he starts laughing. —Don't know *who* I thought had come for us. Just *they*.

You laugh too, but more out of relief than anything else.

—I'm sorry I didn't believe your story, man, he says. —Don't think I ever managed to convince Sally either. Wherever she is now, she still probably thinks the Ecstasy Mafia are after her.

—Yeah, well . . ., you say and can't think of anything further to add.

—I'm glad we ran into each other, though. It was fuckin stupid that we stopped being mates over that.

Nick holds his arms out like he's waiting for a hug. Well, he can keep on waiting; what is this, fucking *Oprah?*

—You wanna do some pills? he says.

—No, mate, I left all that shit behind.

He looks surprised. —You kept that up? Really?

—Yeah, really. I spent a year in Yorkshire watching telly, reading an going down the pub.

He nods his head but it's clear he has no comprehension of the lifestyle you're describing.

—Still, you could do with dipping your toes in the water again, couldn't you, he says. —Specially if you're gonna be dancing to this shit your mate is spinning, you're gonna need something to keep you going.

He reaches into one of the many pockets all over his trousers and takes out a small bag full of bright pink pills. They look like Liquorice Allsorts. Fucking hell, you have been out of circulation a while. Ecstasy is pink these days.

—An what's more, he goes on. —These little darlings are completely legal.

—Legal?

Well, they must be shit then, mustn't they?

—Yeah. Not a trace of MDMA in them anywhere, although they have pretty much the same effect as some of the mellower pills you get. It's some combination of ginseng an cayenne pepper an other weird shit, but they're all legal ingredients so there's nothin they can do . . . fuckin mad, isn't it?

You look at the big pink pills, and at Nick, and at the other blissed out people in the room.

—Come on, man, he says. —I got loads of them. My treat.

Fuck it, why not?

You take one of the pills and bite into it. There's no bitter taste, in fact there's no taste at all. You knew it; they're shit.

He hands you two more. —Here, you got to take these. Three's the dose.

Three sounds excessive to you, especially when you haven't done any for a long time, but if they're as shit as you think they are it's hardly going to matter. Three times nothing is still only nothing.

You put the other two pills in your mouth and knock them back with the last of your Coke.

Later, Nick finds you in the second chill-out area propped up on a beanbag, talking to a girl called Karen with bright red hair and a Welsh accent.

The second chill-out is nothing more than a tent erected outside the back door where monged-out ravers sprawl on the floor and get some cool, fresh air into their lungs. The only music comes from a guy in the corner blowing tunelessly into a recorder. Everyone must be loved-up, otherwise he'd have got a thumping by now.

You've settled into this place quite comfortably. Not long after you sat down, Karen came over and sat next to you, seemingly oblivious to your presence. She sat and smoked three cigarettes in quick succession without even looking at you. Then without warning she turned and asked you if you were having a good one.

It took you by surprise. —Uh, yeah . . ., you said. —Having a ball.

And you are. In fact you'd just been thinking about what a good time you were having, and enjoying the fact that you were having a good time. The pills worked, sort of. There was no big rush and you were sweating like a fucking pig to begin with, but you kept dancing to those manic beats till Tony finished his set and you've had a pleasant glow ever since. More than that, though, you've enjoyed the whole experience again: listening to music pounding against your head, closing your eyes and letting the flashing lights and video images play on the inside of your eyelids, watching people, running into old friends, having attractive women you've never met come up to you and start a conversation . . .

Karen tells you all about herself and you listen contentedly with a smile on your face. You catch a few of the details – she's from a small town near Swansea, she's studying Italian at university, her brother's a half-famous DJ – but mainly you're listening for the tuneful lilt to her voice rather than the actual words. Sounds a lot better than that fucking recorder anyway.

Nick calls your name out as soon as he sees you. —John! There you are, man. Wondered what had happened to you.

He comes over to you. Belatedly, you remember your manners. —Oh, uh . . . yeah. Nick, this is Karen. Karen, this is—

—Nick! she says, standing up and giving him a kiss on the cheek.

They know each other. Of course. As far as you can tell, Nick knows absolutely everyone in here.

They talk for a couple of minutes about people and places unfamiliar to you. Then Karen decides she has to go and find her friends again. She gives you a little wave. —Good to meet you, John. See you round, yeah?

—Yeah, you say, waving back disappointedly.

Nick sits down in her place and immediately begins skinning up.

—It's so good to see you again, man, he says after a while.

—Yeah . . . me too, you say. You hope to Christ he's not going to get all mawkish again.

—So tell me bout this campaign of yours, you ask him for something to say.

And he tells you all about it and you wish you hadn't bothered asking. You fully support his position, of course you do, but people on a mission are so *boring*.

—You must miss the writing, though, you say when you can get word in edgeways.

—Yeah . . . sometimes, he says. —I still do the odd bit, though, you know, for the campaign paper an stuff . . .

He stops his intricate rolling, apparently lost in thought. You didn't realise it was such a leading question.

—Actually I was gonna ask you something bout that, he says finally.

—Yeah?

—Yeah . . .

Go on then.

He seems to be struggling for the words. —It's about that, you know . . . that thing.

For fuck's sake. Spit it out.

—That thing that happened last year. With Fat Cunt an the people up in Leeds an everything . . .

Oh, you mean that thing where you completely fucked me over and slept with my girlfriend, you very nearly blurt out. —Yeah? is all you say, although there's a harshness creeping into your voice.

—I was thinking bout trying to write it up. Thought it might make an interesting magazine article or something. I was wondering if sometime we could go through it all an you tell it from your side of the story . . .

—I've written it up already, you tell him. —I had to do something to work it all out of my system. I'd already made notes in my diary so I just worked from those . . .

He's taken aback. —You keep a diary?

—Yeah. Not religiously, like, but . . . yeah.

—I never knew.

You wish you hadn't mentioned it now. —Well, you know . . . not the sort of thing you talk about really.

—So how come? Your memory that fucked up that you don't trust it at all?

—No, it's not that . . .

You'd rather not go on with this, but he's staring at you intently.

—I don't write about events as such, you try and explain. —It's more how I feel bout things. I'm really scared that when I get older I'll forget what it was ever like to be young. Cause that's what's happened to pretty much everyone I've ever met over the age of fifty: they all seem to have forgotten they were ever our age or younger. So the diary's kind of like a letter to my older self, warning me not to turn into an old wanker.

—Wow, he says admiringly. Then he checks himself. —Yeah, but if you wrote this story up you can only have written it from your side, he says, trying to pull professional rank. —I mean, from a journalistic point of view, it's important to detach yourself from events and try and give a rounded picture . . .

You give a little laugh. How can he possibly know? How can

you tell him what it feels like? That sometimes you're so detached from yourself your soul feels like an extra, lifeless limb dangling pointlessly from your body. That you walk around everywhere you go with your own voice walking right next to you, taunting you, prodding you, insulting you constantly.

He seems on the verge of asking you something else, but just then a couple of his friends come in and tell him they're all about to leave. He thinks about it for a moment, then shrugs and leaves it at that.

—Well, maybe we could talk bout it later . . .

—Yeah.

—See you round then, he says.

—Yeah . . .

—Good to see you again, man . . .

He punches you playfully on the shoulder. Don't try and fucking hug me, your brain is screaming. Don't even fucking think about it.

—I'll give you a call then, he says.

—Yeah . . .

Yeah, you'd like that. It's been a good night. Not a change-your-life fucking brilliant best-time-ever night. But a good night. You're glad you came along, you're glad you ran into Nick. You still have some shit to work through, the two of you, and you're not sure if he'll ever be your closest friend again – not with that fucking goatee he won't, anyway – but it has been good to see him and you'd like to go out clubbing with him again. Not next week maybe, but in month or so. You scribble your phone number on his Rizla packet and hand it back to him.

—See you later.

You sit on your beanbag a while longer. Shortly after Nick and his friends have gone the sun appears, casting patterns of light across the walls of the tent. The guy with the recorder packs up and goes home and truly all seems well with the world. When you feel yourself starting to nod off, you go for a last walk around the whole club to see if Karen's still about. She isn't. In fact the place has emptied out a lot, although the few people who are left are still going for it. Somehow it doesn't seem to matter, though. You're feeling fatalistic; you'll run into her again if it's meant to be.

There are other people leaving at the same time. You walk past a line of mini-cab drivers desperately touting for business and down to King's Cross, where the freaks and ghouls of Saturday night have already been chased away by the light. You're humming one tune after another and you can still hear tribal drums inside your head. You start thinking about getting yourself a couple of decks. With this new job you've got the money now. And fuck, if Tony can do it and get that good, anyone can. You've collected enough records over the years to put together a half-decent set. It's only a question of getting them to co-ordinate, beat for beat, to match up with the sounds you can hear in your head. Tony looks like he has enough contacts now, he could probably get you a gig or two. You've given up your dreams of becoming a top-name DJ and exclusive, expensive remixer to the stars, but it would still be a cool hobby to have. Because the music obviously isn't going to leave you alone.

You walk past St Pancras and the British Library and on up to Euston. It's a long hike back to Shepherds Bush from here; if you still lived off the Holloway Road you'd be pretty much home by now. But it's cool. You're enjoying the walk. You're enjoying the thoughts racing around inside your head.

By the time you reach Shepherds Bush Green there are people milling about. Daytime people. People jogging, walking dogs, shopping for breakfast. You stop at a small newsagents and buy a Sunday newspaper and a large carton of orange juice, which you take out on to the Green. You drink the juice greedily and flick through the glossy magazine that comes with the paper. Then, feeling happily drowsy, you lie back in the sun with nothing on your mind but a tune.